INVASION OF
THE CAT-PEOPLE

DOCTOR WHO – THE MISSING ADVENTURES

Also available:

INVASION OF
THE CAT-PEOPLE

Gary Russell

First published in Great Britain in 1995 by
Doctor Who Books
an imprint of Virgin Publishing Ltd
332 Ladbroke Grove
London W10 5AH

Copyright © Gary Russell 1995

The right of Gary Russell to be identified as the Author of
this Work has been asserted by him in accordance with the
Copyright, Designs and Patents Act 1988.

'Doctor Who' series copyright © British Broadcasting
Corporation 1995

ISBN 0 426 20440 9

Cover illustration by Colin Howard (featuring Scratch, Tarot
and Al)

Typeset by Galleon Typesetting, Ipswich
Printed and bound in Great Britain by
Cox & Wyman Ltd, Reading, Berks

*All characters in this publication are fictitious and any resemblance
to real persons, living or dead, is purely coincidental.*

This book is sold subject to the condition that it shall
not, by way of trade or otherwise, be lent, resold, hired
out or otherwise circulated without the publisher's prior
written consent in any form of binding or cover other
than that in which it is published and without a similar
condition including this condition being imposed on the
subsequent purchaser.

For Gary and Grayson
with more love . . . well, you get the idea

Introduction

Yes, it's that time again, when the tedious author decides to rabbit on unnecessarily and bore you rigid. Promise not to go on as long this time – but this book could not see print without some very important acknowledgements.

Firstly, the entire book came to mind after meeting and falling madly into friendship with Anneke Wills, whose beliefs, fears, loves and passions both inspired me and equalled so many of my own. And whose life across the Atlantic means that we are bereft of her company in Britain for too long. Come back soon!

Secondly, a group of people who helped me research so much of the background and without whom none of it would have even veered towards the accurate (and I hope they forgive me for *Doctor Who*-izing the facts to fit the fiction): Jean Riddler explained all things ley-ish; Ian Martin provided me with maps of the world before, during and after continental shifts; Mark Ayres patiently explained acoustics to me, a total ignoramus when it comes to anything acoustic; Jamie Woolley took me to Cumbria and his parents' gorgeous farmhouse on the coast which I have cheerfully rebuilt into a manor house but the general locale is the same – the story's genesis, therefore, is down to him. Extra special thanks to Porl Cooper for supplying all things mystic, angelic and beautiful. Polly's tarot reading on page 162 was done by him. I picked the cards and shaped subsequent events surrounding Polly and Tim's characters as a result – although the number of coincidences was astonishing. A real case of the characters writing the book, methinks.

For their help in researching the real backgrounds to Ben Jackson and Polly Wright amongst other *Who*-things, Marcus Hearn and Andrew Pixley. Polly Wright's surname is not my invention: it was given in Gerry Davis's character breakdown and audition script sample when, as story editor, he and producer Innes Lloyd created Ben and Polly in 1966. The fact that the name is the same as Barbara's, from a couple of years earlier in the show's history, is probably coincidental and further strengthens my belief that when Davis first came to *Doctor Who* he wasn't particularly *au fait* with its history – hence his repeated use of *Doctor Who* as the character's name: *The War Machines* ('Doctor Who is required'), *The Highlanders* ('Doctor von Wer') and *The Underwater Menace* ('Dr W.'). Despite that, the Lloyd/Davis run on *Who* provided us with Season Four, wherein this adventure is set and, for me, remains the finest season of all the Sixties run.

Immeasurable help also came from the Australian gang – representatives of the most wonderful continent in the world! In no particular order: Fiona, Todd, Kate (still a fiery Pakhar), Nathan, Sarah, Mel, Neil, Lucy, Stephen and Steven.

Also, Paul Vyse who kept my head together when I most needed it. And gave me all that mud! Oh, and Simon Burney for being all the inmates at Wentworth rolled into one. And not forgetting Simon Sadler who had to put up with me traipsing around Oz trying to research everything Aboriginal.

Most importantly: John Ainsworth who always deserved better than he got.

And an extra special mention for Scibus and Mister PeeCee – who took friendship, fun and *The Monster of Peladon* above and beyond the call and without whose time, patience and company this story would have no roots at all.

Frock on, kids!

Foreword

So, there I was, travelling around Mexico when my friend Gary Russell asked me to write an introduction to his new *Doctor Who* book. Not only do I consider this an honour, it also goes to show that I am somehow strangely connected with this show more than any other. And then I have to say I am not surprised, because **magic** happens around the whole thing of *Doctor Who* that continues on and on – into the next century even!

And isn't it strange that so much of what seemed to be way out back then is considered normal now – even this blooming fax machine that I'm sending this on!

So, I hope you enjoy this book as much as I enjoyed playing Polly.

Anneke Wills
Vancouver '95

Prologue

3978 BC
Deep space, approaching Mutters Spiral

The ship was humming along with the complex machinery inside it. So too were the occupants, constantly humming, non-stop, ad infinitum. Each separate component, every individual, all humming together for the benefit of the greater whole.

If they stopped, one of two things would happen. The ship would either blow up or drop out of control, hit an atmosphere at the wrong trajectory and disintegrate. Or, if they were really unlucky, the ship would just drift, the machinery falter and the occupants' brains atrophy and they would fall senseless for an eternity. Faced with such unattractive prospects, the hummers understandably continued humming.

They were elders of the universe, explorers whose researches had exhausted their own planet and solar system. They knew it all. Curiosity was a common failing of many galactic empires and these people were no different. They were many millions upon millions of miles from home. Their humming kept both physical and mental entropy at bay, granting them apparent immortality and allowing them to cross the vast distances in space between the astral bodies they could visit.

And plunder.

They would spot a planet that looked interesting, send down a recon-crew and, if it suited their purposes, leave marker buoys on it to claim it as their own. Every so often one of these planets would have a greater significance. The large blue/green sphere they were approaching now was one such planet. It was only a few million years old, its molten core still raging in turmoil. Not quite ripe but getting that way. Only a few more millennia and it would be exactly what they needed. They prepared a recon-party.

Five of them.

'Information?' sang the commander of the mother-ship.

++PROCESSING>++ There was a pause before the computer hummed back, ++TRACES OF IRON-MAGNESIUM SILICATES<SULPHIDE<OXIDE AND NICKEL IRON.++

'Excellent. This adequately suits our requirements. Prepare the buoys. Physical imparts?'

++THERE ARE TWO VAST LAND MASSES> A REQUIRED AMOUNT OF CLEAR LINEAGE SHOULD BE POSSIBLE WITHIN A FEW DEGREES OF ACCURACY++

'Central base?'

++THE LOWER SOUTH EAST OF THE SOUTHERN CONTINENT HAS THE SHORTEST DIRECT LINK TO THROUGH THE MAGMA> WARNING> PREDICATIONS INDICATE FURTHER MASSIVE CONTINENTAL SHIFT LIKELY> SUGGESTION> RECON-PARTY BE WARNED OF THIS FACT> CALCULATIONS FOR POSITIONING OF THE MARKER BUOYS MUST BE RE-SOUGHT TO AVOID ERRORS++

'Noted. The recon-party shall be informed. Basic readouts?'

++THE ATMOSPHERE IS ESSENTIALLY GOOD ALTHOUGH A HEAVY PARTICLE FLUX EXISTS OVER THE FAR NORTH WEST> READOUTS SUGGEST A MASSIVE MATTER/ANTI-MATTER EXPLOSION OCCURRED WITHIN THE LAST MILLION YEARS> THE EFFECT ON NATURAL LIFE HAS BEEN CATASTROPHIC WITH THE ESSENTIAL BALANCE OF NATURE UPSET IRREVOCABLY> SUGGEST CAUTION> NEW LIFE-FORMS EXIST AT RUDIMENTARY STAGES++

'Mammalian, reptilian or silicon-based?'

++MAMMALIAN, INSECTOID, REPTILIAN AND MOLLUSC>

A GREAT DEAL OF VEGETATION COVERS A MAJORITY OF THE PLANET<BY FAR THE MOST PROLIFIC FORM OF LIFE> LARGER REPTILIAN LIFE MOSTLY ERADICATED DUE TO AFOREMENTIONED MATTER/ANTI-MATTER DETONATION++

'Any evidence of extra-terrestrial influences?'

++TRACE ELEMENTS OF WARP-DRIVE RADIATION WOULD SUGGEST VISITATION APPROXIMATELY FIVE HUNDRED MILLION YEARS PREVIOUSLY++

'Download this information into the recon-party's craft. It is essential that they know and understand as much as possible.'

++CONFIRMED++

In the recon-party's craft waited four of the crew, quietly keeping a melodic harmony going. Around them matter was changing, molecules reshaping themselves into the solid walls of the craft. Next to one of them machinery began to form: the relevant computer consoles were essentially being born, the mainframe's information already loading into its data-banks.

One of the crew reached out with a lazy hand, casually punching a button on the console's top.

'Ident: Atimkos.' As he spoke, his three companions increased their humming. When he finished it briefly resumed its lower level until another of them pressed the button and spoke. The other three then raised their humming to accommodate the loss of voice.

'Ident: Tarwildbaning.'

The process was repeated twice more.

'Ident: Thorgarsuunela.'

'Ident: Udentkista.'

++IDENTS CONFIRMED> THIS SYSTEM IS NOW SUNG INTO ORDER> PREPARE FOR RECON-LEADER++

A shrill cry came from outside the craft and for a brief second the wall melted away to allow entry to the recon-leader. As she stepped through, she cried again and the wall reassembled itself. She crossed to the computer.

'Ident: Godwanna.'

3

++RECON-LEADER IDENT CONFIRMED> SING WELL++

Seconds later a gap appeared in the side of the mother-ship and the recon-craft shot out, down towards the blue/green planet below.

Inside the mother-ship all seemed to be going to plan. The commander hummed softly as he watched the recon-craft tumbling towards its new home.

'Approximate return time?'

++THREE ORBITS OF NEAREST SUN++

'Excellent. Let's make it a leisurely trip. We're in no hurry.'

++CONF >>>> WARNING>>> WARNING>>> SOLAR FLARES> EVASIVE PROCEDURES RECOMMENDED++

To accommodate the commander and his three immediate subordinates turning anxiously to their instruments, the resonance and volume of the other crew increased.

'Helm control. Report!'

'Solar activity confirmed. Adjusting flight plan accordingly.'

The commander nodded and turned to his navigator. 'Information?'

'Plotting a new course, Commander,' she replied. 'We will be five orbits late for the rendezvous.'

'Unacceptable. Make it four.'

'I will try, Commander.'

'Commander!' The cry from his executive officer alarmed him. The exec was not normally given to such outbursts. 'The computer link between us and the recon-craft has gone down. They have no information about our status.'

A few crew quietened their singing but a sharp look from the commander helped them regain their voices. 'Re-establish link. They must be informed.' He turned back to the helm officer. 'Well?'

'Sir, the solar flares are affecting the equipment. The resonance is distorting our harmonies.'

'This accounts for our computer failures,' said the exec. 'We have lost our internal ones as well.'

The commander frowned for a moment and then crossed to his navigator. 'Ignore my previous command – get us to a safe distance, regardless of the delay to our return.'

She nodded her acquiescence. 'I can try for five orbits, sir.'

'No. Safety is of paramount importance. Seven or eight.' The commander shrugged at the exec. 'Further suggestions?'

Before the executive officer could answer, the helmsman gave a shrill yell. 'Solar plasma – observe!' was all he could say before the mother-ship rocked under a massive force of plasma. The commander jumped to the helm-control but it was too late. Caught in the flare, the galley and recreational areas of the ship vanished in a soundless implosion. In less than a second he calculated the effect that the loss of twenty-eight voices would have. 'Sing louder' was the only order he gave before the futility of it overawed him. Without those voices, the ship was doomed. Vast rents appeared in the side leading to the bridge area and he watched helplessly as first his executive officer and then three others were sucked into space.

As the blood rushed through his body, seeking an exit through every available pore, he thought of his stranded crew on the primitive planet. As he watched his friends and officers die he sent out a silent apology for deserting Godwanna and her crew. Death was preferable to exile.

A second before he could be spat out into the vacuum of space the mother-ship imploded.

The glare lit up an already bright, blue sky for a few seconds. The inhabitants of the recon-craft were too busy to notice.

Atimkos and Tarwildbaning were humming as loudly and enthusiastically as they could as the computer console literally dissipated and floated around them. While the

5

molecular cohesion of the whole craft fluctuated, God-wanna was concentrating on maintaining the integrity of the wall between themselves and the propulsion units. Udentkista and Thorgarsuunela were trying to pilot the craft to a reasonably safe landing.

'Brace yourselves,' cried Thorgarsuunela as she twisted the craft towards some shrubbery. 'Prepare for immediate impact –'

The recon-craft smashed into the dry earth at quite some speed, sending portions of it flying out in every direction. Without the humming to sustain them, the pieces quickly faded away to nothingness – leaving five twisted bodies and a couple of crates and a few corporeal components of the ship's drive and propulsion units.

'We should be grateful that the marker buoys are made fully operational before leaving the home-world,' muttered Udentkista as he levered himself up on one of the crates. No one answered him. He began to hum and sway slightly and after a moment Tarwildbaning stirred. She opened her eyes and smiled.

'We have survived?'

'Obviously,' he replied. He looked straight up towards the sky and the sun – but he was trying to stare further out. 'Something has gone wrong. I cannot hear the others singing.'

'It is gone. The whole mother-ship has been destroyed.' They turned to look at Godwanna as she pushed herself away from the hard ground. 'I felt them die.'

'How are we to get away from here?' asked a worried Udentkista.

'We cannot, you fool,' snapped his leader. 'Understand this, all of you. We are trapped here, for good.'

Atimkos staggered over. 'We are going to need shelter soon. This forest is well populated by potentially dangerous animals. The strong vegetation absorbs and reflects the heat. We cannot survive in this humidity.'

'Thank you, Atimkos. Practical as always. What do you plan to do?'

'I thought that *we* could link our songs and build something. Quickly.'

Godwanna shrugged her shoulders. 'Of course. As soon as Thorgarsuunela has recovered, we will do as you suggest.'

Thorgarsuunela crawled over. 'I am all right. Let us sing.'

The five of them sat in a circle, clasped hands, closed their eyes and all but Godwanna began a quiet chant. 'Let the natural power of this planet aid us – use whatever local materials we can to build us protection.' She paused for a second and then released her grip on the others. Quickly the circle was connected again, leaving Godwanna standing in the middle. Throwing her hands upright she closed her eyes and began humming. Seconds later the other four joined in and the air around them began to shimmer. Shapes formed, dark and solid. Four upright struts, then the space between each filling until a box shape existed. Then eight struts across the top, and the spaces subsequently filled in. Finally a doorway appeared, complete with hinged door.

It was a dark, wooden hut.

The door opened and the five figures trooped out, Thorgarsuunela and Atimkos carrying the crates of marker buoys.

Godwanna almost smiled at them. 'Success.' She rotated three hundred and sixty degrees. 'The heat is strong but it will pass over the next few millennia. The ground beneath tells me that the primitive life here is already evolving rapidly. It tells me that we should rest for a while. Then we must look for a safe area. Somewhere raised. A hill or mountain.'

Atimkos frowned. 'But the buoys? The fleet –'

Godwanna swung around angrily, throwing her arms wide. 'What are you talking about? The fleet are billions of light-years from here! We have no chance of being rescued. Once you accept that, you will acclimatize to this situation. We are here for life.'

7

Atimkos looked down at the soft, rain-soaked soil. 'I still believe . . .'

'Yes,' snapped Godwanna. 'Go. Place the buoys. You may be right. We might be rescued. The buoys might be useful. If it provides something for you to do and places you out of my sight for a few hundred years, then so be it.'

Atimkos nodded. 'Thank you.'

'Oh, and Atimkos?' Godwanna was smiling her best, and most insincere smile. 'Take care.'

Atimkos turned on his heel, grabbed one of the crates, hoisted it up on his shoulder and began marching away. Another call from Godwanna stopped him and with a silent sigh he turned back to face her.

'You may need assistance. Take Thorgarsuunela with you. She can carry your RTC units. I expect you'll need them. You'll be gone quite a while.' Both Thorgarsuunela and Atimkos began to protest but a final 'Now. Go!' from Godwanna silenced their comments.

Some hours later, Thorgarsuunela and Atimkos were tiny specks on the horizon. Godwanna and her two remaining hummers were crouched down, singing softly. Before them the air molecules shifted and a tiny wooden box materialized. After a quiet relaxed breath, the three looked at it. 'This planet is too crude,' muttered Godwanna. 'We cannot create what we need here. Not yet. The materials simply do not exist.'

Udentkista frowned. 'What can we do, Godwanna? How long must we wait?'

Godwanna smiled. 'Oh, anything up to about sixty million years, give or take a few thousand. By then we will be able to create a distress beacon that no one can miss. Our brothers and sisters will be able to find us.'

'And if they can't?' asked Tarwildbaning.

'Then,' Godwanna shrugged, 'we will wait and see who does come. And we shall make them take us home.'

Queensland, North-East Australia

Nate Simms loved Australia. He had visited Sydney in his mid-twenties after much peer-group pressure.

'Darling, you simply have to go.'

'Sweetie, it's the most marvellous place. So much opportunity, especially for a Brit. It's reasonably cheap and full of such scenery. You'll regret not going.'

'You've got an aunt out there. Getting a work visa will be easy.'

Eventually he had given in and headed off to Sydney for a five-week holiday. Twenty-four months later, he was still there – settled with a good job at Elton Ward, a prosperous design company in Parramatta. His interest in all things ancient and heritage-based had earned him a sleeping partnership in Acquired Antiques of Leichardt, Sydney. Financially, he was secure for life. Periodically – and much to the amusement of his work colleagues – he would take a few days' leave, maybe just a long weekend, and go off to explore yet another part of the continent that most Australian residents had never set foot in.

He had done the traditional Ayers Rock – or Uluru as he rightfully called it. He had explored the rain forests around Darwin. He had briefly wandered around the deserts of Western Australia until good sense prevailed and he had headed back to Perth before running out of supplies.

The Blue Mountains, west of Sydney, were his favourite place. Kilometres of huge mountains, stretching into a horizon blurred into a blue haze. The forest walks that stretched through the basin of the mountains had kept him sheltered from other humans for six or seven days at a time. He had ski'd in the Snow Mountains, staying in a small wooden house in Jindabyne, where the nearest neighbours were twenty minutes' drive away, and spent many days exploring the harsh, intense but ultimately beautiful countryside that separated New South Wales from Victoria.

Now he was 'doing the rounds' of North Queensland, exploring the area around the Daintree rain forests. His researches into Aboriginal – or Koori – culture had revealed that one particular mountain was sacred in a way nothing else could be. Mount Demi – uniformly believed by the ancients of Australia to be the place where life began. Their equivalent of the Garden of Eden.

Unlike Uluru, there were no polite notice-boards reminding visitors that the Aboriginals would prefer that you did not climb their spiritual mounds. There were no Visitors' Centres, with their huge billboards of Aboriginals in the desert, rare breeds of possum, bilbies or bush rats and tacky gift shops selling books on Aboriginal folklore alongside their heritage.

Mount Demi was merely part of the North Queensland National Park and Nate had not even had to spend $10 on an entry ticket. And like all the world's best and most famous explorers, he had not seen fit to tell anyone exactly where he was going. He just headed off into the undergrowth, crossed the tiny railway line that took the sugar cane to the factory on the other side of Port Douglas, and vanished from the sight of the road. And civilization.

Forty-five minutes later he was at the base of Mount Demi, pushing his way through the bushes, carefully keeping an eye on the dense trees above: stories of tree-dwelling funnel-web spiders that leaped down on unsuspecting British tourists were always foremost in his mind. 'Beware those "funny-webs",' Caldwell at work had joked. 'They'll get you in the end.' One of his cousins had told him of the time her dog had encountered a funnel-web in her children's playroom. 'I covered the blasted thing with a jam jar and screamed for Charlie to help me. He slid a piece of card under the neck of the jar and we righted it, screwing the lid on firmly. As the spider fell to the bottom of the jar, about forty tiny babies

10

fell off her and began crawling up the jar. Forty of them! Charlie grabbed the jar and put it outside the house, away from the dog and the kids. Later, he made a tiny hole in the top and poured smoke in to kill them all. It's the only way!' Crocodiles that snatched unwary fishermen, snakes that injected venom into ankles and even goanna lizards that would run up someone's leg thinking it was a tree and shredding flesh and bone while they were at it – he could cope with all those. But something about spiders, especially the infamous female funnel-webs and those horrible red-backs, scared him witless. He always took care.

As he stared up at Demi, its peak shrouded in a dense cloud of condensation from the thick closed forest that enveloped much of it, Nate Simms shivered. Somewhere, deep within his mind, some primeval fear coursed through him – a momentary flutter of panic. As if he were embarking on a climb best left to the Aborigines of four thousand years ago. As if Mount Demi were more than another sacred site, more than another area of primordial consecrated ground. As if Mount Demi were somehow alive, daring him to climb up, and warning him that he might never go down again. All this flitted through his consciousness in a second. Breathing heavily he forgot his fears (apart from the funnel-webs, of course) and began his ascent.

He never went down again.

AD 1994
Deep space, approaching Mutters Spiral

You are all honoured, my children, and yet in turn you honour us. Those who saw you leave, those who knew in our hearts that your campaigns, your plans, your advances and ultimately your victories would keep you away beyond our lifetimes, wept after you had departed. Not just with grief at the holes you left in our lives, but with the unrestrained joy of knowing that you were

11

going out into space to spread word about the superiority of our forces.

'Know this: wherever you are now, whatever distant speck in the galaxy you currently occupy, all Feles – your world, your people, your birthright – all wait here for your triumphant return.

'We acknowledge you, brave warriors. For ours is the right to dominance, to divinity and to exultation.

'I, Pride Mother of all the Cat-People, salute you.'

A tortoise-shell paw flicked out and punched the remote. The screen fuzzed and then blanked. 'Well?'

'There is dissension, Your Majesty, but nothing that we cannot halt in its tracks.'

'Lotuss?'

'She . . . inspires them, but there are others, across the litter-prides.'

The tortoise-shell paw was licked and wiped slowly across whiskers. 'All right, Chosan. Let her make her move. I shall be ready.'

'And the expedition?'

'I shall lead, Chosan. The Euterpians left exactly what we need here – I wish to ensure we find it.'

'And our contact on this planet?'

The paw pointed at the blank screen. 'As our illustrious Pride Mother would undoubtedly say – we are superior. Our agent is merely an anthropoid, useful for a while. Now, locate the correct planet and obtain some details about it. We must be well informed. Prepare for our approach.'

'Immediately, Your Majesty.'

As the curtain was pushed aside for Chosan to leave, Queen Aysha relaxed back on her cushions and purred quietly to herself. 'Enough power to fuel a battalion, and we are only one ship. Excellent.'

The Euterpians could have had a terrible reputation. They might have been known as a galactic militia; a race of warmongering sadists who wanted nothing more than to destroy everything else and parade throughout space in their massive war fleets.

No one really knew where the Euterpians came from. Evidence of their warlike culture has been discovered during recent Galactic Federation archaeological digs, and their influence has certainly been revealed on many planets spread far and wide.

Unfortunately for the Euterpians, they died out, possibly after some kind of civil strife. No one knows why, where or how. Even their given name is a Federation-given one. None of the historical evidence found so far provides us with any clues as to their real identity. Most of their scripture is a form of musical scribbling. But any attempt to translate it via any known musical instrument provides such a cacophony of discordant noise that even the most avant-garde of musical enthusiasts accept that it is not being played as it should be. Not even renowned musical scholars such as Lock, Proot or even Glasst can provide any meaning to the symbols.

It is therefore generally believed that the Euterpians will have to be catalogued as one of those mysterious galactic races destined for obscurity, both culturally and scholastically.

A shame, really. No one likes a mystery . . .

Extract from *An Even Briefer History of Time*
by High Lord Rhukk
© Bowketts Universal Publications 3974

Episode One

The space–time vortex

'Oh dear, I don't think that can be right.'

The Doctor let go of the elasticated tape measure and with a 'thwick' it quickly rewound itself, slapping across his fingers as it popped back into its casing. 'Owww!' he cried loudly, sucking his fingers.

'Don't be such a baby, Doc,' muttered a young man's voice from across the TARDIS console room.

'Oh, Ben, don't be so unfeeling,' said Polly, quickly going to the Doctor's side. 'He's still feeling vulnerable after his recent . . . experiences.'

Ben rolled his eyes heavenward and murmured something incoherent that included the phrases 'three weeks', 'self-pity' and 'mollycoddle'.

Polly was not listening; instead she was examining the Doctor's damp digits. 'What were you trying to do, Doctor? Maybe Ben and I can help.'

The Doctor smiled, his green eyes twinkling at her concern. 'Oh, that's very kind, Polly. Very kind indeed. But I really don't think —' he saw her look of disappointment — 'oh, on the other hand, maybe there is something.'

Polly brightened and threw a withering look at Ben, who tried to slump further into the Louis xiv chair and read his book.

'Leave it out, Duchess, I'm busy.'

Polly stuck her tongue out at him. 'I didn't know you

14

could read now,' she said. 'Obviously the TARDIS has rubbed off on you.'

'Oh, ha-ha-ha,' retorted Ben.

The Doctor clicked his tongue reprovingly. 'Now, come on.' He grinned at Polly and passed her the tape measure. 'I'm trying to check that the interior dimensions of the TARDIS aren't decreasing. You see, when I regenerated, so did the Ship – to some extent.'

'I thought things had moved around a bit,' said Polly. 'I had a dreadful time finding the bathroom this morning. I walked for ages and eventually found something marked "BATHROOM". It was a swimming pool!'

The Doctor nodded sagely. 'Ah. Yes. Borrowed the plans for that from Claudius Caesar. Nice old chap, but had a dreadful stammer. Good range of baths though.'

Polly smiled. 'I'm glad you're completely recovered, Doctor. You had us worried, you know.'

'Regeneration's a tricky thing,' he said. 'And it was my first one. Always the trickiest. They're supposed to get better as they go on, so long as you don't flitter them. Always used to say to my academy chum Magnus, "Magnus," I'd say, "Magnus, don't throw old bodies away like you would a suit. They don't grow on trees." Or something like that. Never listened though.'

Polly shook her head. 'Just how many of you are there at "home", wherever that may be?'

The Doctor stared at her for a moment and she shivered. Somehow she thought he was not looking at her so much as *through* her – into his own memories. Suddenly he broke into a grin and began twiddling his fingers. 'Anyway,' he said, reverting to his original concern, 'I want to see if this room has contracted.'

Ben looked up from his book. 'Didn't answer the question, Doc,' he said.

Polly turned, aghast at Ben's rudeness. 'Ben! If the Doctor doesn't want to discuss his private life, why should he? You're not exactly forthcoming about your history, are you?'

'Ah, nothing to learn, Duchess. Went to sea when I was fifteen, did my service and ended up here. Besides, the other Doctor – the older one – he'd always answer a straight question.'

The Doctor turned and looked at Ben. 'Oh, I don't think that's true, Ben. Indeed, I can remember many occasions when you got frustrated at things that he . . . I . . . didn't tell you.'

'Yeah, I s'pose so.' Ben suddenly grinned at the Doctor. 'It takes some getting used to, you know. This body swapping or whatever it is.'

'Do you still doubt he is the Doctor?' asked Polly. 'You seemed very dubious on Vulcan.'

Ben looked at the Doctor. 'Nah. He's still the Doctor. He still talks the hind legs off a donkey – and none of it in straight English. He *has* to be the Doc.' He got out of his chair, dropped his book on a cushion and took the other end of the tape measure. 'All right, so what are we doing?'

The Doctor clapped his hands together and smiled. 'Oh, goody. Now, Ben, you stand over here.' He took Ben towards the double doors. 'And Polly,' he said, crossing to her, 'if you'd be so kind as to stand here.' He pointed at the doorway to the rest of the Ship. 'Now, pull it taut and I'll see how long it is.'

Polly gave the tape measure a tug and pulled it towards her. Ben gripped the case-end tightly and the Doctor ran between the two of them, looking at the notebook he had suddenly produced from an inside pocket. Retrieving a pencil from behind Ben's ear (Ben was positive it had not been there seconds earlier), he started muttering and jotting things down.

After a few moments of frantic scampering, scribbling and scratching the Doctor flopped down into the Louis XIV, squashing Ben's book. With a guilty look he retrieved it from beneath him and sheepishly handed it over. In return, Ben gave him the rewound tape measure and a smile.

'Well?' asked Polly.

'Yes, thank you,' beamed the Doctor. 'I think we could all do with some tea and scones.'

'I'll get it.' Polly wandered to the galley area, where the food machine stood. As soon as she was out of earshot, the Doctor beckoned Ben over and pulled him down so that he could whisper in his ear. 'I was right, Ben. The TARDIS has shrunk. Only about fifteen centimetres, but enough to worry me.'

'Centi-whats?'

'I mean, about six inches. I keep forgetting that you haven't adopted decimal measurements in your time. Still, won't be long. Anyway, that's beside the point. The fact is, the TARDIS is getting smaller. Entropy. The time and space traveller's greatest enemy.'

'Is it a serious problem?'

'Oh, absolutely. If I regenerate again, it'll shrink again. By the time I reach my fourth incarnation I predict this room will be tiny – barely room to swing a cat.'

'Your fourth . . . well, excuse me, Doctor, but I hope that's a long way off. In which case, why are we worrying?' Ben patted him on the shoulder. 'You don't half get worked up over nothing.'

The Doctor removed his blue and white spotted handkerchief from his breast pocket. 'I must tie a knot in it, to remind me when I get to my fourth body to do something about reconfiguring the Ship.' He tied four knots in it, one after the other. 'My own special code – four knots for the fourth body,' he smiled. And then frowned. Near the bottom were two knots next to each other. 'I wonder what they are for?'

With a short laugh Ben wandered off to find Polly. It did not take him long as the smell of warm scones drew him on. Sure enough, there she was, pouring tea into three large mugs. 'Wotcha, Duchess.'

Polly started and nearly spilled the tea. 'Oh, Ben, don't do that. You took years off me.'

'Yeah – well, it could be worse. It could be centimetres.'

'Centi-whats?' she asked.

'Oh, c'mon Pol. Centimetres. You know, decimal measurements and all that.' He reached for a scone and popped one into his mouth. 'I'll carry those,' he said incoherently and picked up the plate.

As he wandered out, Polly shook her head and put the three mugs on to a tray. Picking it up she muttered, 'Centimetres? What's wrong with feet and inches? Bet it never takes off,' and wandered back towards the console room.

The solar system containing Earth, part of the Mutter's Spiral

Queen Aysha regarded the bridge of her battle cruiser. Around her, the finest trained crew busied themselves with their jobs, working hard and accurately.

Aysha placed her paw-print on a report form brought to her by first-sired Chosan and nodded at the pattern of stars twisting on the holo display in front of them. 'Is this the system?'

Chosan purred slightly, running a claw down a whisker. 'Indeed, Queen. The message from our agent was picked up from the third planet to the sun.'

'Information, please,' Aysha called down to the assembled crew.

One of the seats was swung round lazily, the occupant licking its paw and then wiping its face. Queen Aysha sighed inwardly. Of course, as tactical officer it would have to be Lotuss who answered. As Lotuss stood up to her full height (she was by no stretch of the imagination tall) she allowed her ears to twitch back slightly, a sign of antagonism. Aysha knew better than to take the bait and kept her own ears erect, her fur flat.

Lotuss had made little secret of the fact that as one of Aysha's first-litter, she had certain privileges. Like Chosan, she enjoyed familiarity and rank aboard the ship but like all litter-runts, the urge to prove physical superiority drove her more savagely than most. One eye socket was gone, its passing marked by a long scar, and her left ear was partially shredded. Quick movements frequently made the unconnected bits flap discordantly. Patches of fur were missing from her back and upper-left forearm. Cosmetic surgery could have cured all of these defects but Lotuss preferred the scars of her battles to be permanently on view. They acted, successfully as it happened, as a warning that her diminutive size in no way mirrored her viciousness.

'Mother,' Lotuss said. Aysha shuddered at the familiarity of the title – even her first-sired referred to her as Queen in company. Only Lotuss would be so bold. 'Mother, it is a world we have been studying for many years. One of only three to have sustained any kind of sentient life in this system, it is called Earth by the inhabitants, a rather obvious name as it is nothing more than a dirt-tray with a preponderance of water.'

Various crew-members shuddered and a few hackles rose at the mention of water, but Lotuss just smiled, bearing her incisor teeth.

Chosan looked over at the holo display. 'Are you sure it doesn't come from the other two?'

Lotuss shook her head. 'The next one on, towards the sun, is too hot for mammalian life and the red planet we're approaching shows signs of a long-lost civilization but for now it is dead. Earth is where our . . . prey is.'

Aysha purred loudly. 'Thank you, Lotuss. But note, we are not seeking out our contact as prey. Not yet. We must find out what this secret is that she has promised us.'

'And then?' hissed Lotuss.

'If it is not to our liking,' Aysha drew back her own mouth and bared her own gleaming teeth, 'well, then we will, as always, destroy all sentient life and strip the planet of whatever minerals and power sources as pleases me. ETA please?'

Chosan punched up some figures and the holo display of space was replaced by a series of numbers.

'Seventeen hours, Queen. Will you use the transporter or take your shuttle?'

Aysha reflected, then shook her head. 'No – even if Tamora has rectified the malfunction, I'm still not willing to risk living beings in it. Use it for inanimate objects only until we can run proper tests on it.'

Chosan made a note. 'I'll confirm with Tamora that your personal shuttle is to be prepared.'

Aysha nodded and waved everyone back to work. 'Thank you. Oh, Lotuss? I will speak to you in my litter-room. Now.'

Lotuss nodded and counted to ten after Aysha had left the bridge. As she mounted the raised dais that led away from the tactical area second-sired Jayde touched her arm. A look but no words passed between them. Then Lotuss left.

As Jayde returned to her navigation console, Chosan stopped looking at her in the reflection of the science console. Something was being planned against their mother. Something that as first-sired, it was Chosan's job to stop. And if that involved the death of the litter-runt, so much the better.

Queen Aysha stood in front of the cage in her litter-room. In her hand was a box of synthesized meat-balls, which she was feeding a morsel at a time to the tom in the cage. He snatched a meat-ball from her in clawless paws and sucked the meat up, getting bits caught in his fur and whiskers and generally making a mess of himself.

The beaded curtain in the doorway swished open. 'It is customary to knock,' Aysha said without turning around.

'It is customary to destroy the spent sire-stock,' was Lotuss's curt reply.

Putting the meat-ball box to one side, Aysha looked at her daughter and curled up on a massive cushion, waving casually to another. Lotuss sat.

'I have had his teeth removed, his claws removed and he can no longer achieve any degree of propagation.

Having him put down seems a fairly pointless exercise, frankly. If we were on the litter-world, I might agree, but as the only male company on board, I choose to keep him. As he is your father, I would expect a degree of respect if not affection.'

Lotuss spat. 'Affection? For that? It has an intelligence quota lower than a rodent. It doesn't even know it ever mated with you, let alone propagated three generations of offspring. It is an abomination and a reminder of how pathetic males are.'

Aysha nodded. 'Maybe. However, let us not forget that we need males or there would be a shortage of crew. Which reminds me. There is a feeling, especially amongst the third-litter, that we should return to the litter-world. With only this wonderful specimen of masculinity aboard, they lack mates and are ready to have litters themselves. But firstly, it does not suit me to have any further litters within our family. The third-litter must accept that like your litter and the second-litter, they will remain barren until they die. Secondly, Feles is too far away. Few of us would still be alive by the time we returned. And thirdly, I imagine you have omitted to point out to them that it was you who mauled the males of your own litter and fed them back to your father without him even knowing.'

Lotuss shrugged. 'Let us be honest, mother. He wouldn't have realized even if I'd wrapped them in towelling and written a note saying "These are your children you are eating".'

'The point I am making, litter-runt Lotuss, is that your continual stirring-up of the second- and third-litters is neither passing me by nor worrying me. No one, bar myself, is indispensable to this mission. I would rather you pent up your savagery and prepare to use it on the creatures that inhabit Earth. A few shock tactics will go a long way to sorting out the first-sires from the runts amongst them. If you will excuse the analogy,' Aysha added insincerely. She then stood, walked towards

21

the milk dispenser, but suddenly changed direction and cuffed Lotuss so hard around the area of her missing eye that the litter-runt not only fell to the floor, but actually mewed in pain. Which satisfied the Queen. 'Be warned, Lotuss. I tolerate your living because you are the best fighter aboard. Accept that honour and prestige and stop trying to usurp your mother's authority, or it will be the death of you. Or worse. I'll put you in your father's cage, minus your claws, teeth and larynx. And I'll make sure he knows exactly who fed him his own offspring.'

Lotuss stared mutely at Aysha . . . Aysha wondered if that look in her eye was terror. Then the litter-runt got up, brushed her whiskers and left.

In the corridor outside, Lotuss coughed up a hairball and rubbed her sore forehead. 'Prepare to die in disgrace, "Queen" Aysha!' She snarled and headed back to the bridge and her station at tactical.

Chosan watched as she returned, silently and sullenly sitting back at tactical, and allowed herself a slight smile. She could imagine what Queen Aysha had done to humiliate the litter-runt. Which was good, because now Lotuss would be full of anger, resentment and fury. And that could be directed at whatever foes they encountered on Earth.

Chosan stared back at her science console. And decided that if she had been a nice, decent member of the universe's population like so many of those that the ship had exterminated, then she would warn Earth that its greatest threat was on its way.

The Cat-People had come to invade, and nothing could stop them.

Earth

Seven Dials. Shaftesbury Avenue. Opposite the MGM, just past the top end of Earlham Street. Wednesday the sixth of July nineteen ninety-four. Five-forty-eight.

Seventy-seven degrees in the shade. Martina had lost the championship on Saturday but departed Wimbledon in style, taking cheers and a sod of the court with her. Poor old Ivanisevic had not been so lucky the following day but what the hell. For him, there was always next summer.

The trains were not working – the railway signalmen were striking – and she had to get a bus home. Despite the glory of the past few hours, it was now raining.

Only a drizzle. Soft and cooling. Not enough to fumble for her umbrella, but enough to be feeling a dampness seeping through her blouse. With a grimace, she hurried a bit faster. And stumbled.

At first she thought she had tripped over a loose paving slab – Westminster Council were not famous for their good road maintenance. But even as she thought this, she became aware that the surface at her feet was Tarmac. As she looked up she saw a young man staring at her, humming quietly, wearing a slight smirk on his face. Was he responsible? Nah, too far away – he had just come out of Orc's Nest games shop. So why the smirk? With a shrug she started on and the man passed by, in the opposite direction, and out of her thoughts. Until it occurred to her that the reason the man might have been smirking was the rain. He had not been even slightly damp – it was as if the rain simply did not touch him. She looked back at the retreating figure and sure enough, she could see an almost man-shaped outline of rain around him. But not on him.

Ignoring him.

The young man suddenly stopped and turned back to stare at her. She shivered – not from the cool water hitting her but from . . . something else. His smirk drooped – became a look of infinite sadness and she felt her breath snatched away. In her head she heard a tiny, faint whistle – probably a noise from the traffic behind her around Cambridge Circus. A strange compulsion washed over her – she wanted to run and hug him. Hold him. Tell him everything was all right, absorb all that unhappiness into herself. As she breathed suddenly heavily, she saw the rain start to land upon him – his strange shield had evaporated. He cast his eyes downwards, turned on his heel and walked on the way he was going.

As she stared at his back, another wave of despair smothered her and a tear escaped her eye. With a slight shake of her head, she walked backwards and stepped on to Charing Cross Road and began to cross.

The driver of the Grey-Green bus number 64 slammed his foot on the brake but the light rain on the previously dry road delayed the mechanics a split second too long.

It took the emergency services half an hour to scrape the unidentifiable woman off the front of the bus, the road, the pavement and three hysterical passers-by.

While they were doing their best, the young man with the invisible shield and rapidly disappearing smirk was standing in a shop in Monmouth Street. Around him, packs of tarot cards, incense burners, joss-sticks and icons made from semi-precious stones and metals all vied for his attention. Ignoring them, he crossed to the far end of the shop and looked at the candles. Male and female. Pink for friendship; red for anger; black for regret; yellow for communication. Then there was green for luck; blue for healing; purple for success; orange for encouragement. Finally, white for peace of mind; gold for justice; and silver for alternate energies.

He reached up and took three – two yellow males, one yellow female. He looked again. And took a fourth. A black female. For the unfortunate woman who had seen the effect of the rain in Shaftesbury Avenue. He hated doing things like that. But maintaining his anonymity was essential. And, if he was honest, he had panicked. That was unusual and irresponsible and it would not happen again.

He paid for the four waxen images and the requisite anointment oils in silence. The pleasant male shop-assistant frowned momentarily at the three crisp, unblemished fivers passed to him. He stopped suddenly as something like the echo of one of the ambulance sirens rang in his head for a fraction of a second. He glanced out of the window, shrugged and looked back at the till.

Surely those fivers had been brand-new? But no, they were crumpled and tatty, one with a phone number etched on to it. He scooped sixpence change out of the open till and passed it to the young man, wrapped the candles and oils carefully in a pink-striped paper bag and said good-night.

The young man was the last customer and the assistant glanced at his watch as the man left. Ten minutes to go. Then it was home to one of Linda McCartney's micro specials, a bottle of red and *Ab Fab* on the video. The sirens seemed to echo again.

He was staring at the till. Why? After all, he had not had a customer for over forty minutes.

Candles wrapped in the pink-striped bag tucked under his arm, the young man wandered into Neal's Yard, whistling to himself. He passed the multicoloured doors of the converted warehouses and sat in a white plastic chair outside the coffee-house at the nape of the yard. He could see everyone who came into the yard, or passed down the passage towards Rough Trade records.

Beside him, two strangely dressed women with silly tufts of hair hacked into tiny pony-tails, wrapped in tin-foil, blathered on about some trendy Icelandic pop singer who would fade back into obscurity, probably the same cultish obscurity she had already emerged from, over the next couple of years.

When a tall, effeminate man minced out of the coffee-shop and asked for an order, the man with the candles requested a wholewheat bap with lettuce and tomato and a bottle of Lemon Iced Tea Snapple. He made sure he paid with a tatty five-pound note.

Moments later, he was drinking slowly and munching

periodically, keeping an eye on all the people that entered or bypassed Neal's Yard. Eventually he saw what he was waiting for.

'You're late,' he said.

'So?' The newcomer, a woman, pulled up a chair. 'I'm off tonight. I'll be in touch.'

'How thrilling for you. Walking?'

'I wish. No, in a . . . I don't know . . . van thing.'

'Minibus?'

'Probably.' She looked upwards and around, staring at the warehouses boxing them in. 'How can you stand all this? It's so . . . close.'

The man shrugged. 'You get used to it. Claustrophobia. Agoraphobia. I adapt. Oddly enough, I like this place. It has atmosphere.'

The woman took a swig of his Snapple and grimaced. 'Poison. Hope it chokes you.' She rose to leave, and then whispered in his ear, 'By the way, do these words mean anything to you? Woman. Bus. Dead.'

He turned away. 'Are you implying something?'

'No,' she said. 'I'm telling you you're getting careless. And obvious. Anyway, as I said –'

'You'll be in touch,' the man finished. ' 'Bye.'

She walked away, right past Rough Trade and down on to Floral Street. Five minutes later, he followed the same route. He stopped outside The Tintin Shop but it was closed. In the window was a foreign translation of *The Land of Black Gold*.

'Tinni and Tobbi and Kolbeinn Kaptienn.' He thought about coming back the next day and buying it for the two women who had been discussing the pop singer. 'No. Bet you couldn't understand a word of it in English, let alone Icelandic.'

Candles hugged closely, he went home.

Later that night an orange-and-cream-that-might-once-have-been-white Volkswagen minibus coughed and spluttered its way up the M6. Barely held together by rust

26

and flaking paint, the vehicle was being driven at a vaguely insane speed by a sullen-looking man with a streak of pure white through the centre of his jet-black hair.

Professor Nicholas Bridgeman sighed to himself, made a mental note not to criticize the driver and wondered what he had done to deserve all this. His co-passengers were two adults and three students, all from London's South Bank Polytechnic or, as it was now grandly renamed, the University of Greenwich.

Seated up front with the driver, staring ahead in total silence, was the bursar, Ms Thorsuun, a tall, ash-blonde Scandinavian woman with a very good grasp of English and known by the male students at the university as Miss Frost. Bridgeman finally decided it was worth the risk but ever the gentleman, he directed his request via Ms Thorsuun.

'If Herr Kerbe went a b-bit slower, Ms Thorsuun,' he stammered, 'this m-minibus might have a b-better chance of getting us up north in one piece.'

The driver turned his head slightly. He was wearing an expensive, plain grey suit which, being a university administrator, he felt he needed to be seen in. 'And if you sat still, Herr Professor,' he said, his German accent broad and aggressive, 'the bus wouldn't vibrate as much.'

The professor promptly flopped into a seat and looked sulkily at his grinning students. After a second, he, too, grinned. 'Did you check –' he started but a sigh from the well-tanned, well-built blond Australian opposite silenced him.

'Sure I did. You asked me so many times I'm beginning to doubt myself!'

'Sorry, Simon,' said the professor. He smiled moronically and nodded his head to imply he was being foolish. He knew that was Simon's opinion of him – but he was not upset or surprised. Bridgeman knew he was considered a bit eccentric and daft by both students and fellow academicians alike. His almost pathological secrecy surrounding his private life was one of the most common subjects of conversation in both the refectory and the staff rooms. Many students had offered interesting Jungian theories as to why the professor with the uncontrollable stammer was sometimes friendly and sometimes so taciturn whenever anyone tried to prise a piece of his past out of him. Bridgeman had heard most of them twenty times over in the last twelve years and none of them approached the truth.

A hand reached out to his knee. 'Everything's going to be fine, Professor Bridgeman. Don't worry yourself.'

Bridgeman ran a hand through his wayward hair. 'You're right, Carfrae. Sorry, all of you.'

The red-headed Welsh girl laughed, her blue eyes sparkling with anticipation of their time away, although he wasn't sure whether it was Simon's film-star looks or Peter's straightforward humour that really interested her. 'I'm looking forward to this, guys. Three weeks in a spook-house. If I'd known that's what an interest in chemistry was going to lead to I'd have done that instead of English.'

Peter, the other student, a second-generation Trinidadian from Wood Green, tugged at his seat-belt which was creasing his precious Ice-T T-shirt. 'But then you'd be a logical, closed-minded scientist. And we'd never have convinced you to come with us.'

'I rather take exception to that comment, Mr Moore,' said Bridgeman.

'Sorry, Prof,' said Peter, smiling at Carfrae. She smiled back.

It looked, Bridgeman decided, as if Peter was the lucky one.

Kerbe spoke up. 'Charnock Rickard services coming up. Anyone want a break?'

Thorsuun spoke for the first time in three hours. 'If you wouldn't mind, Herr Kerbe. I would like time to visit the washroom.' As an afterthought she turned to the professor and his students. And smiled. 'If that is all right with all of you?'

Bridgeman, aware that Peter was saying, 'Oh yeah, no problem. We could all do with a leg-stretch', was amused by the grin spreading across Simon's face. The young Australian had noticed that Thorsuun could smile. And what a legendary smile it was. Undoubtedly, the professor decided, in Simon Griffiths's opinion the journey had suddenly taken a turn for the better.

It was not a very large bedsit, but it serviced his needs. The house had been a fashionable house in the wealthier early-Twenties but had been converted into bedsits during the post-war Fifties after years of neglect and disrepair.

On the first day he had moved in, he passed his hand over the outermost wall, nearest the black front door. The landlady, Mrs Fuller, had given him a strange look as he had mumbled, 'I'm sorry you've been mistreated. Sadly your pain will continue.' On reflection, her bemusement was understandable. He kept reminding himself to be more careful.

Soon after, he had yanked open his weatherbeaten rucksack and taken out a book and a pen. Glancing at his last entry he had written a brief history of the house – noting all its former occupants (and servants), the births and deaths it had witnessed – including a strange one in 1974 which he felt sure the local constabulary would have been pleased to account for and finally close a file upon. Tough.

Seven months later, he felt quite at home – his wanderlust temporarily sated. He had put up his own black curtains and two posters – one with the words *Floodland* and The Sisters of Mercy on it, the other proclaiming that Siouxsie and the Banshees had a new recording called *Face to Face* out to tie in with some moving picture called *Batman Returns*.

He did not really understand the relevance of the words, but over the last few years in various other bedsits he had learned that adopting the appearance of something called 'a goth' made his interest in what ignorant landladies and mentally stunted so-called students called 'weird things and the supernatural' socially more acceptable. The only time it had been slightly risky had been earlier in the year, in Manchester – but he had quickly left the city behind him when the mistrust had got too much.

Sitting quietly he listened for the other occupants of the house. After a few seconds he relaxed – the other rooms were all empty. Only Mrs Fuller was in, down in her basement flat. She would stay there for at least an hour. It was Thursday – *Emmerdale* followed by Des O'Connor. What strange customs these people had – the invention of the television was such a strange event. So much potential and so misused. Instead of a marvellous method of communication, it was usurped for entertainment – a hollow pursuit – and sales.

Wars, famine, global accidents and natural disasters – all could be massively reduced and quickly cured if the television operators were not so totally obsessed with making money.

Modern society was a contradictory thing.

He started to concentrate. He stared at the three yellow candles and reached forward with the anointment oils. Slowly he poured liquid over each one and sat back.

He clicked his tongue. The three wicks flickered into flame. He rocked back and smiled. He stared at the male candle in the centre. And nodded.

After a few moments he rocked forward, and crossed his legs, tucking his feet in behind his knees. Covering his face with his hands, he dropped his body forward, burying his face in his waist and rolled slightly. His body was almost entirely shaped like a ball and he began chanting.

Down below, Mrs Fuller heard the soft chanting and felt a warm glow surround her. She sighed as Des O'Connor introduced his guest for the evening and felt completely satisfied. She liked it when her strange tenant began his Buddhist chants. Somehow, she felt safe. Warm. Soothed. As if all the goodness within him flowed throughout the building. A couple of the other tenants had admitted to similar feelings. Now and again Mrs Fuller was convinced that the paintwork on the house seemed cleaner and fresher the mornings after his chants. It was as if everything that could hear him renewed itself.

'Hear me.'

It was a voice. In a dream. Begging. Asking. Pleading.

Polly turned over in her sleep, unconsciously pulling the pillow over her head as if that would shut out the dream's voice. Instead, it amplified it. Brought it nearer. She moved again, sweating slightly. Acknowledging this, the TARDIS's internal thermostat dropped the humidity in Polly's room but she was heating up faster than even the TARDIS could cope with. Before long, the sweat began to seep through the soft silk sheets and into the mattress.

Polly kept turning and twisting.

'Hear me.'

It was an aggressive shout. It reminded Ben of Tilbury Docks, 1956. As a fourteen-year-old sneaking aboard the cargo ship his late father had worked on. His dad's dock-crane stood rusted to the side of the boat and he looked up at it. Dad was gone – in his place was Alfred. Mum seemed happy enough but Ben, ever the loner, could not get on with his stepfather and so decided to follow his real father's footsteps. The water beckoned.

He hid under the tarpaulin covering the crates destined for Singapore. Rebuilding the country after the failure of the Malay coup. Singapore. Hot. Sweaty. Ben. The TARDIS. The thermostat was unable to cope with his rapid rise in body temperature. He flayed out with an arm, sending his alarm clock to the floor, shattering it into fragments. Still he slept on. Disturbed but not awake.

'Hear me.'

The Doctor stopped polishing the time rotor switch

and stared into the slowly rising and lowering central column of the TARDIS console. The multicoloured shapes turned and gyrated but he was not seeing them. He saw a candle. Yellow. Shaped like . . . a man. No, like *him*. Behind it, two others and beyond them, a curled-up figure.

'Hear me, Doctor. Please. Sellafield. The house. The ghosts –'

The figure suddenly unwrapped itself and jumped up. Behind the man something moved. He was turning back to the candle, moving forward. The two yellow candles to the side tipped, their wicks going out. The figure's hand grabbed at the nearest candle, the one representing the Doctor . . .

It all happened in a rush. The hand gripping the candle dropped away. For a moment the Doctor saw the interior of a room. Bed. Table. Portable stove. Posters on the wall. A room in England, on Earth. Late twentieth century, going by the décor and posters. A student's room? If so, the posters could be a misleading dating system – from what the Doctor could remember of his previous self's visits to Earth, students were never the most up-to-date where music posters were concerned. Nevertheless, somewhere between 1985 and 1995 seemed a good guess.

The Doctor took all this in instantly. There was a flash and the candle melted totally. The hand holding it was bubbling and smouldering from the hot wax. Standing in the now open – no, vaporized – doorway was a creature. A creature with a gun.

'Help me!'

The message was inside his head. Not a shout. Not verbal. It was telepathic.

'Help me now!'

The mirage faded and the TARDIS's central column was once more just an opaque cylinder filled with geometric shapes rising, falling and turning.

The door to the corridor was flung open.

Ben was standing there, his pyjamas clinging to his body contours. For a moment the Doctor thought he had been caught in the rain until the odour told him it was sweat.

If he'd lost that much bodily fluid, Ben had to be dehydrated.

As the Doctor crossed to help him over to the Louis XIV, Ben looked up.

'Doc . . . help Pol. I think she's in danger.' The young sailor collapsed in a heap on the floor.

The Doctor dropped to his knees and felt for Ben's pulse. Strong but fluctuating. He would be all right after some rest and a drink.

Polly!

Polly was flying. Not in a plane but just by herself. Through the night sky above London. Over Seven Dials, towards Covent Garden. The Inferno, the nightclub where she had first met the Doctor on Thursday the thirteenth of July 1966. She was passing over it. Flying towards the river, along the Strand. Passing Trafalgar Square now, turning down the Mall, up to the Palace – and over!

Exhilaration. The cool night air made her goose bumps feel like the greatest goose bumps ever. It was a release – all her problems, her anxieties, seemed to fade away as she whipped up Buckingham Palace Road and up towards Sloane Square. No one could see her, of that she was sure. Otherwise there would be shouts and cries. A woman, flying! Free, like a bird.

She began to descend, involuntarily but slowly, around South Kensington. As her feet neared the pavement she landed as if she had flown all her life. The bump as her foot touched the kerb transformed into an easy step as she casually walked up a small flight of steps to a black front door.

Her hand reached out for the doorbell but there was a flash. She threw her hands in front of her face, her nose aware of the acrid burning of wood. The door was a pile of ashes and framed in the doorway was a creature. A monster.

Polly screamed.

She had faced robotic war machines, bionic Daleks and Cybermen. But an honest-to-God monster was a totally new experience.

Her subconscious mind took in the shape — it stood on two powerful legs, like a man, but the mammary glands told her it was female. It wore a sleeveless red jerkin and outsized red silk leggings, tucked into red leather boots. The flesh was covered in grey fur, flicked back and shining with health. The head, though. It was the head that wrenched the scream from her. It was a cat's head, green eyes staring in mute surprise at Polly. Its whiskers twitched and its ears dropped back flat against the furry skull. Drawing back its lips, it hissed and spat at her. In one paw was a massive hand-gun and as Polly backed away the monster brought it up to fire.

Self-preservation took over and Polly dived. Not back, but forward, under the cat-thing's legs. It turned to follow but Polly instinctively smashed her fists down on its tail.

With a loud catawaul, the cat-thing dropped its gun and its claws unfurled. It lashed out, catching at Polly's sweater, shredding it apart. Polly scrambled back into the large entrance hall. To one side, an elderly woman lay spread-eagled on the bottom steps. Polly was no expert but she had seen enough corpses to recognize another one. Sitting further up the stairs was a young man, rolled up like a ball. Polly had time to be aware that he was moaning softly before the cat used its powerful legs to pounce on her.

Polly's second scream alerted the man who suddenly looked up.

'No,' he yelled. 'No! Not you. Where's the Doctor?'

Polly woke up, screaming.

* * *

34

Friday the eighth of July 1994. Eight o'clock in the morning exactly. The fire services, police and ambulances arrived very quickly. The small blaze was quickly doused and it was of some relief to the occupants of the bed-sits that the only rooms affected were the ground-floor rooms and the hallway.

'It was that goth. Told you he was weird.'

'All those candles and spells.'

'Where is he? Was he burned up as well?'

'Bet one of his stupid candles fell against those black curtains of his and *whommpf*, up it all went.'

'Poor Mrs Fuller.'

'Hey – does this mean we're gonna be evicted?'

The police never found any trace of the mysterious goth who lived in Flat 1. Nothing was left in anything approaching salvageable condition and no one even knew his name.

Maybe he had been completely burned up.

Poor Mrs Fuller. Looked as if she had inhaled the smoke and tripped coming down the stairs; her neck and back were broken in more places than the pathologist had ever seen before. But he could not account for the massive scratch across the back of her neck. Nothing on the stairs or floor could account for that. It reminded him of a large claw mark, like a playful kitten would leave on a hand. Except this playful kitten would have to be lion-sized – or around six feet tall. And there were no reports of animals having escaped from Regent's Park zoo recently.

Like so many mysterious deaths at 164 Cadogan Terrace, SW1, over the last one hundred years, the police report on these two would never be satisfactorily closed.

'Polly? Polly Wright?'

The haze cleared and the lovely voice made her smile.

'Pol, you OK?'

A different voice, but one that was still reassuring.

'Ben? Doctor?'

Her vision cleared completely and the Doctor was beaming at her. He clapped his hands together.

'There you are, Ben. I said Polly would be all right, given time.'

Ben was still looking worried. 'Yeah. Right. Polly, you gave us a bit of a fright.'

'I . . . I'm sorry, Ben. I had the most frightful dream.' Suddenly she sat upright and the Doctor looked back at her questioningly. 'Doctor. Doctor, I was flying. Through London, although it wasn't quite right. It smelled . . . funny. Heavy.'

Ben's eyebrows raised. 'Flying? In an aeroplane?'

Polly frowned. 'No . . . no, just by myself . . .'

Ben laughed.

The Doctor waved him down. 'Quiet, Ben, this could be important.' He smiled again at Polly and crouched down beside her bed. 'Tell me everything, Polly. Don't miss out any detail.'

After she had finished her story, Polly asked Ben to get her a drink. As he wandered off, she touched the Doctor's arm.

'I had an out-of-body experience, didn't I?'

The Doctor shrugged. 'Why do you think that, my dear?'

Polly shrugged. 'I . . . I'm not sure. One of my old flames, Roger, he used to be heavily into that sort of thing. Hare Krishna. Reincarnation, spiritual movement.'

'And you? Did you believe?'

Polly pulled the sodden bedspread towards her and drew her knees up. 'No. Of course not.'

'Are you sure? Not just a little?'

Polly looked at the Doctor and he smiled. Polly relaxed.

'Well, a bit I suppose. Ghosts, or spirits, things like that. I went to a seance once. Contacted Daddy's brother − not Uncle Charles but Uncle Randolph. He died during the war. It was . . . weird. I don't remember much about it, but apparently I blacked out and the others claim

36

Uncle Randolph spoke through me. When I told him about it, Roger said I was possibly a natural medium or something.' She looked at her hands and played with a ring on her finger. 'Devon's funny like that. Once I moved to London to work for Professor Brett, well, those silly things just got forgotten. But just now, dreaming, I felt like I did down in Devon. At the seance. Sort of detached.'

The Doctor nodded. 'Well, Polly, it's not all rubbish, although a lot of people bury true spiritualism under silly mumbo-jumbo that makes it more pantomime than reality. Psionics is not an exact science but quite real nevertheless. Ghosts as such – your traditional sheet-wearing spooks come to haunt you or lead you to buried treasure – aren't entirely real, but some sorts of apparitions can exist.'

Ben walked in with a jug of water and three glasses. The Doctor looked at him. 'I think you ought to get out of those damp pyjamas, Ben. You'll catch a chill.'

'I'm OK –' he began to protest, but a look from the Doctor and he took the hint. 'Yeah. I'll have a shower too, if that's all right.'

After he had gone, the Doctor sat on Polly's bed and poured them both some water. 'Basically, there are two types of ghost, for want of a better word. There is a theory that everything material – bricks, stone, trees, et cetera – are all like tape recorders. Everything that occurs, the echo of every noise and touch and even passing people is somehow absorbed, and when the vibrations are right – sometimes sound, sometimes powerfully strong emotions like fear, anger or hatred – they can be played back like a recording. Thus ghosts. A far more likely alternative is that time is like a silk sheet. It wears down now and again and tiny breaks occur. Before they can be repaired something breaks through from the past or future from that exact physical point in space – a ghost.' The Doctor drank some water. 'I'm not saying which, if either, is right, but they both have evidence to support them and cynics to decry them. I believe in an open mind. I think you do too.'

Polly nodded. And smiled. 'I bet Ben wouldn't be so understanding.'

'Oh, don't count him out. He is brusque and brave but underneath it all, quite sensitive.' The Doctor grinned. 'Mind you, I expect out-of-body experiences are a bit out of his league, so let's not bother him with that right now. No, I think you were receiving a message. From the young man you saw. I had a similar vision. I think he was trying to deliberately attract my attention but your susceptibility to psionic powers caused you to take my place as a physical vessel.'

'He seemed to be in a lot of trouble. And there was that cat-thing.'

'Hmmm. A Cat-Person. The Felinetta are a widespread race of galactic scavengers, I think originally from the Lynx constellation. Like cats on Earth, they are split into many different races across the stars: the Lion-Men of Mongo, the Felinoids of Cait, the Cheetah People and their genetically engineered Kitlings, the mercenaries of Gin-Seng; even the Aegis have been known to use metamorphic cats in their undercover missions. I wonder where your Cat-Person was from? Vedela, perhaps, or Capella? It could have been one of the Kzinti warriors, I suppose . . .'

Polly could see this going on for a while. 'She was well-armed, anyway,' she interrupted. 'I'm fairly certain she'd killed the old lady and was going to kill the man.' Polly shivered suddenly. 'Oh, Doctor, it was horrible.'

As Polly hid her face in her crossed arms, the Doctor patted her on the back. 'There, there, Polly. It's over now. I think we'll go on holiday. I know a nice place in the north-west of England, in Cumbria. Shall we stop off for some Irish Sea air?'

Polly smiled. 'Oh yes, please, that would be so nice.'

Friday the eighth of July 1994. Eight o'clock in the morning.

Peter Moore never knew what hit him.

One minute he was cheerfully gnawing on a rather dry cucumber sandwich, the next he was flat on his back at the foot of the wooden staircase he had been climbing. He was no longer cheerful or eating. Instead his left arm was twisted awkwardly behind his back and although it did not hurt as such – just a dull ache – he was aware that it felt numb and that was not right.

He wanted to call out to the others but as he opened his mouth a blast of chill air swept over him, drawing both his voice and courage away. His eyes widened as something came towards him, floating down the stairs. It was a woman, dressed in a severe black uniform, a tiny white pinny around her waist, tightened cruelly enough to give the impression of a slimness she did not really possess. He stared in mute surprise – although she took very deliberate steps it was as if she was descending an invisible set of treads four inches above the real ones. Her feet were not touching anything.

Peter noticed that she was carrying something in her right hand, cupped out of sight by the other. She clearly had not noticed him, her eyes fixed dead ahead. Only as she stepped a mere three steps from him did her face change. She looked down, not at Peter but to his left. He followed her gaze but there was nothing there, just the dusty wooden floor. He looked back at her and realized that her skin was quite grey and there were dark rings under her eyes. She was either unwell or lacking in sleep and she seemed to be fighting back against some pain.

Suddenly she stopped, her hand falling away to reveal a candle in a holder but Peter saw no extra light from it, or felt even a waft of warmth. Like the woman, it was as if it were not quite there – just a step out of sync with him and the house. Her eyes widened, still looking away from the floor and to his left. Peter could not move because of his arm but knew she was staring at the door he had come out of. Slowly she shook her head and her mouth opened wide in horror. She screamed and dropped the candle.

39

Peter expected to hear her shrill yell but instead his ear drums were buffeted by a rush of wind and a screeching like fingernails across a chalkboard. He tried to put his good arm towards his head to block out the noise but could not. The woman stumbled and fell towards him. Instinctively, he pushed his arm forward to ward off her body although he knew he would never feel it.

In the last second, he heard her yell and his scream joined hers in a cacophony of terror.

There was an almighty crash behind him and he was aware that pairs of hands were hauling him up and away from the stairs into a room. Soothing words were being whispered in one ear by a soft Welsh-accented voice while on the other side, a familiar Australian male was making waspish comments about weight and alcohol intake.

'Si . . . ?'

'Shut up and sit down,' was Simon's response.

The screaming was fading – his own and the woman's. Gradually his eyes focused. He was back in the Ex-Room, the team's concerned faces staring at him. One seemed to detach itself from the others and float towards him, and Peter shook his head trying to restore his vision to normal. He blinked a couple of times and sure enough Professor Bridgeman was there, a pen-torch flashing into his eyes. Peter winced and tried to pull away but Bridgeman's grip was strong.

'N-now, Peter, do stop fussing. You know this doesn't hurt,' Bridgeman was saying.

'Sorry,' mumbled Peter, his vocal chords finally reasserting themselves. 'What . . . what happened?'

'You tell us,' grunted Simon beside him.

Peter turned from Bridgeman's blinking light and stared up at Simon's blond-framed face. He tried to reach out and grasp his friend's arm, but instead a thousand needles drilled into his brain and he cried out.

'Jeez – his arm!' Simon leaned over and Peter felt his arm being moved. It was only a gentle movement but he could not help releasing a further yelp of agony.

'Is it broken?' asked Carfrae.

Peter had let his cries become a soft gasp by now and as he rested his head back he saw the glare that Simon shot Carfrae. 'No, he's making this fuss because he's snagged his sleeve,' he growled.

'I only asked,' she said.

Peter waved the bickering away. 'Hey, guys, not over me, 'kay?'

Professor Bridgeman came into his vision again. 'Let me see that arm p-please, Simon,' he said. Bending down, he carefully ran his hand around it, wincing slightly as he felt near the elbow. Peter found himself wincing as well. 'Not broken, I think. But probably dislocated in a very awkward place.' He tutted quietly. 'I k-keep telling you youngsters to take it easy. Do you ever listen?'

'Apparently not,' snapped a Germanic voice from the opposite doorway. Peter tried to look up but then decided he could not be bothered. It was only Kerbe, probably still dressed as if he were addressing some high-powered executive board meeting, his gelled hair slicked into perfect shape and not a trace of five o'clock shadow. How did he always look so perfect? He carried on barking at them, rude as always. 'It seems that I cannot leave you alone for more than three minutes before you injure yourself. Next time, I will pick my team more carefully.'

'I would thank you, Herr Kerbe, n-not to belittle "your team" so freely in future,' said Bridgeman. 'P-poor Peter has had an accident that any of us could have at any time. An unavoidable one, due to no one and nothing.'

Kerbe stared at Peter and gave a tiny nod and smiled tightly. 'I apologize, everyone. My concern for Mr Moore's injury made me . . . cranky, I think you would say. I apologize.'

Peter smiled inwardly at Kerbe's badly faked humanity. He knew damn well that Kerbe's grasp of English, especially slang and colloquialisms, was better than most British people and even his heavy accent was exaggerated

41

for effect. His humour dissipated however when 'Miss Frost' emerged from the kitchen. The room that only the two of them were ever allowed to enter.

'Herr Kerbe, I think you ought to see these readings.' She handed Kerbe a scrap of paper. He flicked his eyes over it and turned back towards the kitchen. Without acknowledging the others, Thorsuun followed him, closing the door behind her.

'Well, Miss Frost is in fine form,' said Simon to no one in particular.

Carfrae shrugged. 'They deserve each other.'

Peter groaned over-dramatically to remind them of his arm and then felt guilty as they turned their attention back to him.

'Should we get him to a hospital?' Carfrae was staring out of the far picture window at the flat meadow outside. In the distance, the brick pillars that marked the end of the long drive baited her, but she turned back to Peter. For the sake of the experiment, they had been forbidden to leave, they all knew that. Peter saw Simon looking at Carfrae and she averted her eyes, staring at the ground. 'Gut reaction,' she said. 'I'm sorry.'

He reached out to her and touched her arm. 'Mine, too. If only . . .'

Peter almost flinched as Bridgeman suddenly moved away from him. 'All right. I've had enough. Yes, Carfrae, young Peter does n–need a hospital. Blast Kerbe and his restrictions, I'm going to get help.'

Simon grinned broadly. 'OK, Prof, great. But how?'

Bridgeman ran a hand through his thinning hair, and caused a lock of it to fall boyishly over his left eye. With an experienced puff he blew it back into place and crossed to the door leading to the stairway. 'Stall for time if Kerbe comes back out. There's a phone box down by the station. Either I'll call the ambulance from there or I'll take the coastal line to Sellafield and get one of their staff.'

Simon nodded and Peter noted that he put a protective

arm around Carfrae. Raising her eyes to heaven she shook him off and smiled at Peter.

'Good luck, Professor,' he said, trying to prop himself up. 'And thanks.'

Bridgeman closed the door behind him, feeling rather ridiculous and furtive. He looked up the staircase. No one. He breathed out. Of course not; Kerbe had sent the men who had greeted them on their arrival, Smithers and Coates, back to their gatehouse elsewhere on the estate. He crossed quietly to the massive oak front door and slid the bolt back silently. Next he twisted the Yale lock and turned the Chubb key in its mortise. He silently thanked Smithers for keeping everything well oiled and therefore totally quiet. As light snuck in around the opening door a voice from behind froze him.

'Ah, Professor Bridgeman, seeking a little early morning air. You know what they say. Cumbria has England's cleanest.'

Bridgeman straightened his shoulders and faced Kerbe, determined to bluff it out. 'A-actually, yes . . .' he began. Then he saw the compact Mauser in Kerbe's hand.

'One squeeze from this, Professor Bridgeman, and you'll be cut in two before you could finish breathing one molecule. Now, close the door, please. I fear you have already contaminated the atmosphere in here. That could set our work back weeks.'

Bridgeman sighed in resignation and began to push the door closed.

However, at the last second, a scruffy black ankle-boot poked through, stopping the movement. Surprised, Bridgeman stood away and the door was pushed open. Following the ankle-boot was a leg in oversized checked trousers and then the body of a middle-aged dark-haired man in a long black frock-coat. He carried himself as if the words brush, comb and ironing board were alien gibberish and smiled benignly at Kerbe and Bridgeman, seemingly unaware of the Mauser. He straightened the bow-tie attached to the collar of his sky-blue shirt with a safety pin and grasped Bridgeman by the hand. 'My dear Bridgeman, what a pleasure it is to see you again.' The man called over his shoulder, 'Now, come on in, you two.'

Bridgeman just stared as two more people came into the mansion. One was a man in his early twenties; short straw-blond hair topped a deeply tanned face, marked by high cheekbones and he wore a grey polo-necked sweater and grey slacks. But it was the third member of the party that really made Bridgeman gape. She had long platinum hair tied back in a pony-tail, huge false eyelashes and thick black eyeliner emphasizing beautiful blue eyes. She was wearing knee-length red vinyl boots and a matching red skirt which barely dropped below her waist. Her top – a rather ample top, Bridgeman decided – was clothed in a tight orange roll-neck sweater and over this she wore a see-through PVC raincoat, hanging only an inch or so below her skirt.

'There,' said the little mop-haired man. 'There, I told you we'd be welcome.' He turned back to Bridgeman. 'Well, Professor, I hope you remember my old friend Ben Jackson.' He pointed at the man in grey.

Bridgeman just nodded dumbly at Ben.

'Nice to see you again, Prof,' said Ben, gingerly shaking the proffered hand.

The small man presented the platinum blonde. 'And this is my secretary, Polly Wright.'

Bridgeman took her hand. 'Delighted, Miss Wright.'

Polly smiled back. 'A pleasure, Professor. The Doctor here has told me so much about you.'

The Doctor positively glowed at her. He scampered over to Kerbe who was staring dumbfounded at the newcomers. Ignoring the drooping gun, the Doctor held out his hand. 'And you are, sir?'

Automatically Kerbe held out his hand and then realized the gun was in it. Suddenly it was not – it was in the Doctor's, who spun it expertly on his finger like a Western gunslinger and swiftly pocketed it.

'Horrible things. Make loud bangs. I hate loud bangs, don't you?'

Kerbe nodded stupidly. 'Kerbe. Marten Kerbe. How do you do?' He was disturbed by his blonde assistant coming out from the kitchen.

'Herr Kerbe? Who are these people?'

Kerbe suddenly reasserted control. 'A good question, Fräulein Thorsuun.' He held out his hand expectantly, and sheepishly the newcomer returned the pistol. Kerbe slipped it back into its holster under his jacket. 'Well?'

The man called the Doctor suddenly frowned. 'Well, that's not much of a reception, is it, Herr Kerbe. After all, it was you who invited us here. Still, I suppose we could always go again, although I shall want my expenses in full. It's a long way from London, you know, and the traffic was very bad up the M6 –'

Bridgeman suddenly piped up. 'Of course, I . . . I'm sure Herr Kerbe remembers me telling him about you, Doctor. Please come through into the Ex-Room. My students will be overjoyed to meet you at last.'

'Thank you, Professor. Most kind.' As Bridgeman pushed the door open, Ben and Polly trooped through. With a last look of affronted derision at Kerbe, the Doctor followed them in and, smiling at the man's audacity, Bridgeman nipped in and closed the door.

Kerbe and Thorsuun stared at the Ex-Room door.

'Well,' said Thorsuun after a few seconds, 'you handled that brilliantly.'

Kerbe snarled at her. 'Don't talk to me like that –' Thorsuun's right hand slapped him across the face with enough force that it echoed. He stared in shock.

'Don't let us down again, human,' she spat and went back through the door to the kitchen.

Kerbe rubbed his sore cheek and followed her.

He shuffled the deck and closed his eyes. Concentrating. Thinking about the question in his mind – needing to know the answer.

Karen Kuykendall created the Tarot of the Cat People in 1985 – hardly a surprising subject for a woman renowned for her art and literature featuring cats throughout the Western world. It amused him to use her tarot for his readings. The irony was . . . interesting.

He laid out the first pile. Eleven cards – The Four of Pentacles on the top, upside-down.

The second pile. Eleven cards – The Page of Pentacles on top.

With the third pile he only got as far as eight cards before The Ace of Wands stopped him.

Two from the Sapphire Kingdom, one from the Emerald Kingdom. The Four of Pentacles was fairly insignificant – it suggested financial matters, and some sort of failure. Maybe it was not that insignificant actually. Then there was The Page of Pentacles. An excellent card – the reference it implied to a girl fitted perfectly. She would make him proud and there was always a suggestion of travel. The Ace of Wands was the best of all, the implication of a new business venture, and a successful one at that. The birth of new ideas and good news. He was lucky – his question had been answered satisfactorily. The girl – Polly Wright. She was the one. He had been right to contact her after all. Hers was the mind, the power and the belief to help him.

She was his – and heaven help anyone who stood in his way.

Ben frowned as the Doctor rudely dragged a finger along the small fireplace and sniffed at the dust.

'Very nice, indeed. You've been here about three days I assume?'

The professor looked astonished. 'How could you tell . . . ?'

The Doctor's green eyes twinkled and he flexed his fingers. He reminded Ben of a concert pianist about to give the performance of his life. To one side, he was aware of the Welsh girl passing a glass of water to an obviously injured black kid, who winced as he shifted his weight.

'You're hurt.' Polly suddenly sat beside the boy. 'What happened? Can I get you anything?'

'Peter fell down the stairs,' Carfrae said stiffly. She was a bit of a looker, Ben decided. Soft red hair falling straight down her back, and a few freckles dotting her face. Give her a couple of years . . . 'I can look after him,' she was saying pointedly to Polly.

Polly smiled. 'Of course you can. I'm sorry.'

'Don't be,' croaked Peter. 'I can't remember the last time I had so much attention.'

Professor Bridgeman was looking at the Doctor, pursing his lips. 'N-now, I don't wish to be rude, and thank you for sorting out Herr Kerbe, but who are you really?'

Simon, who had heard the scene in the hall, looked at Bridgeman in astonishment. 'You mean, you don't really know who these people are?'

Bridgeman shook his head. 'N-never seen any of them before. Ever.'

The Doctor wiped his fingers on his frock-coat. 'Well, that's all very irrelevant. We are here and that's what matters. Now, why are *you* here, Professor? And why does your Teutonic friend wave a pistol around so casually?'

'He's frightened of something,' muttered Ben.

The Doctor nodded. 'Indeed. Well observed, Ben. But of what? Or who?'

Simon shrugged. 'Miss Frost out there. Fräulein Thorsuun.'

'She looked a bit of all right to me,' Ben said.

The Australian shrugged. 'Looks aren't everything. She's . . . well, weird.'

Professor Bridgeman had clearly decided that a bit of order and less adolescent spite was required. He tutted. 'N-now, Simon. Don't dismiss her like that. She's still the bursar. However unpleasant she may be at times, you should always respect those in authority.'

47

'You know, Professor Bridgeman,' said the Doctor, 'I've never had much respect for people in authority. Least of all those who hide behind guns and thugs.'

Bridgeman coughed slightly. 'Herr Kerbe is hardly a thug, Doctor.'

'Could've fooled me,' said Polly. 'If we hadn't arrived when we did –'

Ben started to cough, but it was too late. Bridgeman decided to question her on that one. 'Yes, where *did* you come from? The house is hardly on the main road.'

'How did you get past Smithers and Coates?' added Simon.

The Doctor stared at a spot of dust that had fallen on to one of his shoes and he bent over to clean it. 'Well, er . . . I don't think how we got here is particularly relevant. I think it was just a good thing that we did. Saved a bit of bother.' Before anyone else could ask awkward questions, he was scurrying over to the equipment laid out on the tables. 'This is an Ex-Room, isn't it? You're ghost-hunting. What fun.' The Doctor beamed over at Peter. 'And you thought you'd found a ghost, it startled you and so you had a bit of a fall. Am I right?'

'Proper little Sherlock Holmes, ain'tcha, Doc?' said Ben. He felt a slight pressure on his arm and turned away as Bridgeman began showing the Doctor over the equipment. 'What's up, Duchess?'

Polly pointed at the equipment. 'I knew we were home, Ben, but I think we're too late.'

'Not 1986 again,' he groaned. 'But at least it's warmer here than at the South Pole.'

'I think it might be later than that, Ben. All that equipment over there – it seems a bit, well, advanced I suppose. I mean, I recognize a microphone, but it's attached to that tiny box. I can't see a tape anywhere. And then there's this.' A quick look to see that no one was watching and Polly slipped her hand into a green ruck-sack by Peter's makeshift bed. She pulled out a thin plastic square.

'What is it, Pol?'

She flipped it open. Inside was a small reflective disc, about five inches across. 'I think it's a record of some sort. There's the hole in the middle and it's by the Beatles. It's called *Let it Be*. But look at the picture on the front. They look so different. So . . . old.'

'I always knew they'd last for ever.' Ben snatched the box. 'There must be a date on it. Yes, here. 1969.'

'Yes, but look. Re-mastered in 1989. Ben, we're nearly a quarter of a century away from home.'

The box was suddenly removed from Polly's hand and dropped back into the rucksack. Ben turned to protest but found himself facing the sardonic smile of Fräulein Thorsuun. 'It's called a compact disc. It's the replacement for the vinyl records you're used to. And I doubt young Carfrae there would like to know that you were being light-fingered.'

Polly stared in shock. 'Stealing?' she hissed. 'Never! We were just . . . just . . .'

Thorsuun held up a hand. 'I know. Trying to work out which year you're in. 1994. I take it you're from the late Sixties?'

Ben nodded. '1966,' he said. This Thorsuun woman seemed to take their time-travelling in her stride. He suddenly felt very wary, and took an instinctively protective step nearer Polly.

'And him?' Thorsuun nodded at the Doctor.

Ben found himself having to answer. He did not want to. He wanted to avoid answering this strange, cold woman's questions and yet he felt he had to. 'He's the Doctor. I don't know where or when he's from. We met him –'

'I know,' said Thorsuun. '1966. You said.'

Ben looked at Polly and then back at Thorsuun. 'You don't seem entirely surprised. Is time travel common by 1994?'

Thorsuun smiled. Broadly. 'Oh, you sweet little creature. Of course it's not. There have been instances over

49

the last few decades, a couple of incoherent references in newspapers and *The Fortean Times*. But on the whole, time travel is restricted to a few lucky people.'

Polly decided it was time to be defensive. 'And you're one of those "lucky people"?'

'Don't I wish. No, I'm merely immortal. An illegal alien, you might say. Immortal and stuck here. For now.'

'Are you going to escape then?'

Thorsuun stroked Ben's cheek and he found it impossible to push her away. 'Of course, little creature. You and the Doctor are going to take me far away.'

'I'm sure if you asked the Doc –' Polly began but Thorsuun's face lost its smile – and it was replaced by a twisted sneer.

'Asked? Asked? You poor morsel. I don't ask. The Doctor will take me – of that I'm sure.'

'Why?' Polly was determined not to be put off.

'Because if he doesn't this rather backward lump of rock is going to be reduced to a radioactive cinder smaller than that CD. In about ten hours. And only I can stop it.'

Ben and Polly looked across at the Doctor.

As if aware that he was being stared at, the Doctor slowly looked up and saw Thorsuun. Ben looked at her and then back at the Doctor. For the first time since he had known him, he saw a look of pure surprise on the Doctor's face. Surprise and something else.

Fear.

Thorsuun smiled again.

George Smithers had lived in Cumbria all his life. For the last twenty years of his working life, he had been an admin clerk at the Windscale nuclear plant – or Sellafield as it had been renamed after a bout of bad publicity in the early eighties.

After his son died of leukemia in 1987, he had begun to question the reassurances he and his fellow workers had been given regarding the safety of fissionable fuels. After his wife had died in 1991 from lung cancer (admittedly she was a twenty-a-day smoker) the questions and doubts had become vocal recriminations. It had been quietly suggested that he take advantage of a good redundancy package and the offer of a rent-free cottage in one of the nearby villages.

'There's scores of youngsters out there looking for work, George,' they had said. 'You're not happy here. You've had more than your fair share of trauma and tragedies. We think you'd be better off out of here, but we want to show you our appreciation and recognition of your work.'

They had given him a quite healthy lump sum and the Gatehouse on the Grange estate, working for some German administrator from one of the London universities. On his last day his colleagues had wished him well, stuffed half a dozen bottles of Jack Daniels in his bag (and a couple of doubles down his unprotesting throat) and seen him to the perimeter fence. He had nodded a sad farewell to old Chalky at the Visitors' Centre and passed through the gates. With a last look at the KEEP OUT sign, with its NUCLEAR PLANTS ACT 1966 addendum, George Smithers had begun his new life.

The move into the Gatehouse was the best thing possible. Selling off the old converted farmhouse had been a wrench but ultimately the memories had faded. He had ploughed most of his redundancy into the Leeds – that Arthur Daley advert had convinced him of the value in that – but paid for a short holiday to Majorca. In forty-seven years, he had never gone further south than Duckenfield and so abroad had been a bit of an adventure.

'I need an estate manager for my Cumbrian house,' the German, Kerbe, had said on the phone. 'I already have a gamekeeper up there. Well,' he chuckled in a way George had come to like, 'I use the term loosely. Poor Mr Coates has no poachers to fend off, nor any game to protect. He's more of a caretaker, but he liked the title of gamekeeper. You British are so proud when it comes to job titles. But he looks after the wear and tear of the place. I let it to students doing research and although sometimes either I, or our bursar, go with them, nine times out of ten, it's just some befuddled university lecturer who might tell you the chemical composition of grass but try to convince him to pay the milkman, and he's panic-struck. That's what I need you for. And since you're already a local, what more can I ask for?'

Two weeks later George Smithers was working on the estate, renovating the kitchen at the Grange and generally doing all that was asked of him. Helping with all this was Charlie Coates, a weaselly looking man who might have played a good armed robber in an episode of *The Bill*. George Smithers was not sure he entirely liked Coates but he had to admit he was not unpleasant or rude. Just a bit shifty. One day he would ask Kerbe where he had found his 'gamekeeper' – somehow he did not fancy asking Coates directly.

Coates had later introduced him to the university's bursar (and rumoured by Coates and others to be Kerbe's 'fancy woman'), Fräulein Thorsuun, who arrived one weekend to prepare for the next batch of students. George Smithers took an instant dislike to her but Coates fawned and doffed and generally crawled. George soon got the notion that if she were kept sweet, all would be well with Kerbe.

George Smithers did not want to move home again. He was nice to Fräulein Thorsuun.

He was dimly aware that Coates was doing strange things to the locks up on the big house but chose not to enquire what. The papers and invoices from the locksmiths passed through his hands, he signed the credit slips and thought nothing more of it.

Until the night of the noises.

Firstly there had been an amazing groaning and wheezing sound right outside his office window. It was dark but he could clearly see a dark blue box outside, in the trees. Where it had come from he did not know but when he went to investigate, he decided upon an answer. It was an old police box. There had been a couple in Carlisle once, huge concrete things. This seemed to be wooden. Students. Normally it was traffic cones and the occasional policeman's helmet. A police box was a new one on him, but it was not doing any harm. And knowing students, it would be gone in the morning.

The second noise was an equally weird one. A popping sound, as if someone had pulled a huge plug or stopper out of something. Again he went outside but could see nothing until he heard voices from behind his Gatehouse. Slowly he walked around the house, hiding in the shadows. He recognized Coates's voice, but there was a strange, feminine voice as well. It sort of . . . purred, rolling its Rs and its Ss were sibilant. He caught a glimpse of Coates and two others, the newcomers dressed in what looked like red leather, with black studs all over. George Smithers's first thought was that they were students going to a fancy-dress party.

As he kicked a dustbin and Coates and his friends turned to look at him, George Smithers's next thought was one so ridiculous and incredible that he could not really comprehend it.

Facing him, dressed in that red studded leather and carrying a massive futuristic rifle, was a standing-upright five-foot something tabby cat with a scar.

He wanted to laugh but it aimed its gun and fired . . .

Episode Two

'An ambulance is out of the question. I'm sorry.' Kerbe was seated at the foot of the stairway where Peter had fallen earlier. He casually ran a hand along the wooden banister and then began tracing the space between the balustrades with the palm of his hand. He was smiling, his head slightly cocked to one side. He neither looked nor sounded sorry at all.

Bridgeman stared at Kerbe with as much obvious fury as he could muster. 'But Peter is injured.'

'And you know, Professor, that I cannot allow anyone to come here and interfere with the project.' Kerbe tapped the bulge under his jacket, reminding the professor that he was armed and prepared to use force if necessary.

Bridgeman shrugged. 'Why? I d-don't understand. They're just children.'

'They are young adults, Professor Bridgeman,' said Thorsuun, emerging from the kitchen. 'I doubt they would appreciate being called *Kinder*. And I don't think Peter's injury is life-threatening.'

'B-but the Doctor says –'

Kerbe stood up abruptly. 'Mr Bridgeman, I don't give a damn what your colleague thinks. You had no right to invite him here in the first place without informing either myself or the bursar.' He waved a hand dismissively in Thorsuun's direction.

She threw him an equally dismissive look – which he did not acknowledge – and suddenly beamed at Bridgeman. 'And anyway, he's a doctor. Surely he can look after Mr Moore?'

'He says he's not that kind of Doctor. H-he says –'

Thorsuun raised her hand to stop him and crossed to sit beside Kerbe. She nestled her head on his shoulder, and Bridgeman noted with a second's worth of pleasure the look of alarm that crossed the German's face. Kerbe was renowned for his dislike of tactility.

'Tell me, Professor,' she continued, 'as he's such an old friend of yours, what is his exact speciality?'

Bridgeman began to stammer and stutter some kind of incoherent answer but before he got very far Thorsuun stood up and stamped her foot. 'Professor Bridgeman, shut up!' Bridgeman fell silent. She pointed at the front door. 'If you want to get an ambulance and check Peter's arm, fine. Go outside and do so. I shan't stop you.'

'But he will.' Bridgeman pointed at Kerbe.

'No he won't.'

'Yes I will.' Kerbe's hand went for his gun.

'No you won't,' emphasized Thorsuun. She smiled at the professor. 'Please, feel free to go. This has got way out of hand. Good luck.'

Without waiting for her to change her mind, Bridgeman rushed to the door, pulled the bolts back and ran outside. There was a phone at the bottom of the road. He had seen it from the minibus when they had driven up the night before. He could use that. Call an ambulance for Peter. Contact the university and tell them that something was wrong – that Thorsuun and Kerbe were up to something.

But what? As the thoughts raced around his already confused mind, Bridgeman realized that phoning the uni and trying to talk about guns, prisoners and strange doctors would make him sound like a madman.

He had stumbled down the road and after about ten minutes could see the red of the phone box on the horizon. Just a few more moments.

A few more yards. A few more steps.

Then he saw them. Staring at him. The one in the wheelchair pointed. And laughed.

'What the hell were you thinking of?' Kerbe was having a hard time keeping his voice calm. 'We can't just let him go for help. We have to keep the house secluded, cut off completely or you'll never get through. You've ruined it.'

Thorsuun swung round on him and he braced himself for the face-slap. Instead she smiled. The sort of smile that Kerbe used to read about in stories of the Medusa turning her victims to stone. 'I think he'll have problems getting through this morning.' She turned away and went back through into the kitchen whistling a strange, compelling tune that Kerbe could not quite place. After she had gone, he found he had to sit down on the steps again. Something was wrong but he could not put his finger on it. He needed Smithers and Coates around. He needed someone to shout at. To bully.

The Doctor's secretary and her man-friend came out of the Ex-Room and wandered towards him. They would do.

'He's sleeping now.' Carfrae pulled the duvet up to Peter's chin and stared at his face, eyes tightly closed, a frown creasing his forehead. She felt a warm hand on her shoulder and looked up at the Doctor.

His eyes were smiling. What a stupid expression, she thought – how can eyes smile? Besides, his mouth certainly was not. Yet as she found herself looking into his blue eyes (or were they more grey?) she felt a shiver go down her back. She relaxed – all her pent-up tension had suddenly been drawn away. It was those eyes. Something in the green (or were they blue?) eyes . . .

'I think he'll be fine.' The Doctor rubbed his finger and thumb together. 'Now, we must try and find out what exactly is going on here.'

'Maybe the place is really haunted,' muttered a surly

Australian voice from beside the boarded-up window.

'That's what we're here to find out, Si,' snapped back Carfrae.

'Oh, I'm sure it's what you're here for, my dear,' said the Doctor. 'Only I'm not convinced that your Herr Kerbe and Fräulein Thorsuun have the same goals as you.'

'Why not?' asked Simon.

'Well, firstly because the average ghost-hunters, especially well-equipped university types, don't walk around with loaded Mauser pistols waving them at their fellow academics. Secondly because there is no reason to be so paranoid about keeping this house secure. We're a good twelve minutes' walk from the village. There's no phone, no television and most of the house hasn't got electricity connected.'

'Just here and the kitchen,' said Carfrae.

'And the main hall and staircase,' added Simon. 'But the upstairs is completely cut off.'

'What about the Gatehouse at the end of the drive?'

Simon shrugged. 'I guess not. I know we had to leave messages about our trip with the post office for Smithers and Coates.'

The Doctor produced a tiny notebook and a pencil, licked the end of the pencil and began to write. 'So. We're cut off in every sense. I really do wonder what she's up to.'

'Who? Thorsuun? Miss Frost is just Kerbe's flunky, surely.'

The Doctor shook his head. 'Other way around, Simon. He's working for her. I wonder if he knows what he's doing. Or what she is.'

Carfrae frowned. 'What d'you mean?'

The Doctor pulled a forlorn face and dropped to the floor, sitting cross-legged. He produced his recorder from an inside pocket of his frock-coat. 'I don't know exactly, my dear.' He stared at the recorder and put it to his lips. He made three toot sounds and suddenly stopped. 'Silence! That's it. She needs silence.' The Doctor was up on his feet again and rushing around the ghost-hunting equipment. 'Simon! Carfrae! Do you use resonators? Any kind of vibratory equipment? Or is it all chalk circles and tape-recorders?'

Simon was beside him in a moment. 'Loads of things. We set up clean fields of course. Ex-Areas. That's what we were planning to do at the top of the stairs until Peter's accident.'

'What's an Ex-Area exactly?'

'An area, roughly square.' Simon was in his element now. 'Right, what you do is put the buzz-dams at the four corners and set up a wave-field pulse. It doesn't last long but it can create a dead zone – an area of complete solitude within a room.'

'Our experiments at uni were quite effective,' Carfrae added. 'I stood inside the buzz-dam field once while it was operating. They played music at me, shouted at me, everything. But you're totally cut off aurally. It's brilliant fun.'

The Doctor nodded, writing copious notes. 'Yes. Yes, I see.' He dashed over to Peter's sleeping form and shook him awake.

'Hey!' Carfrae ran over.

'Hey!' echoed Peter stirring. 'What's going on?'

'Sorry, Peter, but I need you all. We have to try and create an Ex-Area in here. I need all of your help.'

Simon tapped his elbow. 'You don't need to, Doctor. That's why this is called the Ex-Room – it's totally soundproofed. You can't hear anything in here from out there.'

'And vice versa?' The Doctor sounded panicky.

Peter grunted and sat up. 'Of course.'

'Polly!' The Doctor looked even more startled. 'Polly and Ben! Where are they?' He ran to the door and pulled on the handle.

It was locked.

* * *

The Page of Cups.

Flick.

The Tower. A huge seated cat-statue, struck by lightning. Three figures falling from the top.

Danger.

She and her friends were in danger. He leaped up, scattering the tarot pack to the floor. For a moment he stared at them and then swore. Dropping down, he began gathering them together. He needed them. He needed her as well.

Once he had gathered them up he breathed deeply. He crossed to the window where the new candles he had bought that morning stood. He poured oil on the yellow female one and lit the wick.

As he stared into the flame, his mind briefly flickered back to Mrs Fuller's body. And the Cat-creature. He shook his head. That was yesterday or a month ago or twenty years ago. It did not matter, what was time to him anyway. He felt a pang of conscience for Mrs Fuller, but like all her kind, life was ridiculously ephemeral. Now was all that mattered. Now and the girl. Originally he had wanted the Doctor but her mind was even more open, a receptacle for him to dip into. She had the gift and she knew the power. She might even be able to dowse the path, retrace his steps. And the others. She would help him; she had to or life on this planet was doomed to the cat-creature – the dream had proved that much.

Reaching out and grabbing the candle, he crouched down and whistled a shrill note. The candle wavered, re-formed into a perfect waxen effigy of Polly Wright. 'All mine.' He rocked back on his haunches. 'Now, show me. Show me where you are right now.'

He closed his eyes and held his breath. The incense wavered around his nostrils and he breathed it in deeply, letting it flow into his lungs. In his mind's eye he saw a gossamer of light, spiralling outwards like a minute galaxy, spiralling into existence. He concentrated on the very centre of it, ignoring the tendrils of light that circled out, just the centre point. He felt his physical body suddenly gain weight – extraordinary weight – and mentally pulled himself up.

Out. Away. He was floating. Floating in the darkness towards that central zone of bright light. As he felt his astral self drift towards it, the central spot blurred and shaped itself, like a cloud in the blue skies he infrequently saw above London. Clouds that could be seen as anything from the crudest outline of a duck or boat to complicated audio wave patterns governing the mathematical structure of the entire universe. Around him now, the blackness was interrupted by straight shafts of bright light, spearing out from the central zone he was nearing. He shut them out of his vision and mind – only that main point was allowed to occupy his consciousness and it continued its reshaping. It became a face, the one he sought, this Polly Wright. 'Show me more,' he muttered to nothing in particular. The white zone flared up, blotting out all the dark, the various shafts of light blending together to create a more precise picture. He could clearly see Polly and a young man – a fellow traveller of the Doctor's? Yes, he recognized him from the previous night's dreaming – standing talking to another man. He could not hear what they were saying but she did not seem to be in any danger. Where were they?

Of course. The Doctor had taken them to Cumbria, where he had asked him to. Where the songline was strong and where he had first arrived, with her, so long ago. He wondered if she had ever gone back, back to see if the beacon was still operational. He could not explain why he was drawn back there at this time. Or why he had told the Doctor about the ghosts –

The ghosts! Of course, how *could* he have been so slow-witted. That's where she had been going. That's why she worked at that ridiculous learning establishment. She was tracking them as well. Could she have sensed them trying to break through as well? If she had, then Polly, the Doctor and the young man – Ben, wasn't it? –

were in very great danger. Not only would she try to use them, but her motives would not be quite as important as his. He had to get there quickly. Just in case.

Just in case she sacrificed Polly to her own twisted morality.

After such a long walk, he was disappointed that the street was more than just deserted – it was positively empty. Empty of other people, of bird song, of the sound of distant traffic, of everything that a main street in a small village should have. Where were the people? He needed to see people. There was no sign that it had ever been inhabited – just shop façades, a couple of rubbish bins (empty of course) and double-yellow lines painted around the road edge.

And the red telephone box. And the laughing, pointing man in the wheelchair being pushed by the woman in the black dress.

Professor Nicholas Bridgeman was not a particularly self-pitying man, yet the sight of the man in the wheelchair, giggling incoherently, brought a taste of bile into his throat and sent his mind reeling back to his childhood, growing up in Blyth, on the bitterly cold windswept coast of Northumberland. Born a couple of years after the end of the Second World War, the continued use of ration books, passes and general security paranoia mixed with the optimism of a new beginning made his childhood a very bizarre mixture of good and bad – usually a reflection of his father's employment status. Invalided out of the Royal Air Force after ten years as a flight lieutenant on Air/Sea Rescue craft, his father had settled in Blyth along with many other ex-servicemen. The shipyards of Newcastle and the other Tyne regions had been an enormous draw, with the promise of regular hard work, good living conditions and the right atmosphere in which to bring up a young son.

It was just five days after young Nicholas's ninth birthday that the accident happened. Bridgeman senior had been on his way home from the docks, on the forty-five-minute bus ride out of Newcastle, on the old A913 through Whitley Bay, when the bus driver was apparently distracted. The bus spun briefly and mounted the kerb, crashed through a roadside bench and hit a large oak tree bordering the park. The right-hand side of the bus caved in instantly, the driver's body being pulped in his little cab and two passengers on the lower deck equally flattened. The great branches of the oak tree smashed through the upper deck of the bus – and through the shocked frame of passenger Alexander K. Bridgeman. It took the Tyneside fire service four hours to cut the bus free from the tree and get medical aid to the shocked passengers trapped upstairs – trapped because the staircase down was immediately behind the first row of seats and was similarly crushed.

Bridgeman senior was still alive, but despite the best medical efforts of the doctors, nurses and surgeons at the local cottage hospital, the breakages to his spine had whiplashed his neck backwards, fracturing his skull in three places. Bone fragments had jammed into his brain and the once proud and forthright Royal Air Force Flt/Lt officer (rtrd) was now what was unofficially referred to as a vegetable, confined initially to a hospital bed and then moved back home to reside in a wheelchair, looked after by a wife and young son both too much in shock at the sudden change in their livelihoods to know what was happening.

The effect on the family was devastating. Friends, both embarrassed and uncomprehending at the family's altered status, suddenly ceased visiting. Nicholas's mother's frequent jolly nights out at bingo soon stopped and within weeks the smiles of 'we look forward to seeing you back again soon, Margaret,' became behind-the-back whispers of 'well, I doubt we'll ever see Margaret back. Poor cow.' As she struggled to feed, dress, wash and toilet a husband who, to all intents and purposes, might as well have died and been replaced by a silent, uncomprehending and

62

useless stranger, the effect on Margaret Bridgeman was even more devastating. Young Nicholas swore that life drained from her on a daily basis. Every day when he returned home from school, she looked greyer, thinner and less caring. The coalition government's still fledgling welfare state put a paltry bit of money in her purse every week but it was hardly enough. And as his mother's life essence faded away before him, so Nicholas's own interests waned. He began avoiding friends and before long had lost most social graces. He rarely spoke and instead buried himself in medical and science books, naïvely determined to discover a cure for both his parents.

Around the age of thirteen, a sympathetic teacher recognized that Nicholas's obsessive interest in science was something that should be cultivated and arranged for him to take a scholarship exam for the Blue Coats school in Berkshire where, because his father was ex-RAF, there would be no problems with the fees. By then Nicholas's self-absorbed puberty had resulted in a stammer and inadequate drive to push himself socially, so by the time he was eighteen, Nicholas Bridgeman had excelled academically and earned an early scholarship to Manchester University, but was still very much a loner. On one of his first visits back home he explained how much he enjoyed his life in Manchester and saw a glimmer of pride in his mother's eye momentarily replace the more common one of exhaustion and despair. He reached over to his mother, hugged her and, casting an eye over the now very frail form of his father hunched uselessly in his wheelchair, promised that once he began earning money teaching science somewhere, he would see that the family was well provided for. The Sixties were beginning and the 'you've never had it so good' attitude was starting to be believable.

That night he slept in his own bed and dreamed of fame, riches and being able to provide a good home for his mother and the funds to finance his father's future in a well-cared-for environment, freeing his mother to get her own life back on track. It had been nearly ten years since his father's accident and his mother had aged thirty. Nicholas was determined that the future was going to be rosy. He awoke the following morning feeling that something was not quite right. A few seconds later he realized that he had been woken by the Blyth bird song and not by the sound of wooden wheels being pushed over concrete floors. Slowly he dressed and went downstairs. What had once been the living room had been converted into a bedroom for his father and Nicholas went in.

The porcelain colouring of his father's face immediately told him that he would not require the wheelchair ever again. Although the only deaths Nicholas had experienced first-hand were laboratory rats and hamsters he was remarkably calm about his discovery. He checked for a pulse but the cold, hard wrist immediately made it a pointless search. Alexander K. Bridgeman had been dead for some hours, possibly since he had been put to bed the previous night. Rigor mortis had set in and there was nothing for it but to tiptoe upstairs and gently break the news to his mother.

As he left the room Nicholas felt a sudden gut-wrenching guilt – his father was lying dead in front of him and all he could think was what a relief it was. His mother was free of her obligations at last.

Three minutes later he was sitting on the floor of his mother's room, holding an equally pale but less rigid hand in his, reading the beautifully handwritten note, apologizing for what she had done but hoping that Nicholas understood she had done the two most wicked acts possible to free Nicholas to get on with his life. She explained in great detail, for the coroner's sake as much as Nicholas's, that she had obtained a new bottle of sleeping pills from the doctor by saying she had dropped the previous bottle accidentally down the toilet. She then crushed the entire contents of the new bottle up and added it to Alexander's soup and porridge the previous night. She had sat up with him, holding her husband's hand until with a final deep breath he had died. She then tiptoed up to her own bed and took ten or twelve of her original pills herself, written the note, put on her favourite nightdress and gone to sleep. A photograph of herself, Alexander and four-year-old Nicholas lay on the pillow beside her.

The sympathy from both family and personal friends had been genuine enough, although he could have lived without the local Catholic priest proclaiming that his father's murder and mother's suicide meant they could not be buried in the consecrated ground of the local church. Instead, Nicholas paid for the bodies to be cremated and returned to Whitley Bay where he threw their ashes into the sea.

Four years later he succeeded to the professorship of science at the newly formed UMIST in Manchester and soon transferred to London, where his growing interest in the paranormal slowly absorbed all his time. Occasionally he allowed himself to remember his mother and would travel to Whitley Bay twice a year on pilgrimage to stand on the seafront and stare at the waves, as if hoping that the ashes were still lying atop of the water and would one day re-form into two perfectly healthy parents who could one day walk towards him, hug him and tell him the world was all right. Sometimes he would sit in the room at the guest-house he had always stayed in and hold a large bath towel around himself, remembering how big it seemed when he was about six and one, or both, of his parents would wrap him in it after a bath and hug him, telling him how much they loved him.

Nicholas Bridgeman had never found anyone else to love or be loved by. He was fond of his students and knew that those who shared his interest − obsession maybe − with the preternatural were fond of him in return. But there had never been any one person in his life so special that he entertained thoughts of marriage, love or even sex. He was alone but never really lonely.

Until he stood in the deserted, empty village that his

every instinct told him should be bustling with gossipy, insular but attractive life. Deserted except for the crippled man in a wooden wheelchair and a woman dressed in a severe black dress staring at him and pointing. And laughing. Bridgeman watched as the woman slapped the man across the back of the head. 'Stop that, Mr Dent.' Her voice was harsh and bitter, without a trace of humanity, as if scolding her charge was the only attempt at communication she ever made. 'Stop laughing at the shadows.'

'Can't you see him, you daft bleeder!' cried Dent between guffaws. 'There, beside that funny red box. He's just staring at us.'

The woman looked straight at Bridgeman. No, he thought, straight through him. She can't see me!

'You're going on about ghosts again, Mr Dent,' the woman was saying. 'I've told you before, I won't have such unChristian talk from any of my charges. You stop it now.'

Bridgeman watched as Dent seemed to deflate and immediately lose interest in him. 'Oh, all right, you miserable cow.' Then he seemed to brighten again. 'One day, Mrs Wilding, you'll be dead, d'you know that? I hope I'm still alive to see you die. On that day, I promise I'll get out of this chair and dance around your corpse. You hear me? I'll be dancing again.'

Mrs Wilding suddenly began pushing the wheelchair away from Bridgeman, muttering that the chances of Dent outliving her were minimal. 'In any case, I'll kill you myself if you carry on cursing and swearing like that. It's not right.'

As Bridgeman watched the two figures faded away in front of him.

'Ghosts,' he murmured. And then shouted, 'They're bloody ghosts!'

'What are, sir?' said a voice at his elbow.

Bridgeman shook his head and leaned heavily against the red phone box. In front of him, the street was a bustle of activity – people talking, a woman with a pram trying to negotiate the steps of the post office and a small yellow van came to a halt outside the Happy Shopper grocery store. The village was exactly as it ought to have been.

'Are you all right, sir?' asked the voice again.

Bridgeman looked straight at the policeman and frowned. 'I think so, Officer. I–I'm sorry, I'm a bit tired. I need to call an ambulance.'

'Are you hurt then?'

Bridgeman shook his head. 'N–no, Officer. B–but one of my students, up at the Grange, is. I need to get some help.' He stepped into the phone box, and got a twenty-pence piece out of his pocket and placed it on top of the coin-box. It crossed Bridgeman's mind that it was a spanking new call-box with all the latest facilities, coins, phone-card and credit-card slots all together. Obviously encased in the old style red phone box specially for the tourists. Aware that the policeman was watching him curiously through the glass windows, Bridgeman turned his back on him and pulled out the phone directory. 'Carlisle. That'll be nearest,' he muttered.

As he lifted the receiver Bridgeman suddenly started. His vision was blurred by a massively bright white light, blotting everything out. He tried to back away but could not. It filled the confined space of the phone box, enveloping him totally. His last thoughts were that the policeman would help him.

The bright light vanished as suddenly as it had arrived.

Police Constable 452, Gordon M. McGarry, frowned. He stared at the phone box, vandalized six months ago and therefore totally inoperative. Why was he standing there? Something at the back of his mind was nagging him – had he seen someone in there? Something to do with the Grange? No, of course not – he was just tired. He cast an eye inside the call box through the shattered windows but of course it was as grimy, dirty and undisturbed as it had been. Tutting at his own stupidity,

Gordon M. McGarry walked away.

Inside, dripping down the front of the vandalized call box were the very hot liquid remains of a twenty-pence piece.

'Well, that wasn't much fun,' muttered Polly as she slammed the door behind her.

'Yeah, well, he's a bit uptight about something, that's for sure,' replied Ben.

'That still doesn't entitle him to be rude and accuse us of interfering with his work. And what exactly is a bimbo anyway?'

Ben almost answered that one, then thought better of it. Polly's somewhat sheltered upbringing and high society partying probably shielded her from similar accusations said to her face. 'Dunno, Duchess, but I doubt it's anything to worry about.' He was aware that Polly was staring at him. Scrutinizing him, the Doctor would say.

'You're lying to me, Ben Jackson, I can tell.' She jabbed him in the chest with her finger. 'What's a bimbo?'

'Honest, Pol, I don't know. Perhaps it's some Nineties word us poor hicks from the Sixties haven't learned yet.' He smiled. 'It's certainly nothing some poor merchant seaman would ever have heard of,' he lied.

Clearly unconvinced, Polly tucked her handbag over her shoulder and ran a hand through her long hair. 'Well, when he wasn't abusing us, Herr Kerbe told us that Professor Bridgeman had gone to the village for help.' Ben sighed – Polly was doing what he called her 'come here, common little oike, and learn something from me' bit. Luckily it had changed from being an annoying to an amusing little quirk of hers – it was not intended to patronize him. It just did. He then remembered that Polly was lecturing and he ought to listen.

Euston Station, London. A veritable hive of activity at any time of day, any day of the week. And trains to

Preston (where he needed to change for Carlisle and there for Sellafield) were going to be packed.

He stared at the queue, frustrated. What was this human obsession with standing in long lines? Why did the British turn it into an art as they patiently waited in turn, never moaning or complaining at the speed with which the ticket sellers did not work? He cursed the day that queues were invented – about forty thousand years ago. Humans!

He looked at the timetable above platform eight. 14.13, platform five. Change at Manchester! Another change.

'Got any change, mate?' said a scruffy young girl with a moth-eared dog at her heels.

'What?'

The young girl leaned back against Tie Rack. 'Spare a quid? You know, for a cup of tea?'

'Expensive tea.'

'British Rail, mate. Screw us for everything we got, don't they?'

'Anyway, no. Sorry.'

The young girl looked affronted. 'Oh, go on. If not for me, then what about Petra here? She needs some food.'

He stared at them both. 'If you ate your dog, it'd save you begging for food for either of you.'

The young girl reeled back as if she had been hit. 'You what? You sick or something?'

'Oh, do shut up and go away. It was only a suggestion.'

The young girl tried a different approach. She took a step nearer and sneered, 'I hate goths. Bloody Cure, The Mission and all that depressing rubbish. No tune.'

'Yes, yes, I'm sure you're right. Now, excuse me.'

The young girl blocked him. 'I only asked for a quid, mate. It's not that much, is it?' She reached out and blocked the way to the platform.

He stared at the young girl for a moment and sighed. 'I'm sorry.'

For a second the girl relaxed, possibly thinking she was

going to get her money. Instead, he opened his mouth and sang a high note. For a second the girl frowned – she could not hear it. But then Petra yapped and whined and ran in a circle. Around them, the massive glass doors and walls of Euston station cracked as a network of spidery lines snaked across them. The glass front of Tie Rack exploded inwards into a mass of tiny, blunt fragments, showering the stock, staff and customers. Screams started all around and the girl went to cover her ears. And stopped. Her right arm hurt – it ached and throbbed. She grasped at it with her left hand and then started screaming herself. From the shoulder down, both her clothing and her flesh shrivelled and began to fall to the ground in green, foul-smelling chunks. Within a few seconds, her arm was just a blackened bone, fleshy hand at one end clenching and unclenching in uncomprehending panic.

Her pained screaming attracted those already yelling in fear at the fragmenting glass. They rushed over to her but backed away as the smell wafted towards them. Petra the dog ignored the smell and started licking the putrid flesh flopping on the floor.

He only took an instant to realize he had over-reacted. 'Wretched humans,' he murmured. 'I haven't tried this for centuries.' He put his arms upright above his head, let his neck relax and closed his eyes. Opening his mouth, he relaxed his throat and then breathed out deeply, the air accompanied by a long moan.

A few seconds later he stopped and looked around. No one moved. No one even flinched. Petra was standing beside the pile of flesh. The young girl was staring at her arm, her face a mask of pure horror. Around them, people were staring at the cracked glass, pointing and ducking. Around Tie Rack people had scooped up some of the glass, and a man was running away, stolen ties trailing behind him. He had dropped one and it was floating to the floor. Except that it was not. It was just hovering in mid-air. Nothing was moving at all – like a tableau.

He looked around in satisfaction. His internal body

clock reckoned that he had about six hours. He would give it a boost in four. Then another three hours later. That should give him time to sprint up to Cumbria.

It was cheaper than a British Rail ticket, and he did not need to queue.

'What a wonderful library this is!' The Doctor was sitting atop of a set of library steps, about six rows off the floor. Beside him, two candles flickered what little light they could give across the pages of the massive leather-bound book he was studying.

Carfrae stood, her arms folded, at the foot of the steps. 'That's all very interesting, Doctor,' she said, 'but it hardly helps Si and me set up an Ex-Area, does it?'

'What? Oh yes.' The Doctor slammed the book shut and accidentally extinguished the candles. 'Oh, dear. Sorry.'

Simon heard him fumble about and eventually strike a match to relight them. He shivered. 'Bloody cold in here, Doctor. Still, it's secluded enough.'

The Doctor shoved the book under his arm and gleefully hopped off the steps as if he were two feet off the ground, not seven or eight. Without breaking a stride, he landed and wandered to another set of shelves.

'You can learn a lot by reading, you know,' he said. 'I mean, how would Homer have given us *The Iliad* if he hadn't been well read? Mind you, he got it wrong. I was there.' He beamed at the two students as if the secrets of the universe had just been shared out in equal portions and they should give him a round of applause.

'Homer probably couldn't read, Doctor. Or write.' Carfrae shook her head. 'They say he dictated the whole thing.'

The Doctor wagged his finger. 'Well, there you are then. I mean, if he'd done it himself, he wouldn't have got it so wrong. Education – that's the important thing. And you get more education out of reading books than a university could teach you in a lifetime.'

'Yes, thank you, Doctor. Well, if you've quite finished rubbishing our education system, perhaps you could tell us what you found so interesting in that book.' Carfrae gave Simon a look that suggested she thought the Doctor was insane. Simon smiled an agreement and slipped the book out from under the Doctor's arm. He began flicking the pages.

'Looks like a family biography. The people who built this house perhaps?'

The Doctor nodded. 'Very good. Now what are the pages made from?'

'Paper?' suggested Carfrae but Simon was frowning.

'Papyrus?' he ventured.

The Doctor shook his head. 'A bit too modern I think.'

'Papyrus, modern? Oh, come on, Doctor. It's one of the oldest types of paper on Earth.'

The Doctor pulled a book out of a shelf, ran his fingers over the leaves and replaced it. He hummed and hahhed until he spotted a pocket-sized, red-covered one. 'Ah. That's more like it.' Without reading it, he dropped it into one of his frock-coat pockets, causing one of the covers to poke through a tiny hole in the stitching and make it wider. 'No, Mr Griffiths. It's not papyrus. It's not from Earth either. Try tearing a page.'

Simon grunted. 'Always taught to treasure books, not rip 'em up,' he murmured. And then frowned. 'I can't. It won't even fold or bend.'

Carfrae reached for it. And likewise failed to even crease a page. 'This doesn't make sense,' she said.

The Doctor took it back. 'Strange texture, too. It's not polymer nor crystalline. In fact, its molecular structure is rather bizarre – half of it is stable and half unstable, but the actual fractions are in a constant state of flux. Ever seen anything like it?'

Simon shrugged. 'I don't even understand what you're talking about!'

The Doctor began flicking through the book. 'Of

course not.' He stroked a page with the tip of his finger. He held it up for them to see. 'Look at my fingertip. Notice anything?'

'Dust?'

'Paper cut?'

The Doctor sighed. 'Oh dear me, no. Stare hard at the tip.'

'It's a bit difficult in this light, Doctor. Move the candles nearer.'

'Oh, never mind,' said the Doctor. 'I'll tell you. My fingertip is probably three or four months younger now than the rest of my hand.' He beamed as if that explained everything. Simon and Carfrae looked back blankly and he deflated a little. 'Reverse tachyon-chronons. If you put this under an X-ray, it'd probably heat up, and put it under a spectrograph and – well, it'd cause enough feedback to break the machine. Time is flowing backwards and forwards over it in the same way air moves around an ordinary book. Preserves it for, oh, roughly speaking, an eternity.'

'You what?'

'It's time-protected, Simon. A neat trick known only to a few races in the universe. Well, two that I can think of actually. And one of them is only a legend.'

Carfrae tried to form some words and then breathed deeply. She tried again. 'The book is extra-terrestrial?'

'Oh, golly, no,' said the Doctor. 'It's merely been coated in RTCs. It looks as if it was made in about 1895.'

'Victorian,' said a voice from the door. It was Peter. 'Doctor, the old woman on the stairs. She was dressed in a Victorian dress, I'm sure of it.'

'So what?' asked Simon.

'Possibly nothing,' said the Doctor. 'Possibly something. Who knows? But it'll be fun finding out. Now, shall we go back to the Ex-Room with our little find?'

'Hang on a mo,' said Simon, 'I want to know more about that book. And the aliens that wrapped it in your TCRs.'

'RTCs actually,' corrected the Doctor. 'I like an enquiring mind as much as the next me will. Probably. But now is neither the time nor place. Peter, did you find Polly or Ben?'

Peter shook his head, and added that Kerbe hadn't been too helpful when asked why the Ex-Room had been locked from the outside.

'He wouldn't be. I think poor Herr Kerbe is a little out of his depth right now. The less he can try and explain – and therefore fail to do so – the better for his peace of mind.'

'He's a bit naffed off about the mess I made of the lock though,' Peter said, grinning.

'I'll bet. Still, that'll teach him,' said Carfrae.

They were back in the Ex-Room by now and the Doctor pulled the door to behind them. 'Trouble is, it doesn't shut properly now. We won't be soundproofed.'

Peter dipped into his pocket and produced the sliding bolt and socket he had kicked off the outside. 'If I had a screwdriver, I could put it on the inside.'

The Doctor poked around the inside pocket of his jacket and produced three screwdrivers of varying sizes, one of which was absolutely too long to have fitted inside any jacket comfortably, but all three students had given up trying to apply the laws of physics to either the Doctor or his coat pockets. Peter selected the smallest and began making a hole in the wooden door.

'Alien races?' prompted Simon. 'You were saying?'

The Doctor was rummaging through the tape-recorders and wiring that the students had brought with them. 'Later, Simon, later. We need to get this room Ex-ed up as soon as possible. We may need protection and this could be our best defence.'

'Protection? From what, Peter's old ghost?'

'Oh no, far worse than some silly osmic projection. No, I'm talking about whatever Kerbe and his mistress have cooked up.'

'Not ghosts then?'

'Not ghosts. Definitely.'

'Then why do we need an Ex-Area? It's only good for ghosts,' Carfrae asked.

'Nonsense. Any atmospheric seclusion area can be a great defence. You'll see.' He smiled at Carfrae as if he thought he had reassured her.

He hadn't. 'I should've joined the TA,' she said.

'We're getting near the village, Ben,' said Polly, pointing at a red phone box.

'Took the long way though, didn't we, Duchess,' he replied.

'Oh, do stop moaning, Ben Jackson. The walk will do you good. Get some of that fat off you.'

'Fat? Fat? What fat exactly, Pol? I've hardly had a drop of beer since signing on with the Doc. And TARDIS food rations aren't exactly covered in chocolate.' He stopped suddenly. 'Cor, I don't half fancy a Mars Bar. D'you think they still do them in 1994?'

Polly shrugged. 'I really don't know, Ben. And to be honest, I don't care. Besides which, we're not exactly carrying much cash. How much have you got on you?'

Ben dug deeply into his pocket. 'Two and six plus a threepenny bit. You?'

'Nothing. And anyway, Britain is decimal now; remember what we learned at the South Pole. Our idea of money belongs in a museum.'

'Like us, really.'

'I'm sorry?'

'Look at us, Pol. Rejects from the London night-life, *circa* 1966. Thirty years on, our clothes probably look really silly. We're ana . . . anarch . . .'

'Anachronistic?'

'Yeah. I mean, we've really got to be careful what we say and do.'

Polly nodded. 'You know what's really frightening? Suppose we find out something about ourselves. Suppose one of us becomes famous and dies in a car crash. I mean, it'd be in the papers. Imagine if we went through the local library's back copies of *The Times* and found our own obituary.'

'At least that'd tell us something important.'

'What?'

Ben smiled. 'That at some time the Doc got us home.'

'Yes but think, Ben. If we were coming back just to die, would you want the Doctor to try and get us back? I don't think I would.'

Ben stopped walking. 'What would happen if we did find out we'd died in, say, 1982? OK, so we say ta-ta to the Doctor now, in the future when we're still alive. Problem solved.'

Polly was appalled. 'But what about your mother? My Uncle Charles? We could hardly just turn up on their doorstep and say, "Sorry I missed my funeral, but here I am again, looking like I did in the mid-sixties." They'd have a heart attack or some seizure or other.'

'I think we need that Mars Bar.' Ben began walking into the village. 'Or a double scotch.'

Silently, staring at her feet, Polly followed him. 'I'm sorry,' she said after a moment.

'What for, Duchess?'

'Oh, I don't know. Spoiling your hopes. Being pessimistic. Realistic I suppose.' Polly touched his hand. 'I want to go home just as much as you do, Ben, but I don't think 1994 is right for either of us. Just in case. You're right. We'd be too anachronistic.'

Ben nodded. ' One bit of good news though.'

'What?'

'These trousers I borrowed from the TARDIS wardrobe. Like the old Ship herself, the pockets are bigger on the inside than out. I've just found what I presume is a twenty-pound note. It's dated 1993. 'Ere, doesn't the Queen look old!'

Polly flicked it over. 'Faraday. Yucky purple though. Hey, Ben, twenty pounds – d'you think it's still a fortune?'

'Nah, Duchess. Probably wouldn't buy you a hot dog

now. Shall we find out?'

'Hot dog? Oh, Ben, I'm starving. Let's see what's available.'

Ben agreed but held her back for a second. 'Difficult as I know it is for you, Polly, I think this is important. Best not get talking to too many of the locals. We've no idea how easy it is to give ourselves away. They might talk about a football match and I mention a team that no longer exists. Or you might want to talk about that fashion woman, whatever she's called, and her stuff might be old hat now.'

'OK, Ben. I get the picture. Let's just see, shall we?'

They wandered into the street, passing without a glance the vandalized red telephone box and involuntarily held their breath as a policeman wandered in front of them, but he did not give them more than a cursory glance.

They passed a post office with its familiar red posting box outside, a massive GR on the side which Polly found reassuring. Ben had wandered on ahead but Polly was making time to take in the strange things she saw. Granada Rentals, proclaimed one shop. In the window, a group of televisions – but there the resemblance ended. Sleek, black, with flat screens and no visible means of turning the volume up or changing channels, the pictures were so sharp and, above all, in colour. Uncle Charles had once said that he had seen colour television in America. 'It'll never catch on here,' he said. 'Colour's best left for the cinema.' So much for Uncle Charles. He had probably got a houseful now, if he were still alive . . . No, that kind of thinking wasn't worth getting into. Under each set was a thin box, also black. VCRs according to a sign. A pile of 'video tapes: £5.99 for three' were placed at one side. Could these VCRs be some kind of tiny tape-recorder for recording television pictures? But surely they would have to be huge? Then she remembered Carfrae's compact disc. Obviously anything was possible in 1994. £5.99, though. A fortune! People in Cumbria must be very rich to afford those.

She then looked into the window of the Happy Shopper and gasped at the rows of food, people with trolleys and some kind of electronic checkout tills. The rhythmic bleep of items being passed over a square of glass fascinated her but Ben's tug on her arm distracted her. 'A man in a uniform was staring at us,' he whispered. 'Probably thought you were casing the joint.'

'Casing the . . . what?'

'Never mind. Let's just keep going.'

'Oh, Ben, it's Smith's! W. H. Smith's. Oh please, can we go in? Look around. It's something familiar. Something to . . . to hold on to.'

Ben nodded and they went in. Polly went straight for a rack of newspapers and grabbed *The Times*. She found the Society Notices and flicked through the obituaries but there were no names she knew. The same with Births, Marriages and Deaths. Suddenly she realized Ben was not with her. Fighting a surge of panic she dimly remembered from being separated from her mother in Fortnum and Mason's when she was six years old, she carefully replaced the paper and looked around, trying not to be obvious and draw attention to herself. Slowly she walked into the bowels of the shop, past the paperback books (Barbara Cartland was still churning them out?) and stopped as she saw Ben at the biographies. He was flicking through a large paperback. He saw her and passed it over.

'*River Phoenix: A Short Life* by Brian J. Robb. So what?'

Ben smiled tightly. 'So much life has passed us by, Polly. Who was River Phoenix? He made some movies and the author compares him to James Dean. He died young but had a promising future. We've never heard of him. Never seen a film of his. He was born after we went off with the Doctor. This time travel is doing my head in.' He tapped his forehead. 'I'm not sure I'm cut out for traipsing through our future. Daleks, Cybermen, I can cope with. Even those smugglers in Cornwall, but this – this is more alien than anything we've seen so far.'

'Are you frightened, Ben?'

Ben coughed. 'Well, I wouldn't say "frightened" exactly, but, hey, I'm just a bit thrown by it all.'

Polly slipped her arm around his and placed the book back on the shelf. 'I'm sure it's a fab book, but yes, it frightens me too. Let's get some food.'

They left Smith's as quickly as possible and Ben pointed at two similar restaurants in front of them. 'Here, Pol, what's a pizzer?'

'I think it's pronounced peetzah. Italian I think. Obviously very popular nowadays, they're both packjammed.'

'McDonald's?'

'Sorry?'

'Over there? McDonald's. It looks busy but that queue is going down quickly. Let's look.'

They wandered over to the restaurant and Polly pointed at a sign that asked them to pay for their food before finding a seat. They both shrugged and went in.

After standing in a queue for a few moments they realized that a young girl in a red cap was smiling at them. 'Can I help you please?'

Polly was first. 'Yes, I'd like a . . . no, two hamburgers, please. I'm hungry,' she added for Ben's sake.

'Anything with that?'

'Er . . . what?'

The girl's smile faltered. 'Fries?'

Polly stared at her for a second, trying not to panic. 'Well, I don't think I want them blue.' She nudged Ben for help and he leaned against her, keeping his eyes firmly on neither her nor the McDonald's girl.

'Chips,' he hissed. 'I just saw someone asking for fries. They're chips.'

'Oh, fries. I see. I'm so sorry. I'm from nineteen-six– I'm from London,' she said to the girl, hoping that explained everything. She had seen foreigners do it in bars and cafés back in Knightsbridge. 'Yes, I'll have fries.'

'Regular, medium or large?'

'Medium.' Polly hoped that would be satisfactory. It evidently was.

'Drinks? Shake? Coke?'

'Coke please. With ice ... d'you do ice here? Or lemon?'

The girl stared at her. And forced a smile. 'No lemon.'

'Ah. Oh well.'

'Eat in or take out?' The girl placed a Coke on the counter next to the burger and fries. She reached in front of Polly and took a straw from the container and laid it across the top.

'Out,' muttered Ben. 'And I'll have the same. And I'm paying.'

A moment later the two of them were standing in the street, brown bags and Coke in hand, looking which way to go. 'Ben, this is so undignified. I can't possibly eat in the street. It's so ... so American!'

'So, I think, is McDonald's. Besides, Duchess, they're all doing it.'

Polly looked at the people in the street munching burgers, and slurping drinks. 'I bet this is the Kennedys' fault. Uncle Charles always said they were too liberal to be Presidents. I bet Bobby Kennedy sold us McDonald's.'

'I bet he never became President.'

'Shall we find out? That could be fun ... no, perhaps not.'

Ben smiled. 'Yeah. Perhaps not, eh?'

Polly took a bite out of her hamburger and squirted tomato sauce on to the street. More ran down her hand and she felt it around her mouth. Her eyes flicked towards Ben who was hiding, badly, a grin behind his own burger. 'I think,' she mumbled, 'I'd like to go back to the TARDIS now. Can we get to the Grange, pick up the Doctor and go?'

Ben agreed and they wandered back the way they had come. 'Food tastes like cardboard. Nothing changes.'

* * *

The Doctor was stroking the book he had found. Peter was finishing his work on the bolt for the door. Carfrae was setting up four acoustic dampers in each corner of the room and Simon found himself setting up a feedback loop of white noise.

'Any idea what frequency, Doctor?'

The Doctor failed to look up from the book. 'Oh, your usual, Chesterton, your usual. Now, I wonder where Barbara and Susan have got to.'

Simon looked as the other two turned and looked at the strange little man. He shrugged at them. 'Doctor, I'm Simon Griffiths. From Castle Hill, New South Wales. Remember? Who're Barbara and Susan?'

The Doctor still did not look up. 'Sorry, Steven, m'boy. My mind was wandering.'

'Simon. Not Steven.'

Carfrae reached out to the Doctor and he turned sharply. Involuntarily she stepped back.

'Oh, do be careful Dorothea . . . sorry, Dodo!' He stared at her. 'No, it's not Dodo, is it? Hair's wrong, too long. Vicki? No . . . Carfrae! Got it at last. Carfrae Morgan. Simon Griffiths and Peter Moore. I'm in Cumbria. I remember now.' He put the book down and smiled at the others reassuringly, as if putting inappropriate names on people was an everyday occurrence. 'It was the book's fault. Or rather the RTC – made my mind wander back to my previous self. He used to get very confused, poor fellow. Couldn't remember people's names even when they were there, let alone when they'd gone for a walk. Now, are Ben and Polly back yet? I want to get them inside the Ex-Area before we switch on.'

Simon decided it would be best to ignore the Doctor's ramblings but before he could say anything Carfrae suddenly gasped.

'Doctor, who repaired your coat?'

The little man frowned. 'What?'

'Your coat. The hole in the pocket and that stain on

81

the lapel. They've gone. Been repaired or cleaned. But I saw the tear a few moments ago. That little red book you took from the library was poking through.'

Peter groaned. 'Typical. We're hunting ghosts and mad Teutonic mugs with guns and you're worried about a spot of needlepoint.'

'No!' The Doctor jumped up and yanked the red book from the repaired pocket. 'No. Carfrae's right to be alarmed.' He waved the pocket book at them. 'This was the only other one I could find with RTCs on it. And it's altered my coat, time-warped it. That's why I was being strange. Both books in close proximity. No wonder we got rid of them.'

'Rid of who?'

'What. Got rid of what. Books coated in RTC. The libraries on . . . at home used to have a few. Our leaders decided they were too dangerous and banned them. Oh, my giddy aunt, this is bad news. I must keep these books apart.'

With almost comic reverence, the Doctor gingerly picked up the large book and carried it to the door, next to Peter but still within the area outlined by Carfrae's acoustic dampers. Then he crossed back and placed the pocket book diagonally opposite it, near where he was sitting. 'Let's hope that opposites don't attract or we could find ourselves caught in a time storm of sorts.'

'Yeah. Let's hope not, eh,' said Peter warily. Unseen by the Doctor he made a twirling motion with his finger next to his head and Simon grinned.

'And no, Peter, I'm not mad.' The Doctor turned and grinned. 'Just alien.'

'Alien?'

'Yes, Carfrae, alien. Like your Ms Thorsuun. Not from the same planet of course, but nevertheless we're both not from around here.'

'Like not English?'

'Like not human.'

Simon swallowed hard. This was ludicrous. This man

was telling them he was from another planet. And Ms Thorsuun. What was more ludicrous was that he believed everything the Doctor was saying. 'Ghosts?'

'No. Ghosts as such don't exist. Not ghosts as spirits of the dead. Ghosts are a far more scientific reality – after images if you like. Like tea stains on wallpaper that won't disappear no matter how hard you scrub. Your ghosts are etched into walls, floors, everything as sound and picture bytes. The correct resonance or electricity in the atmosphere can bring them back. That's why you don't get ghosts in brand-new buildings. Unless they're from the future and that's a quite different sort of ghost. And I'm not a ghost.'

All Simon could think to say was, 'Oh.'

'What about the woman I saw?' asked Peter pointing to his bandaged arm. 'That seemed real enough. And she saw me.'

'No, she saw something,' corrected the Doctor. 'Roughly where you were standing but back in Victorian times. And it must have been quite alarming because old Mrs Wilding wasn't a woman easily frightened.'

'Who?' chorused the three students.

The Doctor pointed at the pocket book. 'I flicked through Mrs Wilding's diary there. She was the housekeeper and nurse to a Richmond Dent who owned this house. I suspect she was also far more in charge than Dent would have liked.' He stopped and stared at the three teenagers who were staring at him. Or were they?

He stood up but they did not blink or flicker. The Doctor walked towards them but they were frozen, staring at where he had been. Suddenly he felt his leg tingle and found he was having difficulty breathing. 'Treacle,' he muttered. 'It's like treacle.' He managed to step back and the tingle went.

The book. Mrs Wilding's diary. The Doctor scooped it up and dropped it back in his pocket and walked forward, carefully going between the students. This time nothing stopped him. He reached out for the door but his hand went straight through it.

'Or maybe I am a ghost after all.'

The wind from the sea blew into their faces and Polly shivered. She grasped Ben's arm tighter. 'Why did we come back this way? It would have been quicker up the path, past the Gatehouse.'

'Yeah, but I wanted to check the TARDIS was OK, and it's down by the railway line on the beach, remember?'

Polly nodded and pointed. 'Hey, who's that?'

Ben followed her line of vision. A man in a brown duffel coat was digging a hole – or filling one up – on the clifftop.

'Hello!' called Ben.

The wind snatched his voice away but the man heard something because he looked around him before seeing the two time-travellers. He looked back down at his hole and patted the hurriedly replaced soil before Ben and Polly got any nearer.

'My name's Coates. Charlie Coates. I work for your Ms Thorsuun,' he replied to Ben's introduction.

'As in Smithers and Coates. I heard Kerbe mention you,' said Polly.

'Sounds like a revolver to me,' laughed Ben but Charlie Coates did not smile back.

'If you'll excuse me, I got work to do.' He swung his shovel over his shoulder, tipped his cap's peak to Polly and walked away.

'Strange man,' said Polly. 'I wonder what he was doing.'

'Burying his dog or cat I think,' said Ben. 'Look, there's some fur lying around here.'

'Pretty big cat, Ben. I mean –' Polly suddenly started.

'What's up, Duchess?'

She grabbed his arm. 'Ben, my dream. I saw a giant cat thing. Standing with a gun. A giant cat-person.' She pointed at the fur.

Ben smiled. 'Oh Pol, that was a nightmare. Cats don't carry guns. Look, Coates is out of sight now. Let's see what it was.'

'Oh Ben, it might be something dead.'

'Well, don't look then.'

'No, all right. But you dig.' She held her hands up. 'My nails . . .'

Ben nodded wryly and started pulling the fresh earth away with his fingers. After a few moments he felt something cold and soft. 'It's cloth I think.'

After a few moments longer Ben straightened up.

'Clothes. Coates was burying coats. Why?'

'Any idea whose?'

Ben shook his head. 'I'll try and get this one up.' He tugged and tugged and eventually it gave way. Too suddenly. The momentum caused Ben to lose his footing and he staggered back too quickly.

'Ben!' screamed Polly but it was too late. Ben was at the cliff's edge and his feet were still scrabbling for gravity. He fell back, his feet leaving ground and for a split second he was just hanging above nothing except sea and rocks below.

Then he stayed where he was. Polly stayed staring at him, her mouth contorted in a silent scream. There was no sound. No wind, no bird song, just nothing.

And absolutely no movement.

The Doctor stood in the hallway having walked through the closed door. His feet occasionally sank beneath the floorboards and sometimes rose a few inches above. It was as if he were treading across a vat of jelly.

He stopped at the foot of the stairs and waited. He flicked through the diary, nodding at certain passages and at one point stared upstairs. 'So, that's what she saw. How interesting.' After a few moments he closed the book and slipped it back into his pocket. 'Dangerous, Doctor, I know, but not as dangerous as leaving it visible.' He looked towards the kitchen area. 'Oh, do get a move on,

Thorsuun, I object to waiting all eternity,' he called out.

Seconds later Thorsuun walked through the closed door of the kitchen, followed by Kerbe, his Mauser in his hand.

'Oh, very good,' the Doctor applauded. 'You must have some very powerful RTCs to manage both of you.'

Kerbe was astonished. 'How on Earth . . .'

The Doctor tried to look abashed. 'Er . . . not Earth actually, Herr Kerbe. Didn't you know your bursar was an alien?'

'Of course I do,' the German snapped back. 'Didn't know you were, though. That information was withheld from me.' The last comment was directed at Thorsuun.

'Dissension in the ranks, Fräulein.'

Thorsuun just shrugged. 'You know how parochial humans are, Doctor. They are so inquisitive. It's really quite amusing considering how little information their pathetic minds can take before they close down. This one seemed better than most.'

'You mean his greed and aggression made him a better receptacle for your particular brand of mental persuasion.'

Thorsuun smiled a toothy smile. 'Oh, sweetheart, almost right. But it's nothing mental – it's all auditory.' She tapped her throat.

The Doctor jumped up and felt the ground beneath him shift slightly.

'Be careful, Doctor, the gravity fields take a bit of getting used to when time has been stopped.'

'Stopped? Or has the Earth just stopped rotating?'

'Oh, excellent, you spotted that. You're better than I thought.'

'Thank you. I thought you'd reveal yourself eventually.' The Doctor straightened his tie, determined not to die and look dishevelled at the same time.

Thorsuun stared back impassively. 'So, what are you?'

'I was rather hoping you'd tell me about yourself actually. You're Euterpian, aren't you?'

'A what?'

'Euterpian. A Hummer?'

'Probably. We don't have a race name. We know who we are.'

'Were. You died out a long time ago. Sorry.'

Thorsuun shrugged. 'I'm not surprised. We came a long way, Doctor. Across the three dimensions.'

'Three? Space and time and . . . ?'

Thorsuun grinned. 'Oh, my precious, you cannot imagine.'

'Oh, I wouldn't say that.' The Doctor smiled back and tugged his frock-coat closer to him. 'You know, this part of England is rather pleasant. One day, I've always told myself, I'd buy myself a little house here. Somewhere to use as a home whenever I come to Earth.' He paused and then frowned. 'Or was that Kent? The Garden of England. It's so hard to remember.'

Thorsuun waved Kerbe nearer and he pointed his gun at the Doctor. Thorsuun leaned in closer. 'I think my ally will want to meet you.'

The Doctor clapped his hands together and laughed. 'Oh, good, I'd like to meet him.'

'Her.'

'Her. Large, is she? Furry? Feline-based perhaps?'

Thorsuun paused and then nodded reverently. 'You are very good, Doctor. I'm terribly impressed and I think she will be too.'

The Doctor stuffed his hands into his trouser pockets. 'I'm not a commodity, you know. Something to play show-and-tell with to impress your mistress.'

'Ally, Doctor. Queen Aysha is an ally. Equal partners and all that. Just so you know.'

'Of course. *Mea culpa.*' The Doctor turned away but then back again. 'Does she know that?'

'What?'

'That you're equals. I mean the Cat-People have a reputation for, how can I put it, delusions of grandeur.'

'You know of the Cat-People? I'm impressed further.'

The Doctor suddenly screwed his face up in fury.

87

'Know of them? Of course I know of them. Hideous, murderous mercenaries. You can't trust them, Thorsuun. They'll knife you in the back before you can say Kit-e-Kat. They've plundered more planets than . . . than . . .' He stopped and steadily walked right up to her, casually pushing Kerbe's gun away and ignoring the Teutonic curse that followed as Kerbe, still unsteady on his feet, toppled over. 'What do they want here? With you? With Earth?'

Thorsuun lightly kissed the Doctor on the cheek. 'You lovely specimen. You can ask them yourself. They're right behind you.'

The Doctor spun round. Walking through the locked and bolted front door, clearly accustomed to marching on time-shifted surfaces, were seven Cat-People, clad in red leather. A tortoise-shell leader took a step further after waving her troops to a halt.

Kerbe staggered up. *'Mein Gott.'*

'Ihr Alptraum, Herr Kerbe, I think you'll find.' The Doctor again adjusted his collar and pulled his coat sleeves down. He flicked a loose strand of hair out of his eyes, stretched out his arm and strode over to greet the mercenaries.

'How do you do, Your Majesty.'

The Queen ignored him. She turned to Thorsuun. 'My pride, Thorgarsuunela. First-sired Chosan is my executive officer.'

Thorsuun bowed slightly to the sleek black cat, whose weapon was aimed squarely at her chest.

'And this is my tactical officer, Lotuss.'

'The litter-runt. The fame of your . . . abilities to get your way on the battlefield are renowned.' Thorsuun again gave a slight bow.

Lotuss's single eye stared at her, and the hair on her neck and tail bristled slightly. 'Beware, anthropoid, I do not like the term "litter-runt". Do not use it again.'

Thorsuun nodded politely. 'I apologize.'

Queen Aysha surveyed the house. 'Why has time

stopped? You did not warn us. Luckily it affected us seconds after the anthropoid helping froze. We were able to activate our shields and retrieve the RTC unit from our shuttle. That kind of action smells of betrayal.'

'It wasn't me, Your Majesty. If I were going to betray you, I'd hardly have given you my RTC unit to . . .' she waved a hand abstractedly, 'to modify for your own use. Remember, without it, I'm trapped here, ageing slowly again. Besides, I warned you that at least one other of my people survives into this century. I suspect it is his doing.'

'Oh. And why should he do this? Perhaps I should conduct my business with him.'

Lotuss stepped forward. 'An anthropoid-tom? It has enough power?'

'On this primitive planet, tactician, you will find the males just as dominant as the females.'

The surrounding Cat-People hissed their displeasure at this news. 'They should be neutered at birth,' spat Chosan.

'Well, the humans wouldn't last very long, Chosan, would they.' Aysha bared her incisor teeth to Thorsuun. 'My pride is not very fond of males, Thorgarsuunela. Keep yours away from them, and they may avoid sterilization.'

Thorsuun shrugged. 'As you suggest, Your Majesty. By the way, this little thing is Marten Kerbe, the human who has assisted me in setting up this landing site. He helped me find the marker buoy as well.'

'And this one?'

'Oh, this darling little creature is the Doctor. He's not human either. I'm not sure where he's from but he's exceptionally well-read.'

'Thank you,' murmured the Doctor.

'You were not given permission to mew,' Aysha hissed.

Thorsuun smiled. 'Indeed he was not. Well, that's the introductions over. Shall we talk?'

Aysha agreed and Thorsuun walked into the pride and

stood beside the Queen, looking just a little dwarfed. 'Oh, Lotuss, would you like to keep your trigger finger supple?' She pointed towards the Doctor. 'Kill him, would you be a dear?'

With a purr of pleasure, Lotuss swung her gun up and opened fire, blasting Kerbe back against the stairs.

The Doctor stared at the body, and back at Lotuss and Thorsuun.

'Whoops, wrong one,' said Thorsuun. 'Try again!'

Lotuss aimed her rifle-blaster once more . . .

Episode Three

Carfrae screamed. In itself, this was not a very surprising reaction, thought Simon, but nevertheless, it was unusual. Carfrae Morgan was not exactly known for overt emotional expressions and apart from the odd four-letter expletive yelled at someone at college, hearing her scream was almost enough to distract Simon from what had caused her reaction.

But not quite, as he was busy quelling a similar reaction himself. Ghosts, ghoulies and things that go bump in the night he could cope with – indeed, since ganging up with Professor Bridgeman, he had been anticipating them. But harsh reality was something completely new, unexpected and rather horrific.

It had all started when the Doctor was explaining about Mrs Wilding's diary. And had simply vanished in front of their eyes. For a moment the three students had just stared at each other, daring someone else to speak first. It was Peter Moore who had broken the silence.

'Hell, if I believe time-distorting books, alien bursars and a self-repairing jacket I can believe people can just vanish into thin air.'

Simon nodded. 'Yeah. I guess so.'

They were about to go looking for the Doctor when Carfrae had called for quiet. Through the door they could hear the Doctor's voice.

'What have you done?' The Doctor sounded very distraught. 'By what right did you do that?'

'Quiet, anthropoid.' That was a strange voice none of them recognized.

'I'm not just an anthropoid.' The Doctor again.

'Does it really matter?' Thorsuun. No doubting her sneering voice. Then Peter had pulled open the door and Carfrae had screamed.

Lying on the stairway, eyes wide open but a large portion of his chest apparently melted on to the steps, was Kerbe. With a brief flash of dispassion Simon noted he was clearly dead, although his right hand, the gun clutched tightly in it, was still twitching autonomically. Simon turned his head to trace the stranger's voice and blinked. Somewhere from deep within his subconscious an order flashed into his brain. His mouth formed the words, and his throat twitched and gurgled out a barely decipherable 'Quick! Run!' and he slammed the door shut, trapping the three of them in the Ex-Room.

'Simon!' It was the Doctor. 'Use the Ex-Area –' He was cut off by a swift thwack of something and a yelp of pain followed.

'It . . . it was a cat!' was all Carfrae could manage.

Ever practical, Peter, ignoring the pain from his arm, began activating their equipment. 'C'mon, guys. Let's get this up and running!' He waved at their equipment.

'But the Doctor –' Simon watched as Carfrae bolted the door.

'He said to use the Ex-Area. What else can we do?'

Simon felt like kicking himself. The other two were thinking, doing, acting and being. He was just standing there, trying to convince himself that, like Peter, he could accept alien Doctors, dead Kerbes and six-foot cats with guns and red leather flying suits.

'Simon! Please!' That was Carfrae again.

'Yeah. Right. OK, guys, let's get to it.'

One second later the door was blasted off its hinges and two Cat-People stood framed there, guns brought up.

Then there was a thud – the Doctor had thrown the larger of his two weird books into the Ex-Area. Simon bent down as the larger Cat-Person – a white one with a grey spot covering its left eye he noted rather pointlessly –

brought its gun up to cover them.

'Leave the RTC,' it purred.

'Activate!' yelled the Doctor from behind and Simon saw Peter switch their machinery on.

The Cat-People suddenly seemed to shimmer and distort as if there were a massive heat wave in front of them. It reminded Simon of summer schooldays, lying on playground Tarmac and staring at the horizon, trying to see the heat haze create a sort of mirage. All around them everything in the room looked as if it were a mirage.

'And what good does the book do?' muttered Peter.

'I don't know,' said Carfrae, 'but the Doctor obviously thought it was important. We'd better leave it alone.'

'Those Cat-People have given up and gone,' Peter said, pointing. 'But I can't see outside this room.'

'Good.' Simon sat on the floor and looked up at the others. 'Anyone brought a pack of cards with them? I could do with a round of whist.'

'No! Don't kill me!'

'Why not?' spat Lotuss. 'You'd suit me dead.'

Thorsuun waited as the Doctor thought about this for a moment. 'I could be very useful to you and your queen. Your litter would find me exceptionally clever. And I know lots about this planet, its people and how it works. I could act as an intermediary for you.' Thorsuun grunted humourlessly.

'Why?' That was Chosan.

'Ah . . . well, because . . . because I want to live and it's far better to serve you and live than fight you and die. I know far more ways to help you than Thorsuun does.'

'Oh, nice try, Doctor.' Thorsuun tapped Lotuss on the shoulder. 'I thought I told you to kill him, litter-runt.'

There was a moment's pause before Lotuss turned to look at Thorsuun. 'I obey Queen Aysha. My mother. Not you, quisling.' Lotuss was about to move away, when she raised her scarred left arm. 'By the way,

Thorgarsuunela, I hope I don't have to remind you again: the term "litter-runt" is not appreciated. Use it again and I will kill you – regardless of my mother's wishes.' Lotuss signalled to the white Cat-Person with the grey eye-spot, Jayde, and Chosan. 'Let us take these animals with us. Have Aall prepare to use the transporter to take the object that Queen Aysha indicated earlier up to the battle-cruiser. Get the Coates-tom. He can look after Thorgarsuunela and the Doctor-tom.'

Jayde mewed acquiescence and left through the front door. Thorsuun wondered what was coming next. And what object had Aysha found?

Chosan looked at Lotuss and then their captives. 'Queen Aysha has decreed that you will live for a while.'

'Well, I'm relieved to hear that, at least,' the Doctor said.

'If, however, you cause any trouble, you will be killed. Is that understood?'

Thorsuun tried one last tack. 'First-sired Chosan, I am your ally, not some second-rate anthropoid. I insist –'

Chosan's blaster was pressed against her chin in a second. 'I expect that your Kerbe-tom thought he was useful to you, but you proved him wrong.'

Lotuss joined in. 'I enjoyed destroying him. To be honest, I'd enjoy destroying you even more.'

Thorsuun shut up. She just looked at the Doctor who was breathing on a coat button and polishing it with his sleeve. Without raising his head, his green eyes stared hard at Thorsuun. Green eyes which, she suddenly realized, looked just like cat's eyes.

'Hello. Who are you?'

'I-I'm not entirely sure. Where am I?'

'I'm afraid I don't know. My name is Simms. Nate Simms. From Parramatta, Sydney.'

'Y-you don't sound very Australian.'

'Oh, I'm not actually. I'm from Loughborough originally but I moved to Sydney about two years ago.'

'It's very . . . white here. I can't see the walls.'

Nate Simms shrugged. 'I don't think we're in a room, actually. Every so often I feel a bit of a breeze and earlier I saw some movement over thataway. It was a couple of people but I couldn't see them properly. Like watching through frosted glass – yes, that's what it was like! Probably about thirty feet away, I think. I assume it was the people that brought us here.'

'Brought us . . . ? I–I don't remember being –'

Simms shook his head. 'No, I don't either. But I just appeared here, just like you did.'

'When?'

'When what? When did I get here? Oh, about two hours ago. My watch was in my bag – which I appear to have lost.'

'And me?'

'Just now. Literally. I was looking over there . . . or maybe over there and I turned round and there you were. Bingo. At least now we can use each other to give ourselves some bearings. With everything so white, it's been impossible even to know if I've been turning round or not.'

'Can't we just walk towards where you thought you saw something?'

'Ah. No. 'Fraid not. We're inside something. It tingles if you touch it. About three feet around us, in a circle. If anyone else just pops up like you did, we'll get a bit squished.' Simms shrugged again.

'There's nothing to hold on to, is there? Mentally I mean. We can't describe anything, see anything, register it. T–that's rather unsettling.'

'No, you're right. Just as well we can't move I suppose; we'd get lost.'

'Of course, you might have walked for miles and not realized it. There's nothing to set bearings with.'

'Ah, but that invisible wall I mentioned. It won't let you out.'

'Yes, but how do you know it doesn't move with you?

With nothing to get orientated with it might move as well. Fractionally slower, hence you're feeling it, but it could be moving.'

'That . . . that's silly.' Simms grinned. 'I mean, just daft. How can a wall move?'

'Not as silly as standing in a phone box in a village near Whitehaven one second and being here the next.'

'You're beginning to remember things. It took me a while.'

'Bridgeman. Nicholas Bridgeman – that's my name.'

Simms held out his hand and Bridgeman clasped it. 'Pleased to meet you, Mr Bridgeman.'

'P-Professor. Professor Bridgeman of the University of Greenwich. I was in Cumbria with my students – there was an accident of sorts I think.'

'Were you hurt?' Simms gingerly touched Bridgeman's arm.

'No.' Bridgeman shook his head emphatically. 'No, not me. Peter Moore, one of the lads. He fell down the stairs of the Grange. I went for help and there were these two . . . people. One in a wheelchair, the woman was dressed funnily . . .'

'Victorian-like? Yes, that's what I saw. You know, the people I mentioned. Looked like something out of *Upstairs, Downstairs*, I think. I couldn't see them properly.'

'Y-yes, you said. How did you get here, Mr Simms?'

'Nate, please. My friends all call me Nate.'

Bridgeman smiled and nodded. 'All right, Nate, I'm Nicholas. Now, how did you get here?'

'I was climbing Mount Demi, in Queensland. D'you know Oz at all?'

Bridgeman shook his head.

'Oh well, I'm about fifty minutes north of Cairns. Quite near Port Douglas, climbing this mountain. It's quite a sacred Aboriginal site and so I was especially careful about the route I took up. You have to be careful to stick to grazed land rather than crashing through the shrubbery and things. It's their country, you see – white man is just an invader really. Even in Australian schools they use the term "invasion" to describe Captain Cook's discovery rather than "colonization". Interesting semantics that — wouldn't have been the case in the seventies.' Simms stopped abruptly. 'Sorry, was I rambling?'

'In more ways than one, Nate. Y-you were up Mount . . . Demi, was it?'

'Yeah, Demi. Like Bruce Willis's missus. Right, I was about three-quarters of an hour up when I saw a little cave. Rock formations aren't unusual in rain forest areas — indeed when the Aboriginals first settled there, the whole of Oz was rain forest. Difficult to believe, isn't it? Now a majority of it is quite inhospitable desert. Anyway, I found this cave and began to explore it.'

Nate paused.

'And?' prompted Bridgeman.

'Oh, yeah. Sorry, I got distracted. I saw those two people again behind you. Blurred again. I wonder if my eyes are playing up. That light was very bright.'

'What light?'

'Oh, the light at the back of the cave. I was going towards it when it just . . . well, flared up. Really brightly. My eyes hurt and so did my head. And it was really warm. In fact, look at my pen.' Simms produced the remnants of what might have once been a silver Parker cartridge pen.

Bridgeman took it and rolled it around his palm. 'Melted. Fused into a lump. But it didn't actually b–burn you?'

'Not at all. I only discovered my pen was like that a while back. I was going to poke at our invisible wall with it.'

'I remember something similar.' Bridgeman suddenly clenched his fists. 'That's it — the money in the coin box. I remember it just melted, dripped away. And there was a light. Warm, like yours.'

'Did you get the feeling of going up? You know, like in a lift that goes horribly quickly. Like the one in

Sydney's Centrepoint Tower . . . oh, well, you wouldn't know that, would you.'

'No, but I know the feeling you mean. And yes, I-I did feel that. It's all coming back now and . . . What's wrong?'

'Nicholas. Turn around slowly. They're behind you.'

Professor Bridgeman twisted round and stared. Into the faces of two scantily clothed Aboriginals – a female pushing a male around in a primitive wooden cart. The man suddenly let out a shriek of malevolent laughter and was promptly cuffed around the ear by the woman.

'I . . . I know you . . .' Bridgeman tried to reach out to them but instead his fingers touched what he guessed was Simms's invisible wall. 'About one point five volts,' he muttered to no one in particular. 'But I know them. In the village . . .'

'Aboriginals? In a Cumbrian village?' Simms was doubtful.

'No. Not like this then. In Victorian gear. But the faces are unmistakable . . .'

The crippled man suddenly lunged forward in his cart, his hand brushing Bridgeman's shoulder, obviously unimpaired by the electrical forcefield. 'Hiya, Nickie! I'm your worst nightmare!' With a shriek of laughter he rocked back and rolled on his side, curling up like a foetus in the cart and fell fast asleep.

The woman looked down at her charge and then at the two men. 'He's very tired. Forgive him.'

'W-who are you?' Bridgeman tried to reach out again but the voltage pushed his hand back involuntarily.

The woman slowly shook her head and looked at the man in the cart. 'Your past. Your present. Perhaps your future.'

In the cart, the crippled man's right eye popped open and he stuck his tongue out. 'And the death of all humanity. And there's nothing you can do about it. Unless you've a flea collar handy!'

Whatever the meaning of that, it sent him into spasms of

laughter, followed by a hacking cough. Tutting to herself, the woman turned the cart away and suddenly seemed to shimmer, as if caught in a heat haze. Bridgeman tried to refocus his eyes but it was no good. For a moment she seemed to grow taller, wearing her long black dress and the man was back in a wooden wheelchair, wearing the blue velvet smoking jacket and pyjama bottoms Bridgeman had seen him in back at the village phone box.

'Dent!' Bridgeman called. 'Mrs Wilding, come back. Where are we?'

But they had vanished. With a sigh he turned to Simms.

Who had also vanished.

Polly opened her eyes. It was space, dark with white streaks of light stabbing out around her. She had been here before but she could not remember when. Or had she? Something told her this was someone else's dream – that she was just a visitor, a guest inside someone else's memories.

Something reminded her of that time at the fairground, when Uncle Charles had taken her into the old gypsy tent. 'Not a real gypsy, of course,' he had said knowingly, and like all ten year olds, Polly believed him because rich uncles knew everything. 'No, just some local woman dressed in a silly skirt.'

But Uncle Charles might have been wrong. The gypsy woman had looked at Polly's hand, muttered something about a long life and then produced a pack of cards. To ten-year-old Polly, they looked very pretty but strange. There were no aces or threes or clubs or hearts. Instead, colourful pictures showing young girls with wands, looking like fairies. And a tower with lightning which frightened her a bit. And the colourful man tied upside-down, hanging from a tree. She asked Polly to cut the pack and afterwards she dealt some cards out. Polly did not understand for one moment what the point was but all she remembered afterwards was being warned away from a tall, dark stranger.

Years later she would laugh when her friends suggested playing with a pack of tarot cards — the clichéd idea of her dangerous tall, dark stranger stopped her taking the cards seriously.

Now, as she floated around inside someone else's dream (or whatever it was), the warning seemed suddenly unsettling. For some reason she thought that she might actually meet this tall, dark stranger. And then she realized she already had — on a flight of steps in a house invaded by unbelievable Cat-People. The man, curled up in fear, he had been tall and dark and something primal told her this was him. The gypsy's fear.

'It's your dream, isn't it?' Polly breathed for a reason she could not fathom.

'Yes,' said a voice. Warm, soothing and delicious. The sort of voice you could curl up with on a sofa and feel safe. The sort of voice you could trust, give over to, be at peace with. Polly relaxed. 'That's better,' said the voice. 'No one or nothing is going to hurt you. Trust me, please. Trust me and I'll help you.'

The streaks of white light began to shimmer, coalesce into a shape — the vague outline of the TARDIS. 'Is this your home?' asked the voice.

Polly tried to shake her head but did not have the energy. She was too relaxed. 'Yes . . . well, no, not really. I travel in it. My real home is London.'

'Where is the Doctor? Is he in Cumbria with you?'

'Yes,' Polly answered. 'But how d'you know . . . ?'

'That's not important. I need you, your strength and power to help me help him. You saw the Cat-People, didn't you?'

'Yes! Yes, I did.' Polly began to tense up again. 'And you? It was you on the stairs, wasn't it?'

'Sort of, yes. Now, relax again or I can't hold you here. Can't help you escape from the Cat-People.'

'Sorry.' Polly breathed deeply. 'Are they here? In Cumbria?'

'Yes, they are now. I hoped I would get here first but I

made a mistake. I didn't realize how far she would go to escape.'

Polly frowned. 'Who?'

'Thorgarsuunela. We were trapped here together. She's brought the Cat-People here in exchange for free passage away from Earth.'

'What do they want?'

'No more questions. I'm going to try to bring you back to reality. I needed to talk to you like this while your friend isn't around. Ben, is it? His mind is too closed.'

Polly suddenly remembered the clifftop. The coat, Ben pulling at it, getting near the cliff . . . stumbling near the edge . . .

Polly opened her mouth to scream into the darkness –

'Ben!' Polly screeched.

Ben was windmilling with his arms, comically trying to fly like they did in the cartoons. Suddenly there was someone grabbing Ben's wrist and casually lifting him back on to the cliff edge. As his wrist was released, Ben dropped to the ground, panting, tears of fear and frustration on his cheeks. He was wheezing. 'Oh God, oh God, oh God –'

'You're safe. Both of you,' said a safe, warm, soothing, trustworthy voice.

Polly looked straight into the piercing blue eyes of her tall, dark stranger.

More people pass through Heathrow Airport in one twenty-four-hour period than any other installation in Europe. Either as a final destination or as a stop-over, Heathrow sees more passengers and flight crews than anywhere else clogging up the bars, cafés, restaurants, shops and, of course, passport controls.

'Air MidEast announce the arrival of Flight ME 423 from Baghdad. Would all passengers from Flight 423 assemble at carousel 8 for their baggage and then pass through Passport Control. Holders of UK and EC passports to gates 8 to 10, non-EC passports to gates 1 to 7. Thank you.'

'Excuse me, can I get a flight to Manchester from here?'

Passport Control Attendant Philip Jay looked up from his booth and smiled at the attractive, middle-aged blonde facing him. Helping her would make a change from grumpy OAPs who had lost their zimmers en route from France or postnatally depressed young mothers with six kids and a husband playing the slot machines. She might even –

'I said, can you help me?'

Jay coughed, mentally cataloguing this one in his cold 'n' frigid section. 'Yes, madam. You could get a plane to Manchester but it would actually be quicker to take the tube to Euston and catch a train. Our next scheduled flight to Manchester –' his hands flicked over his database keyboard (and he wondered if she noticed the lack of wedding ring on his finger), 'is at 20.05 from Terminal One.'

The blonde stared at him. Wistfully? Helplessly? 'Well, what time is it now?'

Aggressively. Oh well, he had tried. 'A quarter past one, madam. The day is dragging a bit.'

The woman shifted the weight of her shoulder bag. 'That's because your rather pathetic little world has been held in stasis for the last eight hours. I've been stuck on your plane twice as long as I should have been. I ought to have remembered that he'd done that.'

Jay refiled her. Bloody loony. Leave well alone. Call security? Nah, no need. 'Right, madam. The Underground is –'

'I know where the Underground is, mollusc. I've only been away for a couple of thousand years! What day is this?'

Mollusc. That was a new one. He would look that one up in the dictionary tonight. Jay nodded towards a digital calendar suspended above the entrance to the customs area. All the other passengers had gone through, followed by the other support staff. Trust him to be left alone with a bimbo two sandwiches short of a picnic!

'Tenth of June, madam.'

'Excellent. I must get to the Grange by tonight. I have a Doctor's appointment.'

One last try, he just could not stop himself. 'I'm off duty in an hour. Can I offer you a lift somewhere, Ms . . . ?'

'Thorsuun. My name is Thorsuun. And no, I don't think you can do anything for me. I, however, much as I loathe your ridiculous world and its rather dreary populace, will do it a favour.'

Philip Jay smiled. Ms Thorsuun gave out a long, low wolf-whistle, turned on her heel and strode away into customs. Into the green area, naturally. A woman like that would have nothing to hide. Nothing to –

Philip Jay suddenly coughed and hunched up in his seat. He felt extraordinarily tired for no good reason. He shook his head; the lights seemed to have dimmed. He glanced down at his desk; his hands . . . they were not his hands. They were thin, wrinkled, covered with liver spots. They seemed to be shrinking as he watched. He felt short of breath, his head itched, his eyes burned. His chest, his heart . . . his –

If at that moment one of his mates had popped back into passport control they would have been amazed to see a very old, thin man slumped in Philip Jay's seat, wearing his uniform. However, as it was three minutes before anyone ventured out of customs, all they found was his uniform crumpled on his seat, and a pile of dust on the floor.

Charlie Coates was humping a heavy black plastic bin-liner up the path away from the Gatehouse and towards the back of the Grange when Thorsuun and the Doctor were led out of the front door.

'Who's that?' The Doctor pointed at Coates.

'Charles Coates. One of the more reliable thugs that Kerbe employed.' Thorsuun was fuming. How had she let the Cat-People treat her like this? All her plans, all her deals, were they going to be thrown away like so much . . . kitty-litter?

The Doctor gently tapped her shoulder. 'They're all the same, you know.'

'Who are?'

'Space mercenaries. You can never trust them.'

'Thank you, sweetheart. I can trust you I suppose?'

The Doctor laughed quietly. 'Oh no, Thorsuun. Never do that. We're on opposing teams. Whatever your plans, whatever Aysha's plans, Earth is caught in the middle. And my loyalties have to lie there.'

'With this lump of rock? Why?'

The Doctor pointed at Coates. 'Look at him. While the basic physiology is sound, internally and mentally, the humans need protection. They can't fend for themselves against alien aggressors. They can barely fend for them-selves. Right now they're fighting each other in the former Soviet Union, in Bosnia, in Rwanda, in Northern Ireland. All over the place. Sometimes they'll find peace but for every war they end, two more will start up. And it'll take more than these Cat-People to unite them. In the meantime, someone has to champion their cause.'

'Oh, you're so good, Doctor. They should canonize you.'

'Better that than despising you. As a Euterpian, you must have been here many years. Your people vanished a very long time ago. You must have seen civilizations here rise and fall.'

'All of them, Doctor. We were here at the beginning.'

The Doctor nodded. 'I see. How many of you?'

'Five.'

The Doctor stopped suddenly until a shove from Chosan meant he had to keep walking down the path towards Coates, still struggling with the heavy black bin-liner. 'Just five? Where are the others?'

'Don't know. Atimkos and I set off about forty thousand years ago to lay the beacons. We never saw the others again, but we heard the . . . rumours.'

The Doctor stuffed his hands in his pockets, and felt the red book in there. 'Of course. Ghosts. A fellow Euterpian trying to contact you could easily be mistaken for a ghost. What made you latch on to Bridgeman's group?'

Thorsuun pointed back at the Grange. 'There's a large library in there, Doctor. Somewhere within it are some of our books. I can sense them. Messages left by one, maybe more of the others.'

'And where's your chum, Atimkos? Why isn't he helping you?'

'He doesn't know about the books. And,' she waved back at Chosan, 'he wouldn't approve of them.'

'I like him already.'

'Don't be smug, Doctor, it doesn't become you.'

They had reached the struggling Coates. 'Miss Thorsuun.' He touched his cap which promptly fell off. The Doctor bent forward and picked it up.

'So you'll use them to get away from here. Where will you go?'

Thorsuun stopped. 'Oh, Doctor, I felt that.'

'What?'

'Fear. The fear that ran through you then. Yes, you're right – with my knowledge of the multiverse, I can lead the Cat-People anywhere in time and space.'

'Once you re-assert your equality, of course.'

'Of course. I shall put this putrid little world and its ills behind me.'

'How come you're being so accommodating to them? With your powers, I would have thought you could easily . . . omit them from your plans?' The Doctor twiddled his bow-tie again.

Thorsuun coughed slightly. 'Yes, well, I needed a bargaining chip. They procured my RTC unit. We all have one – it stops us ageing. Without it, I'm beginning to grow older – at about the same rate as a human, so it doesn't matter too much. I'll get it back before long.' Thorsuun pursed her lips. 'Assuming that Chosan hasn't remodulated it too much. She's a great tinkerer, I've realized, but hopelessly flawed.'

'How do they work?'

'Very well, thank you. Especially when one or more are brought together.'

'I thought so. I used the two in the house to escape Atimkos's time-stop.'

Thorsuun stopped. 'Oh, and you didn't see fit to tell me. Thank you so much. If I could get my hands on just one of those, I could get rid of Aysha and her moggies when they least expect it.'

'Well, forget it – I left them both there.' Patting his pocket, and feeling the shape of the little red book safely hidden, the Doctor smiled knowingly. 'Now, tell me about the others in your party.'

Thorsuun shrugged. 'Frankly, my dear Doctor, I don't give a damn about them. Atimkos is a fool, dabbling in so-called arcanity trying to find the paths. He's disguised his RTC unit as a pack of cards or something. How parochial.' She ran a hand through her blonde hair and tried to look coy. The Doctor stared impassively back, so she gave up. 'With regard to the beacons, I think I've already found them. The Cat-People can use them, I don't need to.'

'So, if you shut your eyes, it'll all go away. You can just forget Atimkos and the others. As if they don't exist.'

'That's basically it, yes.'

The Doctor spun Coates' cap around on his index finger, ignoring the man's attempts to snatch it back. 'There's a theory – rather appropriately called Schroedinger's Cat – that says something about probability waves and that if you shut something away out of sight long enough it ceases to change – it is everything at once, alive, dead, changing, not changing. You get the idea?'

'I am familiar with the concept.' She smiled.

'Well, old Schroedinger was theorizing that out of sight isn't just out of mind but out of the way of probable change. We perceive what we see and when we don't see it, it ceases to alter until we next need it to. Is that how you see your people? Unchanging. Incapable of acting or doing their own thing unless you're there to actually see it? Isn't that dangerous?'

Thorsuun also made a grab for the hat but missed. 'This is irrelevant. All I need is my freedom.'

The Doctor spun the cap up and Coates caught it, shoving it into his coat pocket. 'Like his cap, Thorsuun. You can't see it, but it's still there no matter how much you pretend it isn't. You owe it to the others to help them off Earth as well.' He pointed at Coates's now bulging pocket. 'Schroedinger's Hat perhaps?'

Thorsuun sighed. 'Don't be such a smart alec. Charles!'

Coates looked up expectantly. 'Yes, Fräulein Thorsuun?'

'What has happened to George?'

Lotuss suddenly pushed herself forward. 'I dealt with him.'

Thorsuun lost her patience. 'Damn you, litter-runt, do you know how difficult it has been finding people who not only accept working for me but aren't afraid to get their hands dirty?'

'George was,' muttered Coates.

'Quiet, Charles. Well?'

Lotuss puffed out her chest and her fur raised. 'One more word from you, and I blast you here and now.'

'Not only do you shoot Kerbe instead of him,' she pointed at the Doctor, who spread his hands apologetically, 'but now I learn you've killed George Smithers. Well, thank you for nothing.' Thorsuun pushed past Lotuss. 'Charles, where's the body?'

Coates pointed at the bag he was hefting. Thorsuun raised her eyes to heaven. 'Where are you burying it?'

'On the clifftop. No one goes up there. Well, except two youngsters I saw earlier but I think they went the other way.'

'Two young –' Thorsuun looked at the Doctor. 'And just where are our delightful Sixties debutantes, eh?'

The Doctor shrugged and shook his head. 'Young people. They will go off on their own.'

'Hi. My name's Tim. Are you two all right?'

Ben was gasping for breath. 'Yeah, thanks, mate. I think you saved my life. Where'd you come from anyway?'

Polly was staring at the man called Tim. 'I . . . I know you?'

'Pol?' Ben got up, putting his weight on Tim's shoulder. 'Where from?'

'I don't know. Have we met?'

Tim smiled. 'I don't believe so. Not in this life, anyway.'

Polly was screwing her face up. 'There's something . . . It's just out of reach.'

Ben smiled sheepishly at Tim. 'Sorry, mate. She's a bit weird at times. Probably saw you in one of her dreams.'

Tim nodded. 'Maybe she did.'

'Yes. Yes, a dream.' Polly put her hand to her mouth. 'Ben! My dream. The cat-thing. This man was in it. It's all coming back to me now.'

'Anyway,' said Tim, 'what were you doing that I needed to rescue you from the drop?'

'Getting a shock, weren't we, Ben?' said Polly pointing at Coates's dig.

Ben shrugged. 'Yeah. That's right. Look here.' He dropped to the newly set earth. 'There's something buried here. Clothes.'

'Murder?' asked Polly.

'Could be, Duchess, could be. But why just the clothes?'

'Distracts the dogs,' said Tim. 'If you bury the clothes and the body separately, the dogs will find one or the other but rarely both. Once the scent is tracked, they find it difficult to start again. Besides which, a body with no clothes means no ID. And clothes with no body doesn't prove murder. Someone knew what they were doing.'

'Blimey, mate, you a detective or what? Proper little expert, ain'tcha. I know someone who'd like to meet you. You could play Watson to his Sherlock.'

'Ben, I think we should tell the Doctor about this.'

'OK, Polly. Let's head back. You coming, mate?'

'Yes, Mr Jackson, I think I should. We need to report this to the authorities.'

The three of them set off. Ben decided to keep the conversation going as Polly had gone very quiet and withdrawn. He noticed she was walking with her face down, watching her feet. 'What d'you do for a job then, Tim?'

'I'm a witch.'

Ben stopped. 'You're joking?'

Tim shook his head.

'But you can't be a witch. I mean, where's your broomstick?' Seeing the lack of reaction, Ben tried a different tack. 'I thought men were warlocks anyway.'

'Not at all. Witchcraft – white witchcraft, which I study – goes back far beyond gender tagging. No, I'm a witch. Of course if you'd like me to supply a cauldron, a black cat, some frogs' tails and go "hubble, bubble, toil and trouble" I could. But it wouldn't do much except look stupid.'

'Oh. Right.' Ben looked to Polly for support but her face was giving nothing away. 'So, how d'you cast a spell?'

'Candles. Chanting. Psionics mainly. I also use tarot cards and have been known to decipher dreams.' Tim looked over at Polly. 'Or use them.'

Ben looked from one to the other. 'Anyway, mate, here's the back of the Grange. Got to watch out for the man with the gun.'

'A warden?'

'No, a university bloke actually. There's something weird going on 'ere, and I bet our murder is connected.'

'Well,' said Tim. 'Let's go.' He strode ahead but Ben hung back and touched Polly's arm. 'What's up, Duchess?'

'Ben.' Polly stared at him with her big blue eyes wide open. 'Ben, how did he know your name was Jackson?'

* * *

'Tickets, please. Thank you, sir. Tickets, please. Yes, all in order. Thank you. Thank you. Yes, change at Piccadilly, cross to Victoria and then change again at Preston. Thank you, ma'am. Yes, that's fine.'

Thorsuun sank deeper into her seat. The door to her coach slid open and shut.

'Tickets, please. Thank you, sir. Yes, that's fine.'

Thorsuun looked out of the window.

'Ticket, please, madam.'

'I don't possess one, little man-thing.'

The ticket collector sighed. 'Where did you get on the train? You can buy one from me now.'

'Euston. But I don't need one.'

The ticket collector smiled with the weary patience of someone who dealt with this situation every twenty minutes. 'And why don't you need one?'

'Who needs them?'

'Everyone who travels, madam.'

Thorsuun pointed to one of the people whose ticket had already been punched. On his knee was a wicker carry-case with a mewling kitten inside.

Thorsuun loathed cats. 'Does that creature need one?'

'No.'

'Why not?'

'Because it's an animal.'

'It's not human?'

The ticket collector was getting bored. 'Yes. It's not human. It doesn't need a ticket. You, as a human like its owner, do need a ticket.'

Thorsuun smiled. 'Wrong.' She looked the ticket collector straight in the eye, and opened her mouth. 'Rrraaaaaghhhh!!' she shouted.

The ticket collector did not even hear the end of the noise as his clothes, flesh and blood were spread across the four seats opposite. Thorsuun looked at his skeleton, standing upright, feet firmly embedded in its boots. She looked around. The other six people in the compartment were similarly dead, the windows, seats and carpet

110

layered with blood and liquefied flesh. Thorsuun wandered towards the cat case and noted with satisfaction that the cat was splattered across the insides of the cage, bits of it oozing through the wicker strands. 'I hate felines of any genus,' she said.

Seconds later the train pulled into Crewe and Thorsuun got off, carefully wiping her blooded shoes in a puddle. The train pulled away and dimly she heard a shriek as some hapless newcomer encountered the mess that used to be the people in coach G.

Thorsuun thought about what had happened. She crossed to an automatic ticket machine and used her Amex card to purchase a ticket to Whitehaven. The next train to Manchester Piccadilly, this one coming via Birmingham New Street, was in twenty minutes. A minor delay.

The inside of the Cat-People's shuttle, parked behind the Gatehouse and obscured by the trees, was utilitarian but striking. Decorated in the same shocking red as their uniforms, it contained a basic helm and navigation console — obviously scaled down from what Thorsuun assumed was on the bridge of their orbiting battleship. Six seats were ranged three-abreast behind it and to the rear was a weaponry storage locker. In front of that was a solitary, softer seat, in which Aysha sat. The Doctor flopped down in the helm seat. 'Well, that was a pleasant little trot, wasn't it?' Everyone ignored him.

Aysha pointed at him. 'You are lucky to be alive.'

The Doctor straightened his bow-tie and stared Aysha directly in the face. 'Yes, I am, I suppose. Of course, we'll never know whether or not Lotuss deliberately missed me or whether you'd already decided to ignore Fräulein Thorsuun's desires and shoot Kerbe anyway. But it's not really important.'

Thorsuun watched the Doctor carefully. Divide and conquer, eh? She looked back to Aysha, who did not respond to the Doctor's comment. Could she have been wrong? Was Aysha going to ignore her? Certainly her treatment at Lotuss's paws left something to be desired but the need to escape Earth frankly overrode a small amount of humiliation. Anyway, she did not trust Lotuss and believed she was perfectly capable of shooting her and claiming it was an accident later. 'Kerbe's use was at an end, Doctor,' she said for good measure – just to let Aysha know there were no hard feelings.

'Yes, I'm sure it was.' The Doctor stared at the controls around him. 'Nice shuttle. Can I press a few buttons? You know, play around a bit? Technology fascinates me, you see and –'

'Shut!' Lotuss brought her blaster up to the Doctor's chest. 'One more prattle and I'll drill your heart out.'

Thorsuun sighed and could not stop herself muttering, 'Oh, how very melodramatic.' She crossed to Aysha. 'Look, Your Majesty, let's sort out these beacons and I can be on my way. He,' she waved towards the Doctor, 'and the others on this planet will all die in the firestorms. Can we get on with it, please? Your Majesty?'

'What are you looking for? Perhaps I can help?' The Doctor was spinning his seat around, and Thorsuun sighed. Did this man really want to die so soon?

'When Atimkos and I left the southern hemisphere, we placed a series of beacons along our path,' Thorsuun began.

'Sort of find-your-way-home-again things?'

'No. Sort of when-viewed-from-space-there's-a-nice-ring-to-cut-through-and-release-the-planet's-energies thing actually.'

'Oh. Like join the dots?'

'Exactly, Doctor. When my people joined the dots on the various planets we encountered, we'd cut the crust open and the resultant magnetic energy that was released would power our ship for millennia.'

'Well, a while anyway,' said the Doctor. 'Allowing for your rhetoric I presume it didn't last for millennia otherwise you wouldn't need to keep doing it.'

Thorsuun sat down. 'You can be such a bore to tell

112

stories to, Doctor. I bet you never believed in Father Christmas.'

'Where I came from, the children were busy learning the quality of life and how sacrosanct all living things were. A way of life such as the Euterpians' and the Cat-People's was abhorrent to us. Evil always is.' The Doctor looked very smug, Thorsuun decided.

'Well, I'm sorry we can't share or even appreciate your honour, Doctor. But we only deal in reality. Survival of the fittest and all that.'

The Doctor stopped moving and then spoke very quietly. Thorsuun actually felt something of a shiver run through her. Those grey eyes of his could be very cold. But they were green earlier . . .

'Tell me about these beacons,' he asked.

'Atimkos and I walked a straight line from our crash site, placing the beacons every few thousand kilometres. With the right resonance and harmonics, they light up and show the path. It's very simple.'

'So what went wrong?'

Thorsuun frowned. 'What makes you think anything has gone wrong?'

'Because no Euterpian fleet has returned to split the planet in half and the beacons obviously aren't working or the Cat-People wouldn't be needing you to show them the way. They'd see it and cut us up without any regard to you, me or the billions of people down here.'

'I've lost the exact path. I tried to light it up many times over the years – we wanted to return to God-wanna, our leader, and the others, but perhaps the beacons have failed. It's taken me this long to interest another species in the properties this planet has to offer and therefore have the resources to commence an operation of this scale.'

'I see. So, if you don't mind me asking, why the Grange?'

'Simple, Doctor. I recognize it. I know we were here once. I can feel it in the ground. There is a line of power

113

running right underneath us as we speak. It's been there so long it's become part of the planet itself.'

The Doctor smiled at her. 'Ah, so you've found a ley line. Indeed, you've created them. Very good.'

'But it doesn't work,' put in Aysha. 'We can trace it across into the nearest continent –'

'Europe,' Thorsuun added, feeling slightly put out that Aysha had interrupted.

Ignoring her, the Cat-People Queen continued: 'They appear intermittently but that is all. It is not enough. Yet.'

The Doctor got up and began to pace the ship, sucking the forefinger of his right hand. 'Well,' he mumbled between sucks, 'that's because, apparently, ley lines are cultural not geographical. England, France and parts of Germany have them, because of the Celtic influences. Scandinavia have similar but unconnected ones. And the Australian Aborigines have . . . the songlines! Of course!' He removed his finger and pointed it wetly at Thorsuun. 'That's where you landed, isn't it! You taught those early men, forty thousand years ago, to sing. They hum things to keep your beacons lit. That's where their legends and myths of the Dreamtime come from.'

'Yes, Doctor, and unlike every other culture Atimkos and I encountered, the Australian Aborigines have kept it going. If I could reach Godwanna and the others, they could force a mass songtime and the beacons would become alight. We could then trace the path exactly. As it is, we only have guesswork to go on.'

'And where are your guesses taking you?'

'Back a few thousand years, before industry destroyed the culture we set up and find the links.'

'So if we can find the links, I can get to Godwanna and together we can stop Thorgarsuunela and the Cat-People.'

Ben and Polly were standing at the back of the Grange, sheltering from the Cumbrian wind behind a coal shed. The man called Tim had just told them he was in fact an immortal alien searching for the path home.

Polly asked the first question. 'And where do I fit into this? Why were you in my dreams?'

Tim smiled. 'Two reasons. I was initially attracted to your friend, the Doctor. His TARDIS crosses all the dimensional barriers: space, time and transcendentalism. We did the same, probably millions of years before his people existed. He is the first alien I've encountered whose powers are similar to ours, although his are mechanical, ours natural.'

'You'd be surprised, mate,' interjected Ben. 'He can do some pretty neat things himself. How many other people can change their bodies for a new one when it burns out, eh?'

'Cellular regeneration is uncommon, certainly, but not unique. Silicon-based lifeforms do it all the time.'

Polly got back to the subject top of her mind. 'OK, but why me now?'

'Your mind is open. You believe, you accept things. The Doctor is essentially a scientist. Ben here is a realist and cynic. But you, Polly Wright, you are open to things.'

Polly nodded. 'You need me to find the ley lines?'

Tim smiled. 'Exactly.'

Ben was confused and pulled Polly closer to him. 'Duchess, what are you talking about?'

Polly hugged herself closer to keep warm. 'Ben, at Leeds University there was a group of us. We did things – silly things. Ouija boards, tarot readings and things like that. We used to go out on to the Yorkshire Moors and dowse. But I was different – I believed, really believed I could feel something there. Dragon paths, ley lines, whatever.'

'Never saw you as a pill-popper, Pol.'

'No, Ben, I wasn't using drugs, it was real. I took a regression session once with this woman who owned a little yellow shop just near the campus. She took me to another life, another place. Told me I was an Australian Aboriginal woman, whose husband was a Dreamer. I used to help him with the Vision Quests; we'd go off for months on end, singing the old songs. The skies would light up – Ben, there was such power, I could feel it running through me. Oh, Ben, I was so frightened when she woke me up, it was so real.'

Tim touched her arm. 'It may well have been, Polly. It would explain why I knew I had to seek you out. I can use you, or your suppressed regressions, to relight those beacons. Get us Godwanna. We need to get to Australia and then go back.'

'Back where?'

Tim smiled reassuringly. 'Only about forty thousand years.'

Ben coughed. 'And do we go BOAC?'

Tim laughed. 'Out of business, chum. Mid-Seventies.'

'Ah well, I always preferred boats meself.'

'Listen, Ben, I had a vitally important task for you. You need to get to the Doctor – ensure he doesn't allow the woman you know as Fräulein Thorsuun any access to your TARDIS. I was hoping to use it myself but I don't think that'll be possible now.'

'Why not?' asked Polly.

Tim pointed around the corner of the Grange. The other two followed his gaze. Facing them was the silver shuttle craft. 'The Doctor and Thorgarsuunela are in there already. Polly and I need to find another way. I can sense things about this house – I recognize the locale. We were here before. I think this house stands on the last beacon we set up. I can try to use it to contact the others – but the power needed will be massive. It'll take time.'

Ben nodded. 'You look after Polly, mate, or you'll answer to me. You OK about this, Pol?'

Polly smiled a small, false smile of confidence which she knew Ben would see through. 'I'll be fine, really. Go on.'

Ben squeezed her hand and with a last stare of warning at Tim, scurried towards the shuttle craft.

Polly watched him and then touched Tim's arm. 'What do we do now?'

'Stay where you are, that's what!'

116

Polly turned and was greeted by a shotgun held by the man she and Ben had spoken to on the clifftop. He was dragging a large black plastic bin-liner and spade.

'Doing some more burying?' Polly asked with a confidence she did not feel.

Coates nodded. 'Yeah – plenty of room for two more. Where's your friend?'

'Gone to stop Thorsuun's plans actually.' Polly heard Tim sigh beside her but it was too late. Coates reacted to the news.

'We'll see about that!'

Tim suddenly stepped behind Polly and pushed his hands against her ears. Dimly she heard him whistle. Although it was faint, it made her head swim – she felt very tired.

The effect on Coates was stronger. He simply let his mouth drop open and he carefully placed his gun on the ground. Ignoring Polly and Tim, as well as the bin-liner, he just turned and walked away.

Tim released Polly's ears. Amazed, she looked over her shoulder at him. 'What did you do?'

'I told him he needed a long rest, that work was getting on top of him and that a nice cup of tea was all he required right now.' Tim picked up the discarded gun, broke it and threw the cartridges into a bush. 'Nasty things, guns.'

Polly smiled, reassured. 'The Doctor always says that.'

'A wise man, the Doctor. Maybe we're more alike than I realized.'

Polly nodded. 'I think so. You'd get on. He's a total pacifist – all life is sacred to him.'

'Me too,' said Tim. 'Now, let's get into the Grange.'

Charlie Coates was tired. Tea. He wanted a cup of tea. And a chocolate Hobnob. And a rest. A long rest. Working for Herr Kerbe and Fräulein Thorsuun was hard work. Especially now George Smithers was . . . was . . . what had happened to Smithers?

117

He could not remember. Had George gone to put the rubbish out? Something about carrying a rubbish bag. Had George come back?

Oh, why did his head hurt so much? Where was the tea? Why was he walking away from the Gatehouse? Was it something that tall, dark strange man had said? Something about rest. Yes, he had told Charlie to go this way – not back to the Gatehouse but further away. He had said it was vitally important to go this way – vitally important to have a good rest. He had ordered, instructed, demanded, insisted that Charlie went this way. Why?

Charlie Coates was still pondering this when, following his instructions to the letter as always, he stepped off the clifftop and plummeted seventy feet on to the black, jagged rocks below, where some soft, torn fragments of his body were quickly washed away into the Irish Sea.

'This explains why no one was ever allowed into the kitchen,' said Polly. She was standing amidst rows of screens, each of them attached to each other in sequence. 'What are they?'

'Computers. Quadra 610s – all brand-new.' Tim followed the wires connecting them. 'They're networked.' He pointed at the images gyrating upon the screens. 'Recognize those?'

Polly stared hard. It was a globe, see-through, each line picked out like a spider's web and rotating on an axis. 'It's Earth. But they're all slightly different.'

'Every map of the full globe issued every time a new country or boundary was established. These must go back four or five hundred years. What was she looking for?'

Polly stared at the screens. 'Did you call these computers?'

'Yeah. Problem?'

'But, Tim, where are the spools? The tapes and lights? These aren't computers. I mean computers are massive things.' For a brief moment she remembered her first encounter with the Doctor and the malevolent computer that could think for itself – WOTAN. She remembered the expanse of room it took up and just a glance at the three-dimensional images told her WOTAN was not ever capable of these designs or images.

'Guess you missed the micro-chip revolution, Polly. It'd take too long to explain and would probably be best if I didn't try. When you get back to your own time, these things will still be fifteen years in the future. You wouldn't want to invent them and upset the web of time.'

Polly shrugged. 'There you go – sounding like the Doctor again. Ben and I discussed this earlier. Don't worry, we'll leave well alone.' She pointed at the screens. 'Nevertheless, what's going on?'

Tim punched a keyboard (although it did not look like any typewriter keyboard Polly had ever used) and one of the globes literally unwrapped itself and became a skeletal flat map of the world. Beside the keyboard was a palm-shaped device which Tim swivelled around and various listings flashed across the top of the screen. Polly gave up trying to understand what he was doing but the palm-shaped thing made a clicking noise and the map filled out into a full colour map like she had seen in atlases. 'How pretty,' she murmured.

'Watch this,' he said and clicked again, turning the map into a relief map. Before Polly could say anything, his fingers darted over the keyboard and the image magnified a few times and she caught a glimpse of Britain . . . north-west England . . . then she recognized Cumbria itself. The coast. Tim jabbed with a finger. 'That's us. This exact spot. There's Sellafield.'

'What?'

'Windscale.'

'The nuclear plant? Didn't they close it down then?'

'Obviously not.'

'Oh.' Polly remembered Paul and Penny getting very het up about nuclear power at university. Always going on demos and putting up CND slogans. She had never taken much notice – nuclear power was something she did not understand and Uncle Charles always seemed to be in favour of it. Mind you, Uncle Charles had been a staunch supporter of Professor Brett and WOTAN, so maybe he was not always right.

'This is the place.' Tim looked around the restructured kitchen. 'This house is right on the top. She probably hoped it was a nexus point. I'm glad it isn't.'

'A nexus point?'

Tim started running around, tapping on keyboards, and the screens started shutting down with warning bleeps. 'This should hurt a bit. I'm crashing all her systems. She'll lose everything.'

'That seems a bit harsh. All that work —'

'Polly!' Tim was aghast. 'Polly, Thorgarsuunela is selling your world for a mess of potage. The Cat-People will use our devices for their own ends and Earth will be destroyed.'

'Isn't that what you would have done forty thousand years ago?' Polly was very confused.

Tim stopped as the last screen bleeped and died. 'Yes. But we didn't know humanity was here then. If we had, we'd have gone off and found an uninhabited world to use.'

'I see.' Polly was slightly reassured. She looked around the kitchen. 'Would you like a cup of tea?'

'They're points in the space-time continuum. Very rare and hard to access.'

'What, cups of tea?'

'No, silly, nexus points. We need to find one to reach Godwanna. She's bound to have sealed herself away from normal space-time in a transcendental hyper reality.' Tim reached for Polly and held her shoulders, staring deeply into her eyes. 'Polly, there's no time for tea. We have to go on a journey. Now, why was she coming back here? Why use the house?' He began to pace the room. 'What's in the house, Polly? What other rooms have you seen?'

'Well, I hadn't been in here before now — all I've seen is the hallway and the students' room where Peter was lying.' She stopped. 'Tim! The students must still be here. They can help.'

'I doubt it. She'll have killed them by now. No, we need . . .'

Polly did not wait to hear the rest – she was off to the students' room.

'Guys!' Peter was calling. Simon looked at him. 'Guys – my arm doesn't hurt any more!'

'Good,' said Carfrae.

'No, wait.' Simon had an idea. They were still inside their Ex-Area, and Peter was standing by the big book the Doctor had chucked in. 'It's that CRT or whatever.'

'RTC,' chorused the others.

'Yeah, whatever. It's making Peter's injury go backwards. We're travelling in time in here.'

'Not properly you're not, but the idea's sound enough.' The voice belonged to a silhouette framed in the doorway; the distorting field of the Ex-Area was bending around him but the light was blotting out his features. Simon realized there was a second figure hovering behind the newcomer – one he recognized.

'Polly?'

'Simon, are you all right? We can't get in. Tim's using his powers to communicate with you.'

'Who's Tim?' asked Carfrae.

'Never mind me,' said the stranger. 'Can you turn your transcendental field off?'

'Our what?' That was Peter.

'He means the Ex-Area,' said Carfrae. 'Have those Cat-People gone?'

'No,' said the stranger. 'They're still outside the house, but they're not in here. You are safe, trust me.'

'It's true, Simon. The Doctor's with them outside and Tim's looking for a space-time nexus so that we can fly to Australia and meet Godwanna in the past and stop Thorsuun blowing up the world.'

'You what?'

Tim sighed. 'Yes. Thank you, Polly, that was a most helpful summation. Simon, is it?'

'Yes.'

'Simon, can you turn off the field you've created?'

Simon looked at the others. Carfrae shrugged and Peter moved to the control bank. 'If we do, what d'you want?'

'Just to come in. See if we can find a way to help the Doctor stop Thorsuun doing what Polly rather haphazardly said.' Tim held his shadowy arms out. 'Please.'

Simon nodded at Peter who flicked the switch. Instantly the room and their vision righted itself and Simon found himself looking at a tall, goth-looking man in black leather. His swept-back obviously dyed-black hair reminded Simon of Dracula but it was his high cheek-bones, pale skin and piercing blue eyes that Simon really noticed. They were compelling, as compelling as his voice had been.

Polly pushed passed him and took Simon's hand. 'Are you three all right?'

'We're fine, thank you, Miss Wright,' said Carfrae, and Simon grinned at the ice in her voice. If Polly so much as looked at him or Peter, she got jealous. He found he quite liked that – so long as she was more jealous if it was him Polly spoke to.

The stranger was looking at the book lying on the floor. He crouched down and passed his hand over the cover. 'An RTC. Where'd you find it?'

'The library. The Doctor found two of them. I presume he's still got the other one.' Carfrae pointed at Peter's arm. 'It cured Peter's injury.'

Tim nodded. 'It would. Good, if he's got one, the Doctor's reasonably safe and can use it to find a nexus.'

'Can we use it, Tim?' asked Polly.

'That's exactly what I'm going to do. And use these young people's trans-field to aid us – protect us from the time winds.'

Simon looked at Tim. Twenty-five – no older. 'Young people?'

Tim stared at Simon and put his finger under Simon's chin to push his head up. Simon suddenly could not move – all he could see were the stranger's eyes. He realized just how blue they were. 'You'd never believe how old I am, Simon Griffiths of Castle Hill, New South Wales, aged twenty-three and four months, height five foot nine, weight ten stone eight, father Daniel Adam, mother Denise Janice, both alive. Need I say anything else?'

Simon felt the finger go and his body relaxed. He almost staggered but righted himself. 'No,' he said, a little hoarse.

'Good.' Tim was all smiles. He scooped the book up and whistled at it. The cover flew open and the pages began flicking backwards and forwards. 'Operate your machines, students. Please,' he added at a look from Polly.

Peter complied and seconds later the distortion returned. Simon stared at the doorway as it wavered in and out of focus. He did not like this at all. Polly obviously trusted this Tim person, but something instinctive told Simon that he was no better than Thorsuun.

For the first time during his three years in Britain he wished he was back in New South Wales.

Ben checked the roll-neck of his sweater, running his finger round the inside to make it look presentable. He ran a hand through his hair and then knocked on the side of the shuttle.

Seconds later a hatch slid open and he was being stared at by a six-foot-tall black cat with a white bib just visible above its red leather spacesuit. Of course – Daleks, Cybermen, why not giant cats? Maybe there was something in this dream of Polly's after all. 'Hi. Is the Doctor here?' He had an urge to add something about coming out to play or asking for a ball back, but the Doctor's cry from inside quickly told him about the severity of the situation.

'Don't shoot him – he's harmless. It's my best friend,

123

Ben.' The cat looked back inside the shuttle for a second and then reached out with a paw and pulled him in. The door slid shut immediately behind him.

A tortoiseshell cat, clearly the leader, eyed him suspiciously. He noted some others — including a white one with a grey spot over its left eye and the rather tatty tabby, much shorter than the rest. Seated by the front of the shuttle was a beaming Doctor and at another console, staring at a screen was Thorsuun. Ben could not see Kerbe or the kids. 'All right, Doctor?'

'Good to see you, Ben. Our hosts won't hurt you, I'm sure.'

'Don't be,' said the tatty tabby.

'Why are you here?' asked the leader.

'Er . . . well, we met this geezer called Tim and he sent me over. He's with Pol, Doc.'

Thorsuun looked up. 'Black hair, tall, wearing leather?'

Ben nodded. 'Pretty good description. Who is he? Seems to know you,' he said to the bursar.

She laughed. 'Atimkos — oh so righteous in his own way. He's probably trying to stop me — he rather likes your planet and wants to stay I think.'

Ben nodded. 'Yup, sounds like it to me.'

'Where is he, Ben?' The Doctor's voice was quiet, almost menacing. Ben took this to require a straight answer.

'He and Polly are in the house. Probably with Kerbe and the kids.'

'Kerbe's dead. Fräulein Thorsuun got bored of him.'

'Charming.'

The Cat-People's leader walked over and looked him up and down. 'Is this human of any value to either of you?'

Thorsuun shook her head and turned back to her screen, watching a drawing of Earth slowly turning. Ben saw multicoloured lines crisscrossing it. The Doctor, however, nodded at the leader. 'Queen Aysha, I would suggest keeping Ben alive. He makes a useful hostage and will keep me in check. If I annoy you, just threaten to kill him and I'll be as good as gold.'

'If you annoy us, I'll threaten to kill you,' said the tatty tabby.

'No, Lotuss,' said Aysha. 'The Doctor isn't stupid. Threatening to kill him wouldn't work – he doesn't fear death like the humans do. Keep this new one alive. For now,' she added, looking at the Doctor. He beamed happily.

'Oh, goody. Now, Ben, you sit there – ' he pointed to the navigation chair next to his – 'and agree to be good. OK?'

'OK, squire, whatever you say.'

Aysha waved over the white cat with the grey spot. 'Jayde, return to the Grange. Find this Atimkos and eradicate him. Bring the female back here – and the kittens . . . What do you humans call your young?'

'Children,' said the Doctor. 'But they'd prefer to be known as students.'

'What are they studying?'

'They think they're ghost-hunting. I suspect they're really being used to find a nexus point into hyper reality. Is that right, Fräulein Thorsuun?'

'Spot on, Doctor,' she said without looking away from her monitor.

Aysha motioned to the door. 'Bring these students as well, Jayde. If there is any resistance, slaughter one of them. That ought to bring the rest into line.'

Jayde saluted, paw across breast. 'Your Majesty,' she said, opening the hatchway, and left.

As the hatchway slid shut Ben nodded towards Thorsuun. 'She's looking for her ley lines then?'

The Doctor raised his eyebrows. 'Your friend Tim seems to have filled you in.'

'Yeah, but there's something funny about him, too. Polly trusts him but I'm not so sure.'

'Polly trusts everyone until she's learned otherwise, Ben. That's her only real fault. But I suspect it's in Tim's interest to keep her safe. My hope is that Simon isn't silly

125

enough to let him know about the book I gave them. The RTC. If Tim is after what I think he's after, him having possession of that could be very dangerous.'

Ben nodded. 'Ah, well. That Aussie seemed to be sensible enough.'

'I hope so, Ben,' said the Doctor. 'I hope so.'

'What's the book doing exactly?' Polly asked. Tim did not reply.

'Time flows backwards and forwards over it,' said Simon. 'It's coated in reverse tachyon-chronons.'

'What does that mean exactly?'

'He doesn't know,' smiled Carfrae, hugging Simon's arm and pulling him just a little further away from Polly than he wanted to be. 'But he likes to pretend he does.'

Simon felt himself go red – partially in embarrassment because Carfrae was right and partially in annoyance at her action. He pulled himself away from her. 'Thanks, Miss Morgan.'

'Quiet!' shouted Tim, contradicting himself. 'We're getting somewhere.' He turned away from the book and pointed at Peter. 'Could you turn the field off, please, Peter Moore. Thank you.'

With a shrug Peter did as he was asked and the room realigned itself to reality. Polly gasped. The others just stared. 'What's happened?'

Tim looked up. The pale-painted and chipped walls and stained wooden door frame had gone. They were in a wood-panelled room and the door was back in place, but with a wrought-iron door handle instead of the bolt Peter had pointlessly screwed on.

'We're in the same place about a hundred years ago. Shall we explore?' Without waiting for an answer he opened the door and walked out. Simon was the last to leave, casting an eye over the incongruous twentieth-century equipment that had been transported with them. Then he wandered into the hallway.

There were plants at the foot of the carpeted stairs,

green drapes hung around the windows and huge front door and where he had expected to see the kitchen door was another wood-panelled wall. He wandered over to a massive mirror by the door where a letter was lying on a silver platter. He held it up to the others. 'Richmond Dent, The Grange, Meckerbet, near Whitehaven, Cumbria. Guess he owned the place. Owns it,' he corrected himself.

There was a noise from the top of the stairs and as one they turned. Standing there, dressed in a severe black dress and cap, carrying a candle was a woman. She was staring at them in surprise.

'My God,' breathed Peter. 'She's who I saw when I fell.'

The woman took a cautious step or two down the stairs and held the candle out further until it cast across the assembled group. With a shriek she dropped the candle and tripped backwards.

'Yes! That's what happened!' Peter was excited.

Tim stepped forward to the bottom of the stairs. 'Yes, drop the amateur dramatics.'

'I doesn't know what you be meaning, good sir,' said the woman timidly.

'Oh, just turn the ruddy lights on!' he snapped.

There was a pause and then the woman got up. 'Spoilsport. I hope none of the locals can see this.' She whistled shrilly for a second and the hallway was bathed in bright light. 'So you got here then. What year?'

'1994.'

'What, a hundred-odd years? I knew this was a waste but he was so sure you'd get here by 1875.'

Tim sighed. 'Yeah, well, he was wrong wasn't he?'

' "Yeah, well," ' the woman mimicked. 'Oh, we have adopted the vernacular. In Victorian times we speak properly. The Queen's English, good sir. And as housekeeper, nurse and local busybody, I have to keep up the pretence.'

'So what name have we adopted? Mrs Dent perhaps?'

'Merciful heavens, no! That sort of thing is frowned upon in this era. I'm Mrs Wilding, widowed housekeeper to Richmond Dent.'

'And where is he? Udentkista, I mean.'

Mrs Wilding suddenly looked very serious. 'In bed. Forty thousand years on this planet have done him irreparable damage. And she didn't help matters.'

'Godwanna?' offered Polly, determined not to be left out.

'Oh, tell the world who we are, why don't you, Atimkos.'

'Yes, and I've missed you too. I wouldn't be here if it wasn't for Polly and these youngsters. They found the books. That was a clumsy way to get to us by the way. RTCs are lethal in the wrong hands. Especially two so close together. I take it the heavy boring one I saw back in 1994 is Udentkista's?'

Mrs Wilding shrugged. 'So. The humans of your time cannot be that advanced.'

'No, they're not, but other aliens are. Thorgarsuunela's flipped.'

'Flipped?'

'Like Udentkista, her mind is not what it was. She's sold the planet out to a race of mercenaries who want to slice it open. You know, like we used to. Trouble is, she's more than happy for the rest of us to stay here and go with it.' Tim wandered up the stairs. 'Get Udentkista up – we need a conference. And I need to get back to '94 to stop her.'

Mrs Wilding shrugged. 'I cannot vouch for his lucidity. She threw us out shortly after you left. Literally. His legs were . . . damaged and I didn't possess the skills to repair them.' She looked at her own feet for a moment, then back at Tim. 'We lived amongst the locals for a few dozen centuries – I lost count very quickly – and then began moving around. I've been nursing him, pushing him ever since. He also has "flipped" but he's not dangerous, just eccentric.'

Simon suddenly spoke up, much to his own surprise. 'Look, it's obvious you know each other, and Miss Thorsuun, but would you mind explaining things to us poor "youngsters". It's our lives as well, you know.'

Mrs Wilding looked at him in shock. 'You're from the landing site?'

Simon did not understand this but Tim nodded. 'Yes, he's Australian.'

'Good to know they made something out of that awful country then. Intelligent, inquisitive humans are rare on this planet.' She looked directly at Simon. 'Nurture it, boy, but when the time is right. Which is not now.' With that she wandered away.

Thorsuun hammered on the door. No reply. 'The shuttle. They must still be in the shuttle. Of course.' She turned and ran towards the Gatehouse.

Moments later she saw Jayde striding towards her and hid behind a tree. 'Of course – Aysha sent her to kill Atimkos. Which means I'm too late – any second now he's going to do it!' She dashed out of the trees towards Jayde. 'Hey, Jayde, it's me! Thorgarsuunela!'

Jayde stopped, clearly astonished. 'I . . . I don't understand.'

Thorsuun nodded. 'No, I'm not surprised. I've spent two lifetimes doing this now. Two lifetimes trying to survive. We've got to stop the Doctor. He's going to trick us.'

Jayde put her head on one side and then the other in bemusement. 'How did you get out of the shuttle ahead of me?'

'I didn't, you stupid fleabag! I'm still in there, plotting my own future. Badly as it happens. Listen, forget Atimkos in the house – there's nothing we can do about that, but we have to stop me making a mistake.'

Jayde shifted the weight of her rifle-blaster. 'You are making no sense, alien. Why have you followed me out?'

'I haven't, damn you. I'm still in there. Twice I've done

this now. Twice I've lived on this dreadful planet. Twice I've watched them make a mess of it. Have you any idea what that's like? Two eternities – one plotting to use you to get away, the other plotting revenge on him for letting me. He used us. Is using you! Don't you understand?'

Jayde was clearly getting irritated – Thorsuun dimly remembered her saying something about doing target practice with Lotuss as live bait. It was such a long time ago. Or maybe it had not happened yet? 'Oh, I don't understand any of this. All I know is I have to stop Queen Aysha somehow, and I can't even alert myself. You see, if I try to talk to or touch my other self – the one in that shuttle – there would be a massive temporal feedback which would –'

Thorsuun felt a massive pain in her stomach and found herself going weak at the knees. As the roaring started in her ears all she could see was Jayde lowering her rifle-blaster. She tried to speak. 'Two damned lifetimes . . . for this . . . it's not fair . . .'

Blackness swelled around her, engulfed her and –

Jayde stared at the corpse at her feet. A massive photon-blasted hole had evaporated most of Thorgar-suunela's midsection. With a furtive glance back towards the shuttle making sure she had not been seen – if Queen Aysha had sent the alien, well, she would report that she never saw anyone – Jayde fired twice more, completely destroying the body.

Wretched aliens.

Polly stared at Richmond Dent, or Udentkista as his real name appeared to be. He was huddled in a wheelchair, a rug covering his withered legs and a blue velvet smoking jacket was wrapped tightly around him to keep out the cold.

Mrs Wilding was seated to one side and Tim was pacing around. 'So you've been trying to follow us throughout time?' he was saying. He made it sound so . . . so casual. Like trying to catch someone on a train. Mrs Wilding was nodding.

'We needed to warn you about Godwanna. She's created herself a hyper reality nexus but blocked off the nexus-access points that any of us would know about.'

'But you've been back and forth?'

'No − not for a while. I remember being there a lot when we lived as Aborigines but I can't remember the entrance. There's one certainly where we crashed, on the mountain. And there's one near here but I think it's in your time-line not this one.' She pointed at Simon. 'A friend of yours was there.'

Carfrae spoke up. 'Professor Bridgeman?'

'Probably. He was safe anyway. But that, I think, is in your time − I knew about these youngsters from listening to him. I try to get through to you regularly but this house blocks me. I can move through time but not space. Saw this Bridgeman chap at one point in the village even, and I saw you,' she pointed at Peter, 'just now. Then you all arrived *en masse* in reality and surprised me.'

'Wow,' was Peter's reaction. 'It all fits.'

Polly nodded. 'OK, but how is this going to stop the Cat-People or Thorsuun?'

Tim looked at Mrs Wilding. 'Good question. I didn't realize she'd actually sealed the hyper reality nexii up. But you think there's one near by, in 1994.'

'Bright light, bright light,' Dent piped up and broke into a fit of giggles. Mrs Wilding casually reached out and slapped the back of his head.

'Hey.' Polly was infuriated. 'Don't hurt him.'

'I'm not hurting him, girl. His synapses are weak, a quick knock gets his neuro-peptides working again. For a while, anyway.'

Dent spoke again, but in a calm, reasoned voice. 'Tarwildbaning is correct, child. My brain is damaged and I can only remain well reasoned for short whiles. Pity her − her entire existence has been wasted looking after me.'

Mrs Wilding − Tarwildbaning − suddenly looked

upset and clasped his hand in hers. 'It is not a waste, my love, how many times must I tell you?'

Polly's heart suddenly went out to these people – a couple locked together in love but with one of them not being the same person ninety per cent of the time. How awful, she thought.

Dent continued. 'Atimkos, this is important. I don't think the two of us dare try to enter your time – my body is weakened and although immortality is a sound idea, we all know that if the body is destroyed, that is it. My body is, effectively, dying. Our RTC units are not enough to help us any more.' Polly could not hide the fear on her face. 'Hush, child – our deaths are not like yours. Imagine your body wasting away but over millions of years, not tens. That's how it is for me. I am dying and it cannot be prevented. However, I do not wish to accelerate it by using the RTC units, my injuries have a reverse effect on them. The chronons are agitated to the wrong frequency by my disturbed neural paths.' He looked at Mrs Wilding. 'We will stay here now – the jaunt into your time severely damaged me.'

'Could you go back?' Polly asked.

Mrs Wilding shrugged. 'If we could remain in the hyper reality where Godwanna is, we would not only be safe but prolonged exposure may help.' She squeezed Dent's hand. 'Remember when we were Aboriginals, how the pain stopped for longer periods. If we didn't have to keep fleeing to avoid her . . .'

Dent put his hand up. 'Let us discuss this if Atimkos is successful. Have you found the songlines yet?'

Tim shook his head. 'They are disrupted. We haven't been able to work out why. Or if Thorgarsuunela has, she's understandably kept it from me.'

Polly frowned. 'Songlines? They're Australian, aren't they?'

Simon nodded. 'Yeah – but they don't really go beyond that.'

'I thought you used ley lines?'

Tim nodded. 'Yes, they're all the same.'

'No, they're not – that's the point, they're cultural. Or adopted by cultures. And they're everywhere – not just on one straight line. How long ago did you land here?'

Tim looked at his fellow travellers. 'I've lost track. Mankind was reasonably new.'

Mrs Wilding shook her head. 'Nonsense – mammalian life existed but mankind didn't come along until you were on your way.'

'That's right,' Tim remembered. 'We stayed in the area for only a few thousand years. Then moved on once we discovered mankind.'

Simon suddenly spoke. 'You landed in Australia, right? You gave the Aborigines the songlines, the dreaming, right? OK – what did Australia look like when you landed?'

'Green. Lovely green vegetation.' Dent's voice betrayed his slipping back into idiocy.

'And when you met the first Abos?'

'I don't remember,' said Tim. 'It was quite arid I think. Yes, hot – the trees were gone. I assumed we'd moved around a lot.'

'You had,' said Simon. 'And you came back after the continental shift. Australia moved away from Asia while it was rain forest and hit the Antarctic before drifting back up to where it is today. That's when you met the Aborigines. Your ley lines, songlines or whatever were in a straight line. You walked around the entire Earth once, but when you came back everything across the globe had shifted behind you.'

'Of course,' said Polly. 'That's why she can't trace the line. It's no longer there. It's not a line but a pattern, all over the planet. How could you miss the obvious?'

'We . . . we never realized how far we'd walked.'

Jayde stood at the doorway to the Grange and blasted the door off its hinges. She enjoyed that. She strode in, sniffing the air but she could not smell the humans. She walked through the hallway and into the kitchen, pausing to note that the computers had been switched off. She opened the back door then jumped back.

'Baaa,' bleated a creature covered in soft white curly fur. 'Baaa.'

Jayde sniffed at it – it smelled good.

'Baaa.'

It would smell better cooked. She altered the setting on her rifle-blaster to microwave inducer and fired at the creature. It started to bleat again but died before it could get the noise out. Putting her gun to one side, she bent down and bit into the rump, tearing a large chunk away. It tasted good and she mewed in pleasure.

A noise – from inside the house like a rush of air. The scent of humans was back.

Grabbing the rifle-blaster, Jayde ran into the house, pausing to wipe warm blood from her jaws. Standing outside the room she had been barred from last time by some sort of force wall was a group of humans. With a hiss she raised her blaster.

'Stay where you are or I'll kill you!'

One of the humans, who smelled different, turned to face her. Jayde recognized the smell – it was like Thorgarsuunela. This had to be the other of her race that she was told to kill. He was holding a book as if it would protect him.

'Put it down, alien.'

'I'm sorry, we've just returned from 1874; my ears are ringing – what did you say?' He took a step nearer. Jayde raised the rifle-blaster but the alien was faster. He seemed to raise the book, flicking the pages at her. Her blaster grew heavy and like some third-born litter-runt she dropped it, cursing at herself. Her head hurt and she put her paws up to fight the pain . . . The man was looming larger . . .

Polly looked on as the Cat-Person fell back, kicking and mewling, shrinking. She realized that what she was seeing was getting progressively younger.

When it was no more than a three-month-old kitten, Tim lowered the book and with a frightened mew it scampered away.

'What now?' Polly asked, feeling just a little bit frightened at how easily Tim had done that. He bent down and grabbed the blaster. Turning to Simon who was about to follow he put a warning hand up.

'Stay here, kid. There's only room for two of us and I need Polly.'

'Only room for . . . what?' Polly said but he yanked her towards the kitchen and she was dimly aware of Simon returning to the others in the Ex-Room. They were in the kitchen, and Tim raised the blaster, shooting the computers. As each one exploded into flame he was scanning the walls, looking for something. Finally he saw a faint glow under the wall. 'Got it – the network transmitter. That's what's linking this lot with the Cat-People's shuttle.' He blasted at the wall, and with a flash it exploded. 'Done it. Let's go.'

'But the others . . .' protested Polly.

'They aren't important. There isn't time!'

In the shuttle, the screen Thorsuun was working on exploded, and she narrowly avoided being blinded by plastic fragments.

'What's going on?' demanded Aysha.

'Atimkos! He must be responsible!' yelled Thorsuun. 'He's cut off my links. We've got to get out of here now!'

Aysha leaped into action, shoving Ben towards the Doctor. 'Chosan, get ready for take-off – this mission is abandoned. For now.'

'No!' screamed Thorsuun. 'You can't! Look here – the lines are lighting up!'

Ben and the Doctor looked at the monitor screen. 'They're all higgledy-piggledy, Doc,' said the sailor.

'Yes, Ben, you're right.' He sat back in a chair and relaxed. 'They've lost it and won't be able to get it back.'

'No, damn it, no!' Thorsuun was determinedly stabbing at controls. 'I must find it – I will find it. There!'

'Where?' Aysha leaned closer. 'That's not what you originally said.'

'No, I know, but the direct link to Australia is lost. If we can pick it up here though . . .'

Aysha looked at Chosan and Lotuss for suggestions. They remained silent. Like their Queen, they acknowledged the mission was unsalvageable. Aysha mewed softly. 'We return to the battle-cruiser. Now.'

'Jayde?' asked Chosan.

'Jayde,' replied Aysha sadly, 'Jayde must be presumed lost to us.'

Thorsuun was purple with rage, saliva at the corners of her mouth. 'You stupid cats, we're going to follow this line regardless. I'm in charge, Aysha. You'll damn well do what I say.'

'You are neither in command nor in control,' hissed Aysha. 'You cannot –'

Thorsuun screamed.

Everyone in the shuttle fell to the floor, writhing. The Doctor was on top of Ben, trying to reach Thorsuun, who was standing stock-still, an unearthly wail coming from her throat. One by one the Cat-People succumbed and even Ben stopped shaking.

Thorsuun stopped and looked down. Only the Doctor was barely conscious.

'Hold tight, alien. We're going back in time and space. I *will* find the trail.'

The shuttle blinked out of existence.

Tim and Polly watched in horror as the shuttle vanished from the clump of trees near the Gatehouse. The TARDIS was now visible.

'Doctor!' Polly was aghast.

'She's on her way. I have to stop her,' muttered Tim. He opened his mouth and let out a piercing shriek.

The surrounding cliffside trembled and Polly tumbled

to the ground, the noise of Tim's cry and the ground's response shaking her violently. 'Tim . . . wha–'

With an almighty bang the ground erupted in a line from the Gatehouse to the Grange, the Gatehouse itself obscured by blinding white light pouring upwards from the ruptured earth. Within seconds it was by the Grange.

Inside the Ex-Room, the students were on the floor.

'He's taken the Doctor's book,' Simon was crying but the others could not hear him. The glass in the window shattered and simultaneously Carfrae screamed. Peter was reaching for the equipment, trying to set up an Ex-Area that might shield them, but with a bang the electrical components exploded, shrapnel of plastic and metal spearing into him, the force sending him sliding across the floor to where Simon was protecting Carfrae. As with Kerbe's body earlier, Simon could tell Peter was dead.

'Jesus Christ,' he muttered.

Polly stared in horror as the white light tore through the house and suddenly it grew piercing and taller, shooting upwards to the sky like water from a punctured hose.

'No!' She desperately wanted it to stop and, with a final, terrible screech of primeval power, the Grange, the Gatehouse and most of the surrounding cliffside were completely and totally atomized.

Episode Four

His mother had always warned him about rushing around too much in the heat, but Adoon never listened. He reasoned that, at eleven years old, he was quite capable of making up his mind as to what he did and didn't do with his time. Mashuk's mother never told him what to do – and he was stinking rich now. A bit of begging, a bit of street dancing and an awful lot of purse-string cutting had made Mashuk the envy of his peers. Adoon reasoned that there was no reason why he could not learn the same tricks and make himself just as much, if not more, money.

Of course, his mother would not approve but ultimately she could not stop him. Adoon's four younger brothers and two baby sisters dominated most of her time now. And since his father had lost both his hands after trying to rob the local Wazir's third wife, Adoon reasoned that it was his job to bring a bit of cash into the household.

Now, rushing through the streets of lower Baghdad, with a red furry demon on his tail, he wished he had stayed at home and helped his aunts weave some carpets.

Behind him was a crash as three or four wicker baskets of fruit crashed on to the cobbled ground. Adoon knew that right now the stallholder would be opening his mouth to yell at the miscreants and would quickly shut it again when he saw the demon. Instead, all Adoon heard was a strange noise, like a stick dragged across bricks, and a sharp scream from the stallholder. A scream so wracked with pain that Adoon found himself stopping and looking – and immediately regretting it.

The demon was standing opposite the stallholder, holding him against the wall. The stallholder was squirming, trying to kick out at the demon but Adoon realized he simply could not reach. After a few more seconds the stallholder stopped squirming and the red demon released him. Adoon stared for a moment longer as the stallholder crumpled in a heap at the bottom of the wall, unmoving. Then he fled before the demon could register him.

He bolted up a flight of steps built on to a nearby block of sandstone houses. Keeping his head down so he could not be seen, he reached the top faster than he thought possible; around him flapped the assembled washing of the ten houses that made up the block, drying under Allah's watchful gaze. No one else seemed to have seen the demon, and carefully Adoon poked his head over the parapet to look down into the street below. He could see the stallholder, who still had not moved, but there was no sign of the red demon.

Adoon tried to calm himself, stop his heart from beating so hard and loud – maybe demons could hear such things. Maybe they could see through walls and roofs. Maybe they could reach up and snatch him down into the great pits below the desert where they came from. Maybe, just maybe, Adoon told himself, if he stopped maybe-ing and did something, he might get home to tell his family. His father would call out the local men and they would go on a demon hunt. Adoon could lead them. He could tell them of the merry chase he had led it, and they would praise him and make him the leader of the local men. Maybe little Jadia would notice him then instead of Mashuk.

Maybe he should get off the roof before the demon worked out where he was.

Adoon looked roughly in the direction of his home. If he could jump on to the lower roof at the back, he knew he could quickly get home – although roof-jumping was forbidden by all the boys' parents, it seemed the right thing to do now. See his mother scold him when he'd led the men to the demon and they'd killed it. And eaten it. And chopped all its bones up and showed them to Allah on Saturday and . . .

'Oh, splendid. I mean, that's really going to look inconspicuous.' It was a man's voice but spoken with a strange tongue, as if he could not speak the language properly.

'Shut up, Dok-Ter.' A woman, but her voice was similarly different.

Adoon poked his head over the nearest parapet and managed to stifle a cry. There, below, on the roof he had been planning to jump on to was a huge silver tent which had not been there yesterday. It was a strange tent: there were no bindings holding it to the stonework, and it was rigid – the wind was certainly strong enough for Adoon to know a tent ought to waver slightly. Who were these two (no, three – there was a second, younger man) people who had put a tent up so quickly? And why on top of this block of homes? As the newcomers moved, the sun glinted on them and Adoon got a second shock. Both the younger man and the woman had yellow hair! That they were strangers was obvious from their voices, but maybe these too were demons. Sand-demons, of course, to match their hair. Then the red, furry demons had to be night-demons, from when the sun went down and the skies lit up red. But, and this was an important consideration for what he would tell his father, were the sand-demons and the night-demons foes or friends with each other? A flap in the tent was pulled back (Adoon had not seen a flap there a second ago) and a red, furry demon came out. Unlike the one which had chased him, this one's red skin gave way to multicoloured fur, as if it had been rolled in wet mud, unlike the grey one he had so far managed to avoid. Still, it answered his questions – the two sets of demons *were* together – and therefore both

140

had to be stopped from whatever evil they planned for the beautiful city of Baghdad.

How exactly Adoon was to do this he was not sure, but he knew that the only way to find out was to get nearer the demons and discover their plans. He crawled up on to the edge of the parapet and lay flat. He could now clearly hear the older man arguing with the female sand-demon.

'What d'you mean, you don't know exactly where we are?'

'Exactly what I said, Dok-Ter. We took off so quickly to avoid Atimkos's meddling that I wasn't able to set the shuttle's co-ordinate properly. I've sung us back quite some way in time but certainly not the forty thousand years I needed.'

'This is . . . unfortunate.' That was the bog-coloured furry night-demon. Adoon noted that it was clutching very tightly a silver club of some sort. It waved it at the female sand-demon and she placed her hands on her hips and laughed. Adoon thought it was a rather nasty laugh, as you would expect of a sand-demon – cold and false. 'Really, Your Majesty,' she was saying, 'please don't bother threatening me. One thing the Cat-People certainly need right now are my powers to track the buoys. Killing me would be wasteful.'

'Yes,' said a new voice, another night-demon, 'maybe, but pleasurable nevertheless.'

Adoon peered over a bit more and saw the grey-streaked night-demon that had chased him returning to its compatriots. He was relieved that it had clearly decided against pursuing him.

'Unfortunately,' it continued reporting (Adoon could imagine that Bog-Colour was its leader), 'my recce was disturbed by an anthropoid-tom, a mere mewling. Nevertheless it saw me.'

Bog-Colour nodded and hissed. 'Did you put it down?'

Grey-Streak looked away, presumably shamed. Adoon was glad he had disappointed Grey-Streak and indirectly

141

its master, Bog-Colour. 'Hopefully we shall not be here long enough for such a puny specimen to interfere with our plans.'

The female sand-demon laughed again. 'Oh dear, we have made a mess of things already, litter-runt. Perhaps your reputation was undeserved?' Adoon almost winced as Grey-Streak lashed out at Laughing-Demon, but she was fast and caught the demon's furry arm. 'Now listen to me – I know what I am doing. I can track the buoys and you can't. Don't even think about ridding yourself of me. Trapped in Earth's past, your ship is no longer in orbit. The raw materials you require are more powerful back here than they were in 1994. Imagine how strong they'll be forty thousand years earlier.'

'Excuse me?' That was the little man with dark hair and clothes. 'Can I just ask what will stop the Cat-People disposing of you once they've got the power they want?'

Laughing-Demon did not look at him. Instead she continued staring at the red-demons, Bog-Colour in particular. 'Because with the merest note I can transform myself into a mobile RTC. I could freeze them for eternity, or reduce them to mewlings themselves. Believe me, Dok-Ter, this alliance is one based only on mutual distrust and one-upmanship.'

'Oh. So long as I know,' said Dark-Hair.

Bog-Colour lowered her silver club. 'Indeed. But remember, we have the protective suits you instructed us to construct.'

Adoon had completely lost track by now. All he knew was that although the demons had come together from within the silver tent, they were not friends even if they were allies. If they were there to threaten Baghdad, then they could be thwarted. Something his father had once said about divide and conquer sprang into his mind – that had to be the solution. He decided it was time to get home, but he also wanted to see the silver tent closer up, then he would be getting as much information for his father as possible. So, carefully and quietly, he started to crawl along the parapet, hoping the demons would not spot him. If just one of them looked directly upwards . . .

He froze. There were sounds he could not place, strange metallic noises. He lay flat but turned his head trying to get a look at the rooftop below but the angle was wrong. If he raised his head, he would be able to look down properly but he would be framed against the blue skyline; raising himself might cause enough of a shadow or movement that one of them might spot him. But he had to see . . .

'Dok-Ter! Look!' Adoon guessed that the male sand-demon had spotted him. There was nothing to lose, so he pushed himself upwards. Not only had the male sand-demon seen him, so now had another five of the red-clad furry night-demons. A jet-black one with a white neck was pointing at him with a silver club. Adoon decided that the best thing to do was shout at the demons, tell them to leave Baghdad before they were sent away by the men of the city, before they were vanquished in fierce battle and burnt within their silver tent. He opened his mouth to yell a threat to them.

'Help!' was the best he could manage. Then Dark-Hair ran forward, pushing Black-and-White's club aside.

'Don't hurt him,' he cried. 'He's done nothing to you.'

Adoon could not help but agree. He stretched his arms out to the side as he precariously got up and balanced on the parapet, then slowly began walking along it. By the time he reached the end where it was safe enough to jump on to the roof where the demons were grouped, Black-and-White was waiting for him, club pointing at him again.

'I think you ought to come over here,' said Dark-Hair. Adoon complied as quickly as he could. 'Now, do exactly as I say and no one will hurt you.'

'Are you a demon, too?'

Dark-Hair smiled and Adoon felt a warm feeling flood through him. Everything was going to be all right. Dark-

Hair, with his deep blue eyes, was going to look after him. Adoon felt relaxed, almost light-headed. He wanted to . . . no, he did already . . . he trusted Dark-Hair and felt safe.

'No, I'm not a demon. I'm your friend.'

Adoon looked at the male sand-demon questioningly. 'Yeah, mate,' it said. 'Yeah, I'm a friend too.'

'Have you quite finished setting up an Arabian kindergarten now, Dok-Ter?' Laughing-Demon pushed between Adoon's new friends. 'Can't we just kill this boy and get on with the hunt?'

'Certainly not! This poor boy is an innocent caught in your machiavellian schemes, Frowline Thor-Sun. Haven't you had your quota of killings today?'

Laughing-Demon stared Dark-Hair in the face. 'No. I have barely begun. Before nightfall, I imagine this city will be a few million displaced atoms floating with the wind. The people will disappear with it.'

'Why?' That was the male sand-demon.

'Because, little human,' she stroked his cheek and Adoon could see the revulsion on his face, 'because when I sing the right song, the beacon we are searching for will illuminate and disclose the path to the others. Of course,' she was still smiling in an insincere way, Adoon decided, 'the illumination will expend the energy of a thermonuclear warhead. I think you can guess the effect on this locality. Fun, eh?'

Adoon's hero, Dark-Hair, was speechless. He tried to say something but could only splutter.

'You'll burst something, Dok-Ter,' said Laughing-Demon. She turned her back to him about to address the night-demons, when Dark-Hair pointed at the washing line running from the wall of the block Adoon had just come from. 'Where does that go to, my friend?'

Adoon pointed to the roadway, just out of sight from their own rooftop. 'Near the market square,' he said. Dark-Hair pulled a piece of blue and white spotted cloth from his top pocket and pulled it tight with both hands.

He then nudged the male sand-demon and pulled at imaginary sleeves. Adoon frowned, trying to work out what was going on. After a second or two, the male sand-demon nodded enthusiastically and pulled the sleeves of his garment over his hands, gripping the ends through the material. Dark-Hair then motioned towards the washing line and nodded towards the street. A momentary look of alarm crossed the sand-demon's face but then he breathed deeply and jumped, swinging his arms up and over the top of the line, his hands looped over the top, gripping each other through his sleeve. Adoon now understood and as Dark-Hair used his blue rag as the connection in his loop, Adoon yanked off his own belt and looped that over the line, holding both ends. One by one they backed towards the parapet and first the sand-demon and then Dark-Hair stepped off into space — and slid downwards.

With a final look towards the night-demons and Laughing Demon, Adoon followed suit. Just as the parapet rose in his eyeline to blot them out, he saw Laughing-Demon turn, and heard her shout. Seconds later, he hit the ground and stumbled backwards into Dark-Hair's waiting arms.

'Well done,' he muttered. 'Which way now?'

'Where to?' Adoon asked.

The sand-demon shrugged. 'Somewhere that lot can't track us.'

Dark-Hair touched his arm. 'Not so easy, Ben. They might not be as good as dogs, but a feline's sense of smell is quite acute. And don't forget, they'll be able to see better.'

'I thought that old guff about cats seeing in the dark was rubbish?'

'Not at all. They can't see in total blackness of course, but they can still see five or six times better than humanoids. And Cat-People, being somewhat larger than the average tabby cat, can probably see very well indeed.'

'Night is falling.' Adoon pointed at the sky. As they watched it grew noticeably darker, and Ben was amazed.

'I've seen night fall quickly from boats, especially in the West Indies, but never as quickly as this.'

'And with the Dark cometh the Cold,' said the Dok-Ter. 'A quote. From a book,' he said as Adoon scrutinized him.

Adoon had no idea what a quote was – he was not entirely sure what a book was, but people had mentioned the word to him before. Something very powerful, he imagined, because people who understood what books were tended to be wazirs, sultans or wizards. Or djinns. 'Are you a djinn?' he asked. 'Was that silver tent your containment?'

'Well, no, not exactly . . .' began Dok-Ter, but the male sand-demon interrupted him.

'C'mon, admit it. You are the Great Genie Dok-Ter – captured by the terrible Thor-Sun and her . . . her . . .'

'Night-demons,' breathed Adoon. Of course – it all made sense now. Dark-Hair, or Dok-Ter, was a djinn, captured and misused by the terrible night-demons, and this poor sand-demon was his friend. Which meant he could not really be a sand-demon, because they never helped anyone, least of all eleven-year-old boys. 'A prince! Yes – are you a royal prince cast into the body of a sand-demon? Is that why you travel with the great Dok-Ter? So that when he is released from his bond, he will return you to your natural form?'

This time, before the sand-demon/royal prince could answer this, the great Dok-Ter bowed. 'You have discovered our secret, young master. Sadly both Prince Ben-Jak and myself are bereft of our powers and riches. Would you help us defeat the demons up there and return order to fair Baghdad?'

Before Adoon could nod, which he was going to enthusiastically, Ben-Jak spoke. 'Doctor, I mean Dok-Ter, d'you mean this really is Baghdad? You know, *The Thousand and One Arabian Nights* and all that?'

'Spot on, as Pol-Ee would say.'

Ben-Jak suddenly frowned. 'Yeah, and what about . . . the princess? She and Atimkos must be wondering what has happened to us.'

Dok-Ter shrugged. 'If Atimkos is as powerful as I suspect, I doubt Pol-Ee is in any real danger. He's using her as a conduit to hone his own powers. He'll get back to Australia with her I suspect.'

'Oz? Why there?'

'Because that's where all this began. It's where Frowline Thor-Sun would prefer to be but hasn't the power to get back. This is the best she can do – about halfway between the two points. She's not going to explode her beacon here to help the Cat-People – she's going to use it to travel back another twenty thousand years. Probably without Aysha and her five friends. Now the sooner we can get away from here, the better.'

Adoon had not understood very much over the last hour, but he had been clever enough to realize that Laughing-Demon, this Thor-Sun woman, was preparing to destroy Baghdad shortly, and he doubted even his father's friends had the power to stop that. And here was the great Djinn Dok-Ter and Prince Ben-Jak preparing to run away and leave the city to its fate. He grabbed at Dok-Ter's sleeve.

'Oh, don't worry, young master,' Dok-Ter said. 'Baghdad is perfectly safe. What Thor-Sun thinks she can do and what she can actually do are miles apart. Literally.'

'How?'

'You see, young master . . . D'you have a name I may be honoured to address you by?'

'Adoon, Great Djinn.'

'Right. Adoon. Well, Adoon, Thor-Sun is searching for something she buried many thousands of years ago.'

'So, she is a vile sand-demon, an evil since the dawn of time.'

Dok-Ter nodded. 'Put like that, yes. Nice turn of phrase by the way.'

147

Ben-Jak sighed. 'Get on with it, Doc . . . Ter!'

'It's very simple, Ben-Jak. Thor-Sun is looking for her mystical path, her geographical ley line. Obviously she's not sensitive to it, or she could have found it centuries ago. Likewise, Atimkos must be the same – hence his use of Pol-Ee. Thor-Sun won't find it in Baghdad because she's using a modern atlas to trace a line from Cumbria to Queensland.'

'Which passes through Arabia, right?'

'Yes!' Dok-Ter clapped his hands together. 'Yes, you've got it.'

Ben-Jak smiled at Adoon. He smiled back and then stopped. The djinn still was not making sense. 'But, Dok-Ter, we're in Arabia. Why won't this Thor-Sun find what she's looking for?'

'Ah, poor child. He doesn't understand, Ben-Jak.'

'Frankly, "great Genie", neither do I.'

'You haven't got it, have you?'

'No.'

'Oh, dear. And I thought we were doing so well. I tell you what, let's talk later. It's dark now and Aysha will be after us.'

'Or Lotuss.'

'Which is a very alarming thought indeed. Yes. Now, Adoon, can you find us some clothes? We look a bit strange dressed like this, don't you agree?'

Adoon certainly did, and suddenly saw what he needed. Without a word of explanation he dived into the darkness and hoped the Great Djinn and his Royal Prince would wait.

The stench was terrible. Had these pitiful creatures never heard of sanitation? Even the most primitive ancestors of the Cat-People knew how to use a litter area and keep their lands clean. Germs and airborne diseases must be in plentiful supply. No wonder anthropoids were so easy to invade.

Lotuss stopped and stared. Most of the anthropoids had

long since scurried back to their stone dwellings to escape the cold air — but she thrived on it. Low temperatures kept her senses clear, her brain alert and her adrenalin running. Memories of previous campaigns for her mother came back: the uprising on Kalidon, when they had been employed to eradicate an entire reptilian species, or the skirmish with the Gargar rebels on the frontier world of the Maskill system. There, Lotuss had fallen victim to a rebel land-mine. Her first-litter-mate Ramuth had been literally shredded apart and Lotuss had lost her eye and blistered her paws.

The medics had offered any number of grafts or pros-thetics, but Lotuss would have none of it. Her diminutive size had saved her life then, just as Ramuth's bulk had cost her hers, and after years of ridicule — most notably from her own mother and litter-mate Chosan — she could use her size and wounds to make a statement. And what a statement it had been, as she battled her way through war after war, battle upon battle, killing and maiming wherever possible. She recalled a victim who had been whimpering in a trench once — a pale-blue anthropoid, splattered with copper-coloured blood and green mud. It had asked her something that she had never forgotten. 'Have you no mercy? No pity or compassion? Is there anything you love more than killing?' Lotuss smiled as she remembered the three answers she had given. A flat, unquestionable negative to all three questions. Then she had blasted his head into oblivion. Chosan had been forced to present Lotuss with a medal after that campaign, much to her chagrin.

Those were good days, before the Queen had become obsessed with power — literal power. Their ships were still the most powerful in the galaxy, capable of years of travel without refuelling. Yet of late, Aysha, her mother, had kept reiterating the need for better, newer forms of energy — this magnetic explosive variety found in the molten cores of worlds like Earth. Lotuss could not see any point in such pursuits. Where was the death and glory in that? If Lotuss was to die, it should be in battle, not searching for fossil fuels.

'Excuse I,' said a voice next to Lotuss. She turned. There was an old female anthropoid, hobbling about, hiding its probably disease-ridden face under a red shawl. 'Excuse I,' it croaked, 'but I cannot see. Which way is the market square?'

'Where I come from, old creature, you would beg for death rather than live a fruitless life unable to contribute to your community.' It occurred to Lotuss to vaporize the creature where it stood, but Chosan had ordered that only the Doctor and his anthropoid companion were to be shot. Lotuss also hoped to encounter the anthropoid-mewling that had escaped her earlier – slaughtering that would be satisfying if not exactly following orders.

'You . . . you are a stranger, yes?' The old woman hobbled a bit nearer, reaching forward.

'Touch me, creature, and you lose your arm,' Lotuss hissed, letting her fur rise, although the old woman clearly could not see it.

Her head still bowed, her face still hidden under the shawl, the woman stopped. 'You have travelled far. I sense weariness in you.'

'Only in your conversation, creature. Leave before you die.'

'As you request, precious lady. But beware the traitor in your midst. She will destroy you all.' The old woman hobbled away, obviously terrified of Lotuss.

Lotuss smiled. Traitor indeed – who amongst the Cat-People would consider treason apart from Lotuss herself? Unless . . . could she mean Thorgarsuunela? Lotuss shrugged, she had heard threats and warnings from experts – some smelly anthropoid was hardly going to hurt her.

Smell!

The anthropoid did not smell like an anthropoid. No it was . . . the Doctor!

Lotuss hefted her blaster and prepared to fire after the

'old woman' but 'she' had vanished. As Lotuss relaxed she knew something was wrong – her blaster! The power pack was missing. The Doctor had managed to steal it during that charade. Lotuss would return immediately to Queen Aysha and tell her that . . .

Of course, she could not. Returning to the shuttle, having encountered a disguised Doctor and lost her weaponry – the shame would be unbearable. Lotuss could picture Chosan's gleeful face at her discomfort. 'Very well, alien, the chase is on. I will have my firepower back, and your head on a stick.'

She slowly walked into the shadows, tracking the Doctor.

Adoon stared open-mouthed at the shambling figure coming towards him.

'I be glad of our little chat, Cat-Person,' croaked the 'old woman', and then it threw the shawl off.

'You are indeed a great djinn, to disguise your voice so.' Adoon wanted to bow to the Dok-Ter but thought that might be considered a bit silly. Certainly neither Dok-Ter nor Prince Ben-Jak had requested such obedience or servitude from him. Dok-Ter threw something to Ben-Jak.

'Is this what I think it is?' he asked, turning it over.

All Adoon could see was a silver box with a glass top.

'Yes,' said Dok-Ter, 'and if we can slip that to Thor-Sun without her knowing, friend Lotuss will be a trifle upset.'

'Good.' Ben-Jak pointed to the sky. 'What about the rest of them?'

'Back in 1994, Ben. Or should that be forward? Anyway, we only have our six here to worry about.'

'And the destruction of Baghdad,' Adoon muttered a little louder than he meant. Dok-Ter turned to him and Adoon expected to be turned into a rat on the spot. Instead, the great djinn knelt in front of him.

'No, Adoon. I'll try to explain.' He coughed to clear

his throat. 'You see, when Thor-Sun and her cohorts arrived here, Earth looked very different. There were no seas separating the continents as there are now. When she laid her . . . lights, they were in one place, but years later the lands slowly drifted apart. Over a long time.'

'Did the djinns push them apart to keep the evil spirits away from good men?'

'Yes, if you like. Anyway, Thor-Sun, your sand-demon, hadn't realized that this thing occurred. She's mistaking her line of twenty thousand years ago for the line as it would be in twenty thousand years' time.' Adoon did not really understand anything Dok-Ter said, and he was glad to see that Prince Ben-Jak was clearly as confused.

'But what's this all about, Doc?'

Dok-Ter looked right and left, apparently checking that no one could see them as he stuffed the old woman's clothes under a nearby market-stall awning. 'Basically, I understand this much.' He held his fingers up, very close together.

'Oh,' said Prince Ben-Jak. 'That's encouraging.'

Dok-Ter shrugged. 'So, what we have are two groups of alien invaders. Group One, who I guess are the fabled Euterpians who died out centuries ago, must have arrived here about forty thousand years ago – Australia by what Thor-Sun has said. Now, they came looking for a power source to fuel their ship – the still cooling Earth's core would be a marvellous supply of magnetic energy which they needed –'

'But forty thousand years ago isn't quite the hundreds of millions of years ago when Earth was created,' argued Ben-Jak. 'What good would it do them?'

'Well, Ben,' said Dok-Ter, 'in cosmic terms, a few million years is a blink of an eye. The core energy would still be powerful enough way back, or when the Euterpians arrived, now or in 1994. The lessening of power would be negligible. Satisfied?'

'Sorry,' muttered Ben-Jak.

'Good.' Dok-Ter beamed happily. He patted Adoon on the head. 'Are you following this, young man?'

'No.' Adoon thought it best to be honest to a great djinn.

'Good,' repeated Dok-Ter as if he had not heard. 'So, they landed and split up. Thor-Sun and Atimkos – your "Tim", Ben – placed a series of marker buoys – in reality massive syphons – that could be seen from space but not closer. These ought to have circumnavigated Earth in a nice curve so that their mothership could slice through the crust and release the energy.'

'Like cutting a slice off an orange?'

'Exactly, Ben, exactly like that. However, they failed. Although they had RTC units to keep the ageing process at bay, they lost any sense of time or distance. I doubt they walked constantly either – even Euterpians must have needed rest now and again. The problem with that was that the ground moved and their little ring of marker buoys was disrupted, breaking their links to each other. So, from space, nothing would be seen.'

'But, Dok-Ter, she must know about the continental shift. Every kid does.'

'Adoon doesn't.'

'Yeah, but Thor-Sun's lived thousands of years. She must be super-intelligent.'

'Why? I can think of lots of long-lived people whose IQ is lower than your shoe size. One day I'll take you home to meet them.'

'But it can't be difficult to find things like that out.'

Dok-Ter sighed. 'Oh, Ben, if only people were that observant. Remember, when it occurred, she and Atimkos were walking and so not as dramatically affected by the drift. And remember there were no newspapers or television to tell anyone what was going on. Even in your time, you don't know what's going on under your feet. Would you know about earthquakes in San Francisco or tidal waves in Hawaii if you didn't hear or read about them?'

'No. I s'pose not.'

'Exactly. Well, bearing in mind that it took nearly thirty thousand years for one man to acknowledge another existed on the other side of the world, is it any wonder that the Euterpians wouldn't know the world had literally changed under their feet?'

'No. All right.'

'So,' Dok-Ter continued, 'so what we have then are a group of people, aliens, disguised and adapted into Earth society. I assume that Mrs Wilding and Dent are two others in the party, trying to reach their friends through time. I found their RTC units in the library at the Grange. Now, I gather from Thor-Sun and the Cat-People that there is a leader somewhere, who has built some kind of sealed-off buffer zone.'

'A what?'

'Like the Ex-Room the students created in Cumbria. It's not quite in this dimension but accessible through a series of points. Presumably it's powerful enough to absorb the power released by the marker buoys if they were set off and return the Euterpians home.'

'So, why don't they go? And why has Thor-Sun got those Cat-things here?'

'Ah,' the Doctor chuckled. 'There's the rub. Our Euterpians don't like each other, going by Mrs Wilding's diary and Thor-Sun's explanations. Certainly she and Tim are usually at each other's throats. I think that our Victorian couple are essentially just trying to discover what the other two are up to. Whether they're working for their leader or themselves, I have no way of knowing.'

'So, do you trust them?' Adoon decided it was time he tried to add something.

'Oh, no, my young friend. We trust no one.'

Ben-Jak nodded. 'Least of all, Frowline Thor-Sun.'

'She's not the real problem, Ben. She's underestimated the Cat-People quite badly, I think. She's brought them here, offering them her RTC unit as a bribe to get her off

Earth if she gives them the power due to come through the beacons.'

'Which she can't find,' said Ben-Jak, clapping his hands. 'Brilliant. She's totally keelhauled.'

'Yes, thank you for the nautical references, Ben. But you're almost right. She used her memory and limited sonic powers to get us here, presumably guessing that she must have placed a beacon here. That would be fine if you drew a straight line from Cumbria to Australia today, but not forty thousand years ago. Baghdad is perfectly safe because she's done her maths and geography wrong.'

'Yeah, and what about those sonic powers?'

'Nasty, Ben. Vicious if misused and I expect she can misuse them better than most. But the Cat-People are immune – as are we in that shuttle – because of the RTC she gave them. That's why I think there's more to Aysha than meets the eye.'

'She doesn't want the beacons then?'

The Doctor shrugged again. 'Possibly. But I think she's thinking bigger than that. I think Thor-Sun told her about the nexus where her leader is and Aysha has guessed that there's even more power to be gained by controlling that. I think she's using Thor-Sun to find a link to that.'

Ben stood up and brushed dust off his clothes. 'OK. So how do we stop them?'

'Divide and conquer?' Adoon asked.

'Jolly good, Adoon. Now, let's go and find Frowline Thor-Sun and give her Lotuss's little present.'

Martin Hickman had never seen quite so much devastation in eleven years in the West Cumbrian Fire Service as that which greeted him at (what was left of) the Grange. On driving the first of the three red fire engines that sped as quickly as possible up the dusty, stone-laden narrow lane that was the only driveway to the Grange, he had been the first to see the result of the unknown events that had clearly destroyed the house and grounds.

The Gatehouse was blazing, the roof already caved in, and as his team dismounted, the west-facing wall collapsed, rapidly followed by the rest. Within three minutes, it was a burning pile of stonework and any hope of recovering articles or, heaven help them, people inside, vanished immediately. Trying to fill out his appraisal forms on this one was going to be nigh on impossible. Arson? Accidental? No one would ever know.

There were other, more inexplicable things as well. That old police box had been there, he was sure. Then there had been a red flash in the corner of his eye and when he had looked back, the police box was gone. No one else saw it, of course. Then there was this long trough which linked the Gatehouse and east side of where the Grange had been. Looking into it, Hickman felt no heat, no damp, no cold. Just a rush of air. He could not see the bottom of the trough, but it was very dark down there.

Of the Grange, there were just fragments. All three storeys had collapsed in on themselves and burned away. A few lumps of stone and the odd piece of wood were all that remained of the Georgian property. Hickman was particularly saddened by this – although the Grange had long been deserted, it was nevertheless a building of character and popularity. The discovery of the overturned, gutted and blistered metal framework of a transit van suggested that the three adults and three students from London were more than likely to have been inside when whatever happened happened. Someone was going to have to tell their friends and families. And there would be nothing concrete to say.

'I'm sorry – we know they died,' someone would have to say, 'but we have no idea how.' Were they burned? Was it an explosion? What about the trough – was there some equipment buried by the students, linking the Grange and Gatehouse, that overheated and literally blew them apart?

PC McGarry had cycled over from the village as soon

as possible, but his notebook and wetted pencil were held uselessly in his hand. Who was witness to the event? Were Smithers and Coates in the Gatehouse or Grange? Hickman did not care much for Charlie Coates but George Smithers had been local for years. And after that business with his wife . . . well, he deserved better than this.

A shout alerted Hickman and then McGarry to the cliff edge, where the trough had continued through the Grange's foundations and out to the sea. A large portion of the cliff edge had also been obliterated – a massive V-shaped wedge had been torn out – and any clues that the grass and earth might have held were gone with it. But there, down on the rocks being lapped by the cold waters of the Irish Sea, was a body.

Thirty minutes later the police from Whitehaven had identified it as Charles Albert Coates. Although no coroner, the SOC had reckoned that he had been killed by the fall – his clothing or skin carried no signs of burns or combustion.

'Could he have been literally blown off the cliff by the explosion?' asked McGarry.

The scene-of-crimes officer, who, Hickman decided, looked as if she had just left college rather than had four years at a busy police station, did not think so. There were not even any slight blisters or fabric scorches. If caught in an explosion, even for a second, the blast would have caused some damage if it had been strong enough to blow someone over a cliff. Having delivered this statement – therefore suggesting that Charlie Coates jumped, fell or was pushed prior to the explosion – she returned to her proper task: trying to ascertain what had happened inside the two buildings. It took her three hours to come to the same conclusion Martin Hickman had immediately. There were no answers, and the questions would remain unresolved for ever.

Hickman's team, however, did find something near the rubble. Mewing quietly to itself, half-starved, was a white kitten, possibly only six or seven weeks old. Its slightly singed fur suggested that it had been near to the explosion and was the one lucky survivor. 'I think we'll call you Solo,' Hickman said. 'You're the only one here and it goes with that black patch around your eye.'

Five hours, twenty-three minutes after he and his team had arrived, Hickman led his engines back to the village. All he could think about were eight funerals, eight eulogies and eight coffins — only one of which would contain a body. And somehow he believed that Charlie Coates's estate would have difficulty finding enough pallbearers, let alone mourners.

As he turned the steering wheel and coasted his engine into the depot, Martin Hickman felt the little white cat with the black-circled eye crawl on to his lap, purring. 'I wonder what you'll be like when you grow up,' he muttered.

'Tickets, please. Oh, you all right, miss?'

Polly looked up at the old man in uniform through aching, red-rimmed eyes. She had been crying reasonably quietly but constantly for nearly five hours now. Every time she thought she had exhausted her reservoir of tears, she just had to think about Simon, Carfrae or Peter and she would start again. Uncontrollably.

'Yes, I'm fine, thank you. Just a bit weary and tired. I'll be fine.'

'If you're sure. Ticket, please?'

Polly momentarily panicked and then remembered what Tim had said. Or tried to — it seemed a bit dim, rather like when he went to buy the tickets. Something about not really needing them, and getting free rail travel. Polly had been sure that was bound to be illegal, even in 1994, but he had seemed so certain. Just as he had been about not being able to do anything about the kids.

'My . . . my friend's got them. He's queueing at the buffet car . . .' That's what he had said she ought to tell the ticket man.

'I see. Right. What does he look like, then? Your friend?'

'What? Oh, you don't believe ... well, he's very tall, wearing black. A leather jacket. Jet-black hair swept back, high cheekbones you could rest a cup on. Blue eyes – deep blue eyes. Soft spoken ...' Polly trailed off. That was a highly emotive description of someone, she thought.

The ticket collector obviously thought so too. He smiled. 'Can't really miss him then, can I?'

'It's all right, I'm here.'

Polly found herself eager to smile at Tim as he arrived back and a strange flush ran through her. He was back and everything would be OK. Tim would sort out this annoying, interfering man with his petty tickets and inane concerns about her ridiculous crying.

'You don't need to see our tickets.'

The ticket collector frowned. 'I think I do, actually.'

Tim whistled. Softly but just audibly. The ticket collector stared blankly at him for a moment and then smiled. 'All seems in order, sir. Thank you. Can't be sure when we'll get to London though, sorry.'

'Why not?' asked Tim.

'Problems earlier in the Chester area. No one's telling us what exactly but it must be quite serious. The whole area has been closed off and we're being diverted via the Leeds line. We'll be arriving at Kings Cross rather than Euston.'

'Thank you. Please don't pass this way again.'

'Certainly not, sir, whatever you say. Have a safe journey.' The ticket collector wandered away, whistling to himself, checking everyone else's tickets and informing them of the delay.

'How did you do that?' Polly leaned across the table and flipped the lid off a steaming cup of British Rail tea. She sniffed. 'Well, here's something that hasn't changed in twenty years. It still smells and looks awful.'

'It hasn't changed in about forty actually. They made a conscious decision to use bad tea when they introduced catering facilities for second- and third-class travellers.'

Polly grinned. 'D'you remember that? How far back do you go?'

'A long way. A proper Methuselah.' Tim sipped his tea and grimaced. He blew on it to cool it down and instead forced a few drops to leap on to the tabletop.

'Messy pig.' Polly wiped up the mess with a British Rail napkin. 'I see your manners are still on a neanderthal level.'

'Fractionally before my time.' Tim tried the tea again. 'You know, if we wanted to, Thorgarsuunela and I could have taken over this world.'

'Thor who?'

'Oh, you know her as Fräulein Thorsuun, bursar of South Thames University or whatever it's called. Miss Frost she said the students call her. They're not far wrong.'

'So why didn't you? Take over the world, I mean. Can you control everybody like you did that ticket man?'

'Yes. If I want to. The humanoid brain is especially susceptible to ultrasonics. There were secret military experiments in the mid-Eighties using sound as a weapon. Restructuring the harmonics of people yelling or screaming. Women in labour, the severely mentally disturbed, accident victims – basically people in pain, which always produces the most natural and violent harmonies possible.'

'That's evil,' said Polly. 'I'm glad I missed the Eighties. Why did people put up with it?'

'Well, the general public were largely unaware of it. Those few that stumbled across the truth were warned to keep out – or face the consequences. Faced with that kind of deterrent, they kept out. But sound is a terrific manipulator. Just the slightest out of resonance harmonic, and the human mind becomes malleable. It does no permanent damage but temporarily makes people susceptible to subliminal or coercive suggestions. Like you saw with that man.'

Polly stared out of the window. 'And Coates? What did you do to him?'

'I simply told him to drop off to sleep. He's probably wide awake now.'

Polly suddenly remembered. 'No, he might have been in the Gatehouse when that went up like the Grange. He's dead, too!'

'Keep your voice down, Polly!' Tim looked around furtively. One of the other passengers was flicking a cold stare at them, clearly annoyed that they were disturbing her concentration but the look from Tim sent her speedily back to the pages of her new Carrie Fisher novel. 'What d'you know about time, Polly?'

'In what sense?'

'You travel in it, right? The Doctor and his dimensionally transcendental machine?'

'Dimensionally what? If you say so, I suppose so.'

'Time is relative, Polly, but in many ways it is preordained. I'm sure the Doctor has told you not to interfere with your own past. One little slip or event halted, and you could cease to exist, damaging the web of time irrevocably.'

Polly nodded. 'He calls it chrono-chaos theory.'

Tim laughed. 'Yes he would. What rot. Anyway, your future is similarly mapped out but of course you don't know it. To someone in 2094, today is history and your part in it is recorded somewhere.' He waved his arm around the carriage. 'Everybody now is someone's past. But what if you could see the future?'

'I wouldn't want to.' Polly folded her arms. 'That would be . . . pointless. Why live if you know what's coming?'

'Good philosophy. However, no one is immune to a little warning. You've used tarot cards before?'

'I had mine read years ago. My friend Claudia used to do readings. I don't think she was very good.'

'Few people are. But to me, these are a gateway to the future. To reading your destiny. Here, cut the pack.' Tim produced a pack of tarot cards and placed them face down on the tabletop. 'Go on.'

Polly cut the pack twice and tried to pass them back, but Tim shook his head. 'Only you can hold them or the majik won't work.'

Polly turned the first card over. 'Oh, look. A pussy cat.' Suddenly she stopped and stared at Tim. 'The Cat-People . . .'

'Quite deliberate, I assure you. You are woven into their future as much as they into yours. Keep going.'

Polly laid out four cards. The Sun. The Three of Cups, upside-down. Also upside-down was the High Priestess. Finally, the Knight of Swords.

'I'm not going to comment on any of these,' Tim said. 'Merely interpret them for you. The two reversed cards are interesting. Carry on, three above.'

Polly turned another three. Another reversed card, the six of Swords. Then the Ace of Pentacles, followed by the seven of Swords.

'That one,' Polly pointed to the seven of Swords, 'reminds me of the cat in my dream. At the house in London where I saw you.'

Tim looked at the card, showing a female warrior carrying a sword. Six others were embedded in the ground and in her other hand rested a tabby cat. 'Needs the scar, though.' He motioned for her to continue.

Two cards above the three, the four of Pentacles and a reversed Knight of Wands.

'Now I want you to put one card, face up above them to create the pyramid. Then above that another solo card, but face down.' Tim pointed to the cards. 'OK?'

Polly nodded. 'When I had my tarot read by Claudia, I had the High Priestess, only it was the right way up.'

Tim smiled at her. 'Strange that – it's a common card for women but not so for men. Now, are you happy with that lot?'

'A few too many reversed ones for my liking but that's random choice for you.'

'I Ching is another science altogether. Let's not get into that. OK, turn the top card over.'

Polly did so – another reversed card. The Lovers. She smiled.

'Before you say anything,' Tim said, 'it's a common misconception that the lovers means anything romantic. It's more of a suggestion of a partnership or friendship, often in business. The fact that it's reversed implies you've made a bad choice somewhere along the line.' He pointed at the Sun. 'A strong card because although it's not high up in the pyramid you've created, it was nevertheless the first card you turned over. It suggests joy, pleasure – often associated with travel. Somewhere hot perhaps.'

'Travel? Well, we're on a train now.'

'True. The six of Swords directly above also means travel but as it's reversed, it suggests a delay. Which, as that nice ticket collector told us, we're experiencing whether we like it or not. Back to the cards, Miss Wright, if you please.'

'So, this upside-down three of Cups?'

Tim sipped his cooling tea. 'Hmmm. Fun and frivolity but again, as it's reversed, a hoped-for union might not take place. It's placed between a sun and relationship card – unfortunately indicating that whoever you've got designs on might not be the right person. You'll enjoy their company but it won't lead to anything permanent.'

'Well, travelling with the Doctor hardly gives me time for anything romantic.'

'Ben?'

'Ben?' Polly laughed. 'Oh, he's very sweet, but we're not really a couple. Just good friends, as they say. Besides, Uncle Charles would have a fit, giving me away to a working-class sailor.' She swallowed some tea and pointed to the upside-down High Priestess. 'I don't like the look of that if it's meant to represent me.'

'Oh, don't worry. The High Priestess is normally cool and collected – it's a card of extremes in many ways. It embodies the female psyche. Reversed it just goes to another extreme; it suggests that you're someone who is forever caring about people more than yourself – you put them ahead of your own happiness or safety. Take it as a warning – someone you're committed to caring about might turn out not to be worth it.'

'The Doctor?'

'Could be. Why him particularly? Why not Ben? Or me?'

Polly shrugged. 'Don't know. Just seems the most likely candidate.'

'Fair enough. The Doctor could well be represented here by either the Knight of Swords or the Knight of Wands. The Swordsman is frequently associated with medical things though. He could well be linked to your reversed Lovers card but maybe not. You need to think quickly about him though, he has a tendency to rush in where others fear to tread.'

'Sounds like the Doctor all right.'

'Now, this is interesting. Between your two Knights is the seven of Swords, featuring our dream cat. This card usually suggests a rip-off, a swindle. Could be referring to either Knight but as it's the Knight of Wands rather than our Doctor-card, the Knight of Swords, which is reversed, it probably applies to him. He's almost certainly someone working against you, a swindler and very insincere although you will have spent a lot of time building up your trust in him. Again, this links to the reversed High Priestess and your putting too much energy into someone over your own needs. The Knight of Wands is not only reversed but he's below the reversed Emperor card – a definite fall from grace. Possibly the most important card in the warning sense in the whole hand.'

Polly was nodding. 'And this upside-down Emperor?'

'He's a man of status but he's fallen from favour. Again, another liar or maybe you're just getting a distorted picture of him because other people put him on a pedestal.

He's not so much unreliable as unable to deliver on his promises.'

'Charming.' Polly drained her tea. 'OK. Last two.' She jabbed at the two Pentacle cards.

Tim nodded and shrugged. 'Basically, they're both money cards. In some tarot packs they're Coins not Pentacles. Both their presence, their position and their right-way-upness would suggest you could be in for some riches – not necessarily monetary though. Possibly spiritual. In fact given your constant travelling with the Doctor I should guess that money is the least of your problems. Flitting through time and space means you're hardly going to have a reliable bank account. No, I think it means soulful rather than material wealth. The Ace tends to suggest a change of circumstances leading to this alteration though.' He sat back and waved at the cards. 'Want to do something else?'

Polly shook her head. 'I'm a bit tired. And that's given me a lot to think on. I wonder which card you are.'

'Me? Oh, I'm all the bad ones.'

Polly laughed. 'Never. You're too nice to be bad.'

Tim smiled and began clearing the cards away. Then he stopped and reached forward, putting a finger under her chin. 'Polly,' he began. 'Polly, listen to me. Think about the events in Cumbria.'

'Yes?'

'Concentrate on them.' Tim began humming quietly.

'Tim, stop that, what about . . . about . . . ab . . .' Polly sighed deeply and flopped back in her chair. 'Oh, it's such a nice day outside. I wish we were going to the seaside – or back to Cornwall. Oh, Tim, do let's. Cornwall is so nice in the summer. I could take you to Lizard Point, or the stone circle above the cliffs. There's one not far away with a huge upright circular stone with a perfect hole through it. A prehistoric Polo mint . . . Do you still have Polo mints in 1994?'

'Polly.' Tim hummed again and Polly yawned. 'Polly, your friend the Doctor. He's nice, isn't he?'

165

'Oh, yes, he's lovely. You'd really like him. He's a bit kooky at times and all that but he has some fab clothes in the TARDIS and let's us play around with them whenever we want.'

Tim nodded. 'Of course he does. He's certainly "fab", but will he trust me? Will he understand what I'm doing? And why?'

'I expect so, Tim. What are you doing? What are you doing to me?'

Tim's humming stopped. 'To you? Why do you think I'm doing anything to you?'

Polly yawned again and stretched, speaking through her yawns. 'I don't know. Of course you're not.' She flopped her arms on to the table, letting her fingers gently stroke Tim's thumbs. 'You're dead nice, you know that? Dead nice.'

'Yes, Polly, I am. And it's very important that you remember that whatever I do is for the good of Earth. For everyone on it.'

'Oh well,' giggled Polly, 'you'll get on fine with the Doctor. That's all he ever wants.'

Tim nodded quickly. 'I know, I know. But I think our methods might clash – he might not see things entirely the same way I do. And it's very important that he does. Or, failing that, it's just as important that he doesn't know exactly what I'm doing.'

'What are you doing?'

'Oh, that isn't important. You wouldn't, couldn't understand. What matters is that you trust me. Implicitly. Do you trust me?'

'Implicitly.'

'Good. How tired are you?'

'Not very, a bit exhausted that's all.' Polly tried to sit up. Tim hummed. 'I think you're very tired.'

Polly yawned yet again. 'You know, I think you're right. Dead clever, like I said. If I didn't know better, I'd think you were using your reso-whatnots on me.'

Tim smiled. 'As if.'

Polly settled back and fell asleep.

Within a few seconds she felt herself rise up. Her eyes popped open and she could see her body below her, curled up on the train seat, a soft smile on her face. Polly knew that she ought to be happy, the smile told her that. Yet something was wrong. The sleeping Polly was happy, so why wasn't she?

She looked around her sleeping self. Tim was gone. In fact the carriage was empty of life apart from her. She wanted a better look and saw the outside of the train as it sped below her. Fighting an instinctive twist of vertigo, she heard herself mutter, 'More. I want to see some more.' To her astonishment, the roof of the train melted away to reveal nothing – not one living person except her sleeping self. And the shadows. Each seat that she thought ought to have been occupied but seemed empty actually had a shadow on it. It reminded Polly of the leaflets the anti-nuclear protesters at Leeds had shown her. Human beings caught in an atomic blast reduced to silhouettes burned on to brickwork. A dark blob was moving down the centre of the train. The ticket collector, of course.

Where was Tim?

'Gone, my dear. Never really there. He's not what he seems.'

'Who . . . who are you?' Polly whimpered. The voice, soft, feminine but slightly mocking, had reverberated all around her but seemed to lack any point of origin.

'I am a friend, Polly my dear. A good friend. You can trust me. You must, if you want to save Earth.'

'Everyone wants to save Earth. Everyone wants me to trust them. You, the Doctor, Tim . . . why?' The train had vanished completely. Polly was in space, blackness, just tiny pinpricks of light in the distance wavering and flickering. She could feel movement and realized it was herself – she was not exactly falling but nevertheless definitely unstable. 'Well?'

'You are right, my sweet one. Better to trust none of

us. That way, you cannot be let down. Of course, you can have no firm beliefs, no opinions and no sense of righteousness from which to argue, fight or protest, but perhaps in the coming war that is good. Yes, I think it is good.'

'War? What war? Please,' Polly felt frightened, 'please tell me who you are.'

There was a flash and Polly closed her eyes.

'Open them, my child. You are quite safe – your astral form is neither subject to harm, nor visible to any other than ourselves.'

Polly opened her eyes. To nothingness – vast, white nothingness. She turned a complete circle or assumed she did. The lack of any colour, any shade, any landmark made it impossible to judge if she had turned slightly, a lot, ten times or not at all. 'What . . . what is this horrendous place?'

'It is my domain,' said the voice. 'Observe.'

Images flickered into existence, but unclear. To Polly it reminded her of the girls' toilets at school, where the windows were long strips of frosted glass that you could run your pen down and feel the bumps. Impossible to see out of, just brief snatches of shade rather than colour, and distorted shapes. The shapes she could see now were moving slowly and the more she stared, the more she could see that it was a person pushing something.

'Away,' said the female voice and the shapes began to fade.

'No, wait,' called Polly and for a brief moment the figures formed actual shapes – a dark-skinned woman in rags, pushing a similar-looking man in a cart. He had his foot pulled up to his mouth and was sucking his toe. The woman looked at Polly. The bone structure, the proud forehead, flattened nose and almost feverish eyes that bore into her, screaming with ignored intelligence instantly told her these were Australian Aborigines.

'Yes, I can see you. Ignore everyone. Trust no one – especially me. And him.'

The man giggled and plucked out his saliva-covered toe. 'No, ignore no one – just me!' He began to laugh and the woman slapped his head. Immediately he stopped laughing.

And changed.

Both the man and woman were suddenly Victorian: she in a severe black dress, he in a smoking jacket, seated in a wheelchair with a chequered rug on his knees. 'Hello again, Polly. They told us you were coming.'

'We made a mistake,' the woman said. 'We trusted Atimkos – and she recaptured us.'

'Don't trust him at all – he's using your powers to destroy us all.'

'Enough, cretins.' It was the all-pervading woman's voice. The Victorian man and woman distorted and opaqued again, then vanished.

'There, child. Confused?'

Polly nodded.

'Good. Because if you are confused, unsure and bewildered, no one can use you. Atimkos is one of us. Like me. Like Udentkista and Tarwildbaning who you saw earlier. Like Thorgarsuunela who no longer exists in your timelines. We are the singers, we created much of your culture and existence. We can also destroy it.'

'Why are you telling me this?' Polly called out into the bizarre whiteness that enveloped her.

'Because the other humans I tried to enlist have proven to be unusable. Like you, they possessed a strand of the natural powers of this planet within their life essences, but none have ever been strong enough. I fear my manipulations may have damaged them. You are your only hope.' There was a pause, then the voice continued and Polly could almost see the smile in the tones. 'Remember, anechoic. That's all you need to use. Anechoic. Goodbye for now, sweet creature.'

'Wait!' Polly automatically cupped her hands around her mouth as she shouted, 'You mentioned some others. Where are they?'

'Goodbye.'

Polly felt herself being pulled gently away from the whiteness. As she began to lose what little sense of balance she had achieved in the past few moments, two figures blurred into view. At first she thought it was the Aboriginal/Victorian twosome but instead their clothes gave them away: two twentieth-century men, huddled together on the floor. The young one, possibly in his twenties, had his back to her and all she could see was dark hair and a tanned cheek, but the other faced her, staring. His head hung slightly to the left, his eyes stared forward, blinking rapidly. His brown hair was a straggly mess and foam and saliva grouped at the lower point of his mouth and his breathing was heavy and irregular. As she finally winked out of existence, Polly tried to reach out to him, recognizing him.

The last thing she heard was her own voice, screaming out: 'Professor Bridgeman!'

The leader of the night-demons was very, very angry. She was waving her silver club at Thor-Sun (who was not a laughing demon any more) and pointing at their silver tent, still set up on the roof of the building behind them. Adoon could not hear everything that was said but he had got the idea: Thor-Sun had brought the night-demons to Baghdad to find something important and she had failed to find it. The mysterious light that would destroy the city presumably which Dok-Ter had assured him certainly was not here. All Dok-Ter wanted to do was put the pretty shiny box in Thor-Sun's jacket and 'retire to a safe distance'.

Adoon had immediately offered to do this – even Ben-Jak had agreed that Adoon's experience at, well, removing objects from various traders and visiting businessmen's pockets made him the obvious choice. Replacing was just as easy as removing. They had approached the building but Adoon had suddenly felt nervous and afraid. At first he had tried to hide it, but the

170

nearer they got, the worse it got. He almost called out in panic at one point, wanting to know where Dok-Ter was. Ben-Jak had found him first and agreed that even he was frightened. Adoon had relaxed slightly. If a prince could be afraid, so could he. There was no shame in it. Dok-Ter and Ben-Jak had then talked about a magic lantern that the night-demons had brought with them. Adoon did not exactly understand what it did, but Dok-Ter explained that they used it to keep everyone else away. Anyone approaching the area would feel afraid and leave. Dok-Ter had then darted off and after a few moments returned with the magic lantern in pieces. He was very happy and Adoon had announced that all his fears disappeared then. Although he did not tell the others, this was not strictly true – they had lessened certainly, but Adoon was not foolish enough not to acknowledge to himself that the night-demons really terrified him and although Thor-Sun was only one person, she was also very scary.

Right now he weighed the silver box Dok-Ter had given him in his left hand, staring at Thor-Sun. The coat she wore had two big pockets on either side and one inside. Inside pockets were easy to get stuff out of, but impossible to put anything in. He chose her left-hand pocket – she always pointed and demonstrated with her right hand, suggesting that she was right-handed. Therefore, her left side was slightly more vulnerable.

He bit his lip, waiting for the right moment. Behind him, out of sight, he knew Dok-Ter and Prince Ben-Jak were watching, counting on him to achieve his mission. Swallowing hard, he again stroked the silver box, feeling his sweat oozing around it.

Thor-Sun turned away, her back to him. This was his chance.

He bolted forward, yelling as if the night-demons were chasing him. As if he had not been looking, he careered into the startled Thor-Sun, knocking her sideways. Adoon reached out to steady her, muttering hurried, breathless apologies. 'I'm sorry, my lady . . . be warned, there are creatures of the night here! Night-demons, they will destroy us all –' He suddenly froze. Walking towards them were the night-demons, two at the back talking to a third – the one that Dok-Ter had stolen the silver box from! 'Demons!' he cried and ran back the way he had come.

He was aware that a couple of the night-demons were giving chase but then he heard Thor-Sun order them to stop. He dived behind a bazaar awning and whipped around to watch them, completely hidden from their view.

'It was only some pathetic human child. If your deflector field was set at a less emotion-stimulating level, he probably wouldn't have blundered in here.' Excellent, that was exactly what Dok-Ter had hoped she would say. Adoon slipped backwards to where he knew Dok-Ter and Ben-Jak were waiting. They greeted him enthusiastically.

'Good on yer, mate,' was Prince Ben-Jak's praise. Dok-Ter just smiled, and Adoon could see from the richness of his blue eyes how pleased he was. 'Now,' said Dok-Ter, 'all we have to do is wait.'

They did not have to wait long before the screech of 'traitor!' was heard from Thor-Sun. They strained to hear, knowing that risking an actual look could be suicide.

'Oh yes, it was the Dok-Ter all right. Your accomplice!' That was clearly the night-demon that Ben-Jak called Lotuss.

Thor-Sun was angry. 'My . . . my accomplice? What are you on, stale catnip or something? What possible reason could I have to associate with him, litter-runt?'

The night-demon's leader shouted for them to stop. 'Clearly this cannot go on. We will settle this by finding the Dok-Ter once and for all.'

'How, Your Majesty?' That was Thor-Sun.

'Easily. If the Dok-Ter has Lotuss's power-pack, we can

trace it. Chosan, get the fellinite tracer from the shuttle.'

Chosan obviously left because there was quiet, interspersed with the occasional hiss, which suggested to Adoon that Lotuss and Thor-Sun were facing off in frustration. After a moment Chosan must have returned because the night-demon's leader commanded something to be operated and Adoon heard a strange beeping noise. It suddenly grew faster and louder.

'My power-pack. It's near here!' said Lotuss.

The beeping suddenly peaked and Adoon put his hands to his ears.

'What? No, get off . . .' Thor-Sun was struggling with something and then she stopped. 'What the –'

'My property, I believe,' Lotuss hissed. 'Traitor.'

'Explain this,' demanded the leader.

Dok-Ter was grinning at the exchange. He and Ben-Jak put their thumbs into the air – Adoon took this to be a ritual sign of success and joined in. Ben-Jak ruffled his hair and Adoon smiled. He had helped the two strangers succeed in stopping the demons. 'Now comes the tricky part,' said Dok-Ter. 'We need to get caught and taken back aboard their shuttle.'

Ben-Jak was staring as if Dok-Ter were insane. Adoon wondered if in fact he was. 'But Dok-Ter, why?'

'Because we need them to get us back to the TARDIS. We're going to need it to stop both Queen Aysha and Thor-Sun's people. Of course, in the meantime all I have to do is convince Queen Aysha not to kill us.'

'And?'

'And what?'

'And how do you do that?'

Dok-Ter jumped up. 'Easily, Ben. I give them Frowline Thor-Sun on a plate.'

Frowline Thor-Sun came crashing towards them at that moment, chased by Lotuss and two night-demons.

'*Et voilà*,' said Dok-Ter. He stood directly in front of her and pulled her down into their hideaway behind the bazaar stall. He put his fingers to his lips and although she gave him a murderous look, she nodded. The demons ran on by and when they sounded safely far away Thor-Sun relaxed.

'Loathsome as you are, Dok-Ter, I offer you my congratulations. A brilliant ploy. I don't know how . . .' She stopped, seeing Adoon for the first time. He felt her eyes bore into him, he could almost see the hatred in her as if it were a stick poking at him. 'Of course,' she continued. 'The clumsy boy – and you were on the roof as well. I should have recognized you. So now we all have Aysha and her stupid cats chasing us. Any suggestions, Dok-Ter?'

'Yes. Escape.'

'Oh, great. I mean, even Ben might have thought of that one. How?'

Adoon suddenly thought of something. 'Great Djinn Dok-Ter.'

'Yes, Adoon?'

'Can you make a carpet fly?'

Dok-Ter smiled. 'Alas, I can't.'

'But,' Ben-Jak said, 'I know someone who can.'

Dok-Ter frowned, and then nodded. Together they turned and looked at Thor-Sun. Dok-Ter shrugged. 'You are, after all, a demon, Frowline Thor-Sun.'

Thor-Sun quietly pulled at the back of the bazaar stall, revealing a lot of carpets. She picked a large one. 'This big enough? Are we taking your young friend?'

'Yes.' Adoon was determined to come along. A flying carpet . . . He tugged at Dok-Ter's sleeve and put on his best 'oh, pleeeeeese' face.

Dok-Ter shrugged. 'All right. Adoon can come too.'

Thor-Sun grimaced. 'I'm not taking any responsibility for the child. Or, for that matter, either of you. Where are we going?'

'Back to the shuttle. I trust you can pilot it without Aysha's cronies?'

'Of course.'

'Dok-Ter,' began Ben-Jak, 'you can't consider leaving

the Cat-People in this time? I mean, they could rewrite history.'

Dok-Ter was stroking the carpet, letting the tassels on one corner fall through his fingers. 'Oh, I think Adoon's people would swiftly make mincemeat of them.'

'Oh, the compassion. The concern for life overwhelms me,' said Thor-Sun. 'I thought you loved life in all its myriad forms. Or is that so much hogwash to disguise your true, selfish side?'

Dok-Ter slowly raised his head and stared at her, his eyes the same bright green as the night-demons Adoon had seen earlier (but his eyes were blue moments ago?). 'A few savages are a price worth paying to save the planet from their rapacious greed, don't you think?'

'Wouldn't know, *mon chéri*. I'm more than happy to see Earth reduced to molten slag, just for the hell of it. Watching it grow and expand over the last forty thousand years has been about as interesting as counting Aysha's fleas. I don't care if it survives or not. So long as I don't have to stay here much longer.' She sat down on the carpet, laid out on the cobbled ground. 'All aboard the Flying Carpet Express. First stop, the Cat-People shuttle. Hold tight. Fasten your seat belts and –'

'Get on with it,' growled Ben-Jak.

'Miserable human.' Thor-Sun leaned towards Dok-Ter. 'Still, if you only lived three score years and ten, you'd be grumpy too. Lucky, aren't we.'

Dok-Ter pointed upwards. 'Don't even try to suggest we are similar, Thor-Sun. The concept makes my stomach turn.'

Thor-Sun began to hum quietly to herself, a rhythmic pattern which Adoon found pleasant. It reminded him of the songs his mother would sing when scrubbing the family clothes. Suddenly he realized he was moving. The carpet was rising up.

'Blimey,' said Ben-Jak. 'It's working.'

'Of course it's working, Ben. Euterpians are very clever. Let's hope Aysha doesn't spot us though.'

Adoon decided to take a look at Baghdad from the air – and literally found his breath taken away by the spectacle. They were only a few man-heights from the ground but it was enough to give him a perspective he knew he would never forget. The wind was stronger but cooler and his ears felt slightly funny. He tried rubbing them, but it did not do anything much.

'Air pressure, mate. They'll get back to normal after a few minutes back on the ground.' Prince Ben-Jak knew everything. If he said it would be all right, Adoon knew it would.

Dok-Ter pointed down. 'OK, Thor-Sun. Take us down.'

Still humming quietly, she nodded and the carpet gently began to descend. Seconds later it was flat beside the silver tent.

'How do we get in?' asked Ben-Jak.

Without waiting for an answer, Thor-Sun whistled and a gap appeared in the side. Adoon stroked the tent – it was cold and metallic. He decided that he would not want to live in it. Dok-Ter smiled at him and Adoon was positive he could read his thoughts. Then again, he was a Great Djinn. 'It's all right, Adoon. You don't need to come in.' He waved at Ben-Jak and pointed. Unseen by Thor-Sun, Ben-Jak nodded and slipped into the tent, coming back out with two silver clubs. Thor-Sun was looking for the night-demons but with little success. 'Now, Adoon, I have a job for you,' Dok-Ter was saying. 'I want you to go back home and raise your family. Get them to tell everyone about the demons and to come and chase them away. And thank you for everything you've done. You are a very brave boy.'

Adoon wanted to tell Dok-Ter that he was staying, that he wanted to travel in the silver tent and fly on another magic carpet. But Dok-Ter's eyes stared at him (his eyes were blue – or green – but not grey) and Adoon knew he had to do as he was told. With a bow of thanks he headed for the parapet and climbed back on to the roof from which he had first set eyes on Dok-Ter, Prince Ben-Jak, Thor-Sun and the demons. There, he would go down the stairs and back home.

He gave a last look, preparing to wave goodbye. And stopped.

Dok-Ter and Prince Ben-Jak were aiming silver clubs at a protesting Thor-Sun. Dok-Ter called out, 'Queen Aysha, this is the Dok-Ter. I have Thorgarsuunela – she's yours if you take us back home.' What Dok-Ter had not seen were the night-demons, led by Lotuss coming up behind them. There was nothing he could do as the demons jumped them, and the leader stepped out of the shadows. 'Thank you, Dok-Ter. Your usefulness has not ended. Unlike Thorgarsuunela's.'

Thor-Sun stood upright, angrily. 'Stuff and nonsense. You still need me to –'

'We need nothing from you. We now know what we are looking for. We also know that you are ignorant as to the whereabouts of the beacon. The Dok-Ter will help us or we will kill his companion.' She turned to Dok-Ter. 'Which, if I remember correctly, was your suggestion.'

Dok-Ter looked at Ben-Jak and shrugged. The two of them were herded into the tent. Thor-Sun went to follow, but Lotuss stopped her. A look – Adoon could not see what exactly – obviously passed between the leading night-demon and Lotuss and the leader entered the tent.

'I never liked you, sub-anthropoid. Killing you will be a pleasure.'

Thor-Sun drew herself up. 'So, litter-runt, how are you going to do it?'

If Adoon could have seen Lotuss's face clearly, he knew she would be grinning. 'Knowing how much you've enjoyed living on Earth, you're going to die here. It'll be about two thousand years early, but never mind.'

Adoon did not understand a word of what was meant but he was shocked when Thor-Sun suddenly fell to the floor. Lotuss was bending slightly – and Adoon knew what was coming next – he'd seen Mashuk do it often enough. Thor-Sun was feinting and as Lotuss's silver club got close, she grabbed it, pulling Lotuss to the ground.

'Now, litter-runt, I think you're going to let me back aboard.'

'Wrong,' hissed Lotuss. 'I'd rather die.' They stared at each other.

Then Thor-Sun gasped. 'Your Majesty . . .'

Lotuss turned briefly and Thor-Sun smacked the back of her head with the club and jumped towards the tent. The gap vanished.

'No,' murmured Thor-Sun. 'No, you can't leave me here. I've had one lifetime on this pathetic planet – I won't live it again. You can't do this to me!'

Lotuss was upon her and Adoon winced as her claws raked across Thor-Sun's back. The laughing demon shrieked and twisted, Lotuss falling back towards the tent. The gap opened briefly and Lotuss scrambled in.

The tent vanished. Silently and instantly.

'How did you do that?' called Thor-Sun to no one in particular. 'Dok-Ter! Aysha! Lotuss – don't leave me here!' But it was too late. As Adoon decided that getting home was a better option than listening to Thor-Sun's ranting, he heard her screaming, 'I'll get you for this, Dok-Ter. You set me up. You'll pay – in two thousand years I'll be waiting for you and I'll stop you.' Then slightly quieter she added, 'Or at least I'll stop myself getting involved.'

Adoon headed home.

Inside the shuttle, Aysha stared at Lotuss. 'Well?'

Lotuss preened herself with a damp paw. 'She put up a surprisingly good fight.' She popped her claws out, displaying red blood on them. 'Her blood was not that of a true warrior, though. She is dead.'

Ben asked, 'How will the Cat-People fly back to 1994 without Thorsuun's help?'

'We recorded everything Thorgarsuunela said, sung

or hummed,' explained Chosan. 'Our battle computers translated the exact meanings of the notes while we wasted time in Arabia. We can now fly this shuttle under Euterpian power by ourselves.' Chosan nodded to Queen Aysha. She noted Lotuss standing stiffly by the hatchway. 'And I don't think our tactical officer has quite forgiven you for disarming her under such less-than-honourable circumstances.'

Lotuss stared at the Doctor. 'No. I'll have my revenge.'

The Doctor turned to Chosan and Queen Aysha. 'So, if you can now travel in time and space using harmonics, why do you need us?'

'We know how to use Thorgarsuunela's methods, Doctor,' said Aysha. 'We still don't know why. You're a time-traveller, and an alien. You've got a machine.'

'The TARDIS?' said Ben. The Doctor groaned. 'Sorry, Doc.'

'Exactly,' continued Aysha. 'This TARDIS will take us back forty thousand years as Thorgarsuunela promised us. There, we will wipe out the Euterpians and take the power source ourselves.'

The Doctor frowned. 'But your main ship is still in 1994, in orbit. It still begs the question of how you are going to move that amount of magnetic force through time.'

'We're not,' said Chosan. 'You are. Using your TARDIS and the RTC equipment Thorgarsuunela provided us with.'

Six rifle-blasters rose and focused on Ben. 'Any problems with our plans?' asked Aysha.

The Doctor said nothing.

'Oh, good. I knew we could rely on you.'

Episode Five

Hot. So very hot. Far hotter than anything he had ever encountered before. He reached out to her, but she didn't notice. She hadn't noticed anything for some days now – or was it weeks? He'd tried to make contact, let her know he was still there, but it was pointless. All she did was walk.

Walking free.

In a straight line, following her instincts as the sound led them across the plains. She was the more accomplished of the two – her tracking skills had been invaluable on so many previous expeditions, while he was there more as a craftsman, making physicality from the harmonics created. His own notes and resonances were good, but impure – they could form an image, a lumpy almost-there – and that made him particularly useless in a society where perfection was essential. But there was a certain symbiosis between him and her. She could bring matter into existence through her oscillations, he could add to that molecular soup, carefully sculpturing a finished product, fully functional as if it had been in existence for years and with parts that never needed replacement. Organic and inorganic; silicon, vegetation or sentient – it was all the same. It existed, perfectly or imperfectly, depending on his mood. But it was always his choice. It was this ability that made them immortal. If something went wrong with their own physiology, they simply sang it right again.

Freedom was something that couldn't be sung for. Ever.

They had been on the planet for a few hundred years now judging by the rotations around the sun. He had calculated the planet's daily rotation to be eleven spans. An awkward number: the ship had artificial days of fifteen spans. It took some time to realize that they were becoming accustomed to the planet's rotations and natural spans. For the first few years they had insisted on keeping ship-time, sleeping every eight spans for seven. However, it had been she who first adapted to the planet's own alarm clock and slept during its night periods. And she who gained the wrath of their recon-leader. The recon-leader could not accept this adaptation and began to become more and more obtuse and irrational in the demands and orders given. Eventually it had become too much and an argument ensued. Without any real surprise, the recon-leader won – and banished the two of them to walk the deserts.

When they had first come, the basin had been full of lush green vegetation but now, during their walkabout, they had realized the trees and flowers and bushes and plants had died. No amount of singing could bring them back, which he couldn't understand. After a long time (days, weeks, years, who knew?) the Walkers had encountered an intelligent life. Dark-skinned and strong, they had been warriors. They had tried to kill the two of them, despite being sung beautiful songs of creation. As a result, the Walkers tried to ignore the people and their spears and brown bodies covered in natural dyes and their faces painted to accentuate their aggression. They wandered in many directions over the days/weeks/years trying to teach the New Men to sing the songs of life, to understand the beauty in creation from pure sonic harmonies, but the New Men simply weren't interested.

Then one afternoon, the Walkers found themselves in a slightly greener part of the world/island/country and saw strange shapes on the water, coming in from the north-west. As the shapes approached the beaches, they realized these were more men, similar in appearance to the vicious New Men but with a fire in their eyes, a depth and intelligence denied their aggressive cousins. An inner peace and beauty. They carried spears, but at the rear, not as part of their forward party. They carried bizarre carved wooden objects, curved at the centre. Perhaps sensing the Walkers' curiosity, one of the men hurled his wood away from him and it sailed through the air, perfect aerodynamics causing it to twist and turn, until it retraced itself, coming back through *the air to the Peace Man who threw it. The Walkers were immediately impressed and she began singing.*

The Peace Men were awestruck as beautiful things began to stir under the sand on the beach. Animals began to claw their way up, pushing their way to the surface where they breathed in the beautiful fresh air. Tall animals with massive tails which hopped rather than walked, small furry ones with snouts and big eyes, wingless birds who waved their long necks as they sought out the smells and sights with their newly created senses. Lizards of all shapes and sizes, more birds and mammals.

'These shall all be yours. Uniquely. No one else may have them and they will honour you if you love them,' she said.

'Treasure them and this world can be yours,' he said.

'Teach us,' said the leader of the Peace Men. 'Teach us to sing like you. To continue the beautiful life. To build homes, lives and roots for ourselves. Please.'

Before they agreed the Walkers explained about the violent New Men.

'Show us how to sing and we will protect this beautiful land, these beautiful creatures, for the rest of time from the evil New Men.'

The Walkers, now accustomed to having lost their own roots, agreed – in the Peace Men, they had found purpose and reason. 'This is your land – your aboriginal sites,' she said. 'The others are the invaders, who would be evil and desecrate the world. The animals we have given you are gods for you to revere and honour.'

'It will be done,' said the Peace Man. Together the Walkers –

'Tell me about the battles,' Dent giggled. 'Tell me the bit about the Aborigines wiping out those other evil ones and how beautiful they made this country.' He sat back in his wooden cart, staring at the endless expanse of white above, beside, behind and below them, rubbing his blunt nose and staring at Mrs Wilding in fascination.

'Another time,' she said. 'I have other patients to tend now.' Wilding ran a hand through Dent's scraggly black hair, trying to disguise her fondness for him by pretending she was making him look tidy.

Instantly, they changed, re-adopting their Victorian appearances. Dent's brain improved. 'Tarwildbaning, I don't now how much longer I can keep rejuvenating my synapses. One day I'm going to regress to our Walker state and lose it.' He snatched at her hand, a tear pushing its way down his face. 'I don't want to lose my mind!'

'We have to leave this world and get back amongst the stars where we belong. Only there, away from Godwanna's plans, can your brain properly readjust. Unless . . .' Mrs Wilding straightened her pinafore. 'But until then I have to find a way. Remember – I love you.' With that she smacked the back of his head and he twitched, his giggling old-man personality instantly re-engaged. 'We must conserve your resources,' she said.

A tear, as desperate as his had been, fell down Mrs Wilding's face as she left him chortling at some insane private joke and went to tend her new charges.

'Hello, Mrs Wilding,' dribbled one. 'Have you come to clean me?'

'Yes, Professor, I'm here to look after you. Always.'

'Is Mr Dent not well again?'

Mrs Wilding nodded mechanically. 'We keep trying to reach Godwanna's hyper-reality. We could all be safe there, but she's still sealed the final nexus.'

Bridgeman nodded. 'I like this place. It's clean.'

'It's white. Is it heaven?'

Mrs Wilding looked across at a second man wandering aimlessly in circles, trying to keep his balance walking around an imaginary circle. 'No, Mr Simms. Not in the way you mean. But it's not exactly your home planet either.'

'So where are we?' asked Bridgeman. 'Nate and I have been wondering that for . . . oh, yonks and yonks and yonks.'

Nate walked over. He put his head on one side and

stared up into Mrs Wilding's face. 'You've been crying. Do you love Mr Dent?'

'Oh, Mr Simms, what a question! I do apologize for him, Mrs Wilding.' Bridgeman pulled at Nate's sleeve, trying to pull him to sit on the ground with him.

As he allowed himself to go down, Nate giggled. 'I can see right up your nose!' He pointed at Mrs Wilding. 'It's very dark up there!'

Bridgeman went red. 'Nate, please.'

Nate Simms suddenly looked at Bridgeman as if noticing him properly for the first time. He reached for Bridgeman's nose. 'You've got a nose, too.' Then he frowned. 'Do I know you?'

Bridgeman nodded. 'Yes. We were playing together earlier in the garden.'

Mrs Wilding stopped her ministrations. 'What garden, Mr Bridgeman?'

'He's a professor, you know. A clever man. He went to university. He's got qualifications.'

'Lots,' agreed Bridgeman. 'Lots and lots and lots and lots and –'

Mrs Wilding put her hand on his shoulder. 'What garden?'

'What garden?'

'I asked you that. What garden were you in?'

'No garden. No garden. No garden.' Nate rolled on his back and kicked with his legs in the air, as if he was riding an invisible bicycle. 'No garden.'

'Nicky?'

Bridgeman looked at his knees and began picking at an invisible scab there, ignoring his trousers. 'He told me not to tell. Big people are bad. Tell us off.'

'I won't tell you off,' said Mrs Wilding. 'Look, tell you what – you tell me how you found the garden, and we'll go together. That way, it can't possibly be bad, can it?'

Bridgeman pouted. 'I don't know, Mrs Wilding . . .'

'Can I come?' called a voice. Pushing himself across the white nothingness in his Victorian wheelchair was

Dent, his eyes alight with excitement. 'Oh, let me, please, please, please, pleeeeeeze,' he whined.

Mrs Wilding shook her head. 'No! If she finds us there, she might do anything!'

Dent was suddenly back into his rational self. 'But they know where it is, how to get there. Tarwildbaning, what else can she do? She crushed my legs, she probed my brain and fudged it. What more harm can she do? Kill me? It might be a blessed relief!'

Mrs Wilding suddenly burst into tears. 'Don't you understand, any of you? What if she does something to me? Who's going to look after you?'

The sudden outpouring of emotion spurred Dent on, knowing he had to be as rational as possible before the insanity kicked back in. He grabbed Mrs Wilding's hand. 'But that's the whole point – eventually she's going to do something. She's like that. We know that Thorgarsuunela has let us down and despite our meeting with Atimkos, I doubt he'll be much help. It is down to us.'

'Atimkos will . . . he must help,' murmured Mrs Wilding. She knelt beside the chair. 'We spent so long looking for them both, they must help us.'

'Yes – we spent millennia looking for them, believing that they could solve our problems. They can't. We were wrong. Thorgarsuunela totally betrayed us. Atimkos simply hasn't got what it takes.'

'The Doctor?' Bridgeman shambled over. 'I remember a man once. Little chap with grey eyes. Or were they blue?'

'Purple?' suggested Nate.

Bridgeman sighed. 'Don't be a silly-billy. People don't have purple eyes – he had green eyes, that was it. Ah, he was clever.'

Mrs Wilding stared at Dent, mentally begging his sanity to stay longer. 'That girl with Atimkos mentioned the Doctor. Who is he?'

'Was he in the garden with us?' asked Nate. 'Lots of people were there.'

'No,' said Mrs Wilding. She pulled away from them and walked a few paces. 'No, the only people in the garden are others like you two, like Udentkista, people whose minds she has deliberately shredded to try to find her way home.' She continued pacing, this time in a circle. 'But if you could get in and out, there must be a way. How did you get there? Was it a nexus? Did you sing it? No, you couldn't have. How did you manage it?' She rushed over to Nate Simms and sat with him. 'Please tell me, Nate. How did you get into the garden?'

'Easy.'

'Go on, tell her,' egged Bridgeman. 'Tell how we did it. Then she'll love us more.'

'She already loves me,' said Nate proudly. He smiled at Mrs Wilding. 'You do, don't you? You do love me?'

'Yes, she loves you,' said Dent, but Mrs Wilding put her hand out to quieten him.

'Yes, Nate. Yes, I love you. Both you and Nicky. I love you lots.'

'But me more!' shrieked Nate, scrabbling away. 'Say you love me more!'

'No, she loves me best.' That was Bridgeman who dashed over and pushed Nate on the floor. Mrs Wilding looked at the two grown men – each minute saw them regressing further. Another day or so and they would be adults with totally undeveloped brains, nothing more instinctive than foetuses. Only Dent's power, his singing and the constant battle to produce peptides had stopped him going the same way.

She thought back to their one visit to the garden – a lush, green garden full of rose bushes, conifers and wrought iron gates. Behind the sculptured hedges loomed a marvellous hillock, with a magnificent Gothic folly upon it. Beautiful flowers grew around its base and by standing on tiptoe, you could see out of the garden and almost smell the flowers. Once one of the poor idiots created by severe mental probing had climbed over the hedge, cutting himself and screaming in pain. Still, he had crawled to the folly, hauling himself up the steps inside. He had got to the top and looked back to where his fellows watched in awe. And where two aliens, Tarwildbaning and Udentkista, had joined in the cheering as he waved.

Then the sky had darkened, the bird song vanished and the winds blew up.

And up.

Trees began to bow under the onslaught and the inmates began screaming, running in pointless circles trying to escape. Heads of flowers snapped off and rain began to fall, turning the ground to mud in seconds. Grass, instantly destroyed by the running feet, was replaced by swirling pools of muck and then the lightning exploded. Udentkista had bravely tried to calm the inmates while Tarwildbaning had attempted to entice the inmate in the folly to return. He had refused and started yelling about freedom. Tarwildbaning remembered that he was once a soldier, from an era when the planet was dominated by its people, called Romans. He had shouted something about Jupiter and then vanished as lightning struck the tower. Tarwildbaning was sure that for a brief second she had seen a blackened skeleton standing in the same pose as the lightning faded and almost instantly serenity returned to the garden.

The trees righted. The flowers grew new heads and grass shoots pushed their way through the solidifying ground. Udentkista and she had stared in astonishment as the inmates began laughing and cheering. Udentkista had pointed at the hedges – they had grown three feet in height – the folly hidden from view.

Then she had arrived. No one saw her come but she was there, amongst her mentally crippled flock, like some grand mother-figure, touching their hands and foreheads as if that made up for their condition.

Udentkista had said what they both thought. 'If you hadn't been so quick to meddle with their brains, they wouldn't be like this.'

187

She had smiled. 'I like them like this. They are controllable. One day I shall learn their secrets – learn the paths created by Atimkos and Thorgarsuunela. Find what you two failed to do. One day.'

'One day,' Udentkista had continued, 'one day you will have eradicated all sentient life on this planet and still we'll be trapped here. Be patient – our people will return for us eventually.'

And she had frozen, and then sprung forward, sending disturbed humans flying, weeping and wailing like hurt children. 'You are not recon-leader. I am. What I say is law here.'

'What I say, Godwanna, is that you are totally and utterly insane!' spat Udentkista.

'No . . .' Tarwildbaning had begun, desperately wanting to sing time back, erase those words, but knowing their powers would not work on each other.

Not the useful, constructive powers. Not like the ones used to create the animals, tame the savage men and create a society of trust and belief as they had done thousands of years before.

No, but they could be affected by the darker, sadistic, untapped powers of their minds. And before either she or Udentkista could say a thing, Godwanna had lashed out with her hand and poked intangibly into Udentkista's brain, solidifying the tips of her fingers and causing him to scream with more primal, unreasoning anguish and hurt than Tarwildbaning thought it possible for a thinking, rational sentient to manage. He was still shrieking as Godwanna removed her hand, and as Udentkista fell on his face, his mouth chewing into the earth and grass in autonomic shock, she rammed both intangible hands into his calves, solidifying slightly and moving down both his legs.

Tarwildbaning heard every crack and splinter as Godwanna shattered both his legs, moving her hands slightly sideways every few inches to ensure the breaks were savage and unmendable.

'Never, ever, argue with a recon-leader, Udentkista. Constructionists are replaceable. Recon-leaders are not.' And with that she had moved away from him.

Godwanna waved at two of her whimpering retards. One was a dark-skinned woman from what Tarwildbaning could only guess was the twentieth century (her clothes were clearly synthetic), the other was a man, an Oriental. She hugged them and they smiled. She smiled as well. And with a soft moan, made not only her hands intangible but their heads. She rolled the heads together and then solidified them. The humans barely had more than a few seconds to scream before they died of massive internal haemorrhaging but the effect on the others in the garden was instant. They went silent. 'No more badness,' Godwanna said simply and dropped the bodies to the floor.

Eagerly, like admonished children seeking approval, they nodded and darted in different directions to play – the Roman outside, the two corpses and the slowly moaning Udentkista forgotten. The sun was shining again, the birds began singing.

Tarwildbaning never saw Godwanna again.

But she swore that if she ever did, she would kill her.

Then she found herself dressed in rags, her skin darkened and her face feeling differently formed, standing amidst nothing but red sand under a scorching sun. Beside her, still moaning, physically changed but just recognizable through the distorted features, was Udentkista. She knelt beside him and rolled him on to his back.

And his eyes cried insanity.

The ship was a mass of activity. When the shuttle's reappearance in space and time had been reported, engineering officer Aall, second-litter, first-sired, was third in command of the ship; but as both Queen Aysha and first-litter, first-sired Chosan had gone to the planet, Aall was given the responsibility of running the ship and crew.

She was also aware that some members of the crew, notably the more aggressive members of the third-litter, were openly disrespectful of their mother. Aall was no fool – she knew that queens could not always curry favour with their litters, but it had been tactical officer Lotuss that had stirred up the problems. Litter-runts from any litter were renowned for their unsuitability for senior tasks, but as a fighter Lotuss had proved herself again and again. Queen Aysha clearly admired that but in Aall's opinion, that admiration might be a mistake. Even members of the first-litter, such as Jayde, had gone over to Lotuss's way of thinking. Aall decided to await their return before making any hasty decisions about her loyalties. Queen Aysha and first-sired Chosan may already be fur-bagged, and if Lotuss had been responsible she would undoubtedly proclaim herself a new queen.

'Shuttle approaching, engineer,' said the helm, Nypp. Beside her, the navigator – and Nypp's twin, both third-litter – Tuq confirmed their trajectory. 'Bay eleven, engineer.'

Aall mewed. 'Prepare recompression.' She stabbed a button on the communication's console near the command cushion. 'All crew. Observe respect. Queen Aysha's shuttle returns. Communications blackout now on-line. Queen's Guards to bay eleven. Engineer out.' Aall rolled off the cushion, and flicked her fur upright, straightening her tail. She waved a paw at the comm's cushion. 'Jodi, you have the conn.'

A smooth-haired brown first-litter acknowledged and moved on to the command cushion.

Aall exited the bridge and walked towards bay eleven, down a short stairwell and passed the mess hall. As she went by, the door-curtain swished aside as the Queen's Guard emerged, twitching their whiskers in deference to Aall. She followed them to the bay and waited for the green light to announce the return to oxygen and safe entry.

After a moment, there was a buzz and the voice of

Tamora in bay control purred over the intercom: 'Shuttle returned safely. Atmosphere returned to bay.' The light flashed green and the door raised inwards.

Without hesitating to confirm the bay controller's statement, the Queen's Guard strode in, forming a neat flank on either side of the shuttle door. The door to the shuttle slid away and Chosan emerged, nodding almost imperceptibly to Aall. The Queen was fine – Lotuss had made no attempts. Aall noted that all the Queen's Guards' rifle-blasters were primed. At a flick of her tail, their red charge lights were uniformly changed to green. Unless Chosan had swapped sides, everything was safe.

Queen Aysha was helped out of the shuttle by two of her guards and then the other Cat-People, including Lotuss at the rear, jumped out. Lotuss turned back and called into the shuttle, 'You can come out now. We're here.'

Aall twitched a whisker (but was glad to notice not one of the guard did likewise) in surprise as two aliens jumped out. One, short, about Lotuss's height in fact, dressed in a baggy black jacket and checked trousers. The other was taller – but still shorter than any Cat-Person – with fair fur on its head. Both were clearly male but both – especially the smaller one – were by no means either idiotic or drugged as toms were on the ship or Feles, the litter-world.

'Anthropoid-toms,' muttered Chosan as she drew beside Aall. 'I'll explain later. Who has the bridge?'

'Jodi.'

'Excellent. Nypp and Tuq will be annoyed.'

Aall smiled back. 'I thought so.' She looked in the direction of Lotuss. 'Any problems?'

'Not at all. In fact,' Chosan put a paw on Aall's shoulder, 'we had a tragedy. We lost Jayde.'

Aall breathed deeply. 'Indeed. A sad loss to the Litters. And especially Lotuss and her rebellious pride.'

Queen Aysha, having acknowledged her guard as befitted the occasion, had caught up with Chosan. Aall began to bow but Aysha spoke. 'Leave it, Aall. I want these two toms defleaed and brought to my chamber in twenty minutes. Chosan, who can you leave on the bridge?'

Aall spoke up. 'Your Majesty . . .'

Aysha barely flicked her head but the message was clear. She wanted Aall with her as well as Chosan.

Chosan licked her incisors. 'Jodi is there now. If we can keep Lotuss away, our only potential trouble is from Nypp and Tuq. However, their duties ought to keep them busy.'

They passed under the raised door, Chosan having to duck very slightly. 'These two toms are important. Repulsive but important. Lotuss will seek to eliminate them even harder than she wants to kill me.' She called over her guard commander. 'Protect them, Nihmrod.'

'Your Majesty.'

'Could we not remove the problem of Lotuss now?' Aall asked.

Aysha smiled slightly. 'You underestimate martyrdom, Aall. Lotuss's direct supporters are few – the third-litter are merely grumbling. But destroy her and they'll rally, attach themselves to her first- and second-litter supporters.' Aysha flashed her eyes. 'But we'll set a trap that'll do the job for us – quickly, efficiently and without creating a martyr. A hero maybe, but we can live with that.'

Chosan hissed, 'Excellent, Your Majesty. When?'

Aysha shrugged. 'When do we invade this planet?'

'As soon as you give the word,' Aall said.

Aysha purred and licked a paw, then wiped her whiskers clean. 'Well, let's not bother restocking Lotuss's larder beyond the next few days.'

On their eventual return to London, Tim booked plane tickets for Sydney (she still could not understand how he could afford it for both of them) and then insisted on taking her shopping. 'A train ride's all very well, but

192

arriving in Sydney looking like a reject from Mary Quant isn't going to enable you to hide in the crowd.' On impulse, he claimed, he took her to Austin Reed in Piccadilly and sat patiently flicking fashion magazines while Polly tried various jackets and skirts on. Eventually she chose the cut of a nice olive-green riding-jacket, pure wool of course, and a dark grey skirt that hung uncomfortably just below her knees. Polly preferred her own mini-skirt but she noticed that a majority of younger women were slightly more conservative in 1994.

Tim paid for the clothes with something he called a store card – if they were there on impulse, how did he have one with him? Polly was amazed: everyone seemed to be using little plastic rectangles to pay, lots of different colours and shapes. She was fascinated by them, and the bleeps and whirls that came out of the machines they pushed them through. 'The average computer in 1966 took up a room the size of this shop,' Tim laughed. 'The black magnetic strip here,' he pointed to the back of his store card, 'is the equivalent of that in basic terms. It reads, digests, feeds and correlates information in the blink of an eye.'

Polly gaped. She didn't ask how. She didn't want to know. 'If anyone asks,' said Tim, 'say you've been away for a while. That'll explain your ignorance. And I don't mean that unkindly.' He slipped his arm through hers and gently eased her closer as they walked.

Polly did not mind. She liked his company and protection. 'I could say I've been at the South Pole since 1986 if that would help.'

'Credit cards are a bit older than that, Polly, but it's a start.'

They walked up Regent Street. 'It's busier,' she said, looking up, around and across at everything, 'but basically recognizable. Oh. Hamleys never used to be here.' She looked towards Liberty. 'It was nearer Beak Street, I'm sure.'

'Probably,' said Tim. 'Even the greats cannot avoid

expansion and commercialism. Ever been to Carnaby Street?'

Polly gripped his arm tighter. 'Have I ever? I practically lived on Carnaby Street. Bette and I used to go every Saturday and buy heaps of kooky things. I mean . . .' She stopped walking, ignoring the curse of the couple behind who nearly collided with them. Tim carefully eased her into a shopfront – Gap for Kids. 'I . . . I can't go to Carnaby Street, Tim. I can't.'

'Why not, precious?'

Polly suddenly felt very small. Very frightened. All around her, people, wearing strange clothes, reading strange books, eating strange food, using strange plastic cards to buy things, tiny coins of decimal currency everywhere. Noisy, dirty buses with doors at the front that opened by themselves. Taxis that looked like hearses. People with tiny earphones in their ears, surely deafening themselves with what passed for music in 1994. 'I can't cope with that, Tim. Please, don't let's go.'

'But there's a great shop there. Buy you the best tops in London.'

'But it'll look different. I've coped with Euston station, all that concrete. I've managed that awful underground with that grafti –'

'Graffiti.'

'Whatever. Gosh, Tim, I even don't mind Hamleys moving a few hundred feet. But Carnaby Street – that really represents 1966 to me. It was my life. What if I meet Bette, or Kitty or Brenda or –'

Tim grabbed her gesticulating hand before it made contact with one of the wary pedestrians trying to avoid this mad woman waving at them in Gap's doorway. 'Hold on, precious. Whoa. Who are Bette and Brenda and Chitty?'

Polly caught his eye. He was staring at her, his deep blue eyes twinkling, reflecting the smile his mouth was creased in. She had immediately relaxed, letting her arms fall limply down. 'I'm sorry,' she whispered.

'No probs. Now are Chitty or Brenda –'

'Kitty. Kitty, or Brenda or my cousin, Bette. I mean, they used to come every Saturday. With me. To Carnaby Street, shopping. And if I see them, I'll still be young and they'll be . . .' She drew in a breath. 'Old.'

'Old. I see.' Tim shrugged. 'Fine. They'll quickly realize that you aren't you; after all, how couldn't you age like they have? If they are there, if they see you, if they think they recognize you, the most likely thing is that they'll put it down to a look-alike. Someone similar. No two people look identical, but some people can look surprisingly similar. Believe me, it'll be fine.'

Believe me.

Two words, begging for trust. For acceptance. For . . . belief.

Tim took her firmly but gently by the hand and slowly moved her towards Beak Street. Seconds later they turned into Carnaby Street and Polly stopped. And stared. And then realized she had been holding her breath. As she let it go, it hit her. Her fears had, on one level, been totally ungrounded. And well founded on another. 'It's completely changed. Completely different. I don't recognize any of it.'

Tim frowned. 'Oh, c'mon, it's not *that* changed. A few shops, maybe, but –'

'No!' Polly put a hand to her forehead, as if she had been hit. 'No. Nothing is the same except the brickwork. I . . . I don't recognize anything at all.' She caressed the brickwork. 'The only thing that hasn't changed . . .' She shook her head. She circled three hundred and sixty degrees, seeing Carnaby Street rotate around her, absorbing the sights and smells. She caught glimpses down the side streets – Karen Millen was still there and, by the look of it, still selling the same fashions. Probably twenty times the price now; Tim had said on the train down how sixties fashions were back in vogue. 'OK, where's this fab shop of yours? If you're paying, I'm buying.'

'And Bette? Brenda? Chitty?'

'Kitty!' laughed Polly. 'If I see them, I'll cope. I'll be strong.'

Again, Tim took her hand and squeezed it. 'I know.'

The touch made her think back. To one other person she associated with Carnaby Street – a young man called Roger. They had gone out for a while, only half seriously, on his part at least. Polly's trouble was, she had fallen for him in a big way, but to Roger, Polly was just another brief fling. Oh, he had talked passion, said all the right things. Told her how he had never felt as relaxed or comfortable with anyone else.

They had spent happy days and nights walking around London, heading for the pictures, holding hands in the dark, so that no one else would know. No reason, just a silly pretence at furtiveness they both enjoyed. He had given her a flower once. She had kept it for a week and then pressed it between the pages of *Alice's Adventures Through the Looking-Glass (And What She Found There)*. Then, one day, walking down Carnaby Street, dipping in and out of the favourite shops they had dipped in and out of loads of times before, he took her hand and squeezed her fingers. He had smiled at her. 'This is silly,' he had said. 'I mean we like each other, but it's rather daft. We don't actually love each other, do we?'

'Don't we?'

'No. I mean you're almost twenty-one – lots to explore, see and do. I like being friends – good friends.' Roger had squeezed a bit harder. 'Hey, we'll always be friends, won't we? But I'm not looking for anything serious right now. I just don't want to be tied down – no, I don't mean tied down exactly, but responsible. Let's just have fun. As friends.'

And like a fool, Polly had nodded. 'Yeah. Sure, just friends.' Friends with Roger was better than no Roger. It had to be if that was all that was on offer. One minute it had been love all the way, the next it was gone just like that. No discussion, no time to think. Just a *fait accompli* that she had to go along with because to argue might have cost her everything instead of just his love. She could not make him love her like she loved him. That would not be right.

A week later, shopping with Kitty (and feeling more than a bit lost without Roger) she had seen him with Lucy Miller. Dipping in and out of the same shops. Laughing. Snogging, open-mouthed. In public. He had never done that with Polly. But, surely, he did not want a relationship. No responsibilities. What about responsibilities to your friends? she had wanted to scream. That's what she would say after she had hit him. After she had stuffed that beautifully preserved flower down his throat.

Instead, Polly had just turned away as if she had seen nothing and said to Kitty that she was bored of being a debs' delight, lazing around in dives like Carnaby Street. Yes, she would take that job boring old Uncle Charles had fixed for her. The Post Office Tower – that was new and hip. That was really swinging. And she would be nearer Covent Garden, where Kitty worked. They could go there and see real life.

She did not need Roger. Only she did. He had been like a drug, she had needed her fix of him and she had never got over him. The way Tim squeezed her fingers right then, on that exact spot – that was all the reminder she needed.

That's why she had wanted to travel with the Doctor. And Ben. To get away from everything that places like Carnaby Street represented. 'Let's shop,' she said to Tim. 'And then, let's get that plane.'

Smiling he pulled her towards Muji and they went in.

Ten minutes, three blue roll-neck sweaters and something called a baseball jacket later they left, laughing, joking and without a care in the world. Polly could not think why she had not wanted to come here. With Tim. Roger was years ago. Weeks ago. It did not matter. He was probably old, wrinkled and boring now. Tim was fun, with a very large F.

'Hey!' A woman shouted. 'Hey, surely it isn't . . . it can't be . . .'

Polly froze. No! Surely she could not be right? No one could have recognized her! Yet, here was this woman, hurrying over.

'Ignore her.' Tim tried to pull her away, but Polly could not move. Would not move. This was it – someone who knew her in 1966 was about to get a shock. The woman stopped and stared, her mouth opening and shutting slowly, trying to form words.

'Is it . . . ? Are you . . . ?'

'Can we help you?' Tim stood suddenly between them. Polly thought he looked three inches taller. And broader.

The woman visibly blanched. 'I'm really sorry. It's just that your . . . friend looked like someone I knew years ago. But that's daft. I mean –'

Polly carefully moved around Tim and asked the silliest, stupidest, most astonishingly dangerous question she could. As soon as the words left her brain on their way to her mouth, little impulses of panic and regret tried to chase them, overtake and close the mouth, sever the vocal cords – anything! 'What was her name?'

'Michelle.' The woman started to go red with embarrassment. 'Michelle. She went to Spain years ago and I haven't seen her since.'

'My name's Polly. Polly Wright. I'm so sorry, but I've never seen you before in my life.'

The woman looked down to her feet. 'Sorry. I'm so sorry. It's just that I never hear from Michelle any more and I miss her. I thought, hoped, you were her, but you look like she did then. Twenty-eight years ago.' She looked up and smiled. 'You must think I'm very rude. And silly.'

Polly smiled back and touched her arm. 'Not at all. Believe me, I know the feeling.'

The woman stared at her and then turned away, slowly disappearing back into the crowd.

198

'That poor woman,' said Polly. 'She so desperately wanted me to be her Michelle. Do you think Kitty and the others look at people in crowds and hope to see me? Or ask complete strangers if they are me?'

'I don't know.' Tim looked at his watch. 'We ought to go.'

'I don't like this, Tim. I don't like being in the future. It was bad enough in Cumbria, where just the things were strange. But here, London, it's too near home. I want to find the Doctor in Australia and go back to the TARDIS. Get away from here.'

'All right. Let's go fly.'

'Are you sure he'll be there?' They walked into Golden Square, on their way to Piccadilly tube, where they could get on the underground to London Airport. Or Heathrow as Tim said it was called now.

'He'll be there. I promise. Believe me.'

'I do.'

'Hey!' Tim suddenly bounced ahead of her, like a puppy. If he had a tail, it would have been wagging. 'Hey, how many terminals were at Heathrow in 1966?'

'Terminals? One, I suppose. Why?'

Tim had skipped around her. 'Oh boy, are you in for a surprise.'

He was not wrong. Polly could not ever remember seeing so many people crammed into one place. Four terminals and even that did not seem to be enough. She felt the fear building up inside her – was she becoming agoraphobic? Claustrophobic? Peoplephobic? All she knew was that the sooner Tim got her away from all this, the better.

He thrust a ticket into her hand and booked their baggage in. Ten minutes later, they walked towards the departure lounge for flight QF003 to Sydney via Singapore and Melbourne.

And here she was now, seated in seats 75A and 75B, just the two seats with plenty of baggage room beside the window, near the rear of the plane. Polly had not had a chance to tell Tim that she had only flown once before but what the hell. She had been to a colony on Vulcan and back. What was a little trip to Australia? Surely it was not that different to the TARDIS?

Except that the TARDIS did not take twenty-three hours. And the Doctor was in it.

While Tim went to the toilet, Polly took out the pack of tarot cards, shuffled them and turned the top one over – the Lovers. It showed a tall man with a woman, both dark-skinned with pure white hair, their young faces portraying love and comfort in each other. They were draped together under a massive cloak, he offering her flowers. At their feet, two cats, both almost pure white, the male rubbing his chin over the female's head.

According to the little instruction book that came with the set, the cloak represented a youthful and carefree existence that they share, its circular patterns symbolic of eternity. An eternal friendship/relationship/whatever. Their pale hair glowing in their love for each other. The flowers are a token of his affection for her. They are headed for a deep, meaningful friendship – possibly more –

Polly slipped the book back into the pack. Tim was coming down the aisle from the toilet and she felt guilty about examining the tarot cards. It was almost as if she were refusing to accept what he had read. Much of it had been negative – the thing about the Knight of Wands and the Knight of Swords, warnings not to trust people. Both in their way had pointed towards the Doctor. But, she reasoned, both could mean Tim. Or Ben. Or anyone. Was Tim trying to tell her something when he joked about the bad cards all representing him?

'Oh, what's the point?' She stuffed the pack back into her pocket.

As Tim sat beside her, casually stroking the back of her hand and sending a little thrill up her spine that she simply could not keep ignoring, she wondered what the Doctor was doing right now.

* * *

'I wonder what Polly's doing right now,' muttered Ben as he was pushed along the carpeted floor of the Cat-People's battle-cruiser. He stared at the carpeted walls and carpeted ceilings. It occurred to him that maybe Persian cats were employed to weave carpets for the ship.

The Doctor was walking backwards, forwards and sideways, apparently trying to take in every nook and cranny, count every bolt and bulkhead, and generally making Ben dizzy. 'Oh, don't you worry, Ben. She'll be all right for now. Tim ought to be taking her to Australia as we speak.'

'Why?'

The Doctor suddenly dropped to the floor by a guard. 'Bit worn here, old chap. Chap-ess.' He corrected himself sheepishly. 'What's your name? You weren't on Earth, were you?'

The Cat-Person raised her rifle-blaster a bit higher. 'I am Nihmrod of the Queen's Guard.'

'Ah.' The Doctor stopped moving and stared upwards, sucking his finger as if trying to remember something. 'Nihmrod. Someone once told me that means Little Hunter. Are you a hunter, Nihmrod?'

'Only of fleshy animals like you. To capture and kill. The hunt is all that matters.'

'Oh, absolutely.' They came to a blunt-ended corridor. Then a panel slid away, revealing a lift. 'In here? Oh, good.' He jumped forward as if over an invisible trip-wire. With a sigh, Ben walked in normally, followed by Nihmrod, her red leather suit creaking slightly. The Doctor, smaller than Ben and Nihmrod, stood at the back of the lift. 'This is a terribly nice guided tour, Nihmrod. Do you do them often?'

'Quiet.'

The Doctor stuck his tongue out at the back of her head. 'Suit yourself.'

The lift door slid open and they were in another long, carpeted corridor. Instead of sliding doors, each entrance-way was covered by hanging beads of soft curtains.

'Living quarters, Doc,' said Ben.

'Yes. Probably. They like their comfort, don't they?' Without waiting for an answer, he darted through the nearest set of hanging beads, letting them clack behind him. Nihmrod and Ben were after him instantly, and they found him sitting cross-legged on a cushion. 'Queen Aysha's perhaps?'

Nihmrod lowered her rifle-blaster. 'No. First-sired Chosan's actually. Queen Aysha's is further down this corridor.'

'Easy mistake.' The Doctor got up. He turned and patted the cushion, removing his indentation. 'Wouldn't want to upset Chosan, would we, Ben?'

'No, Doctor. Any more than we want to upset Queen Aysha.'

'Ah.' The Doctor wandered back into the corridor. 'You're quite right.' He turned to Nihmrod. 'Well, come on, come on. Don't keep Her Majesty waiting.'

Nihmrod pushed past them. 'Follow me.'

The Doctor winked at Ben and nodded slightly. Ben frowned and then got it. Nihmrod was now in front, and there was nothing behind.

He slowed to let Nihmrod get a couple of paces ahead. He was going to ask the Doctor what they were going to do next when he suddenly realized he and Nihmrod were alone.

The Doctor had vanished.

Circling Sydney Airport. Five o'clock in the morning, local time. Pitch-black. Little lights. Water. Tired. Needing a wash. Furry teeth, scraggly hair. Creased Muji pullover. Tim's morning breath on her neck.

Polly had managed to stay awake just enough to register the rather dreary thirty-minute video showing her the delights of Sydney, complete with behind-the-scenes footage of new movies, some theatre productions and a brief 'guided tour' of, oddly enough, the tourist attractions. The graphics that flashed around the screen, pictures flipping in and out and over each other had been almost too much. So many technological advances in thirty years – all down to computers, she was sure. That seemed to be the catchword of the Nineties: 'It's amazing what they can do with computers.'

She had sleepily murmured at some point to Tim what was the point of employing actors if computers could do it all? He had nodded and gone back to sleep. Very useful.

'Botany Bay,' murmured a rather fey steward. 'Where James Cook eventually settled when he found he couldn't see directly into Sydney harbour. So the airport was built here as well. Are you here for long?'

Polly immediately assumed he wanted to see her passport and dug around in her bag for it. Her new bag that Tim had given her at Heathrow that contained a passport (a small, burgundy one, not the chunky black one Daddy had got for her when they went to the Seychelles a couple of years earlier), credit cards, a brush, $250 and a crumpled photo of her and Ben on the Cumbrian cliff tops – none of which Polly could account for.

Triumphantly she flourished the passport but the steward laughed politely. 'I'm not checking. Just asking.'

'Oh.' Polly felt silly. 'Sorry. Anyway, I don't know. It depends on Tim.'

The steward stared for a moment at Tim. 'Is he your boyfriend?' he asked cheerily.

'Yes,' said Tim, suddenly sitting upright and not looking as if he had been on a plane for twenty-plus hours.

'Oh.' The steward wandered away.

'Cheeky git,' muttered Tim.

Polly laughed. 'Actually I don't think it was me he was interested in.'

Tim nodded, 'I know. As I said, cheeky git.'

Ten minutes later, the plane landed safely. 'Still got their one-hundred-per-cent safety record, then,' Tim muttered. They grabbed their hand luggage – Polly's handbag and a plastic bag of T-shirts of Tim's – and made their way down the aisles as quickly as the mass of people would allow. 'Should've gone First Class,' Polly said but Tim shook his head.

'Business, maybe, but in First they're over-attentive.'

They arrived in Passport Control, were smoothly processed, collected their luggage and walked into the Arrivals terminal. 'Do you drive, Polly?'

'No.'

'Shame. Neither do I. We need a car.'

'Mr Atimkos?'

Startled, they both turned to greet a scruffy Aboriginal man, his teeth gleaming in a broad smile through a matted beard. His breath smelt of cheap beer but his manner did not suggest to Polly that he was in any way drunk.

'Hello. Who are you?' Tim offered his hand and the Aborigine shook it.

'Sidney. And you are?'

'Polly. Polly Wright. Hello, Sidney of Sydney.' Polly realized he had slipped her luggage away and was turning his back, carrying it towards the doors. They slid open and the cool, but humid July air hit her. Tim smiled encouragingly as she began to sweat. 'What's it like by lunchtime?'

'Hotter,' called Sidney. 'You cover yourself up with block, Miss Wright. Your skin is pale, you'll burn easily.'

Polly shrugged and looked back at the airport. 'I'm not planning on sunbathing, Sidney.'

'No matter, Miss Wright. Half a day walking around the shops and you'll begin to cook in this weather. Sunblock and time, that's what you need. Your body adjusts if you are careful.'

Polly said she would remember that and looked at Tim. He made a face that said he did not understand either, which Polly was glad of in a way. Something strange was happening that Tim was not aware of. She remembered the tarot cards: The Knights. Was Sidney one of these? One to be trusted? They got into the car, Tim in the front and Polly clambered over one of the Muji bags that Sidney had failed to cram into the boot. The car looked tatty and uninspiring from the outside, like any cheap mini-cab might that was looked after by a boozy Abo. Inside, it was a palace! The seats were soft and clean, a feeling of fresh water in the air and an almost dizzying mixture of smells, reinforcing the feeling that Polly was halfway up a mountain rather than in a taxi. Music was playing from somewhere; it sounded like a recording of Tibetan monks chanting and humming. It was constant, no change in rhythm or harmony. She was not sure how long she could cope with it. The dashboard on the car looked very futuristic but Polly just assumed she was not used to it until she noticed Tim staring in equal fascination. 'Nice car,' was all he said.

Sidney laughed. 'Mr Udentkista's, I believe. He's always tinkering with things, you know.'

Polly leaned forward. 'Can I have the window down a bit? I can't find a handle.'

Sidney slapped his head with his hand. 'I knew something would get forgotten. Sorry, Miss Wright.'

The top third of the window beside Polly simply melted away and a cool draft of air seeped in.

'Very good, Sidney. You've mastered the art well,' was Tim's response.

'Not really, Mr Atimkos –'

'Tim.'

'Mr Tim. Not really – it's all one really. No joins.'

Polly looked about the car and realized it was true. There were no joins, each thing simply grew out of another: the seats, the armrests, the rear-view mirror, the fluffy dice. It was as if the inside of the car were one huge blob of matter that things were shaped from. Like Plasticine.

'Very good.' Tim poked Sidney's arm. 'You as well?'

'Of course. Best of them so far according to Mr Udentkista.' Sidney shrugged a lump out of his arm and it

205

formed a large hat with corks hanging from it. 'Best play the tourist for now, Mr Tim.' The hat darkened until it was jet-black and Tim tugged it off Sidney's arm.

'Doesn't hurt, Miss Wright,' Sidney said, clearly seeing Polly's look of astonishment in the mirror.

'No. No, I'm sure it doesn't,' she breathed. 'Sorry, I'm not following all this. Is this a car or not?'

'Yes,' said Tim.

'No,' said Sidney.

'Thank you both,' said Polly.

'Well, all right, I suppose it isn't,' agreed Tim. 'I mean it looks like a car, behaves like a car and feels like a car. It just isn't really.'

'It's better for the environment than a car. No fuel needed. Just this.' Sidney tapped the dashboard and pointed at a speaker grill where the annoying humming and chanting came from.

Tim nodded. 'He always was an improviser.'

'Look, I know I'm a bit dim but would someone mind explaining things to me?' Polly stared at Sidney's reflected eyes and forced a lopsided grin. 'I'm from 1966.'

'Ah. You're the Doctor's friend. Tarwildbaning mentioned him. And you.'

'Oh. Good. I think.'

Tim turned to face her and left Sidney to navigate the Sydney traffic as he bypassed the city centre (no tour of the Opera House, Polly decided) and passed under a series of bridges to emerge in the bizarrely named Ultimo, following signs for Chatswood, and the North Shore for Newcastle.

'Sidney's not real. Not like you or me. He and this car are sonic constructs, sung into existence by Dent, as you know him.'

Polly frowned. 'If I remember my Aboriginal legends correctly, aren't the Songlines here meant to represent pathways where everything was sung into existence?'

'Their fault,' said Sidney. 'Him and Tarwildbaning showed my ancestors how to do it, so the legends say.'

206

'Which legends?' asked Tim.

Sidney laughed. 'Tarwildbaning and Udentkista of course. Living legends!'

'Surprise me further,' muttered Tim.

'OK.' Sidney passed through Chatswood and out past some huge red and white space dishes. 'Television aerials,' Sidney explained. They did not look like any television aerials Polly had ever seen. By now they had reached Wahroonga. 'By the way,' continued Sidney, 'Thorgar-suunela's dead.'

Polly was surprised to see this did not phase Tim. 'I thought as much. I felt something just before the house in Cumbria was destroyed.'

The house in . . . Why did that mean something to Polly? She tried to remember the significance of it, but she could not concentrate because Tim was whistling at her. She wanted him to stop so that she could concentrate on . . . on . . . now what was she thinking about? Oh yes, Fräulein Thorsuun was dead. Tim was not upset. Funny that. Neither was she.

'How?'

Sidney shrugged. 'No one's too sure. One minute she was there. The next, albeit briefly, there were two of her. Then both vanished within a minute of each other. Tarwildbaning can't trace her at all. She must be dead.'

Tim smiled. 'No loss. Where are Tarwildbaning and Udentkista now?'

Sidney swerved around a large truck pulling out of a road to the left. Polly saw that a sign was pointing them to the M3. Presumably not the same one that linked London with Winchester or Winchester with Bournemouth. It flashed through her mind that by now the link between the two must have been completed, making London to Bournemouth available to all traffic. So much must have happened . . .

'. . . trying to get into the garden.'

'She's created a garden? Here? Why?'

'Same reason as always,' said Sidney giving a finger to a

driver passing dangerously close. Polly did not want to ask
what the finger represented; somehow she could guess.
Sidney carried on talking as if nothing had happened.
'They're in the nexus area, waiting to get in and then on
to her. They've got two loonies who've been in but got
out again. They're not sure how.'

'Who?' asked Tim. 'The loonies or Tarwildbaning and
Udentkista?'

'Don't know.' Sidney turned on to the M3, a massive
six-lane motorway leading to Newcastle.

'Can one of you explain what you lot mean by a
"garden"? I take it it's not full of trees and shrubs.'

'Actually, Polly,' replied Tim, 'it is. Exactly that. It's a
sort of a dumping ground. It's like the human brain has a
repository for things it doesn't need – a mental warehouse
if you like. You know, you know things but you tuck
them away until you need them?'

Polly frowned. Warehouse? House? Things tucked
away in the memory? 'Yes?' she prompted.

'Well, my people created physical warehouses, places
to put things that we don't want or need to deal with. But
rather than passing thoughts, this is where we store real
things, physical things. We create it to look like a garden
simply because it's attractive. It'll keep the things happy
until they're retrieved.'

'These things,' said Polly, 'd'you mean people?'

'Oh yes,' said Tim. 'Frequently when we'd have aliens
volunteer to come with us to broaden their minds, we'd
put them in a specially created garden until we found
what we wanted to show them. They don't need feeding
or monitoring there.'

Sidney joined in. 'Sort of cryogenically storing them
without actually putting them to sleep. Like a video on
pause.'

'A video?'

Tim looked at Sidney. '1966 not '86.'

'Oh. Sorry, Miss Wright.'

Polly decided she could not hope to follow all this.

'Where are we going, Sidney?'

'Good question,' said Tim.

Sidney pointed at a passing road sign. 'Newcastle. Booked into a motel for the night. Tomorrow, off to Byron Bay. Then to Cairns.'

Polly thought of her Australian geography. Byron Bay, she knew, was where lots of people had headed to Australia to hang out. A couple of her friends from Leeds University had gone there – cheap pot and lots of communes. Something about peace, love and harmony. Free love, they had called it. Said that within three years, the whole world would come to know, respect and belong to the hippy communities. Byron Bay was going to be the new cultural centre of Australia. Polly had doubted it then. Looking at Earth thirty years on, she doubted it now even more. But Cairns? What was there? The Barrier Reef? *Flipper*? She had seen an episode of that just before she met the Doctor. No, that was American. And Skippy was a bush kangaroo but there was little bush near Cairns. A few rain forests though. Polly thought back to her training as a courier – a job that had lasted only a few weeks after she had told the tutor that he was as pompous and stuffy as Daddy. They had told her that rain forests were going to vanish over the next fifty years. Maybe by 1994 they had all gone. She would soon know. 'Why Cairns?' Asking seemed the best way of getting answers, and it was too early in the morning for her head to sort this out clearly.

Sidney ignored her question. 'Newcastle is about another hour. Relax, Miss Wright.'

Tim frowned. 'We got out of Sydney very quickly, Sidney. Have you been chrono-tunnelling?'

Sidney grinned. 'You caught me out, Mr Tim. As soon as I sensed your RTC, I knew we'd be safe.'

'RTC? What RTC?' asked Polly.

Tim turned and smiled, reached out and took her left hand, running his thumb across it in circles. 'Go to sleep, Polly, there's a love.'

Polly slumped back in the seat. No one told her anything any more. Like, what happened at some house. Why couldn't she remember . . . why couldn't she . . . The last thing Polly could really sense was Tim letting her hand go.

Blackness.

'Well? Well, did you manage it?'

'Manage what?' Dent squirmed in his Victorian wheelchair, staring ahead into the whiteness.

Mrs Wilding was behind him. 'Did you collect them?'

Bridgeman and Nate Simms crawled over. 'Is someone coming?' asked Bridgeman.

'Someone new to play with?' wondered Simms.

Mrs Wilding patted their heads. 'Yes. But before they get here, we need to get you two sorted out.'

Dent suddenly struggled in his chair, his adrenalin pumping, putting his mind totally back in control. 'Is that wise?'

'I have to do it.' Mrs Wilding waved around the open space. 'We can do nothing here. We need to be in the garden when the nexus opens. These two have been there.'

Dent pulled on her sleeve. 'We don't know that. Not for sure. Their brains are as addled as mine. They could have heard us mention it and decided to tell us they'd been there.'

Mrs Wilding came round the front of Dent's chair, her black dress suddenly looking less severe, her whole demeanour softer. 'My love, I know that's a possibility, although I don't think we did mention it. But like this, they're no use to anyone. Least of all themselves. Now I know I can try and do something.'

Dent took her hand. 'I've never challenged you before, beloved, but I ask you to consider this. You tried rectifying her meddling once before, remember?'

Mrs Wilding lowered her head and rested it on her knees. 'Do you hate me?' she asked softly.

He ran a hand through her hair. 'No. I love you. But

210

trusting you with my brain and trusting you with theirs is different. I gave myself knowingly. They can't. Humans don't have the knowledge or the shields. If they did, she'd find it harder to destroy them. I can't stop you doing this, but I can't give you my unconditional support either.'

Mrs Wilding looked up at him, her eyes glistening with tears. 'If only I'd left you alone, you might have cured yourself eventually. Instead, I condemned you to this constant pain. Constant brain-slides.' She looked across at Bridgeman and Nate Simms, chasing each other with the energy and enthusiasm of eight-year-old humans. 'If I succeed – and I know it's a big if – if I succeed, will they remember these days? Will they hate themselves, each other and me for forcing them to come to terms with it?'

Dent pulled her closer and kissed her gently on the cheek. 'Do what you must, my love.'

She kissed him back and stood up, wiping her face with her pinny. She gave a last look at Dent's uncommonly lucid face, tried to smile and then turned away. 'Boys!' she barked, adopting her sternest voice. 'Boys, come here now!'

Bridgeman and Nate Simms stopped and looked around, as if hoping she was talking to some other boys, but Mrs Wilding's indicating finger was aimed at them. Sheepishly they came over, Nate Simms put his arms behind his back, and kicked something invisible on the floor.

'Haven't done anything, Mrs Wilding. It wasn't us.'

'Not true,' Mrs Wilding said loudly. 'You've both been very bad boys. Very bad.'

Bridgeman sniffed and started to cry. 'Wasn't us.'

'Bad boys. Now look at Mr Dent.'

They did so and Mrs Wilding pointed at him. 'Mr Dent says you pushed his wheelchair over. Did you?'

'No!' they both chorused.

'Yes you did!' called Dent. 'Punish them, Mrs Wilding. Punish them so they'll never forget it.'

The two men who thought they were boys shrunk away from him, dropped to their knees and pressed into Mrs Wilding's pinny for comfort.

'He's a hateful man, isn't he? A mean old bitter man with no legs and you hate him because he's always so mean to you. Isn't that right, boys?'

Bridgeman looked at Dent and then Mrs Wilding and burst into tears. 'Yes!' he sobbed. 'I hate him.'

'Me too,' grunted Nate Simms. 'Silly ugly old man. I hate him lots.'

And Mrs Wilding bent down to them. 'Scream out how much you hate him then. Scream it out now!'

And the two men screamed the word 'Hate!' out as loud as they could. Over and over again.

And Mrs Wilding suddenly screamed and shocked the two men into silence. They stared at her, strange feelings of hate and fear coursing through them. Remembering another scream very like hers.

And Mrs Wilding plunged an intangible hand into each of their brains and solidified her fingers.

And they began screaming too.

'*whatsgoingonwhereami?*'

Who are you, little bright light? Why are you here?

'*whereisherewhoareyouhowdidigethere?*'

An interesting question. Now, if you relax, we'll try and sort out your questions. You are frowning.

'*myheadhurtsgodithurtssomuchwhydoesithurtpleasemakeitstop!*'

All right, but it won't stop until you relax. Now. Open your eyes and tell me what you see.

'*lighticanseelighticansee —*'

Stop! Too fast. Calm down. I can't help if I can't understand.

'*sorryit'sjustthatit'sso . . . so . . . so fright*ening. I'm frightened. Please help me.'

What can you see?

212

'A room. I'm in a room. White. The ceiling has lights and there's someone at the end of a corridor. I'm in a hospital, aren't I? Have I had an accident?'

Of sorts, yes.

'Where am I?'

We're going to help you. This place is what you want it to be. If you're seeing a hospital, that's good. Hospitals are good. They'll help you be mended.

'The person at the end of the corridor, he's coming towards me.'

Good. Is he nice?

'I think so. He's smiling. I know him, though.'

Is he going to help you? Is he a doctor? Hospitals are full of doctors and nurses.

'Yes. Doctor – he's a doctor . . . no, he's *the* Doctor.'

So. Do you know him?

'He saved my life. He's a bit strange but he's weird.'

If he saved your life before and you're seeing him again, then he's probably here to help you. That's good.

'Hey. He can't get to me. I don't understand. He's running, trying to reach me but he's getting further away. Why can't I go to him?'

If he's having trouble getting to you, it's because you won't let him. How would you describe him? As a person I mean?

'Oh. All right. No, nice. I mean, he's very confident.'

More than you?

'Oh yes, far more. He sorted Kerbe out and took his gun from him. Very clever.'

How did he 'sort out' this Kerbe?

'He just bulldozed his way in, took charge I suppose.'

Weren't you in charge, though?

'No. No, Kerbe was. Or Thorsuun. I've never been in charge really. Not very good at it.'

I'm sure you're being harsh on yourself. You're a university professor it says here. You must be in charge of your students.

'Nominally, yes. But frankly, not very often. They rather take the . . . er . . . mickey out of me.'

Why?

'I don't know . . . yes, I do. It's my stutter. Somehow I let them get me down. They're not a bad bunch of kids but it's so easy to lose control if you can't talk properly.'

You sound fine now. You're not stuttering at all.

'No. No, I'm not. Why not?'

Who knows. Maybe your need to stutter has gone. Why did you stutter?

'I don't know. It just happened one day. I didn't really notice it at all. People say it's a confidence thing but I'm not so sure.'

Most people stutter because of their past. Let's examine your past shall we?

'Why?'

Because we might find an answer and make you better.

'No! I mean, the stutter's gone. I am better.'

Are you still in the hospital with the lights and the white walls?

'Yes.'

Then you're not better. Sorry but that's the way it goes. Hey, who's this?

'Oh God. That . . . that's my mother.'

She's beautiful. Look, she's waving at you – oh no, not at you, at him. Who's he?

'Father? Oh God, it's my father too . . . where am I?'

Is your father dead? Is that why you're crying?

'Yes! Yes, they both died. Together. On the same night – and I was there and didn't do anything to stop it!'

Could you have?

'What?'

Could you have saved either of them? How did they die?

'Do we need to do this? Can't I just go with them?'

Is that what you want? Really want? Oh, I see it now. Your mother killed your father and then took

her own life, isn't that right? . . . Hello? Am I right?

'Yes. Yes, and I was there. And I did nothing . . . nothing at all . . .'

'Hello, son. How are you?'

'D . . . Dad? You can see me? Hear me?'

'Of course I can, son. Hey, Margaret, it's Nick. Come and say hello.'

'Hello, love. How are you. Still ghost-hunting?'

'Mother? How do you know I ghost-hunt?'

'Because the ones you find told us. You're looking for us, aren't you? That's why you do it, isn't it?'

'Is it, son? That's daft, you know. I'm sorry but we're dead. Even tracking us down as ghosts won't bring us back.'

'But . . . but I never had a chance to say goodbye. To say I love you. I . . . I miss you so much.'

'We miss you too, son, don't we, Margaret?'

'Oh yes, Alex, we do. But we're also so proud of you. We always have been.'

'Really? But why? I haven't done anything.'

'Oh, Nick my son – not done anything? Of course you have, you're successful in a nice, modest way. You're good to the kids at the university. Frankly, you'd never have got to university and to teach if I'd been around. Too stubborn, me.'

'Yes, that's true. Your father wanted you to follow him into the navy.'

'I'd have hated that.'

'Of course you would, son. We know that now. By the way, the bit at Whitley Bay, the ashes and all that. Nice touch. We both appreciated that.'

'Oh yes, Nick. Very nice. But you keep coming back. It's a nice gesture, but so pointless. We're not there really. We're here. With you.'

'Where exactly is here?'

Inside you.

'Who *are* you?'

'Oh, he's you, Nick. He's the piece of you you keep

215

bottled up – the strong, assertive part. He always asks you questions, but you never answer them properly. I think now's the time to do so. Leave us – don't forget us but don't think about us so much.'

'Mother's right, son. Let us go and help your kids. And the others. The Doctor – he seems a good fellow. Probably ex-service, seen a bit of action. Join up with him. He needs you. They all do.'

They're right, Nicholas. Everyone needs you. The strong Nicholas Bridgeman that's always been here. The one who coped. The one who really coped when the world crashed in on him.

'Go on, Nick. For me and your father. We'll see you again. One day. Remember us.'

'Mother? I love you. Please don't go.'

'We love you too, son. We love –'

They're gone.

'What now?'

What do you see?

'Whiteness. Not the hospital – I've been here before. There's a woman. And a man. In a chair. And there's someone else with them, curled up. Asleep. Hello? Hello? Where are you?'

'Professor Bridgeman?'

Nicholas Bridgeman opened his eyes and looked up at someone he knew was called Mrs Wilding. He felt a warmth rush through him, as if a thermostat had just triggered. He tried to get up but stumbled. She was reaching to help him, but he pushed her away. 'No. No, thank you. I'm fine.'

He looked around him. It was the same whiteness he had seen when he first arrived. After the telephone box. Mrs Wilding was the woman he had seen there, in that odd village that was not quite real.

'We distorted your perceptions, I'm afraid. In Cumbria. Our efforts to get through to 1994 altered the reality nexus. That's how you got brought up here.

216

Godwanna saw us and you and decided to remove you in case you interfered with her plans.' Mrs Wilding went over to the crippled man he somehow knew as Dent.

'Hello, Professor,' said Dent. Shouldn't he be giggling, mad or something? 'No, my peptides are all right for a while. Good enough for me to read your mind in fact. Sorry, it's a bit of a liberty I know.'

'That's fine,' Bridgeman said, aware that he didn't know if it was fine or not. No one had ever read his mind before. 'I feel strange. What's happened?'

Mrs Wilding breathed deeply. 'Suffice to say you were in a bad way after Godwanna finished with you. I had to try and set you right – I'm sorry if I caused you any pain.'

Bridgeman shook his head and smiled. 'No. No, I feel fine. Quite light-headed actually.'

'I meant mentally. Spiritually. I had to bring out your fears, your phobias in order to quash the other things that Godwanna brought out. Your deeper, frightened self. You managed to override them all. You should be very proud.'

'I would be if I had any idea what you were talking about.' He suddenly saw the curled-up man properly. 'Nate? Nate Simms?'

Mrs Wilding held Bridgeman back.

'I'm sorry. I tried to do the same with him, but his fears are too deeply scarred. The real Nate Simms couldn't get out. I lost him inside his own psyche. He's lost.'

'For ever?'

'I'm afraid so.'

Bridgeman suddenly turned round. 'Where is he?'

'Who? Nate Simms? He's here.'

'No, not Nate. The other man I saw. The Doctor. He was trying to get through to me. He needed my help – it wasn't me that needed his! He was trying to get to me.' Bridgeman suddenly understood everything – and he grasped his temples. 'My God – you probed my head, didn't you?'

'Yes. I'm sorry.'

'Don't be. You did me a great favour. Everything's coming back. The garden. You need to find the garden. The Doctor's going to meet us there.'

Dent pushed his chair towards them and grabbed Bridgeman's arm. 'Yes. Well done, my friend. How do we get there?'

Bridgeman smiled. 'Easy.'

The whiteness vanished and the three of them looked around. Sweet roses. Trees. Blossoms on the peach trees and the gentle buzz of bees.

'The hedges. They're low,' said Mrs Wilding.

'I wanted it that way,' said Bridgeman. 'Your God-wanna has twisted me around. Now it's my turn.' He looked at Dent. 'Are you with me, sir?'

'You are a changed man, Professor Bridgeman. Beware you don't get over-confident.'

'Point taken, Mr Dent. Are you both with me?'

Mrs Wilding clasped Dent's hand. 'Of course we are. We want to go home. If we could get out amongst the stars again, Udentkista's health would return. I'd have enough power to save him, make him whole.'

Bridgeman was laughing. 'But don't you see? It's all an illusion. The garden – this is reality. That white place – we were here – we just couldn't see it. Godwanna was altering our perceptions. Twisting us.' Bridgeman took Dent's other hand. 'Come on. Let's get her.'

Dent stared at him. 'Are you mad, human? I can't just run along with you! Look at me.'

'He's crippled, Professor. And his mind could go at any minute.' Mrs Wilding frowned. 'I thought you realized that.'

Bridgeman laughed. 'Do you know something, Mrs Wilding? Thanks to you, I feel complete for the first time in years.' He plucked a flower for her. 'Here, a token of my gratitude. But you haven't done anything. Not physically. You just opened my mind – the bits I'd closed. I'd told myself they had to be closed, but you opened them. I'm the same man I was but now I actually believe I'm complete. That's all it takes. Belief.'

Dent looked from Mrs Wilding to Bridgeman and back. 'I don't understand this.'

Mrs Wilding hugged Bridgeman. 'You're right. I could do it to you but not see it myself.'

'But you did do it, didn't you?' Bridgeman looked at Dent. 'She tried to cure you?'

'Years ago,' said Dent. 'It didn't change a thing.'

Bridgeman suddenly pulled Dent forward, kicking out at the chair, which sped back and crashed into a tree and promptly fell on its side.

Dent was standing. His Victorian clothing faded – for a brief moment he was an Aborigine again. Then he was standing tall, younger, dressed in a tight grey survival suit, bulging with his muscles, a lithe, strong frame. As he had been when he had first arrived on Earth, forty thousand years before. And he burst into tears.

'You mean . . . he's always been able to . . . to stand?' Mrs Wilding stared at the chair, one wheel spinning uselessly. Likewise, her face was younger, her survival suit tightly wrapped around her. 'And his brain isn't addled?'

'You cured him, Mrs Wilding. Centuries ago. But your Godwanna stopped you realizing it.'

Dent stepped forward, a little unsteady. 'I think I can get the hang of this, Tarwildbaning.'

Mrs Wilding hugged him. 'Are we ready to face Godwanna now?'

'Yes,' said Dent.

'Good,' said Bridgeman.

'Oh, this I've just got to see!'

Godwanna was standing, her arms folded, leaning against the tree that the wheelchair had hit. 'Darlings, are you the best army that can be raised against me? You haven't a hope.' She clicked her fingers.

Out of the bushes, dropping from trees and clambering around flowerbeds were the other occupants of the gar-den. Insane, traumatized and completely bewildered. But

Bridgeman could see it in their eyes – they would follow Godwanna to the bitter end. They were her army.

Godwanna raised her arms forward and flicked her hands upwards. 'Kill them.'

Sand, drifting through her fingers. Like my memories.

Polly jerked herself back to reality. 'Since when did I get so poetic,' she said to no one in particular. She stood and looked across Byron Bay. In the distance was a little island – at least it looked little but it could have been massive. It was hard to say, the mist around it distorted her perceptions. She was annoyingly aware that a lot of her perceptions seemed to have been distorted recently but could not think in what way exactly. Something about a house.

She had taken a long walk. Sidney and Tim had stayed in the motel, looking at road maps for Cairns – or rather Port Douglas, another hour further up the coast. She had never found geography interesting and as a non-driver the need to become fascinated by red squiggly lines criss-crossing with blue and yellow ones bored her to tears. Because Daddy's surgery was so far down in Devon, people like Roger and Uncle Charles were always trying to get her to show them the route on a big RAC atlas, but it was all Greek to her. She remembered once having to get Miles, her youngest brother, to call Uncle Charles up and tell him. And Miles was only twelve and he could read maps. Typical.

So she had walked around this supposed hippy commune only to discover it was as commercial and lacking in love, peace and freedom as everywhere else. Presumably the hippy dreams had died shortly after they started. She'd taken a very long stroll up a path to Australia's most easterly point and watched dolphins playing in the water below. She had wandered past a white lighthouse and dodged past tourists posing for any number of ill-focused and ill-constructed photos. There had been some students, English ones, and that stirred something in her memory. Maybe this elusive house had something to do with students.

'Whoops, sorry, lady.'

A young blond Australian had knocked into her, trying to evade his girlfriend's plastic bag of water. The thrown bag exploded at Polly's feet, wetting them.

'Oh Jeez, I'm sorry.' The girl had her hand over her mouth.

The boy just stared. 'Laurel, you can be so dumb at times!' He scooped the bag up and saw Polly's soaked ankles. The water had gone inside her shoes. 'I'm really sorry.'

'It's all right,' Polly murmured. In her mind's eye, she saw the white bag explode at her feet over and over again. White. Explode.

The train trip. Short. The plane trip. Short. The passport, the money. False. No Newcastle stopover. The unreal car and equally unreal driver, Sidney. The short trip from Sydney airport. Polly's mind had been manipulated. Time had been accelerated.

Once upon a time, Polly described herself as weedy, easily frightened. Once upon a time, that was true, but her brief time with the Doctor had begun to cure that – she was learning to stand on her own two feet.

And she had been tricked. Manipulated. Those poor kids in Cumbria, they had been left to die. The Cat-Person, reduced to a kitten. Charlie Coates – had he really gone back to his Gatehouse and been blown up or was he already dead by then?

The tarot cards – an attempt to throw doubt on the Doctor and Ben – but Polly believed in the tarot, her internal powers, her long-mocked dowsing prowess and in ley lines. She had been manipulated; she was being used by someone who needed her power to find his way home.

Tim.

Atimkos.

No hero. No tall dark stranger to whisk her off her

221

feet. Polly understood it all now – and she did not like it.

Now, sifting the sand through her fingers, her memories painful but intact, her whole mind and body bewildered but strong, she was ready for a fight. She stood up and walked the short distance to where Sidney's 'car' was parked.

Tim and Sidney were leaning on it, looking at a map.

'Don't bother with the map, Tim. You can take us directly there now. Your charade is over.' Polly whipped the map out of Sidney's hand.

'Hey, Miss Wright, that's my –'

Polly ignored him. She pointed at Tim. 'You used me. Tried to tap into whatever natural powers I may or may not have. All you had to do was ask nicely.'

Tim smiled. 'No, asking wasn't enough I'm afraid, Polly. I need strength – your strength. The strength of anger or fear.' He waved around him. 'And I'm using it now. Feel it, Polly. I can see a songline linking us to Godwanna's hide-out already forming. The Earth is reacting to your strength, lighting the beacons.' He raised his arms up. 'Yes, feel that power.'

Polly was furious. 'Stop it, you pig! Stop using me!'

Tim shrugged at Sidney. 'Sorry, mate.' He touched Sidney who, along with his car, vanished leaving a ball of white light glowing on Tim's hand. Pure psychic energy. 'Use it, Polly! Use your anger!'

Polly could not stop herself. She was crying in frustration. 'Stop it, you'll destroy the world!'

Tim was yelling incoherently. Polly stared around her, the sky was flashing like some strobe light, black, white, black, white. Polly watched as the glass in nearby cars cracked and then splintered as Tim's pitched screams got higher. The roads were trembling. The glass in the hotels, houses and shops similarly exploded. People inside and in the street did not have time to panic. In her mind's eye Polly could see the boy and girl with the bag of water hugging each other as their world began to shudder and crumble. She saw them, all the tourists, all the people

222

around her, freeze and begin to change. Starting from the ground and going up, their bodies stiffened and became glass. For one instant all life on planet Earth except herself and Tim (if he was really alive anyway) was made of glass. Every tree. Every blade of grass. Every house, car, train and aeroplane in the sky. Every cloud, every puff of cigarette smoke — all glass.

The sun was glass. The moon was glass.

Only she and Tim were flesh and blood.

The ground shattered open and the white light, the energy like that in Tim's hand, roared up into the heavens as it had in Cumbria. Then, with the largest shattering she had ever heard, Earth and everything on it shattered into atom-sized particles of glass and then winked out of existence for ever.

It was all over.

Episode Six

The trouble with letting aliens aboard the ship, Aall decided, was that they had an annoying tendency to get themselves lost. Frequently, a long, protracted search would reveal them to be somewhere in the depths of the ship's engine rooms, mewling pitifully for food, succour and warmth. Aall would then have to drag them back to the main areas, warm them up, feed them and then report to the Queen that the problem was solved.

Normally Queen Aysha would execute the stupid aliens and that was that. Aall would then consider the last hour a total waste of time and wonder what would happen if they just left the silly creatures to starve/freeze/jettison themselves to death.

This one was different — Queen Aysha clearly had no intention of shooting it, or offering it to the neutered sire-stock to play with. No, she wanted it dragged to her litter-room and talk with it. Talk? With an anthropoid? After all the years of campaigning they had been involved in, Aall had yet to meet an anthropoid with an IQ larger than a house mouse. Still, Her Majesty seemed rather taken with this Doctor-thing. Even Chosan seemed slightly awed by it. Aall decided it must be a very special anthropoid to warrant awe from first-sired Chosan.

To her right, Tensing was sifting through the litter-trays that had yet to be expelled into space. Not the most pleasant of jobs but one which, as a ginger, Tensing deserved. Genetic throwbacks alarmed Aall, not through any bigotry on her part, but simply experience. A genetic throwback rarely had the instinct for battle and by rights a ginger female ought to have been a cook or menial, or a courtesan to keep the sire-stock amused until the breeding season was right. Instead, Tensing had been promoted by Lotuss to her Tactical Corps (a rather grandiose word, Aall decided, for security team) and Aall was therefore using her to hunt the alien Doctor.

On her left was the somewhat more reliable lithe black form of Tamora, a veteran of the Cadmore campaign who had distinguished herself by bringing her scout team back alive and safe, if not entirely in one piece. Tamora and her sister Feebi were now highly ranked in Lotuss's Tactical Corps, but Aall also knew they were loyal to Queen Aysha. Tensing's loyalty to anyone other than herself had yet to be proven.

They slowly walked down the tubular corridor, Aall's nose twitching with the rather heavy smell that permeated the stale air – the unsurprising but pungent residue of forty-five Cat-People (or rather forty-four since the oh-so-sad loss of Jayde). Tensing seemed not to worry – she was either being a model Cat-Person or was too stupid to know how unpleasant her task was. Tamora was far more alert, swinging her rifle-blaster around at every flickering shadow, ready to shoot anything she saw. Well, that was the intention anyway – her blaster was of course powered down: a stray shot puncturing the bulkhead could be rather unfortunate for all concerned. Hopefully this Doctor would not realize that. Mind you, if he was intelligent as they said he –

'Ah! It's Lieutenant Aall, isn't it? We met in the shuttle bay.'

The Doctor was sitting on top of a particularly rancid section of used litter, kicking his heels into it and sending tiny pebbles cascading down. Aall wondered if the anthropoids of Earth ever washed; if they did, the sheer repulsiveness of the litter ought to have stopped him ever going near it. 'Doctor. What are you doing up there? My associates and I have been searching everywhere for you.

225

And I'm the chief engineer actually.'

'Sorry. Is that demotion or promotion?'

'Neither. It's an executive job; it has no military rank, merely a command base.' Aall waved Tamora's (useless) gun away. 'Anyway, I doubt you've been hiding down here pondering the hierarchy of the Cat-People. And if you have, I'll be rather . . . shall we say, disappointed.'

'Why's that then?' He stared at her and she was struck by his green eyes. Very similar to those of her own people. Interesting.

'Because, Doctor, your intelligence is reported as being far higher than that. And hiding in our refuse area to discover the secrets of said hierarchy doesn't immediately suggest an above average IQ.' Aall held out a paw and he took it, allowing himself to be led down. She sniffed a little too loudly.

'Oh, don't worry, I don't mind the smell.' He smiled and turned away from her, pouncing towards Tensing who, for a Tactical Corps, jumped back in ill-disguised alarm. Aall sighed. 'I was actually examining the bomb that's been placed here. See? Right behind this pile of . . . er . . . unwanted stuff.'

Aall nodded at Tamora who shouldered her rifle-blaster and wandered towards the Doctor. 'See, right there,' he was saying. Before Tamora got a close enough look he was running back over, pointing back to the 'bomb' with both hands. 'Now, if you'll listen carefully to me, I can defuse it. Well, I hope I can.' He suddenly looked rather lost. 'Yes, I do hope I can because if I can't, then this ship will explode and we'll all die.'

'Explosions do that, Doctor. Every kitten knows that.'

The Doctor nodded furiously. 'Yes, yes I'm sure. The Cat-People are famous for their ruthlessness. But look at this. It's one of your own bombs.'

Aall shot Tamora a glance and the black cat nodded in confirmation.

'Oh, thank you for your trust,' said the Doctor. He was getting quite agitated. 'Now, can we try to defuse it or is a

226

visit to your Queen Mother more important?'

Aall considered. 'Why would a Cat-Person place a bomb on the bulkhead down here? It would not destroy the ship, merely put a hole in it.'

'A large hole though.'

'Yes, all right, a large hole. A very large hole. But not a life-threatening one.' Aall waved her paws around the tunnel. 'I mean, let's face it, blowing a wall out of a toilet is hardly going to destroy us, is it? The sealants would activate instantly.'

The Doctor held up a finger. 'Ah, it's not where it's been placed but *where* it's been placed that's important.' He smiled as if his double-talk should have explained everything.

Aall scratched her head. 'Important? Oh, of course it is. Doctor, as an engineer I can tell you that the positioning of that bomb would open a hole approximately three metres square. The door seals would come down within forty seconds. The air in here and a great deal of waste products would be shot into space – not a bad idea, I concur – but no lives would be lost and my engines would quickly compensate.'

The Doctor shuffled his feet. 'I'm sorry, Engineer Aall, but you have overlooked something. Something that I thought was rather important.'

'And that is?' Aall saw Tamora prepare to wander back over but she signalled for the trooper to stay put. For now. Tamora nodded her acknowledgement.

The Doctor dropped to the floor, cross-legged. He started riffling through his pockets, producing an assortment of objects of various shapes and colours so rapidly Aall gave up trying to follow his movements. Within a moment there was a pile of . . . of rubbish that simply couldn't have existed inside two tiny pockets. As if sensing her astonishment, the Doctor looked up and smiled, his blue eyes glinting in the low light.

Blue eyes . . . ?

'Marvellous pockets, aren't they?' He suddenly

produced a small round object on a gold chain from the centre of the pile. 'Ah, there it is — given to me by an old school friend at our academy's graduation ceremony. Last I heard he was into selling illegal fake TARDISes to the Andromedans.' He held it up and it managed to glitter in the dim surroundings. 'It's a fob watch. It tells the time.'

Aall dropped to her haunches. 'I'm sure this is very interesting, watches, pockets, bombs —'

'Cat-People bombs,' he reminded her.

'Yes, all right. Cat-People bombs. But, to coin a phrase, so what?'

The Doctor looked shocked. 'Don't you want to know what the bomb's for?'

'Going bang!' Tamora clearly could not contain herself any longer.

Aall did not blame her. 'Was Being Infuriating a course at this academy of yours, Doctor?' She stood up again and waved Tensing over. 'Take the Doctor back up to the Queen's litter level.'

Before Tensing had taken a step the Doctor was up and back over by the bomb, ignoring Tamora who, rather pointlessly, swung her rifle-blaster off her shoulder. He pushed it away. 'It's empty,' he muttered. 'You're all too good at your jobs to carry primed energy weapons in this confined space, so close to a bulkhead.'

'Oh, just take over, Doctor. Be our guest.' Aall caught up with him. 'So, what's this bomb for?'

The Doctor grinned. 'Caught your attention at last, have I? Good. Now look at the bomb. When is it set to go off?'

'You tell me.'

The Doctor sighed and turned his head slightly. 'Oh, really, Aall, you're not being at all helpful. If I could read Cat-People writing I wouldn't have had to wait for you to catch up with me, would I?'

Tensing obviously decided to use her initiative. 'One hour from now,' she said.

228

The Doctor said thanks and Aall sighed at Tensing's childish grin. 'So,' he continued. 'It'll go off in an hour. Bang. Kaput. Tell me, Chief Engineer, using your expertise as a mercenary killer as well as a starship engineer, what will be the effect on this section of bulkhead when it goes off?'

Intrigued, despite herself, Aall traced around the bomb with her paw. 'Interesting. The bomb has been attached manually, rather than magnetically as they're designed to do. It's angled downwards.'

'Which means?' hurried the Doctor, waving his hands around in every direction.

'Which means,' Aall concluded with professional pride, 'that it will explode out and upwards at around thirty-five degrees.'

'Velocity?'

Aall sighed. 'Difficult.'

The Doctor nodded. 'OK. How much bulkhead goes with it?'

Tamora spoke up. 'None, surely. The bomb will destroy, not remove.'

Aall shook her head, twitching her whiskers at the sudden excitement of the alien's theory. 'No, Tamora. Not at this angle. The explosion will rip the bulkhead open first, before the main ignition vaporizes it – which by exploding straight upwards will be extinguished by the outrush of air.'

The Doctor grabbed Aall's paw. 'Yes, you're getting there. Go on!'

Aall wrenched her paws free. 'So up goes a small but immensely powerful lump of bulkhead – three square metres, as I said, but fused into a smaller, heavier lump.'

'Dwarf star alloy, I presume?' said the Doctor. 'Most battle-cruisers I've seen use it.'

'Technical secrets, Doctor, but there is a certain trace element of DSA in the metalwork.'

'Enough,' the Doctor spoke slowly and clearly, underlining his points by jabbing a finger at the bomb, 'enough to turn our shard of metal bulkhead into a very heavy lump akin to a small meteor. Am I right?'

Aall nodded.

'And what is three levels above us?'

Tensing spoke up again. 'Shuttle Bay Eleven. Why?'

'Because,' the Doctor dropped down and began shoving everything back into his pockets, 'that's where I was brought in. Which means that's from where Queen Aysha's shuttle will depart when she leaves to invade Earth. In, oh about . . . ?'

'One hour,' Tamora hissed.

'I think your Queen owes me one, as my friend Ben would say.'

Aall watched aghast and the Doctor turned and walked out of the tunnel and towards the light. He was playing a little tune on a pipe he put to his mouth.

Able Seaman (Radar) Ben Jackson was mentally kicking his heels. He felt rather out of place standing next to a pile of plush red cushions in a room full of silk drapes, soft rugs and a beaded hanging curtain that represented the door to the corridor outside. Give me the hard metal of a ship's bows, with the thumping noise of engines, sweat and swearing and a distinct lack of charm and glamour. That was a ship. This finery, this comfort, was a total antithesis of what Ben considered 'a ship'.

Queen Aysha was curled up on a cushion. Chosan and Nihmrod flanking her. All three were watching a television screen (in colour – for a moment Ben had assumed it was imported from America and then realized where he was). On it another Cat-Person was speaking and without having to listen to her rasping hisses, Ben knew she was very, very old. He guessed that she was some kind of commanding officer and even he felt like standing to attention. He was, therefore, surprised to realize that, considering how strict a disciplinarian Aysha was, neither she nor her two cohorts seemed particularly reverent about listening to the old CO.

Deciding it must be a bit like the Queen's Speech on the Home Service on Christmas Day – and some of his shipmates found that boring – Ben strained to listen.

'. . . *and so it becomes imperative that all manned battle-cruisers return to Feles as soon as possible. The requirements for energy are getting more and more desperate. No matter which end of the twelve galaxies you are in, head back now. If only a few of you manage to return within twelve months, all will not be lost. Feles will use whatever energies you have acquired to replenish itself.*

'*Hurry, my kittens. Your people need you now.*'

Aysha cleaned her whiskers nonchalantly and twitched her tail towards the remote, cutting the screen off. 'Delay?'

Nihmrod consulted a pocket diary-sized contraption that Ben couldn't hope to understand. She popped her claws and flicked them rapidly over some indentations, and Ben saw a tiny green screen glow, strange squiggles that he assumed was Cat-People writing flashing across it. 'Twelve days, Your Majesty.'

Chosan snarled. 'Our Pride Mother has dishonoured us. She has used an open-subspace channel to communi-cate a message of despair and panic. Any number of our foes and predators could have intercepted it.'

Aysha considered this. 'And so?'

'And so,' Chosan was angry, 'we should ignore her.'

Nihmrod dropped her device and stared at Chosan. 'Ignore the Pride Mother? Even with a twelve-day delay, that message could still be important. Our friends and family –'

'Are long-since dead, I suspect,' said Aysha. 'If Feles is that desperate for energy, rest assured what reserves there are, or were, will have been fed directly to the Pride Mother and her retinue. I see little point in returning to a dead world before our mission is accomplished.'

'And what exactly is your mission?' Ben had not seen the Doctor enter but was very glad he had, despite the rather rude tone of his voice. Cat-Person or not, Aysha

231

was Queen and clearly preferred to be treated as such.

The Queen unfurled herself and stretched upright, preening the fur around her mouth as she did so. 'Ah, Doctor. So good of you to join us. Did you have a nice exploration?'

'Oh yes.' The Doctor was all smiles and expansive gestures. 'It was very rewarding. Wouldn't you agree, Chief Engineer Aall?'

Ben had not seen the tall, long-haired grey cat hovering in the doorway. She looked a little flustered, her whiskers twitching in a manner Ben had come to associate with worry. 'The Doctor has made some disturbing . . . discoveries, Your Majesty.'

'Go on, Doctor.'

Ben listened in astonishment as his fellow traveller explained about the bomb, its priming and the trajectory of its ultimate explosion. Queen Aysha seemed to take it all very matter-of-factly. Ben was reminded of the very first captain he had served under who, on discovering Ben's lack of years, instead of keelhauling him (or whatever they did in the merchant navy), just sat and listened to his explanations about his step-father, his mother, his late father and other angst that most fourteen-year-olds consider the worst things in the world. The captain had merely nodded at the relevant pauses and in the end offered Ben a proper job on his fifteenth birthday.

'But, sir, that's four months away!' he had complained.

The captain had just shrugged. 'And we're in the Far East now, Jackson. How long d'you think it takes a cargo ship to return to Tilbury?'

'Four months?' Ben ventured.

The captain had smiled. 'I'm sure we can keep you occupied in the galley or engine-room, earning your keep until then. Unless you'd rather be put off at the next port of call?'

'No.' Ben had saluted. 'No, sir. Thank you, sir. Very good, sir.'

Aysha had taken the details with the same calmness,

and however much he disliked her, Ben admired her. Respected her. All a good CO could ask for really. After a moment she pointed towards the corridor and Nihmrod went out, looked around and returned, shaking her head. 'Good,' the Queen said. 'What about Tamora and Tensing? How was the test?'

Aall straightened her shoulders and made her report. 'Tamora's loyal to you, I'm sure.'

'I hope so,' said Chosan. 'If she were working for Lotuss, by now the discovery of the bomb would be known and Lotuss would have to find another way.'

'Wouldn't have to if the Doctor hadn't saved your hides,' murmured Ben.

'True, anthropoid-tom,' said Aysha. 'A fact that I have noted.' She looked to Aall again. 'And Tensing?'

'Difficult to tell exactly. By rights, she's well in Lotuss's pride. However, she was certainly as astonished by the bomb as us.'

Chosan took Nihmrod's device and poked at it herself. 'Interesting. Lotuss has assigned her guard duty for you, Your Majesty. On the invasion shuttle.'

Aysha cocked her head slightly and hissed a smile, her tongue caressing her teeth. Ben noticed how sharp they were. Very sharp. He would not like to think how quickly she would be able to disarm him. Literally. 'A shuttle that we won't be taking. Lotuss has made her move slightly earlier than I expected.'

'Excuse me,' piped up the Doctor, 'but Ben and I aren't really part of all your politics and catawauling.' Ben winced, but the Doctor continued. 'Couldn't we just go back to Earth?'

'Sorry,' said Aysha without any trace of apology. 'Sorry, but we need you here. For now. We need your TARDIS, remember?'

'Why?' Ben still had not figured that one out.

The Doctor answered. 'Because, Ben, Queen Aysha has a weird idea that I can take her back forty thousand years in it, to find the beacons when they were new.'

'But I thought they were more powerful in 1994.'

'Yes, but Fräulein Thorsuun saw to it that we couldn't find them.'

Chosan joined in. 'The ridiculous creature had forgotten where they were.'

The Doctor nodded. 'So it's better to get less of something than nothing at all. Hence the TARDIS.'

'But don't they realize,' Ben laughed, 'that you can't control it? If you tried to get us back forty thousand years, we'll probably end up on Venus in a million years' time!'

The Doctor frowned. 'Thank you for your confidence.'

Ben was not giving up. 'Yeah, but I'm right, ain't I? Haven't got me and Pol back to July '66 yet, eh?'

Aysha hissed. 'Is this true? Can you not pilot your own craft?'

The Doctor cleared his throat and shoved his hands deep into his pockets. 'Yes. Well. Ben puts it a little less tactfully than I'd have liked, but fundamentally, that's true.' He looked up and grinned. 'Sorry.'

Aysha stared for a moment. Then: 'Oh well, eject his TARDIS into space, Chosan. I don't need extra weight on board.'

'What? You mean the TARDIS is here?' The Doctor almost jumped for joy. 'That's excellent.'

'While we were in Baghdad, Aall located it and transported it here. Why?'

'Because, Your Majesty, I can get in it with Ben and leave. Go away. Leave you behind.'

'Then what?' Chosan was frowning in that way that cats do, Ben decided. Cats always had that haunted look back aboard ship when they thought their food was late — a sort of disdainful glare that made their eyes look heavy and therefore wrinkled their foreheads. Chosan looked just like that now.

The Doctor smiled expansively. 'Then you can invade Earth in 1994 and try to find the beacons. You'd get about two miles into the atmosphere before they launched an all-out atomic strike and you'd be destroyed in about thirty seconds.'

'Like the Z-Bomb at the South Pole?' Ben asked.

The Doctor nodded. 'Exactly, Ben, but another eight years has made their cruise missiles and the like even more powerful. Mankind has developed some very impressive weaponry by this decade, Your Majesty. I doubt you'd find the combined might of the USA and USSR quite as easy to kick aside as a few Arabian peasants.'

Aysha shrugged. 'We were safe in Cumbria. We could infiltrate slowly and cripple their world before they knew we were there.'

Ben started laughing aloud. 'Oh, come on. Overgrown pussycats? You'd be spotted in an instant – if they didn't kill you, you'd be in a zoo.'

'Ben's right. A curiosity is all you'd be, Queen Aysha. Prodded and poked by those you despise.' The Doctor waved his hand around the room, catching one of the silk drapes and nearly tugging it down. He extricated himself. 'You could say goodbye to all this.'

Queen Aysha looked at Aall. At Chosan. At Nihmrod. Then at the blank screen from where the Pride Mother had delivered her plea. 'You're right, Doctor. I have no desire to lead my pride to death or dishonour. I thank you for alerting me to Lotuss's bomb. It seems only fair to allow you to leave peacefully – Nihmrod, escort our . . . friends to their blue box. Cargo bay 2.'

Confused but obedient, Nihmrod moved towards the bead curtain. 'This way, Doctor,' she said.

The Doctor bowed to Queen Aysha. 'Your Majesty, I sincerely hope you return home safely.'

'Thank you, Doctor. You are most kind.' She waved a paw at the curtain.

Ben let himself bow just enough to be polite and followed the Doctor out. 'What was that all about?' he whispered. 'We can't just leave!'

'Why not?'

Ben was appalled. 'Polly! What about Polly? You can't leave her stranded in 1994!'

Nihmrod called the lift. 'Oh, she'll be all right, Ben,' she said cheerfully. 'It's only about thirty years out of time. She'll adjust in no time.'

'Oh. And what about your famous "web of time"? Won't that be a little disrupted?' Ben couldn't believe it. Abandon Polly? 'The old Doctor –' He stopped, but it was too late. As they got in the lift, the Doctor glared at him.

'The "old Doctor what?" Ben? Hmm? Wouldn't be callous? Wouldn't dump Polly? Rubbish, Ben, you know nothing about "the old Doctor". The old me! If you ever get home, look up Ian and Barbara, my old friends. Ask them about the caveman. Or should we ever return to find poor Steven, just mention the name Anne Chaplette and see what effect that has on him. Even Dodo – she'd have some stories to tell. Don't presume to place your pathetic human morals, ideology and nuances upon me, Benjamin Jackson.'

'Oh, do shut up!' snapped Nihmrod. 'You two bicker worse than three-month-old kittens in the breeding pens!'

'Shut up yourself,' replied the Doctor. 'And – whooaa!' The Doctor suddenly careered into Ben, pushing him against the side of the lift. The Doctor then fell back against Nihmrod, slamming her into the lift controls. An alarm went off immediately. 'Oh, do excuse me,' he said, suddenly pushing Nihmrod aside. 'I'm so sorry about that. I must be getting giddy. Let me try to repair it.' He wrenched open the lift-control panelling, and Nihmrod tried to stop him. For a second Ben, confused, angry and alarmed, saw the Doctor wink at him. And then it became clear. He was up to something – all that shouting was a distraction for Nihmrod. He was not really going to abandon Polly after all. 'Oh, what have I done?' the Doctor wailed and wrenched a few feet of clear plastic cabling out of the panelling.

'I don't know,' Nihmrod wailed back. 'I'm not a technician!'

'Hold this, Ben.' The Doctor held some cable out. 'And you.' He passed a dead end to Nihmrod. 'Now, if I put that in here – or is it here – that should stop the alarm.' He wrenched out another cable which began sparking and spitting in front of him. 'Oh dear, oh dear,' he cried, holding the wire in front of him as if it were a snake wriggling to escape. 'Oh, Ben, I can't control it!' With which he stepped back and jammed the end against the dead end Nihmrod held. 'Ben! Drop it!' he yelled. The cable was already hitting the floor as a blue arc of energy whipped around their heads, catching Nihmrod at the centre, smashing her against the back wall of the lift, unconscious. There was an uncomfortable smell of singed cat fur.

'You enjoyed that,' Ben panted.

'I did not,' the Doctor retorted.

'Yes you did.' Ben checked Nihmrod for a neck pulse. 'She's stunned.'

'Oh, good. In that case, yes, I did enjoy it. Now, let's get out of here. Can you force the door?'

'What if we're in between floors?'

The Doctor sighed. 'Oh, Ben, give me some credit. We're on level 2 – where the TARDIS apparently is.'

Ben shrugged, pushed his hands against the sliding door and pushed. And pushed. 'It . . . it's giving,' he said.

'Well, save your breath and push.'

'You could . . . help, you know,' Ben felt the door begin to give. It gave and he fell through the gap on to the soft carpet of level 2.

'You only had to ask.' The Doctor marched past. 'Cargo bay 2. This way I think.'

As the Doctor and Ben were led out, Chosan turned to her Queen. 'I don't understand, Your Majesty.'

'You will, first-sired, you will. Meanwhile, we have a litter-runt to deal with.' She looked across at Aall. 'How long before the bomb goes off?'

Aall consulted her own data-pad. 'Fifteen minutes.'

Aysha punched a control on her screen remote-control and the bridge popped into view.

'Your Majesty.' Jodi bowed.

Aysha bowed back. 'How is the conn?'

Jodi paused for the briefest of seconds, acknowledging the coded question. 'Secure at command. Helm and nav report no problems but are wary, as always.' Jodi was telling her Queen that Nypp and Tuq, Lotuss's agents, were still there. 'Tactical is calm. Communications are ever ready.'

So, Lotuss was not there. Good. But Tensing was, at the communications console. She must have returned there immediately after leaving the refuse area. Which meant Lotuss could not know that the bomb had been discovered – and Chosan wondered where she might be.

Queen Aysha threw Aall a look and then back to Jodi. 'I am ready to begin the invasion of Earth, Jodi. I require Nypp and Tuq at Shuttle bay eleven in five minutes. Keep communications at standard.' In other words, Chosan realized, keep Tensing on the bridge.

Jodi paused. 'Shall I join you?'

Chosan smiled. Jodi was very good.

'No, Jodi.' Queen Aysha twitched her whiskers. 'You keep the conn.'

Jodi bowed. 'Good hunting, Your Majesty.'

'Good hunting.' Aysha smiled and broke the connection. 'When this is over, Aall, I want her promoted.'

Aall laughed. 'I understand that there could be a vacancy for tactical officer shortly.'

Chosan also smiled. 'I'll send out the application forms when we get back.'

Aysha looked serious. 'We must play this carefully. Aall, I'm risking a lot on the fact that Lotuss is too paranoid to have told anyone in her ridiculous pride about the bomb. Therefore Nypp and Tuq will be as unaware as Lotuss.' She crossed to the doorway. 'Chosan, you and I will collect Lotuss from her quarters. Aall, prepare the shuttle. Get them aboard before we bring Lotuss.'

Aall bowed. 'Mother.' She left first.

Chosan led the way. 'Lotuss won't go to Shuttle bay eleven easily.'

Aysha laughed. 'Oh yes she will, daughter. Watch.'

Moments later they were in Lotuss's quarters. The litter-runt rose, none too quickly, from her cushion. Chosan knew she was pushing Aysha to see what she could get away with.

'Lotuss. I require your help.' Aysha smiled. 'I am leaving for Earth with Aall immediately.'

'Shall I prepare you a shuttle?' Lotuss was so polite.

Aysha shook her head. 'No need, my child. The one we returned in is ready – you know how I hate to waste time. Shuttle bay eleven will do adequately.'

'As you desire, Mother. What can I do to help?'

'Two things. Firstly, I do not trust Jodi on the bridge. You will remove her from command once I am gone, thereby not reflecting the action on me. After all, once I am in deep space, I cannot stop you doing whatever you believe is right for command.'

'I am not joining you?'

Aysha shrugged. 'I know you enjoy killing, Lotuss, but Chosan needs you here more. I want you to work together on improving our weaponry. The Doctor was certainly right about Earth's defences. I want a pulse trigger built that will set off every nuclear-powered device on the planet simultaneously. If nothing else, it'll rip the thing apart and we'll absorb the energy that way.'

'And when do we use it?'

Aysha smiled again. 'Preferably when I return empty-handed. I am trying to locate the buoys one last time.'

They began walking towards the shuttle bay. 'I wish you good hunting, Your Majesty,' Lotuss said.

Aall stood outside the bay entrance. 'Your command crew are aboard the shuttle, Your Majesty.'

Aysha twitched her whiskers. 'Good. Shall we go?'

Lotuss opened the bay doors, revealing the shuttle. Chosan looked into the bay control room.

Tamora. Excellent.

The bay door dropped behind them. Aall, Chosan and Aysha began walking towards the shuttle. Lotuss paused and then followed.

'Why are both hatches open?' Aysha demanded.

Aall shrugged. 'I'm sorry, Your Majesty, I don't know.'

Chosan nudged Lotuss and pointed at the rear hatch. With a sigh, Lotuss nodded and went to close it.

The alarm screamed at them, followed by Tamora's panicking voice over the intercom. 'Decompression! The outer doors have circuit-jumped. They're opening!'

Lotuss, near the open hatchway at the back of the shuttle, heard the alarm and Tamora's voice. Decompression took four seconds – she hurled herself into the open hatchway, praising Chosan sarcastically for sending her there. Slamming it shut with the emergency lever, she saw Nypp doing the same with the side one.

Nypp? Why was she here? And Tuq. And . . .

'Nypp! State of decompression in the bay?'

Nypp stabbed at a control. 'I don't understand – there's no decompression. It was a false alarm.'

Lotuss looked through the window and saw Chosan and Aall escorting Aysha through the closing bay door, back into the corridor.

'Whoops. Sorry about that. False alarm.' Tamora's voice crackled through the communicator. 'Shuttle preparing to launch now. Strap yourself in. Good hunting.'

Tuq was frowning. 'I thought the Queen was –'

Lotuss leaped forward, pushing Tuq aside. She stabbed the comm-switch. 'Tamora! Don't you dare!'

'Decompression completed. Your navigation controls appear to be locked out, Lotuss. Sorry, I'll guide you out with the tractor beam.'

'I confirm that,' said Nypp. 'They're moving us. Controls should re-engage when we're outside the ship's shields.'

'No! No, no no!' Lotuss slammed her paw into the console.

The shuttle was free of the bay and in space. The tractor beam — or rather Tamora — gave it a push.

'Free of shields in ten seconds.' Nypp punched her navigation and helm controls. 'Still locked.' She frowned. 'I don't get it.'

'Time,' shrieked Lotuss. 'What time is it?'

She did not hear Tuq's response. All she saw out of one window was a flash from two bulkheads below the shuttle bay. The refuse area.

She breathed deeply and allowed herself a grim smile. Outwitted in a style she thought only she was capable of.

'I misjudged you, Mother.' As her missile struck the shuttle the floor erupted. Nypp was sucked straight out, Tuq crushed by the missile as it hit the propulsion unit. In her mind's eye, Lotuss saw Aysha, Chosan and Aall laughing at her.

'Damn.'

The shuttle, and litter-runt Lotuss, disintegrated in a burst of fire that was instantly extinguished by the vacuum.

'Are you all right?'

Polly opened her eyes and promptly shut them again — there was a glare of brilliant white, which she recognized. From where?

After a few more seconds she tried again and quickly adjusted to the brightness. Looking at her were two vaguely familiar people, but she could not place them straight away.

'Well done, Polly. You got us here.'

She recognized that voice, even if she could not see him. Her heart sank. Despite her beliefs, Polly knew in her heart that the concept of Heaven as a physical place you go to after dying was a nonsense. Wherever she was, she was both alive and trapped. With Tim. She propped herself up on her elbows and looked around. Tim was sitting cross-legged about four feet away from her. He looked different – his face less weathered and his hair more meticulously shaped. He was wearing a dark one-piece jumpsuit. So were the other two people near by – although, as they were standing over her, they were far enough away from Tim to let her know that they were not best friends.

Mrs Wilding and Mr Dent. Looking younger and, in Dent's case, somewhat less crippled. They too were wearing the black suits. Polly reasoned that this was all three's real appearance.

Mrs Wilding held out her hand to Polly who gratefully allowed herself to be pulled up.

'Excuse me. Everyone else turned to glass and I'm feeling fragile myself.'

Tim laughed. 'I didn't know you were such a wit, Polly.'

'I didn't know you were such a –'

Dent took Polly's arm. 'Let us tell you what is going on, shall we?'

Polly looked at him, looked into his younger, less-pain-wracked eyes. 'That would be nice. Is the Doctor here?'

'No. Not yet, anyway, although we believe he will be soon.' Mrs Wilding moved aside and Polly saw the two men she'd last seen in her dream: Professor Bridgeman and the stranger.

'Professor! Are you all right?'

'I am now, thanks to Mrs Wilding. How are Simon and the others?'

Polly began to say something, and then realized she couldn't. The memory, now unburied, flashed through her mind – the Grange enveloped by the white light, the unbridled energy of Earth released in its purest form. Destroying everything.

'They're dead, Bridgeman. Vaporized. Burned. Crisped. Zappo.' Tim got up. 'Terribly bad show, old chap. Still, plenty more back in London, eh? Students are two a penny, I think.' He paused to take in Bridgeman's reaction. There wasn't one. The human was just staring. Tim shrugged. 'Actually, I'm wrong. There aren't any more. We activated the beacons and destroyed Earth. Sorry and all that.'

'Where are we?' Bridgeman gently eased the man Polly did not know to the white floor. 'I take it we're not in the garden any more?'

Dent agreed. 'We're actually within the nexus itself. Outside normal space and time.'

'Why?' It seemed a logical question to Polly.

Tim just laughed again. 'Because I brought you all here.'

'Wrong. *We* did.' Another voice Polly recognized – this time from the same dream in which she had seen the sick Bridgeman.

As one they turned.

'Godwanna,' breathed Mrs Wilding.

Polly saw their nemesis – dressed in another black jumpsuit, but this one dotted with reed decals. Her jet-black hair was tied back and up in a severe pony-tail, and her face was set in the most insincere smile Polly could ever imagine seeing. It was like someone had taken a corpse and fixed its mouth into a rictus grin. If the eyes were not so staring, so powerful, Polly could have believed she was the embodiment of the traditional zombie. Her skin was stretched tight over her bones, giving her an attractive but harsh appearance.

'Welcome, my children. Welcome, survivors of the human race.' She nodded to Tim. 'A shame you couldn't find your way to returning Thorgarsuunela to us.'

Tim shrugged. 'She's dead. Sorry.'

'No matter.' She walked over and stroked his cheek. 'You served me well, child.'

Mrs Wilding took a step forward. 'He was working with you? All this time?'

'Of course, Tarwildbaning.' Godwanna put her head on one side. 'Pitiful fool, did you never once consider I

243

had help? Am I considered so all-powerful that you believed I arranged this by myself?'

Polly frowned. 'Arranged what?'

Godwanna threw her hands in the air dramatically. 'You, my dear. You and your powers.'

'I don't have powers.'

'Nonsense, sweet child of Earth. All your race have powers. From the earliest men of Africa and Australia to the newborn children born at the very second of your planet's destruction. Your brains have untapped codes and pathways, linking you to the very construction of your world. You all have the power of geopathy: to control, cure, communicate and cultivate. Your planet gave you all these gifts and it has taken Atimkos millennia to find what I needed. Someone whose brain has been opened to its possibilities.'

Polly stared at her. 'When I was younger . . .'

Godwanna waved her down. 'Yes, child, I'm sure your powers have manifested themselves slightly. They do with a few million of your race every thousand years. But your travel with the Doctor, crossing the boundaries of time and space, they cleared those neural pathways even better. Gave us something to focus in on.'

'The dream . . .' Polly frowned. 'The Cat-People I saw?' She looked at Tim. 'You put them there?'

'Sort of. The dream was your own brain's attempts to warn you, cloud your judgement as I broke through to you. The human brain is quite delicate, you know.'

Dent joined in. 'So it knew it was being manipulated – showed Polly the Cat-People as a warning of the future if she allowed herself to become involved with you.'

Bridgeman nodded. 'This is all fascinating. And true, I'm sure. But why am I here? And Nate Simms?' He looked down at the dribbling childlike face of Nate, who stared back in abject terror.

Godwanna looked him up and down, casually. 'Like everyone in my garden, you all had the potential in you. The beginnings of the power growing. But none of you

244

had the minds capable of coping with my manipulations. Looking at your lucidity now, I fear I misjudged just how powerful Tarwildbaning could be.'

'We helped each other,' Mrs Wilding put in.

'Of course you did, dear. How much more fruitful if you had aided me instead of fighting me.' Godwanna held her fist out and unclasped it. Floating fractionally above her palm was a small ball of light. Energy.

Polly recognized it: it was identical to the one she had seen in Tim's hand just prior to the destruction of Earth.

'It's all here, you know, children. Life, energy, matter. Everything that was the planet Earth is here in my hand.'

'Put it back. Please.' Polly did not know why she said that, it just seemed appropriate.

'Oh, I don't think so. I need this energy. I'm going to use it to add to our own powers. We will sing ourselves home now.'

'What about the Cat-People?' Polly stared at the glowing ball. Life. All life from Earth condensed into one small globe of energy.

Tim answered her question. 'Thorgarsuunela had roughly the same idea, unaware that Godwanna and I had been communicating all these years. She was going to get the Cat-People to release it and use the power to sing just herself home.'

'But I thought the Cat-People wanted the power?'

Tim shrugged. 'Who cares. All Thorgarsuunela had to do was collect the energy and go; she could erase the Cat-People from existence with one note. She just needed their machinery to tap the marker buoys.'

Mrs Wilding and Dent looked at each other, then at Godwanna and Tim. 'This is wrong, recon-leader. We have no right to destroy life like this,' Dent said.

Bridgeman interjected, 'I thought it was too late. Earth is destroyed.'

Polly was beginning to understand. 'No. Not yet — it's been transformed into that ball. Until Godwanna uses it, everything still exists but re-formed.'

Tim clapped sardonically. 'Very good. The bimbo secretary from 1966 finally grasps the physics of the situation.'

'But,' Polly continued, 'if you explode that ball, release the energy and use it to sing yourself home, that will destroy, once and for all, all life on Earth?'

Godwanna nodded enthusiastically. 'Oh dear, so it will.' She gestured expansively. 'Pass on my apologies to the humans, won't you. As you join them of course.' She began to cup the ball in her hands. 'Oh, Tarwildbaning? Udentkista? I'm afraid Atimkos and I will be travelling alone. We only need two voices with all this energy. And we don't need a ship – the nexus can store all this lovely energy. Thorgarsuunela could have discovered that, if she'd bothered to ask. Such a waste.' Godwanna waved insincerely. 'You've been very nice company but it's time to say goodbye. Please don't hate us.'

'Hate,' said a quiet voice beside Bridgeman. He knelt down and hushed Nate, who was frowning.

Tim produced the old brown book the Doctor had retrieved from the Grange's library. Mrs Wilding started. 'You kept the RTC! No wonder those poor human children couldn't save themselves.'

Tim began flicking its pages. 'Speeds up the absorption of the power into the nexus. Devastating in the wrong hands, these things. Can do terrible things.' He smiled at the group in front of him.

'Hate,' muttered Nate Simms.

'Goodbye, y'all.' Tim opened the book and held it out, pages facing Polly and the others. He began flicking the pages, activating the tachyon-chronons . . .

Ben's hand was blistered. He had been hitting the TARDIS door for ages now, trying to force his way in.

'It's no good, Ben,' said the Doctor gloomily. 'Aysha knew we'd do this. She's used an RTC unit' – he pointed to a small bank of equipment to their left – 'to place a field around the lock. The TARDIS exo-shell is built of the hardest, densest and most indestructible materials. You can't force your way in.'

'We can't stay much longer, Doc,' Ben protested. 'Lotuss's bomb'll go off any sec.'

The ship shuddered slightly, as if caught in a wave. It righted itself. 'I think it just did.' The Doctor sighed. 'I think we just have to wait, Ben.'

'Not for long, Doctor.' Queen Aysha, Aall and Chosan stood at the cargo bay hatchway. 'Thank you for waiting. Aall and I would like a lift to the nexus.'

'I told you. He can't fly this thing properly,' Ben said.

Chosan pointed to the RTC unit. 'A gift from Thorgar-suunela. It's tuned in to her people's wavelength. We can't find her marker buoys with it, but it'll lead us to her home dimension, this nexus out of time and space. Or whatever.'

Ben was puzzled. 'Why go there?'

The Doctor clapped his hands. 'She was double-crossing you and you knew it. Our Fräulein Thorsuun seriously misjudged you, Aysha.'

'She saw us as a band of warlike thugs, Doctor. Not our fault.'

'Pretty good description if you ask me,' said Ben.

Chosan crossed to the RTC unit and switched it off with her remote device. 'By the way,' she hissed at the Doctor, 'you'll be pleased to know that Nihmrod will recover. I thought it wise to restrain her in medi-care. Otherwise she might claw your throat out.'

'Nihmrod's like that,' added Aall. 'I just can't seem to correct her violent streak.'

'And Lotuss?' The Doctor stared at the RTC unit.

'Gone, along with the ringleaders of her pride. Tamora is . . . cleaning up the residue.' Aysha noticed his interest in the RTC unit. 'Impressive, isn't it? Chosan adapted it.'

The Doctor seemed genuinely impressed. 'And how is this going to help?'

'Your TARDIS, Doctor. I believe your companion when he says you can't control it. But it can be con-trolled. With an RTC.'

'How?' asked Ben.

The Doctor was nodding. 'It's like a homing beacon. It'll track down other RTCs. Like the ones at the Grange. Or in the nexus.'

Chosan and Aall hoisted up the RTC unit. Aall removed a segment and pocketed it. Chosan carried the rest back towards the doorway. 'Good hunting, Your Majesty.'

Aysha hissed in satisfaction. 'Your door will open now, Doctor. Please take us to their leader.'

'Hate.'

Polly stared in alarm as the odd man she now knew was called Nate, hunched beside Professor Bridgeman, suddenly jumped forward. And ran towards Tim – Atimkos she corrected herself – and Godwanna.

'I hate you,' he cried.

Polly saw a look of panic go between Dent and Mrs Wilding.

Tim looked up, his face a mixture of surprise and amusement. He turned the book/RTC slightly and caught Nate in its chronon-field.

As Polly watched, Nate seemed to stagger, his clothes deteriorated and he grew older. But his momentum kept him going. His cry of 'Hate!' seemed to slow down to a guttural roar and as he thundered into Godwanna, he was now aged about sixty-five. She staggered back, the globe of energy dropping from her hand.

Mrs Wilding let out a screech, causing Polly to put her hands over her ears, but the globe did not hit the floor. Instead it floated and as Mrs Wilding altered her pitch, the globe started to move towards her and Dent.

'No!' roared Tim, dropping the open book to the white floor.

'No!' Godwanna yelped as the pages faced towards her.

Nate Simms was already dead, his flesh vanishing, and within three seconds his skeleton was fading dust. But

Godwanna was now caught in the RTC field. She shook and convulsed. Her mouth opened and closed in soundless shrieks of pain and rage.

Tim stopped and looked at her. And grinned. ' 'Bye, recon-leader.'

Godwanna waved her arms frantically towards the book but it was no good. Tim whistled and the pages flapped over faster.

Polly could do nothing but stare as Godwanna began finally to grow grey, her skin stretching until her face looked like a decayed prune. Her now thin body flopped to the floor and wriggled like a fish out of water.

Then it stopped and she was dead. A few seconds later, her skeleton began snapping and she was dust.

'Oh dear. Poor Godwanna.' Tim stood facing Dent, who held the energy globe. 'Come on, Udentkista. We might not be friends but at least let's use the power to go home. Leave this sector.'

'We've been here for forty thousand years, Atimkos,' Mrs Wilding said. 'This is home now. I doubt our own people even exist any more.'

Tim snarled at her, 'Don't be so pathetic. Let's find out.' He waved his arm towards the dust that had been Godwanna. 'She had us trapped for all that time. Without her, we can do anything.'

'I like Earth.' Dent stared at the globe. 'Everything I like about it is here, in my hand.' He looked at Tim. 'And you want to expend it, destroy it just to go back to a dead world.'

'We don't know it's dead!' shrieked Tim. 'We'll never know unless we go and find out.'

There was a thump from behind them. Polly turned and saw the Doctor, carrying the book, having closed it. 'A dangerous toy, Atimkos. You shouldn't be playing with toys like this.'

Tim was furious. 'How did you get here?'

'We brought him.' Polly saw two Cat-People and Ben standing by the open doorway of the TARDIS. One of

249

the Cat-People was carrying a strange contraption.

'Your world is dead, I'm afraid. By 1994 it had been gone for ten thousand years. You've destroyed Earth for nothing.'

Dent caressed the air around the globe, unable to completely touch it. 'Not destroyed, Doctor. Transformed. With this young lady's help,' he nodded at Polly, 'Tarwildbaning and I can restore it.'

'You can't!' yelled Tim. 'You mustn't!'

'No!' said one of the Cat-People suddenly. 'No, give it to us. We need to power our ship. Return home.'

Ben walked towards Polly. 'Don't believe Aysha. She has no intention of returning to Feles, her world. She just wants the power to continue destroying planets.'

The Doctor tossed the book between his hands. Then he smiled at Aysha, his green eyes glittering. 'Is that so, Your Majesty?'

Aall raised her rifle-blaster. 'That is no concern of yours, alien.' She moved the blaster to cover the Euterpians. 'Please surrender the energy globe.'

Tim laughed. 'Shut up, pussycat. You have no idea of the power you're dealing with here. None of you have.'

Aall stepped forward. And began dying as Tim shrieked a long, piercing note straight at her. For a split second her body vibrated, and she staggered, lumps of fur and flesh vanishing. As she dropped to the ground, her rifle-blaster clattered in front of Aysha. 'Mother . . .' she hissed and disintegrated.

'Who's next?' spat Tim. 'I'm not joking. I am going home.'

'Good hunting,' murmured Queen Aysha at the fading dust that was once Aall. She bared her teeth and hissed, 'Your life is mine, Euterpian.'

Dent suddenly darted sideways, tossing the globe at the Doctor, who in turn threw the RTC/book to Mrs Wilding.

'Well done,' the Doctor called as he, Polly and Dent ran to the open TARDIS.

Tim shoved Ben aside as he followed, but the TARDIS door was slammed in his face. 'No!' Tim yelled angrily, smashing his fists against the door.

Inside, the Doctor stared at Dent.

'Can you really reassemble Earth. Intact?'

Dent nodded. 'At a cost. But one that seems appropriate.'

'Your own energy?'

'Mine and my beloved.' He looked around the TARDIS. 'Hmmm, interesting. Transcendental engineering. We were once investigating something similar.'

The Doctor smiled. 'Maybe that's where we got the idea from. Certainly your RTCs found their way to my planet, often disguised as books.'

'Paper makes an excellent trigger, Doctor.' Dent touched the console. 'Tim will kill to get his hands on this and that energy globe, Doctor.'

'I thought he might. That's a nasty scream he's got. Poor Aall.'

Polly suddenly frowned. 'Doctor, what does anechoic mean?'

Dent started. 'Why?'

'Well, this'll sound silly but I met Godwanna in a dream, after Tim used his powers to manipulate my mind. She said it. Like a warning.'

Dent looked at Polly. 'She knew. She knew Atimkos was possible danger, even to her.'

'I can do it, Mr Dent.' The Doctor's face had one of the grimmest expressions that Polly had ever seen him wear, regardless of his body. He reached below the TARDIS console and opened a flap. Inside was a tiny golden rod with black tips at either end.

Dent frowned. 'What does that do?'

The Doctor stared at the rod. 'My TARDIS is made up of two objects occupying the same space – the exo-shell and the interior. If I remove this time vector generator unit, the interior dimensions are literally tucked away in an alternate dimension, leaving just the exo-shell both in here and out.' He tugged at it and there was a flash.

The Doctor, Polly and Dent were standing inside a box the same size as the police box exterior. Only the energy globe gave them light.

'The TARDIS is no longer protected by the field generator. There's nothing to stop Atimkos getting in.' He gave Polly responsibility for the globe.

It tickled her hand and she thought it peculiar that she couldn't actually touch it but knew it was there. She could feel something.

The door opened and Tim virtually fell in.

Dent and Polly shoved him towards the Doctor and fled, leaving the door open.

'Not much room for two is there?' The Doctor edged towards the door, clutching the time vector generator behind his back.

'I thought this was a spaceship of sorts?' Tim stared at the metallic blank walls.

'Actually, it's a time/space capsule. Of sorts,' said the Doctor. And jumped through the door, slamming it shut. Breathing heavily he tried to relax.

And then staggered as Tim launched himself against the doors from inside. The Doctor looked at the time vector generator. 'Can't keep you out for long, can I, or we'll never repair the damage.' He looked across at the others. 'Dent, Ben, Professor, your strength, please.'

'Typical man,' muttered Mrs Wilding. 'Only men have strength apparently.'

Polly smiled. 'I'm sure the Doctor is right . . .' she began.

Mrs Wilding ignored her and went to add her weight to the door.

Inside the TARDIS shell, Tim stopped pounding on the door. 'Say goodbye to your ship, Doctor,' he muttered. Tim opened his mouth and let out what ought to have been a devastating high-pitched shriek. It went nowhere except into the TARDIS walls and bounced back into the centre again.

Atimkos, or Tim as he had let himself be known on Earth, ceased to exist as his own sonic scream separated his atoms from each other and blasted them into nothingness. The whole procedure took less than a second.

'I made an anechoic chamber of the TARDIS exo-shell. Instead of absorbing sound and then spreading it around, it merely bounced it straight back.'

'Is he dead?' asked Mrs Wilding.

'Yes. I'm rather afraid that the Euterpians are represented only by the two of you now.' The Doctor opened the door and wandered into the TARDIS, followed by Ben. He knelt down and reinserted the time vector generator into a tiny hole in the floor. Instantly the familiar TARDIS console room popped back into existence. 'I do hope nothing got too scrambled,' said the Doctor. 'Polly wouldn't like to find her room at the bottom of the tin-mine, would she?'

'What tin-mine?' asked Ben.

'Oh. Haven't I shown you that?'

'Doctor!' Dent's call stopped them both. 'Polly!' they said together and dashed outside.

Sure enough, Polly was standing in the distance, Aysha holding her in a throat-lock, a stubby hand-blaster aimed at her forehead. Professor Bridgeman was trying to talk Aysha down but to no effect. She was carrying the mechanical RTC unit Aall had brought in her hand.

'Give me the energy globe, girl, or I'll kill you.'

'Why do you want it, Your Majesty? How would you utilize it in your engines? Chosan obviously understood more about the RTC unit than Fräulein Thorsuun realized, but does Chosan know how to convert that amount of energy?'

'Do you really think me that foolish, Doctor? Of course she does. I'd be a very stupid Queen if I took this much power aboard one small ship if I wasn't confident

253

that we could use it safely.'

'Oh. Fair enough.' The Doctor pondered, then smiled. 'All right, Polly. Let her have the globe.'

Polly's eyes widened. 'Doctor!'

'No, honestly, it's all right.' He whispered to Ben, 'Ever played cricket?'

'Not since the fourth form.'

The Doctor slid a cricket ball out of his coat pocket and into Ben's hand. 'All you have to do is knock the globe out of her hand.' The Doctor turned to Dent and Mrs Wilding. 'If one of you would do the honours?'

They both nodded.

The Doctor cleared his throat. 'Right. Well, Queen Aysha, if you'd like to activate your RTC, the link to your ship is still strong. It'll bounce you straight back there – now the coordinates are fed in, you don't need my TARDIS.'

Aysha studied him, weighing her newly acquired energy globe. 'I don't trust you, Doctor. This is too easy.'

The Doctor shrugged. 'That's the problem with world conquerors. You get paranoid so easily. Believe me. I'm not going to hurt you.' The Doctor held his hands out. 'Honest.'

Polly squirmed free and fell into Bridgeman's arms. He smiled at her.

'Now, Ben!' yelled the Doctor.

The cricket ball sped from Ben's hand and struck the globe and was instantly vaporized. But the surprise made Aysha instinctively back away as Dent shrieked, capturing the globe in another sonic net. Quickly he vocally dragged it back to himself.

Aysha stared at the victorious group. And smiled. 'You win, Doctor. Watch your back, though. I'll be watching for you.' She activated the RTC unit and a yellow glow began to envelope her and the machine. Both vanished.

A blast of yellow energy shot upwards into the never-ending whiteness until none of them could see it.

* * *

'Report!'

Jodi looked up from tactical. 'Sorry, Commander, but I cannot evade it.'

'Science?' Chosan looked up at Tamora.

'It's energy of some sort, on a direct bearing for us. Impact in twenty seconds.'

Chosan stared at the bridge crew. Then at Jodi again. 'Blast it. Whatever it is, stop it in its tracks.'

Jodi nodded and fired the ship's weaponry.

Mingled together the two blasts of energy flared briefly but the incoming burst flared brighter, absorbing, enveloping and reversing the ship's fire-power.

It sped straight back again.

'Damn,' muttered Chosan as it hit the ship. There was a flash, and Chosan watched as, almost in slow motion, the interior of the ship sparkled. Webs of yellow energy arced across it, disintegrating sections as it went. Out of the corner of her eye, Chosan saw the immobilized forms of Tamora at science and Tensing drafted into nav were surrounded by the energy as it traced the contours of their bodies and stations. Then they, along with the hull integrity, vanished. Dimly aware that Jodi at tactical was mewling in pain as the energy killed her, Chosan thought she saw a face etched into the energy arcs that destroyed her.

Queen Aysha, screaming in pain.

The battle-cruiser of the Cat-People flared yellow and exploded into billions of tiny fragments.

Dent stared at Mrs Wilding. Without saying a word, she nodded.

'Return to your TARDIS, Doctor. We will get you to Earth eventually.'

'When?' asked Polly.

'As soon as we can, my dear,' Mrs Wilding replied.

'No, literally when?'

'Now?'

'How about –' Polly glanced at her watch, 'how about

255

yesterday afternoon, just before the Grange was destroyed?'

Mrs Wilding nodded. 'As you wish. Goodbye.'

The Doctor pushed Ben, Polly and Bridgeman into his TARDIS. At the last minute he turned back to the last two Euterpians.

'Are you sure about this?'

Dent nodded. 'We'll be together. Who knows, we might find a physical form as well. Either way, we'll be alive.'

'But trapped, possibly floating around Earth non-corporeally? Is that what you want?'

Mrs Wilding smiled. 'Goodbye, Doctor.'

He looked at them a little sadly. 'Good-bye.'

Seconds later the TARDIS began to dematerialize.

Udentkista kissed Tarwildbaning and let the globe drop.

The white nexus ceased to exist.

The TARDIS rematerialized.

In the Ex-Room.

Inside the Ex-Room, the students were on the floor.

'He's taken the Doctor's book,' Simon was crying but the others could not hear him. The glass in the window shattered and Carfrae screamed simultaneously. Peter was reaching for the equipment, to try and set up an Ex-Area that might shield them, but with a bang, the electrical components exploded –

and a huge blue box appeared between Peter and the console.

'Jesus Christ,' Simon muttered.

A door on the box swung open. 'Simon! Quick! In here!'

'Professor?' yelled Peter.

Ben and Polly ran towards them, Polly helping the shaking Carfrae up. Ben was the last one in just as the Ex-Room, along with the Grange and a large section of the clifftop, were consumed by a massive burst of Earth's natural energy.

* * *

Ben bit hungrily into his McDonald's burger.

Polly stared at him, disdain on her face. 'You've got tomato sauce on your chin, Ben Jackson.'

Simon, Peter, Carfrae and Professor Bridgeman were at the next table, discussing their plan of action. How to tell the university they were alive. How to explain the disappearances of Kerbe and Thorsuun. How to explain the Doctor's involvement.

Carfrae touched Bridgeman's arm. 'Whatever has happened, Professor, it's done you a lot of good, hasn't it?'

'Yeah,' said Simon tactlessly. 'Yeah, you've stopped stuttering.'

Bridgeman laughed. 'Do you know, that's the only evidence I have that this isn't just some awful dream. Mrs Wilding made me . . . accept things in my past. Come to terms with myself. Some evidence. That and the Doctor's help of course –'

The others were staring at a half-eaten burger left on the table.

'Where've they gone?' Peter wondered.

The TARDIS was where it had first arrived, in the trees – now burned – by the Gatehouse. Or rather, the large hole where the Gatehouse had been.

Polly stared at the cliffs. 'He really played with my memories, Doctor. Made me forget all this until shock forced me to remember.'

'Tim was not a nice man, Polly, despite his pretences. He killed a lot of innocent people.' The Doctor opened the TARDIS door and Ben slipped inside. The Doctor looked at Polly and she smiled.

'One moment.' She dug into her pocket and took out the tarot pack. The tarot of the Cat-People.

The Doctor took it from her. 'Tim's RTC unit. If only I'd known you had it.'

'It's a horrible weapon, Doctor. You didn't see what it did to that poor young man in the nexus. And Godwanna herself.'

'People always end up destroying themselves, Polly. And usually with their own weapons. Don't shed too many tears for Godwanna.' He passed the tarot pack back, patted her arm and disappeared into the TARDIS.

Polly looked at the cards. 'If only they'd known there really were Cat-People,' she murmured, then drew back her arm and threw the pack as far away as she could. 'Bimbo yourself!' she yelled.

It bounced across the charred lawns and landed beside the massive split in the ground from which the energy had been released. The box split open on the final bounce, sending most of the cards spiralling into the chasm. Of the few that remained, one lay face up in the blackened grass.

The Lovers.

They sat around campfires, telling the stories of the Dreaming and the Songlines. Remembering their history, their culture and their heritage.

Twenty or thirty Aboriginals, determined to maintain their way of life despite attempts by the Australian authorities to change them. In the distance came the sound of a car engine. A couple of the men hugged their coats tighter to them and walked towards the sound.

The car stopped and two white people got out, a man and a woman.

'Hello,' said the woman. 'Can you help us? We're a little lost. We're trying to get to Alice Springs.'

One of the Aboriginals pointed to his left. 'Two hours. You got fuel and water?'

'Stacks,' said the man. 'Thanks anyway.'

The Aboriginal stared at them. 'You're not like the travellers out here. What are you doing?'

The man held out a hand. 'My name is Chris Dent, and this is my fiancée, Emma Wilding. We're part of a survey trying to ensure that the new rail-link from Alice to Darwin doesn't cross or damage any traditional sites of yours.'

The two Aboriginals pointed to the campfire. 'You want to eat?'

'Yes, please,' said Emma Wilding. 'That would be great.'

As they sat and nodded introductions to the rest of the Aboriginals, Emma relaxed. 'Hey, do you know the stories of the early settlers here, how they were shown how to sing life into the planet?'

The Aboriginals nodded.

'Good,' said Chris Dent. 'Just checking.'

While not intended as a replacement for the readers' own imaginations in visualizing characters, situations and settings, it may be of interest to note that as this story was being written I was constantly casting and re-casting the leading players. Were *Invasion of the Cat-People* to be a television programme instead of a book, the following would be my preferred cast list.

DOCTOR WHO
A six-part adventure in space and time
starring
PATRICK TROUGHTON
as Doctor Who
with
Jacqueline Pearce, Susan Engel, Jude Law, Carolyn Seymour
and
Anneke Wills, Michael Craze
★

Invasion of the Cat-People
by Gary Russell

Cast in order of appearance

Atimkos	JUDE LAW
Tarwildbaning	STEPHANIE BEACHAM
Thorgarsuunela	CAROLYN SEYMOUR
Udentkista	JOHN NORMINGTON
Godwanna	JACQUELINE PEARCE
Pride Mother	CYNTHIA GRENVILLE
Queen Aysha	SUSAN ENGEL
Chosan	PATRICIA MAYNARD
Nate Simms	STEVEN MACINTOSH
Doctor Who	PATRICK TROUGHTON
Polly Wright	ANNEKE WILLS
Ben Jackson	MICHAEL CRAZE
Lotuss	MYRA FRANCES
Jayde	ROWENA WALLACE
Nicholas Bridgeman	ALAN DAVID
Marten Kerbe	MAURICE ROEVES
Simon Griffiths	SIMON FENTON
Carfrae Morgan	SIRI NEAL
Peter Moore	NATHAN CONSTANCE
George Smithers	GERALD JAMES
Charlie Coates	COLIN JEAVONS
Aall	MAGGIE KIRKPATRICK
Nypp	LOIS BAXTER
Tuq	LOUISE SIVERSEN
Nihmrod	ROSALIND LLOYD
Tamora	MAGGIE DENCE
Tensing	JULIE T. WALLACE

Directed by Graeme Harper
Music by Mike Fillis and Adrian Pack
Produced by Michael Chapman
© Virgin Films 1995

Available in the *Doctor Who — New Adventures* series:

The next Missing Adventure is *Managra* by Stephen Marley, featuring the fourth Doctor and Sarah Jane Smith.